Robert Sargent is a first-time author. He was raised in the suburb of Crumlin, a working-class area of Dublin city. He is married and a father of three daughters. Robert still lives in Dublin to this day.

In memory of my da, pity you never got to read it.
R.I.P. Jim, 1948–2019.

Robert Sargent

THE BLACK POOL

AUSTIN MACAULEY PUBLISHERS™

LONDON ∗ CAMBRIDGE ∗ NEW YORK ∗ SHARJAH

A CIP catalogue record for this title is available from the British Library.

ISBN 9781398406988 (Paperback)
ISBN 9781398406995 (ePub e-book)

www.austinmacauley.com

First Published 2022
Austin Macauley Publishers Ltd®
1 Canada Square
Canary Wharf
London
E14 5AA

I would like to acknowledge the support of Austin Macauley Publishers for taking a chance on me as a first-time author.

Of course it goes without saying, I would like to acknowledge the support and belief I have received over the past ten years from my beautiful wife and children. Without their love, support and belief in me, I would never have taken the step to go for publication.

Huge thanks also to my extended family and friends for their support too.

Table of Contents

On the Run

Introduction

The word 'Dublin' is actually a composition of two Gaelic words: 'Dubh' meaning 'Black' and 'Linn' meaning 'Pool'. The literal translations of the words are 'An Dubh Linn' or 'The Black Pool'. In bygone years, the Pool itself was a dark tidal pool located within Dublin's city centre, close to Dublin Castle.

To understand the modern social and political demographics of Dublin, one must try to understand the city's past and how it formed a tiered class divide that is a feature of the city to this day. When history reflects on the formation of Dublin city in the twentieth century, it will tell us that during the later decades, certain quarters of Dublin became well-known unemployment black spots, which led to poor living standards with an ever-increasing crime rate. These social problems were primarily located within newly planned local authority housing estates across the county along with a number of multi-storey flat complexes that were in general situated within the boundaries of the Inner City.

Not long before the formation of the Irish Free State, the city of Dublin became a struggle for survival as people lived in overcrowded and unhealthy tenement buildings scattered around the city centre. What also came with the tenements was poor sanitation and family upon family crammed into single-room flats all because of the failure of Dublin Corporation, the city authority, which in conjunction with the government of the day did not develop a meaningful policy to improve tenement life.

In time, modern plans were put in place to build decent housing for Dublin's residents and they began as far back as the 1930s and then continued into the 1970s with substantial progress being made as thousands of Dublin's working-class population were moved to suburban housing estates around the county. New and growing suburbs like Crumlin, Drimnagh, Coolock and Finglas were built in the 30s, moving many, many families from the Inner City tenements into two- and three-bedroom terraced housing on the outskirts of Dublin city.

Add to this the number of local authority flat complexes built up around the Inner City over time, which included Dolphins Barn, St Teresa's Gardens, Fatima Mansions, York Street and Dominic Street flats. Understandably, the successes of these projects were mixed because although the tenement buildings were largely removed, the urgency that grew from day one from both tenants and community activists highlighted that little or no planning went into the building of the new public housing and the lack of amenities would see problems in the future, and how right were they.

These problems would be abundantly clear in later years in all the aforementioned areas but especially during the 1970s, when massive building projects were put in place, namely Tallaght and Ballymun. Unlike the flat complexes that had a small number of residents, these areas instantly acquired a huge population growth, especially in the case of Tallaght where, in a very short time-frame, the population rapidly grew overnight. The planners got the go-ahead without any provision for shops, public transport or employment for such a huge population intake, again creating problems for years to come.

Since the early 1970s, Tallaght has developed from a small village into a huge suburban area, with a population of over 100,000 people and is still a rapidly changing area to this day; mind you, the same can be said for Ballymun as this area on Dublin's north fringe has seen massive social and economic problems over time along with a number of community rebuilding initiatives over the last 50 years.

Now it must be said that not all of Dublin's social and economic problems can be laid solely on the planners' doorstep as the state departments were not to blame for all the woes of Dublin, no matter how loud some may shout. Truth be known, over the years, many of these estates and complexes went to rack and ruin due to—yes, at times underfunding by the state—but it must be highlighted that an underappreciation by a small percentage of residents who showed little or no sense of community or respect for those living around them tarnished a community by their actions; fact of the matter is that it only takes a few to ruin it for the majority. You see, social deprivation fuels its own problems and when people are left to fend for themselves, sometimes something has to give.

As stated, many residents do not care about community but the majority do fight back and by this, I mean they drive to have a better life for their loved ones and are happy to get up and go to work day in and day out, living the normal life across Dublin's fair city. On the other hand, others take and take, be it on social welfare, or view crime as a career and way of life to get rich fast, not caring about those who get in the way or those who get hunted along the way. This, of course, leads to social inequalities and increased crime rates within social estates that became a major problem over the years; some are still suffering to this day.

You must understand that what was built on the city's faltering social foundations, a society, grew and was developed to make Dublin the great city that we know today. In saying that, what also grew was a bitterness and hate from a certain breed of man and woman who were also fighting back, not like the working class but as they conveniently saw against a society that made no room for them and gave them nothing to believe in. They would thrive on this, using it as an excuse to take their frustrations out on everyone else.

In the twentieth century, the Black Pool would see its young people taken not just by revolution, civil war or emigration but also by the devastation of the illegal drug trade and gangland feuds, which would take hold of her communities. Over the years, a number of these close-knit communities were to be absolutely decimated by heroin abuse but again, it must be said, not in any way the fault of the vast majority of the residents. You see, this is not a story of heroes but a story of how the reality of gangs and crime can get hold of a city.

Some of Dublin's gangsters engage in extortion, intimidation and bribery to wield influence over their victims and others have been known for attempting to manipulate the decisions of civil institutions, such as court cases. The fact of the situation is that the reality of gangland is not as it is portrayed in the movies but a deadly ring that only the strong survive; well, until someone stronger comes along to take their place.

Dublin City is no different to any other place on Earth and gangs and violence go hand in hand just like any major city around the world. It is here in the decades of years gone by where this story begins, in a time of uncertainty as a nation was seeking out a glimmer of hope in a life with nothing to look forward to and no reason to go and find it.

People may tell you that time is a healer and I do tend to agree, but only in certain circumstances because not everything can be healed by time as some things are just too raw to come to terms with, no matter how much time has passed.

For instance, take the loss of a loved one; this is one of those scars that run deep because it is that hidden pain that will always stay with those who have loved and lost. Many suffer in silence, battling those hidden demons that can never be explained to another as they do not and cannot feel that sense of loss.

What must be understood is that the City of Dublin has had many children, some of them good and of course, some bad; this is a fictional story of one such son of Dublin; this is the story of one Thomas 'Little Don' Moran.

It will tell the tale of this man from his humble beginnings living in the Inner City Dublin flats to becoming Ireland's most revered and vicious gangland boss. The world that Thomas 'Little Don' Moran was about to enter along with his ruthless gang would bring the 'Black Pool' to its knees through violence, intimidation, drugs and murder over many years.

This is not a story of heroes but a story of how the reality of gangs and crime can get hold of a community and bring it to its knees. Is it the bravado of becoming a household name and main man on the block or is it a stain on society that young men and women turn to crime to make ends meet?

Well, it just might possibly be that it's a combination of both. Violent men come and go and only sad memories of a misled life is all that remains of them, but their time on this planet will never go away.

This is one fictional story of the Black Pool, Dublin City.

Ireland, sir, for good or evil, is like no other place under heaven, and no man can touch its sod or breathe its air without becoming better or worse.

-George Bernard Shaw.

Chapter 1
Thomas Moran Jnr

The date was 30 January 1968 and all across the city of Dublin, a savage wind was blowing, a biting icy chill that came quick and sharp through the narrow streets like a thief in the night. As the sun finally set and night began to close in on a bitterly cold winter's day, Dublin was shimmering under a clear starry sky as she began to freeze over with the temperature rapidly dropping below zero. Snow was lying in patches on the ground, causing disruption to residents who carefully made their way home to get inside, away from the biting wind and treacherous conditions, to heat themselves beside a warm fire.

Inside the Coombe Women's Hospital on Cork Street, the normal routine within the delivery suites were being carried out as one of the hospital's many midwives was giving comfort to a young woman who had just brought a new child into the world. The time was 7.11 pm and Marie Moran had just given birth to her first-born child; while outside the delivery suite, a young father, Thomas Moran, filled with both fear and hope nervously waited for some news.

'Thomas Moran, Thomas Moran, is Thomas Moran here please?'

'Yeah, yeah, I'm Thomas Moran,' answered a young man with expectation and eagerness in his voice.

'Please Mr Moran, this way,' said a polite nurse.

Thomas, with his cap held tightly in both of his now sweating hands, nervously followed the nurse as she led him up a long bottle-green corridor, with cubicles covered by large white drapes on either side. The drapes concealed the new babies and the tears of exhausted mothers who had just experienced the ordeal of bringing a new life into the world.

'Where is Marie, Nurse?'

The nurse pointed to a set of double doors at the end of the corridor. 'Just down here, Mr Moran, just down the corridor.'

And seconds later, at the end of the corridor, Thomas was met by the double swing doors and in big red writing, he read: *Delivery Suite, Do Not Enter*.

'Nurse, is it okay like?' Thomas asked, pointing towards the doors with a nod.

'Indeed, Mr Moran, go straight in; someone is waiting to meet you,' smiled the nurse.

With those words of comfort, Thomas entered the delivery suite where his young wife, Marie, was waiting patiently. As the young man entered the room, a new sound caught his attention, his heart started pounding with a feeling he had never felt before. Thomas thought to himself, *what is this sound that filled him with such joy?* It was like his favourite sound of the bells at St Patrick's Cathedral ringing out across the Inner City, but for Thomas, this was different. A second later, what Thomas was met by would never leave his memory, the echo of a baby's cry volleying throughout the room; it was the cry of his new-born son, weighing in at a healthy eight pound nine ounces.

Thomas was full of pride when he saw his baby son for the first time; a small tear ran from the corner of his eye down his cheek. The young father watched as the midwife placed the new-born child, fully wrapped in a cotton blanket, in the arms of his weary young exhausted mother.

'Congratulations, Mr and Mrs Moran, you have a beautiful son. Now Mammy, here you go, your new baby son.'

'Thomas, Thomas, isn't he beautiful?'

'Of course, he is, love, of course, he is. So Marie, what are we going to call him?' questioned a proud young father.

A tearful young mother suggested in a voice that was forcing out words through the exhaustion of the long process of childbirth, 'It's Thomas, yeah, Thomas Junior, after you.'

The proud father, with glee in his voice, asked the midwife, 'So Nurse, when will he, Thomas Moran Junior, be home cause I gotta get back and get the flat ready and tidy it up for him?'

'A week, Mr Moran, around a week if all goes well.'

On hearing the words of the midwife, the worried voice of the young mother called out in distress, 'Thomas, Thomas, what does she mean if all goes well?'

Thomas, with worry in his voice and holding the hand of his wife, turned and asked the midwife, 'Nurse, is anything wrong?'

As the midwife gently put the infant back into his cot, she approached the young couple and explained in a reassuring voice, 'No, no; it's just precaution, Mr Moran; we make sure that baby Thomas is fine and also Mammy that she has no infections. So Mr Moran, I think it's time you left, as Mammy will need all the rest she can get after the birth.'

'Oh right, yeah right, I get you,' replied a relieved Thomas. 'Look love, I am off to the flat to start sorting things out. You relax, all is well and our son is in the best of hands.'

The tiring voice of Marie Moran, as her head hit the pillow, spoke to her husband, her eyes closed, 'Okay, love, see ye tomorrow.'

Thomas went over to his new-born son now lying in the hospital cot. 'Goodnight, son, my beautiful little Thomas. I love you so much.' He kissed him on the forehead.

These joys of childbirth would in time disappear as unknowing to Thomas and Marie, they had just given Ireland its most notorious and ruthless criminal that the country would ever encounter. Their pride and joy would bring communities to their knees, destroy lives and break families. This was the birth of a monster that would bring nothing but hardship, death, fear and intimidation to the Island of Ireland over the next few decades to come, because Thomas Moran was the name that would send fear and terror into the bone of many in time to come.

At the time of his birth, Moran's parents—Thomas Senior and Marie—were renting a two-room flat in number 13d Barrow Street, an old-four storey tenement complex situated in the heart of Dublin's South Inner City. The very humble dwelling was divided into two small basic rooms, a bedroom and a kitchen-dining room that were separated only by a plasterboard partition that shook when the wind blew or a door opened or closed in their or a neighbouring flat. Even the old ceilings were sunken from age and badly damaged with holes in places where, on rainy Dublin nights, the water would run through the holes to waiting pots and basins strategically placed to stop the flow of water gathering throughout the rooms. In general, the conditions were appalling and not a home to raise a new-born baby.

The night of Thomas Jnr's birth, his father arrived home where he and his young wife had lived since their wedding the previous year; he turned the key in the lock and, forcing his shoulder onto the door as it always got stuck, pushed the door forward to gain entry. He entered the flat only to be met by the hard freezing cold of a Dublin winter that sent a chill throughout his body.

He stopped in his place, pondered a moment and looked around the room, thinking about what he had made of his life and the circumstance he was bringing a child into. Crying in silence, the young father knew all too well that he must do something about the situation because he did not want his son to be raised in the same world he had been brought up in. He then proceeded to light a small fire in the old decaying fireplace in the corner of the small tenement home to combat the freezing Dublin weather.

Thomas was determined to leave the tenements behind and move to one of the spacious two- and three-bedroom corporation housing estates surrounding Dublin's Inner City so that his son and the possible additional siblings could have a better life than he and Marie had.

Every day, he would visit Dublin Corporation to see if any houses were available for his family to move into but to no avail. The rejection by Dublin Corporation was nothing new and continued for the next number of months as Thomas made his daily pilgrimage in search of a new home for his family.

To make things worse, one year later came the arrival of Thomas and Marie's second son, Patrick Moran, who would later be known as Gonzo. With the arrival of Patrick, Marie became even more frustrated with the surroundings she found herself in and added even more pressure on Thomas to get them away from the squalor of the tenements.

Crime was a regular thing in the Inner City with plenty of bounty on their doorsteps; for many of the men from the tenements with no work, they had to somehow make a quick shilling— legitimately or not. Marie could not understand why Thomas did not turn to crime like many of their neighbours and this infuriated her even more; Thomas was a decent honest man who could not bring himself to steal. Top all of this off with a landlord who did not care just as long as he got the weekly payments from his tenants, who did not have the money to pay most of the time.

The landlords could do as they pleased because there was nobody to stop them as government restrictions had not been enforced back in 1970's Dublin. As usual, when wanted, the landlord was nowhere to be found until rent collection day—the one day when families did not want the landlord calling. The fact was that nine times out of ten, tenants could not afford to pay the rent but the fear of eviction from these slums terrified families as it was better than raising a young family on the streets. The overwhelming fact was that the landlords were the master of their destiny as the tenants had nowhere to turn or nobody to fight in their corner.

The landlord for the building the Morans lived in was a Mr O'Leary, a grumpy middle-aged man who cursed the world he lived in, blaming it on his failures to make his—as he thought—rightful fortune. O'Leary owned a Bric-a-Brac shop on Dorset Street and became a rent collector so that he could feel better within himself, seeing that there were actually people less well off than him; he loved to see people beg at his feet. Marie hated him and in time turned Thomas Junior against him too.

Ten years later in 1980, a young man was to break in and burn the shop to the ground the unmannerly way O'Leary had treated his mother; that young lad was a certain Thomas Moran Junior.

It was on 22 June in the early hours of morning in Dublin when Moran left his building and headed towards Dorset Street. It was a very humid night with a serious lack of air to breathe as Moran approached O'Leary's shop; there was not a sinner to be seen so it was full ahead with his plan.

Even at such a young age, Moran had carefully planned his assault on O'Leary and his shop; days before, when he had paid a visit to the area, and had noticed that at the side of the shop was a wooden fence where the planks were rotten and a small gap appeared just enough for an eleven-year-old boy to squeeze through. Within seconds, Moran was in the yard and had reached the back door. He found to his surprise that the door was already open, luckily taking away half his job of not having to break the glass and alerting any nearby residents to the rear of the shop.

In his right hand, Moran was carrying a 2.5 litre plastic container full of fuel he had stolen from cars in the local school. Once inside, Moran began to remove the rag that kept the fuel from spilling and then began to carefully pour the petrol in the room, when a flashlight startled him, leading him to fall over a lamp table and the petrol dousing him. The flashlight had come from a local Garda patrol on his regular beat just checking to see if all was well.

After the Garda had gone, Moran finished spreading the petrol that was left in the container and stood at the door he had entered; he lit a Zippo at arm's length, careful not to catch his fuel-covered clothes. Click, click! Went the flint on the lighter as a flame rose and Moran tossed the lighter towards the area where the petrol was doused. Within seconds, the old decaying building was a mass of flames with Moran Looking on with a sense of satisfaction as this was not just for his mother but also all who O'Leary had bullied in the past.

Within twenty minutes, there were three fire engines on the scene; around twenty firemen tried to stop the fire from spreading as they fought with smoke billowing out of the building and flames rising into the now not so calm Dublin night. As the patrol Garda, who was still on his beat, approached Moran and asked, 'Well, well, now what have we got here? Is it not a bit late for you to be out and about at this hour of the morning?'

A cheeky Moran with a wry smile on his face explained to the Garda, 'Sure, Jaysus Garda, how can anyone sleep with that racket going on? I just live in there and I sneak out without me ma knowin, ye know, to see what all the noise was about.'

The Garda smiled and sent him on his way. 'Go on home, young lad,' replied the Garda, unknowing that he had just let the man they would be searching for walk away. It was only in later years that Moran would tell the story of how stupid he and the Garda were; Moran was covered in petrol and must have stank to high heaven. Moran had taken his first steps outside the law and it felt good, it felt really good. This was the first of many, and burning down an old building was only a drop in the ocean of what was to come.

Chapter 2
Little Don

In Ireland, certain political mind-sets will say that everyone has a choice in what the direction of their life will take, but the fact of the matter is that in some cases, many people have no choice or control over their own or family's destiny. When you take people like Thomas Moran Junior who, under the position of his social standing, he was never going to take the straight and honest road that society expected of its people. For Moran, when he was growing up in such poor conditions and at times surrounded by dishonest and dangerous people, there was only one way this young lad was heading and that was a life of crime.

He would actually proudly embrace the life of being at one against the world and the world he fought against being united to stop him. In his mind, crime was not a bad thing; it was a necessity of life and the people who worked day in and day out for a living were the fools. Criminals think differently from law-abiding citizens but it is easy to understand why young people rebel against a system that denies them their legitimate right to a job or decent home and contributes to widening the gap between those living in affluence and those living in relative poverty.

Times were changing and the 1970s rung in a decade of change that saw Ireland go decimal as shillings and pence were replaced by the Irish pound or the Punt as it was more widely known in Ireland.

Next up was Ireland's introduction to the European Economic Union and the first McDonald's opened its doors to an adoring public. The Moran family had more pressing issues to take care of and a bit of luck did come their way at last.

Still living in Barrow Street, Thomas Senior got a bit of good news when he was offered a job as the caretaker in the local school by the parish priest, Father Donnie O'Grady, because like most people, O'Grady was fond of the well-mannered man.

'It's not much money but it might help, Thomas,' explained O'Grady.

'Thank you, Father, thank you so much. Marie will be over the moon and the extra money will help ever so much.'

If this was not good enough, months later the Morans got some more good luck when Dublin Corporation offered the young family a new place to live—St Christopher's Mansions, one of its newer flat complexes on the outskirts of Dublin City, not a million miles from Bride Street.

The complex sat on the banks of the Grand Canal in the heart of Dublin's southwest Inner City under the shadow of the world-famous Guinness Brewery. It was thanks to the extra income from the new job that gave the Morans just about enough money to rent from the local authority. So in May of 1971, St Christopher's Mansions was to become the Moran's' new place to call home, and C Block was the new place of residency for Thomas Moran and family.

The new flat had two bedrooms, a kitchen, private bathroom with a bathtub and separate dining room so compared to their earlier tenement; this was like moving into Buckingham Palace. But over the decades, poverty, exclusion and the scourge of drugs changed all that and brought a once vibrant and happy community to its knees.

Unknowing to its tenants, the new neighbour's son, Thomas, was one of the men who would destroy their little piece of heaven in years to come. St Christopher's Mansions were to be the launching pad for Thomas Moran's criminal empire and where he would form a young gang of local thugs and would be surrounded by people he could trust as the law had no meaning unless it was the law of the street. Thomas Moran was home.

From an early age, Moran possessed the right combination of brawn and brains to make him successful in his chosen field and his mother understood this from the get go; all Marie had to do was ask her son for something and the young thief would get what she wanted, whenever she wanted. Thomas senior did not condone his son's actions, which led to Marie arguing with him on many an occasion and saying that at least he was trying to make her happy; it was because of this that the relationship between father and son faltered, never getting back on track.

The final straw was to be in the summer of 1980 when Thomas senior had enough of his family and he left Marie after she had been, once again, drinking heavily one night; as she staggered home, she fell over and burst her eye open, leaving herself with a number of stiches and a black eye. The next day, three of her brothers called around to Thomas and beat him severely because Marie—too embarrassed to tell the truth—had blamed her husband for her injuries. Thomas rightly, or wrongly, turned his back on his family forever and moved to Birmingham, England, never to return.

As the years passed, Thomas Junior became well known in the Inner City as the person prepared to sort out problems from unwanted parties, such as violent boyfriends, gangs causing problems on his patch or even going on jobs as a lookout for the more senior gangsters. What held him in good stead was that he would always adhere to strict methods of discipline that would hold good in the years to come.

Moran loved the feeling of respect and loyalty he garnered and this became a serious factor when he joined up on jobs and all through his adult life, as he would never respect anyone who would turn in a friend; it was an unwritten law in the criminal world—you did not grass under any circumstance.

Amidst all of his minor local dealings, Moran strove to become rich by whatever means necessary and nothing or nobody was going to stand in his way. He had also grown up with an anger that was the seed of a total and utter hatred for all establishments, with no respect for authority, never trusting anybody outside his close circle, which stuck with him throughout his life. One of those close allies was the one man who would become his best friend, right-hand man and confidante—his neighbour, Noel Slattery—and over the following decades, both young men would become inseparable.

The first time Moran and Slattery met was on Halloween night in 1984 when both young men were just sixteen. Moran had just started out from his home when something on the stairwell startled him and the curious youngster asked himself, *what the fuck is that?* As he got closer to the stairwell entrance, he noticed, hidden under the shadow of the enclosed concrete circular staircase, a young man sobbing. Concerned but cautious, Moran asked, 'you alright?'

Sobbing, the young man replied, 'Yeah, why wouldn't I?'

'Only askin, for fuck sake. Tryin ta help, that's all, ye can go fuck off now,' snapped Moran as he began to walk off down the stairs.

'I'm just sick of that cunt,' replied the young man.

'Who?' asked Moran.

The stranger proceeded to tell Moran about his mother's boyfriend. 'Me Ma's fella, he's fuckin pissed and he's after knockin the fuck outta her again. So

I got up to stop him and he gave me a fuckin hidin as well. The cunt is always doin this.'

'So d'ye want a bit of help sortin him out or wha?' inquired Moran. Slattery was more than interested but puzzled at what he was hearing from this stranger. Was there a ray of hope to sorting this problem once and for all?

'So you're saying that we do that cunt?' questioned Slattery.

'Yeah, I am, revenge, ye silly bollix. I saw it in *The Godfather*. It's a fuckin great film. Have ye seen it, it's me favourite film ever.'

Slattery still puzzled replied 'Yeah, of course, I've seen it. What's your fuckin point?'

Moran, now standing in front of Slattery with his arms stretched out wide, replied, 'My fuckin point! Are we gonna sort this cunt or wha?'

Slattery, not knowing exactly what was happening, put out his hand and introduced himself to Moran. 'Okay then, I'm Noel Slattery, and who the fuck are you? Don fuckin Corleone or somethin?'

'I'm Tommy Moran, nice to meet ye. Live just there.'

A smiling Slattery wiping the tears from his face and christened his newfound friend, 'Well, 'Little Don', nice to meet ye.'

Moran looked up, quite happy with himself, and replied to his newfound friend, 'Little Don, I like that. I really like that. Yeah, Tommy 'Little Don' Moran. Fuck it, why the fuck not!'

As both youngsters broke into laughter, Moran asked, 'so we gonna do this?'

'I'm not messin now; he is a big bastard,' explained Slattery.

'Let me sleep on it, Noel, let me sleep on it,' replied a confident Moran.

Slattery, with a gleam in his eye and the spring back in his step, cheekily asked Moran, 'So, fancy a little house crawling tonight?'

Moran burst into laughter. 'For fucks sake. Yeah, I'll give it a go.'

True to his word, over the next few days, Moran plotted his plan for revenge on Martin Downey, a man he had never met, for a newfound friend he had only met. The plan by Moran was simple; the aim was to catch this man being a bully on Wednesday night of November 7 at closing time in his local pub.

It was perfect as Wednesday was the day Downey received his dole payments, so he spent the day drinking from morning until night. Moran's idea was simple; with Downey being tanked up from a day of drinking, it would make it easier to beat a bigger and much stronger man. Slattery agreed but knew well they had to put him down, and fast, because if he got away from them, he could kill one or both of them.

When the arranged night of the attack arrived, both Moran and Slattery stole some nylon stockings—to hide their identity from their victim—from the lines that hung in the courtyard of St Christopher's. Both youngsters had agreed that a laneway just a few hundred yards from the pub would be the place to carry out their mafia-style revenge. Their weapons of choice on the night were not what the conventional gangster would carry but still weapons that were intended to inflict ultimate damage to their unknowing victim.

Moran was in possession of a pickaxe handle and Slattery a hurling stick with nails hammered into it. The plan was: as Downey passed by the laneway, Moran was to come from behind, push him into the laneway then both men would serve out a serious beating on the unsuspecting victim.

It was at 12.15 am when Slattery noticed Downey approaching the laneway and he alerted Moran by pointing him out. Moran, checking the coast was clear, came behind the man, pushed him into the lane and quickly got him to the ground with a single blow to the back of his head. As planned, both young men, without an ounce of remorse or hesitation, beat their victim so badly he was hospitalised for three weeks. The line into a world of serious crime had just been crossed but the chilling thing was that Moran and Slattery enjoyed it and basked in the feeling of invincibility.

Over the coming days, news travelled fast around the area of the attack but unknown to Moran, Slattery went around bragging to everyone close to him about the attack and giving a blow-by-blow account. When Moran found out that Slattery had opened his mouth, he was furious and called Slattery's home to confront his friend.

'Noel, ye stupid cunt, everyone knows we did your aulwans fella, for fuck sake.'

'So fuckin what, Tommy?'

'So fuckin what, so fuckin what! We could get fuckin done for it, that's fuckin what! We're in this together, Noel, together so we have to trust each other and nobody else, got that?'

Slattery knew from that moment that he had messed up big-time, realising Moran was right.

'These fuckin rats around here would have the law on us in no time. Fuckin rats, Noel, that is what they are, rats in our fuckin flats, scum like. We got to stay loyal to each other.'

Slattery soon learned that Tommy 'Little Don' Moran was no fool; he was a serious individual and he swore to keep the silence from then on.

'What we do is not for every cunt under the sun to know about, right? You are my lieutenant, Noel. If I can't trust you, who can I trust?'

Slattery, trembling with fear and excitement, acknowledged his friend. 'Together, mate, we are in this together, Tommy.'

'Okay Noel, but you must remember trust and loyalty. It'll keep us strong and protect us because let me tell ye, if I have my way and do the things I want to do, they'll come after us and that's when we have to stand together.'

Moran had drawn the line; Slattery clearly knew who the boss was and stepped right into line as any good lieutenant would. The outstanding factor for Thomas was he would actually proudly embrace the life of being at one against the world and the world he fought against being united to stop him. In his mind, crime was not a bad thing, it was a necessity of life and the people who worked day in and day out for a living were the real fools. Evidently, from a very early age, Moran possessed the right combination of brawn and brains to make him successful in his chosen field. From that day, 'Little Don' was officially born.

Chapter 3
The Young Tearaways

Ireland in the 1980s was a country rocked by financial and political turmoil, both north and south of the island, as the Irish government's focus turned away from the pressing social issues at hand. The faltering economy in part turned the heads on Kildare Street as did the Provisional IRA due to the havoc they were wreaking not only on the island of Ireland but within Great Britain too. The politics of social change were not to the fore by the political class as they continued to ignore their own backyard, which was falling deeper into major social dysfunction such as increasing crime, huge unemployment rates and a heroin epidemic breaking out across the country. The economy was rocked but truth be known, the power brokers looked after interests that lay far from the broken streets of Dublin and more towards bankers and business.

These were tough times, but for Thomas Moran, the Dublin he lived in was a million miles away from the troubles of the world and the changing city around him. Moran did not care that the country was thrown deeper into a state of complete instability because for him, life just moved on. Following on from the attack outside the pub on Martin Downey, both Moran and Slattery had unknowingly acquired a band of devoted foot-soldiers who were more than willing to join the ranks of Little Don's new gang. Even if he did not admit it to anyone, he secretly enjoyed all of the attention he was getting as he quietly relished in the adoration of his young band of loyal followers.

In December of 1984, Slattery called on Moran to introduce him to many of the youngsters in the area but being the shrewd and calculating young man that he was, he chose only the most suited and trusted to become members of his gang of teenage tearaways. It would be from here that a certain core of this new gang would become Moran's most trusted soldiers and confidantes for the next number of years.

These new gang members included Noel Slattery and a pretty young local girl called Jean O'Shea, who had already fallen for Moran's charm and charisma while finding the entire buzz that surrounded him too much to resist. Strangely, for such a very headstrong and forward-thinking young man, Moran could not pluck up the courage to ask Jean out but instead called on ladies' man Noel to ask her on his behalf; this was to Slattery's absolute joy and Moran would never live it down.

'The fuckin great Little Don afraid to ask a bird out!' joked Slattery.

'Fuck off, Noel, but okay, sort it out, will ye?' asked Moran as his face turned the colour of a bright red balloon. In the end, after the piss-taking had finished, Slattery agreed to help his woman-shy friend; with Moran and Jean both living in the same complex of St Christopher's, it was easy for Slattery to sort the young love-struck teens out.

On New Year's Day, 1985, both Moran and Jean went on their first date to the Savoy Cinema on Dublin's O'Connell Street to watch the Christmas blockbuster of the time—*Ghostbusters*. In years to come, Moran would treat Jean to a lot better than a trip to the cinema because from that day on, Thomas Moran and Jean O'Shea became inseparable; and in a very short time, Jean had Moran wrapped around her little finger, the young gangster was besotted by her.

Nevertheless, behind this pretty and seemingly timid nature hid a violent young girl who would resort to anything to protect her man; Jean would not only become his wife in time but she was to become one of his closest partners in crime. It was a Bonny and Clyde relationship and it suited them both to have it that way.

Next was Moran's younger brother, Patrick 'Gonzo' Moran. Gonzo really looked up to his big brother and just wanted to tag along with the gang as he loved the protection he got from Thomas. In saying that, even though Gonzo was a tagalong, Little Don was very, very protective of his little brother and always looked out for his well-being because Patrick was his world along with his mother Marie and his newfound love, Jean.

Another of the St Christopher's residents recruited to the gang was 17-year-old Danny Moore, a school dropout who found it hard to make his way in life due to his lack of reading and writing skills. Moore's mother had passed away two years previously, leaving behind four young children in the care of their aging grandmother while their father was in and out of prison for theft and armed robbery.

Moran was everything that Moore needed and Moore was just the fool that Moran could find very useful. To be seen as an associate of Little Don's was good enough for him but for Moran, it would later become clear that Moore had a gift that would prove very useful in years to come.

Next up was all the gang's favourite, the fun-loving comedian and youngest member of the group—14-year-old Darragh 'Dar' O'Leary. Moran loved O'Leary like a brother as his Dublin humour and his zest for life always cheered him up.

Away from the young fun-loving members, love interests and family within the gang, there were the more heavy-handed members—two extremely violent and unstable young men named Brian 'Pudner' Smyth and Frankie McCann. In time, these two men would terrify the city of Dublin as Little Don's violent enforcers.

Of all the gang members, Pudner Smyth was the only man not living in the St Christopher's complex but he was accepted in because he was a close friend of Noel Slattery and his word was good enough for Moran. At the age of seventeen, Pudner was very intimidating-looking, being a heavyset young man standing over six feet three inches and weighing more than seventeen stone—just what a new gang needed.

The last piece in Moran's jigsaw was the mysteriously dark and frightening figure of Frankie McCann. Born in Dublin on 23 April 1968, Francis 'Frankie' McCann in time would—with only the mention of his name—send shivers down the spines of even the hardest of men. McCann would carry out some of the most vicious crimes the city would ever witness for his newfound boss, Little Don. When he was introduced to Moran, 17-year-old McCann lived directly above Moran's family home in St Christopher's and again, like all the other members, he worshiped the ground that Thomas Moran walked on. He saw Moran as the man who could get him involved in a world that would give him a chance at life like nobody else could ever imagine.

It all came about in March of 1985, when speaking with Pudner, Frankie showed an interest in joining the gang and without hesitation, Smyth swiftly explained to Noel Slattery who McCann was and what he was capable of. A couple of days later, Slattery met McCann and, impressed with the young man, introduced him to Moran; McCann from that moment became a vital cog in the group but in time, it became clear to all that McCann was a mentally unstable young man who had an extreme tendency for violence. Moran did not care because it was all too clear that Pudner and Frankie together made for a very powerful and deadly duo.

With his crew now in place, Moran knew that a bounty lay in wait not too far from the Inner City in the more affluent areas of Terenure, Rathmines and Renelagh. It was a thief's paradise and with house security not overly sophisticated in the 1980s, it made things quite easy for these young but talented housebreakers to fill their pockets.

The gang knew how to spot if a house was empty by taking notice if a car was parked up in a driveway for a number of days or if the post was left in the door or milk gathered on the doorstep; 99 times out of 100, these were hints that people were away on holidays. But the gang also broke into homes even when people were home; nothing was safe from Little Don's gang. Moran and Slattery actually got so good at house-breaking that they started taking orders from local people as birthdays and Christmas became a very lucrative time for the two young thieves.

A regular occurrence when breaking into a house was that the gang members would try to locate car keys and if successful, they would take the car out on a drive around the Inner City with their bounty placed in the backseat to be sold to their neighbours the next day.

One night in May of 1985, things did not go to plan when Moran and Slattery, then aged just seventeen, were out on a job in Terenure. The time was 3.15 am as the two unsuspecting thieves were leaving a house on Eaton Square when they were spotted by a Garda foot patrol, who immediately radioed in for backup from the local station not too far from the house.

When the two finished loading their bounty into a car they were about to steal, they were oblivious to what awaited them. As they reversed out of the driveway, a burst of flashing blue lights startled them as a Garda car pulled out in front of them with another behind, blocking their escape.

'Bollox, Noel, it's the law; leg it.'

'Fuckin hell, where did they come from?' shouted Slattery.

Both youngsters bolted from the car, trying to get away from their would-be captives as a Garda called out, 'Stop, stop there.'

'Get them. Get the little bastards,' shouted another when both young men tried to run but they were overpowered by a number of Gardaí.

As they were put to the ground, Slattery called out, 'Get the fuck off, ye scumbag cunt.'

'Shut your fucking mouth, ye little bastard,' shouted a Garda while another slipped on the handcuffs.

Moran called out to Slattery, 'Say fuck all, say fuckin nothing!'

It was a calm fresh night in this quiet middle-class area of Dublin until it was woken up by the ructions on the street and by now, a small crowd had gathered. In the crowd were members of Moran's gang who were alerted by the sirens and could only watch as both Moran and Slattery were put into separate Garda cars and sped away to the local Garda station in Terenure.

When they arrived at the station, Moran kicked out at a female Garda and a fight broke out in the main entrance as the two young men fought with members of the Gardaí. Moments later, a number of Gardaí had overpowered the young men and they were taken to separate interview rooms. As the sun rose on Dublin city, Moran and Slattery were charged with breaking and entering and car theft only to be released on a small bail, which was paid by an anonymous source.

The two young criminals were ordered to show up in the Kilmainham District Court at 10 am on 25 June 1985. The District Court could try a child or a young person under 18 for any offence except homicide, provided that in certain cases, the child's parent or the young person has been told of their right to trial by jury and has consented to be dealt with by the District Court.

Coming from a poor background, Moran and Slattery had no money to hire a private solicitor so had to make do with the free legal aid that was offered to them by the state. The morning of the trial, Little Don's gang turned out to support their leaders along with his girl Jean and mother, Marie. The judge presiding that morning was the Right Honourable Mary Ann Hooper, a well-known long-serving judge who was known for her stern courtroom manner, controlling the room with an ironclad fist. Hooper was a no holds barred judge who followed the book of law to the extreme and Moran and Slattery were about to find out just how tough she was.

Hooper called her courtroom to order, 'Thomas Moran and Noel Slattery, please stand.'

The court case took fifteen minutes in total and the judge announced her verdict. 'I will not tolerate this sort of behaviour and I will not have the circumstance of living in a deprived area as any type of excuse. Mr Thomas Moran, I am sentencing you to twelve months for breaking and entering and driving a stolen car. Mr Noel Slattery, I am sentencing you to nine months for your part in the breaking and entering. My verdict is that both sentences are to be served immediately. Take them away.'

Marie, sobbing at the verdict, shouted out to her son, 'you'll be alright, love, be strong.'

'I'll be sound, Ma; everyone, keep the patch sorted. I'll be home soon.'

With that, a loud cheer came from the devoted gang members. This was Moran's first serious brush with the Gardaí and the courts but most certainly, it was not going to be his last. His criminal empire was only just beginning.

'Silence in my courtroom; these are not the streets; please take them away, Guard.'

As the two young men were led away, Slattery cheekily winked at Judge Hooper and said, 'See ye again, love.'

Luckily for the young wannabe gangsters, still under the age of 18, they were charged as juveniles and would not serve their time in Mountjoy adult prison but next door in St Patrick's Institution for Young Offenders. Founded in 1858 and situated beside Mountjoy Jail alongside the Royal Canal, St Patrick's was Ireland's largest young offenders' institution, holding inmates aged sixteen to twenty-one serving a wide range of sentences.

Moran's time in juvenile prison did nothing to steer the young criminal away from his life of crime; in fact, it had quite the opposite effect. While inside the walls of St Patrick's, he associated himself with young criminals from across Dublin who taught each other new and improved ways to continue their way of life outside.

The one thing Little Don and Noel Slattery learned quickly within the walls of St Patrick's was that good behaviour gets you out of prison quicker; both became model inmates, befriending the guards and even the warden. The two even took reading classes and it was in the prison classroom where Little Don excelled and took to reading like a fish to water. If Moran was nowhere to be found on the prison landings, it was in the peaceful surroundings of the prison library where he would be found with his head in a book. *The Godfather*, obviously, was the book he always returned to when he had nothing new to take his fancy. This love for reading though was more of a weapon, for the intelligent young criminal read books to help feed his brain of how criminals of the past had operated; they fascinated him and he would learn from them.

On 15 March 1986, Moran was released from prison after he had been locked up for only nine months of his twelve-month term with Noel Slattery following just two weeks later. On his release, Little Don Moran had only one thing on his mind—money, and he wanted plenty of it. Only days after his release from St Patrick's, Moran went right back to work and within weeks, Moran had his gang drilled and prepared for any scenario. Nothing moved in or out of the Inner City without Moran's knowledge as the gang ran the streets around the south Inner City like a military operation, always keeping a lookout for Garda patrols when they brought in their bounty from the previous night's haul.

The gang had grown during his time inside as Frankie had trained a well-organised group of younger members to keep lookout on the jobs so that mistakes of the past would not happen again. Outside of the Inner City, the gang's rise to notoriety brought them deeper into Dublin's underworld as they began to get a reputation as a ruthless but professional bunch of young thugs within both the criminal underworld and the Gardaí.

Over time, the house robberies became obsolete because they came with a much smaller haul and a much bigger risk of being caught so Moran needed a new line of income. In Dublin's city centre, the gang found an Aladdin's cave full of riches as so many of the main shopping departments lay on their doorstep. Breaking and entering into shops and warehouses became a speciality of the young gang and soon, this became their main source of income. It was easy pickings for Moran's gang.

The operations were simple. In the 1980s, like with the houses, security on warehouses was poor so the gang found it easy to get in and out of the department stores and warehouses with ease. Most often, they would enter through the skylights in the roof of the building, find an unsecured area and let the rest of the gang inside the premises. When inside, it was mass rewards for the organised bunch of young tearaways; Little Don's gang was the best-dressed gang in Ireland and the women around the flats loved the knockdown prices they were receiving from the Robin Hoods of the Inner City. Little Don was now fast becoming the lord of his Inner City manor but he knew he had to keep things in order; the young gang leader became very protective of his patch and its inhabitants so if another gang tried to come in and take over, they would be met with some serious repercussions.

One such occasion was in November 1986, a neighbouring gang leader and two of his cronies beat up Danny Moore after trying to get money from him, knowing all too well he was flush with cash from doing jobs in the city. Moore was left in a badly beaten state and when Moran heard this, he was furious.

'I want this cunt done, I want it done now! Frankie, get your bunch of lads to find out where the cunt and his boys hang out and then we take them fucking down, nobody fucks with us, fuckin nobody! This is where we show this city we mean fuckin business, these cheeky cunts!'

Frankie, under strict orders, organised the gang to find the attackers, making sure that not one stone was left unturned until they were found and it did not take too long for the news Moran was waiting for. The information that arrived informed him that the gang he wanted hung out at a local youth centre close to the canal near Rialto Bridge every Monday night and that it closed at around ten o'clock. On the night of Monday, 10 November 1986, Moran, Danny Moore, Pudner, Slattery, Frankie McCann and two other young men from St Christopher's went out looking for the rival gang to teach them a lesson and show everyone exactly who the number one gang in the Inner City was.

The plan was in place and the day before, Frankie had made up weapons from pieces of 2 x 1 wood with three six-inch nails nailed into each piece. Moran and his gang lay in wait until Moore spotted the opposing gang leader heading home from the youth centre accompanied by two associates and he promptly pointed him out to his friends,

'That's the cunt there, lads. The taller one, Tommy.'

'Okay boys, do this bastard good. Right, Danny, fuck off,' was Moran's order.

Moran and his gang swooped on the three unsuspecting young men, inflicting a savage punishment, the like never seen in the area before. The word on the street the next day was that in certain parts of the area, you could hear the young victims scream from the beating they received breaking through the silence of the Inner City night. The three young men had been beaten so savagely that one suffered a punctured lung while another was told that he would never be able to walk properly again. It even made the morning newspaper headline:

Savage attack on teens causes concern to Inner City residents

As ever, the newspaper got it wrong as not too much concern was shown, the silence that surrounded the attack from residents was far too evident. Over the next few weeks, a blanket silence came over the Inner City as the Gardaí hit dead ends everywhere they went, with nobody hearing or seeing anything on the night of the attack. The Gardaí soon gave up hope of catching those responsible for the attack because unbeknownst to them, the word had spread that if anyone was to speak to the Gardaí, they were signing their own death warrant. 'Little Don' and his gang had sent out its letter of intent to all in the Inner City or anyone who wanted to cross them.

Little Don's gang was officially born.

Chapter 4
Fast Cars

The summer of 1987 had arrived and the sun shone brightly down on the city as temperatures were reaching an irregular high of twenty-eight degrees to give Dublin one of her best summers ever. The capital's residents were not going to let it pass without making the most of the sun and everywhere you looked—from street corners to flat courtyards—people basked in the heat wave with a happy and positive vibe embracing the city that only the warmth of summer sunshine can bring. As schoolchildren were just beginning their summer holidays, the feeling of expectation of the long lazy days of summer hit the streets with a buzz that was far too exciting to hide.

In the midst of this heat wave, now aged nineteen, Thomas Moran had been out of prison for sixteen months and with his St Patrick's schooling now paying off, he became a more careful and callous criminal. He had earned himself a reputation among Dublin's criminal elite as one to watch and he was held in high regard within the criminal fraternity. Some criminals even joked that if there was an actual annual gangster award ceremony, Moran was set to become the Best Newcomer.

Carefully staying away from the watchful eye of the authorities, Moran had continued recruiting and nurturing some of the most violent and ruthless teenagers from the Inner City into the ranks of his gang. By June of 1987, he had a timely and welcome end to his parole terms just as a new social problem was escalating in Dublin and the Moran gang took to it like a fish to water. That social problem was car crime and this was to become widely known across the city as 'joyriding' and the Moran gang had garnered a passion for fast cars and the adrenalin rush it gave them.

Housing estates across the city were scourged with reckless driving by out-of-control youngsters who were using Dublin as a racetrack at any time of the day or night. Many unsuspecting victims would awake in the morning to find that their car had been stolen; some seeing their livelihood literally go up in smoke as the gang set the stolen cars on fire after they had finished with them.

Like all of Thomas Moran's best-laid plans, the gang's operation for stealing cars was simple and uncomplicated but done to absolute precision because Moran did not want to get caught cold ever again like in Terenure the previous year. Certain members of his gang became experts in breaking into vehicles; some of them even became top-class drivers with their favoured cars of that time being the Porsche 944 Turbo that could hit top speed of 157 mph, the Toyota MR2 and the Honda Prelude, all cars of high performance for a night's joyride.

It was on the night of 24 August that joyriding would come to haunt Moran when his self-adopted brother, now 16 years old, Darragh O'Leary, died in a car crash having had a falling out with his father. O'Leary, with a temper burning inside of him, stole a high-powered Porsche Coupé in Templelogue, another middle-class suburb of the city. Taking his anger onto the streets, the youngster took the car and hit the streets hard and after an hour, when he eventually decided to head home, he was recklessly driving down the Crumlin Road at 110 mph when a Garda patrol car spotted him and subsequently began to give chase.

Under chase, unlike the older members of the gang, O'Leary was not the most experienced of drivers and as he continued to speed towards his home patch leading him down Cork Street and approaching the very sharp turn at Ardee Street, he spotted another oncoming patrol car on the opposite side of the road.

In a panic, trying to get away from his pursuers, he began to do a full handbrake turn around a sharp corner when he lost control of the car, turning it repeatedly until it came to a sudden stop against a wall and within seconds, the fuel tank exploded and the car was amass with flames. It was at 2.33 am on the morning of 24 August 1987 when 16-year-old Darragh O'Leary instantly died in the stolen car and it would leave a community numb and shocked.

It was only hours after the accident when residents of the Inner City awoke to meet another glorious summer's day but the relaxed sunshine atmosphere was rocked as word spread around the streets of O'Leary's death. The rumour mill was in overdrive and stories spread like a game of Chinese Whispers. When the news eventually reached Moran through a young gang member, Deco Dunne, the story being told was that a Garda patrol car had deliberately rammed O'Leary's car and forced him into a spin, ending up running him into the wall.

Moran did not need or want another version of the story as he believed it to be typical of a corrupt anti-Inner City Garda force.

Seven days later, at Mount Jerome Cemetery in Harold's Cross, Darragh O'Leary was buried never to be seen again by his friends as a community was still getting to grips with the loss of one of their own young men. While the funeral party watched the coffin being lowered into the grave, Moran and his gang swore revenge on the people who took their young friend's life and a few short months later, they got their wish.

The long hot summer days had now long gone only to be replaced by a cool crisp clear Halloween night with all the young children now wrapped up warm in bed after a good night of trick or treating. A sharp frost was beginning to settle all around the city as Thomas Moran and his crew continued with the festivities into the late hours; it had just passed midnight and the gang of over twenty youths was still drinking around a bonfire giving off just enough heat to keep them warm when out of nowhere, a loud roaring sound startled them. The sound came from the dark of the green area around the flats and as the startled group turned and looked, they saw a car speeding across the green towards them as a loud voice shouted out, 'It's fuckin Frankie, the mad cunt!'

McCann began speeding around the gang in a brand-new Mercedes without a care, which saw the group run in all directions to avoid being hit as he drove the car right into the middle of the fire. McCann quickly jumped out and onto the grass to safety and moments later, the car was engulfed in flames. The on looking gang, momentarily subdued at the young gangster's outlandish behaviour, then began to scream and shout at the top of their voices.

'Frankie, ye mad cunt, go on!'

'Burn, yeah bastard, burn, yessss, come oonnnnn!'

'Wreck the fuckin place, boys. Do it for Darragh!' roared Moran as his gang began to wreak havoc on the Inner City with more cars being added to the fire, bottles being randomly smashed, shop windows kicked in and out of nowhere, a gang of now over forty young men began to loot the area.

Amidst all the mayhem, an emergency call had already been made and received at the local fire station close by in the Dolphins Barn area. On arrival, the firefighters found themselves under a barrage of stones and bottles and even firebombs hitting the engine. One firefighter had glass lodged in his eye when a bottle smashed into the side window of the fire engine and another was stabbed in the shoulder as the mob was now completely out of control. Moments later, a local Garda patrol arrived to assist the firemen but this was like a red rag to a bull. Moran saw this as the perfect opportunity to get revenge for Darragh's death.

'Take out that fucking pig's car, boys, and kill those cunts!' screamed their now demented leader.

With the order given around, a dozen young men and girls attacked the patrol car, smashed every window and burst all four tyres. The gang continued to attack the occupants of the car and one of the Gardaí got hit with a steel bar point-blank in the side of the head, eventually needing twelve stitches to close the wound.

Within seconds of the attack, Frankie McCann came charging towards the patrol car, repeatedly sounding the horn and flashing the headlights of another stolen car and again the gang had to scatter as McCann rammed the patrol car and knocked it across the street by around fifteen feet. The two Garda members, clearly shaken by now, narrowly escaped with their lives as their car lay in a wreck, leaving them to take off on foot, looking back only to see their vehicle set alight by a rampant gang of teenage thugs. Frankie McCann drove the now battered Ford Escort into the bonfire to yet more boisterous cheers of joy.

The Halloween celebrations still spiralling out of control, Moran decided to make his way back to the flats so he could watch over his men taking control of his area. He sat on the roof of the flats with Jean looking down at the bedlam below and he told her, 'Jean, one day I will run this fuckin city and we'll never want for anythin, I promise, I fuckin promise.'

'I know, Thomas, I know.'

The next morning, as Moran walked the streets, he found a battleground with broken windows and doors, and the smell of burnt-out cars and petrol irritated his nostrils as it went wafting through the cold Dublin air. He grinned when he noticed the patrol car where he and his gang had chased the enemy away from their doorstep. Moran thought to himself, *well now, that was a good fuckin night out.*

It was on that same day Moran was to hear from Noel Slattery that Pudner Smyth was arrested for the Halloween night disturbances. He had been charged for being the driver of a stolen car and was to appear in Kilmainham District Court later that afternoon.

'What the fuck, how was he caught, Noel?'

'He was tryin to leg it when the Garda came in from all over the place and there was a car with the engine on so he fuckin jumped inta it and before he could drive away, a fuckin gang of the pigs tore him out of it and arrested him. Poxy thing was he wasn't even in any of the fuckin cars last night; he was just tryin to leg it.'

'Fuckin eejit, the stupid fuckin eejit. And they done him for being in a fuckin stolen car, wankers,' replied Moran.

'Yeah, and he might get stung for one of the people causin the riot too, Tommy.'

'The cunts!'

'Joey Flynn, Marko Dunne and Tommy Hopkins were arrested last night too, Tommy.'

'Fuckin hell! What time are they up at?' asked Moran.

'Not one hundred percent sure of the time, Tommy, but I'll find out and let ye know.'

'Okay, do that and come right back to me, Noel. Fuck!'

It was later that afternoon when Slattery was informed that Smyth was to appear before the judge at 10 am on 2 November in Kilmainham so he and McCann went to the court to find out their friend's fate. The news was not good as the judge had heard reports of the riot, stolen cars, looting and attacks on the fire brigade, patrol cars and the injuries to members of the Gardaí and fire services. The judge was not in a forgiving mood but luckily for Pudner, he could only be charged with driving a stolen vehicle and not for organising the riot.

'This sort of behaviour will not be tolerated and I will not take light of it. I find you, Brian Smyth, guilty as charged and I will pass sentence on these matters. I will retire to my chamber to decide your sentence and court will resume at 3 pm tomorrow.'

Smyth was sentenced to twelve months on Spike Island, a jail for young offenders in Cork Harbour, which held up to 100 inmates. Smyth was to serve only six months of his term.

Life went on as Pudner was inside; when on 25 March 1988, Moran, Slattery and McCann were in Dublin city centre and short of money, they had only one thing on their mind—someone was going to pay up. When they came across 31-year-old Sean Gallagher, a van driver from Santry who was only out doing a day's work, he never expected what was going to happen.

'Lads, I'm fuckin starving but I'm fuckin skint,' spoke Moran.

'No problem, Tommy, leave it with me,' was McCann's reply.

As Gallagher began to put the key into his van door, McCann approached him on Sackville Place, a small side street off O'Connell Street, and without thinking, McCann pushed him to the ground and ordered him to give him all of his money while in the background, his friends laughed at their friend's brazen attack.

A terrified Gallagher, who was only a slight man, was no match for the big burly thug and within seconds, the laughter had turned to a more serious mood as Moran and Slattery kept a lookout for the Gardaí. McCann served a severe beating on Gallagher when he refused to hand over any money then pulled out a fishing knife, stabbing the helpless and terrified Gallagher, leaving him lying in a pool of blood to die alone. McCann was cold and callous in his deed but without remorse, Moran and Slattery emptied his pockets before they left.

'Nice one, lads, let's get some grub, yeah?' suggested Slattery who was sniggering away.

The next day, Sean Gallagher's family appealed for information on the TV in a brief statement released through the Gardaí.

'Devastated at the loss' and asked for 'anyone with information to please go to the Gardaí'.

The phones never rang and Sean Gallagher became another unsolved crime and a soon-to-be statistic. What was more frightening for the city was that this would not be the last time the violent gangster Frankie McCann would take a life for his boss.

As a family grieved the loss of a loved one, Moran and his gang celebrated on 13 June 1988, when Pudner Smyth got out of prison and the gang went out on the town to celebrate.

'Welcome back, Pudner' was the toast from Noel Slattery.

As the celebrations continued, the members of the gang were unaware that their lives were about to change forever. This gang of loose cannons was being kept under close watch by an interested party and he was about to come looking for the new king of the kids, Thomas 'Little Don' Moran, as a new era was dawning.

Chapter 5
Benny Jewell

During the early 1980s, the scourge of illegal drug use had taken a savage grip on Ireland largely; it must be said, at first within the capital city of Dublin as communities were destroyed with heroin becoming the most popular drug of choice. Dealers delivered their poison with little or no fear of arrest due to a very small and uneducated Garda drug squad of the day, in saying that addicts and Gardaí alike were uninformed about the effects of this killer drug. So many addicts were getting caught up in the heroin epidemic as dealers were gathering an army of poor unfortunates who would never fully recover from this addiction.

Indeed, heroin took many lives but many recovering or recovered addicts would never get back to a normal life from their time on the drug due to underlying medical conditions such as collapsed veins, bacterial infections of the blood vessels and heart valves and other soft-tissue infections. Many years of abuse also result in clogging the blood vessels that lead to the lungs, liver, kidneys or brain that can cause infection or even death of small patches of cells in vital organs.

The fact is that while on heroin, the actual intake reacts to send the addict into a momentary state of relaxation and euphoria, what is called a 'downer' effect. This blocks the brain's ability to perceive pain but only for a short time until the drug intake wears off. Other symptoms such as shortness of breath, dry mouth, small pupils, disorientation, cycles of hyper alertness followed by suddenly nodding off are all signs of heroin abuse.

Other less obvious signs are repeatedly stealing or borrowing money from loved ones, or unexplained absence of valuables, a more hostile behaviour towards loved ones, including blaming them for withdrawal or broken commitments, a decline in self-esteem or worsening body image plus even wearing long pants or long sleeves to hide needle marks, even in warm weather.

Users build tolerance to heroin, leading to increases in the frequency and quantity of heroin consumption. With growing tolerance, more definitive physical symptoms of heroin abuse and addiction emerge, such as extreme weight loss.

This wave of addiction accentuated a social crime rate into its north and south Inner City flat complexes and many a housing estate across the capital. Heroin addiction caused a wave of petty crime such as muggings and an array of robberies as addicts tried to secure cash for their next 'fix' by whatever means necessary; addiction is a cruel mistress and nothing, and I mean nothing, can come before that next fix. This made many of the affected areas all but uninhabitable for the rest of the population; it was reported and actually told to my face by ex-addicts that within the North Inner City area, young children were mugged on their First Holy Communion day as addicts knew they had money on their person, that they stole from their own homes and even turned to prostitution to feed their habit; it was a daily battle.

Other such pitfalls for addicts came from when they began dealing to feed their habit, getting payment by a steady flow of fixes in return. The problems really began when they were using more than they were selling and as a result falling into the hands of the deadly drug gangs who were not very sympathetic when they did not pay up, leading to severe punishments or even death.

The saddest part of this entire epidemic was that over the years, many a family would lose loved ones to drugs from overdosing, bad drugs or even suicide when the addiction became too much for these poor lost souls. You must remember that for the addict, the only thing that mattered to them was that everything was good once they got their fix to take away the pain for a while but when the pain returned, the routine would start all over again.

In many parts of the city, in front of all to see, addicts would openly feed their addiction in public places by the preferred way of injecting heroin into a vein. If taking heroin was not bad enough, needle-sharing became the norm for many; many heroin users across the city were unaware that with needle sharing, there were even more deadly consequences. The threat of contracting diseases like Hepatitis C and HIV, however, soon became a stark reality and again it must be stated that there was a serious lack of education or warnings of the possibilities of contracting such diseases as these dangers were not explained by the government or health authority when the heroin epidemic broke so nobody knew or cared if the person they shared with was clean from any possible transmitted diseases.

The illegal drug trade saw the establishment of serious organised crime syndicates across the city, flush with money and heavily armed while controlling the streets with violence on a level largely unseen before on the streets of Dublin city. The lives of a whole generation of Inner City youth was blighted by the heroin epidemic as young people were dying with frightening regularity across communities.

Just take a short stroll from Leinster House, the home of Ireland's Parliament buildings, where you will find yourself in a very different world from that depicted in the Board Fáilte adverts or the glossary of pretty travel programmes they issue. Young people were caught in the grip of this epidemic and there was no way out for them in a society who did not understand the level of abuse or in many cases did not care about this problem as long as it was not on their own doorstep.

It was an epidemic, make no qualms about it, this was completely out of control. Sadly, in time, it would be proven that the governments of the time had underestimated the escalation of the drug problem while ignoring a city who was crying out for help, help that never arrived in time to try to save a generation of lost youth. Another major factor in the rise of drug addiction was that the Gardaí had pretty much no funding made available from Central Government for the anti-drug unit to combat these spiralling problems. In the early to mid-1980s, there were only thirty-five members in the Dublin Drug Squad, which meant that the Gardaí and Garda Special Branch were stretched beyond their limits.

In 1983 and 1984, the government of the day, led by Fine Gael, did establish a task force to combat the drug crisis and co-ordinate a response but this all came to no avail as heroin had already gotten a hold of Ireland and it was too little, too late.

This was partly due to the fact that no parliament was around long enough to issue proper legislation on national drug policy as government after government cabinet rapidly fell when Ireland went to the polls five times in total during the 1980s. The way many communities saw things was that the majority of the ruling elite in Ireland were more than happy to ignore these problems with people at the end of their tether as drug gangs worked with little or no hassle from the undermanned Gardaí; Moran was about to fully embrace this opportunity.

By 1988, Thomas Moran had garnered such a reputation that it was no surprise when one of Dublin's leading underworld figures called the young gang leader to a meeting to propose a new business venture. On the night of 3

September 1988, it had just turned dark when a knock on the door interrupted Marie Moran who was watching TV in the sitting room; she rose from her seat and upon opening the door, Marie was met by a strange face and was immediately cautious; this man was not like anyone she had seen before; the stranger looked more like a movie star and not a resident of the Inner City. Standing quite tall, the man was clean-shaven, neat and tidy and wearing a well-cut pinstriped suit; to Marie, he looked important, and that bothered her.

'Yeah, what ye want?'

'I'm lookin for your young fella, Tommy; is he in?' replied the stranger with a strong Dublin accent.

'For what, has he done sometin?' Again, with a tone of caution, asked the concerned mother.

'Ahh, nothin much. I just want to ask him about sometin.'

Moran was home at the time and overheard the conversation that was taking place so he made his way to the door to confront the well-dressed man. Appearing from behind his mother, Moran confronted the stranger.

'Yeah, I'm Tommy, wha do ye want?'

'Someone wants to see you about a job,' replied the stranger.

'Ma, its okay so can you leave me alone here?'

'Yeah, okay son,' said Marie, returning to her soaps on the TV and leaving Tommy to look after his own business; after all, he was now the man of the house.

'So, a job, you say. Who wants a job done and what kind of work are you and your friend inta?' asked Moran in a tone of interest and caution.

'Benny Jewell wants to see you on Wednesday night down in the Black Horse on Cork Street at 7 pm sharp.'

This rattled the young gangster as Jewell had a reputation and not many people got a visit from Jewell or one of his henchmen to organise a meeting. Moran quickly changed the tone in his voice from cocky to a nervous inquisition as he asked the stranger, 'Benny Jewell wants to see me, for wha?'

'How the fuck do I know; just be there. Okay!'

'Okay, okay, for fuck sake, calm down, will ye. Tell Mr Jewell I'll see him on Wednesday at seven.' The stranger left, leaving Moran's mind running wild as to why Benny Jewell wanted to see him of all people.

Drug lord Benny Jewell was a renowned gangster in Dublin's Inner City and a man who had the respect of near enough all who were involved in the Irish underworld and further afield due to his professional workings and friendly persona. Forty-year-old Jewell was an educated man who came from a well-to-do middle-class family in the leafy suburb of Donnybrook in Dublin 4, one of Ireland's wealthiest postcodes.

Excelling at university, Jewell had a brilliant mind and quickly realised how much money could be made from drug dealing and he wanted to know more about this illicit trade. It was in his second year of university when studying law, Jewell first encountered the world of illegal drugs during a fresher's party when he was introduced to marijuana.

Jewell befriended some local small-time dealers and in time would gradually become the leading figure in the marijuana trade on campus. From then on, Benny realised that law was not for him but Jewell being Jewell, he decided that he was going to finish university as he saw the future and realised that an education in law could become useful as drug trafficking and street selling was the future for this bright young academic.

Only a couple of years out of college, Jewell became a man known by reputation as a shrewd businessman and a source who could organise major drug deals and increase profits better than many of the uneducated drug dealers of the day. Jewell, not the biggest of men, hired well-known hardened Dublin gangsters to carry out extreme acts of violence on his behalf when needed but these men were also providing him with some well-needed protection.

It was a close-knit group and for those who worked directly for Jewell always stuck by him as he was very loyal to his people in return. It was well known that Jewell kept his men on-side by playing fair and paying handsomely while sorting out his gang financially, when required, due to bad gambling debts or alcohol issues; at times, he would also help with some legal matters by getting them off with minor and sometimes serious criminal offences.

Nevertheless, other gang leaders thought Jewell was mad to share so much of his spoils but Jewell saw it as an insurance policy, and none of his men ever turned, whereas other gangs had informers in the ranks or foot-soldiers wanting to take over from their bosses. He had, in a way, the steady ship in a stormy business.

Business was very good and Jewell needed to expand and he had a new man in mind to join his ranks, and that was Tommy Moran. Unknowing what was happening in the background, the visit from one of Benny's men had Moran at his wits' end and he called on his right-hand man, Noel Slattery, for advice.

'Noel, he wants to see me at seven next Wednesday,' explained a worried Moran.

'Tommy, I'm not too sure bout this, ye know. That Jewell is in a different league to us. Tommy, I tell ye, he is one clever cunt and those fuckin animals he hangs about with—'

With Slattery's outburst, Moran cut across him, 'I know, I know, Noel! Look, he called so I can't turn him down now, can I?'

Slattery replied in a stern voice while frantically walking around the sitting room of his flat, running his hands through his hair, 'No, no, ye couldn't. Okay but I'm goin along with ye and I'll have Frankie and Pudner in the pub in case he tries any shite.'

'Yeah, good idea. Right then, let's go see the lads,' gasped an uptight Moran.

It was 7 September 1988 and the meeting between Moran and Jewell was due to take place in the Black Horse on Cork Street, not too far from Moran's home. Outside the pub, Moran handed out the orders to Noel Slattery, Brian 'Pudner' Smyth and Frankie McCann, just in case, as Slattery said, 'If anyone was goin to try any shite on their leader'.

'Okay, Frankie, sit at the bar and Pudner at the jacks. Noel, you stick to me like fuckin glue.'

With nods of approval given by each of the young men, Moran took a deep breath. 'Right then, Noel and meself will go in first and then you two follow one by one about a minute apart and sit where I just said. Right Noel, let's go ahead in.'

Both young men entered the bar and found Jewell sitting at the rear of the bar accompanied by a heavily built man, a man named Andy Russell. Russell was a career criminal hailing from the Joyce House flat complex in Bluebell on the outskirts of Dublin city centre and had been in and out of prison since his teens for an array of crimes.

All his life, Russell was open for work to anyone who would pay for his services because he was an established enforcer and was known to have at least three homicides to his name, including his own brother. Russell had never been charged with any of them due to the lack of evidence and witnesses suddenly getting amnesia when it was time to bring the case to court. A feared and callous gangster, he was recruited by Jewell for his undoubted talent, but Russell's loyalty to Jewell stretched even further.

On his release from prison in November of 1986, Russell had no one to turn to and nowhere to stay, bar Benny who took him in. Everyone he associated with before blanked him when he was sentenced to five years due to him raping the fifteen-year-old daughter of a close friend, and bad blood ran deep after this. After the rape, Russell was warned never to be seen in the Bluebell area again when a death penalty was put on his head, but Jewell saw a useful pair of hands and took Russell under his wing without hesitation, even if it did ruffle a few feathers within the Irish underworld.

'Over here, lads, come have a seat!' called out Jewell.

Moran patted Noel on the back, pointing the way as both young men sat down. As soon as their arses hit the seat, Moran went straight into questioning Jewell's reason for calling on him.

'So Benny, what is it ye want with me?'

Russell took offence to Moran's brazen questioning. 'You shut your fucking mouth and speak when spoken to, ye cheeky little bastard.'

Slattery got annoyed by this outburst and stood up to leave. 'Bollix to this, Tommy, let's get the fuck outta here.'

'You can shut your fuckin hole too, boy, or I'll make shite of that pretty little face of yours,' replied the now clearly frustrated Russell.

Moran stood up to challenge Jewell over Russell's brazen outburst and with Frankie and Pudner now inside the pub, both approached the table where the four men were situated.

'Right, enough of this shite; what the fuck is going on, Benny?'

'For Jaysus sake, Tommy son, will ye fucking relax for a bit, have a drink and I promise we will talk business soon,' replied a cocky Jewell, laying back, arms stretched out across the back of the pub sofa.

'What fuckin business, Benny?' barked Slattery but within seconds, Jewell changed his mood and looking right into his eyes he warned the young gangster.

'Call your boys off now, Tommy, or I will have them cut into little pieces and fed to the fucking fish.'

Suddenly, around ten men appeared out of nowhere and Moran, realising he was vastly outnumbered, called his lads off.

'Okay boys, sit down and relax,' ordered Moran.

Jewell, calming down the situation, called on the barman, 'Derek, my good man, drinks for my young guests please and keep them coming. It's all on me.'

A couple of edgy hours later and after a few pints had been downed, Moran put the question to Benny Jewell again, 'So Benny, out with it. What is it you want with me?'

'Okay Tommy, okay. Right, so it's business time, that is fair, I guess.' Benny sat upright, clapped his hands and then continued to rub them together.

'But first, before we get down to it, you boys head off to the bar. I want you to answer me this one simple question, Tommy, in private. So, pretty-faced Noel, big man Smyth and you scary-looking cunt, fuck off for a sec. I want to talk to your boss,' ordered Jewell, pointing at each man as he spoke to them.

'What?' protested Slattery.

'You heard me,' Jewell replied, giving Slattery a long hard stare.

'Go on, Noel, its cool,' said Moran.

Noel Slattery got up and went to stand at the other end of the bar with Frankie and Pudner as Jewell put the question to Moran.

'Okay Tommy, tell me this. Can you trust these three little pricks?' asked Jewell.

Moran, sitting forward on his seat, answered the question firm and prompt, 'With my fuckin life, I would die for them and them for me. These are the best lads around this area, Benny. Why do you ask?'

A very impressed Jewell nodded his head on hearing the answer. 'Okay, okay, then let's talk. Call your boys back over.'

'Right boys, come on over and have a seat,' called out Moran.

Jewell nodded at Slattery. 'Okay, we all settled down now?' All four men nodded and began to listen to what Benny had to say.

'Yes? Grand so, but I must admit something that you lot must be baffled about.'

'What would that be now, Benny?' inquired Slattery with a puzzled look on his face.

'Let me explain, young pretty Noel. I was the one who posted bail for you pair the time you were arrested for breaking and entering a couple of years back.'

Shocked, Moran asked, 'It was you, Benny? Always wondered where that money came from.'

'It was indeed, Thomas, it was indeed.'

'But…' stuttered Moran.

51

'But my hole,' laughed Jewell. 'Let's just say I invested in you lot because I saw a bunch of lads who I could have some use for in the future and so far, you have not let me down. You lot are capable people who work well and I like that.'

Again, a puzzled Slattery questioned, 'You invested in us? I don't get ye, Benny.'

'We have been watching your goings-on for the last couple of years.'

'Oh yeah?' asked a smart-arsed Pudner.

'Yeah Fathead, we have. Look boys, how the fuck do you think you got away with some of the shite that you've pulled off? Well!'

Slattery cockily remarked, 'We are good, I suppose.'

'Suppose!' Jewell paused and contemplated his next words. 'Well yes, I will give you that, you lot are quite good at what you do and that is why you're here with me now. You see, boys, it was I who put the word out that anyone who grassed on you especially after the job you did on that young fella after he left the youth club, yeah, I fucking know who did that,' again pointing at the four young men individually as silence came over the group.

'So if anyone grassed on you, they answered to me. You do not have the pull that you fucking think you have, Little Don Moran. It is 'Little Don', isn't it, big shot?' asked a sarcastic Benny Jewell.

Moran, embarrassed, answered Jewell, 'Fuck off, Benny.'

Jewell broke into laughter then he turned to a more serious tone as he put a proposition to the young gangsters.

'Okay, enough of this bollox; let's get down to the real business of why you lot are here. Right, you lot know who I am and what I'm into, right?'

Nods of acknowledgment came from Moran and his men.

'Okay, look…I want lads who I can trust and who will follow orders and won't fucking rob me. We have plenty of money to be made here, lads, if you want it, and I fucking mean plenty of it. The thing though, how much do you really want it is the million-dollar question. It's not easy but it is financially huge. Do you want it, boys?'

'What is this work, Benny, for fuck sake?' snapped Slattery.

'Watch your fucking mouth, Noel. Don't you ever be so fucking sharp like that with me again!'

Moran replied, 'It's cool, Benny, relax. Noel is just curious like the rest of us. So what is the work you have for us, Benny?'

'Okay, okay then. I need people to look after my backyard, especially in and around the South Inner City, I need people to look after my drug business, are you and your boys up for it, Tommy?'

A dead silence came over the group again as they all turned to see what Tommy Moran had to say.

'Well boys, are you fucking interested!' barked Jewell.

'Fuck yeah,' was the answer from a delighted Moran.

'Yeeesssss, that is what I want to hear Tommy, 'Little Don', that's the good lad. Okay, this is how we work…' And Jewell began to explain the workings of his heroin business as an excited gang listened with bated breath as Jewell detailed the running of the operation they were about to take on. Over the next hour and a half, the plans were laid out but Jewell also explained to his new young gangster about the threat from sources out to stop drug dealers and how they would have to be careful.

'You'll have to watch out for the Mockeys, the Provos, the Garda and the last lot are the CPA fuckin D cunts, so keep your fuckin eyes and ears open,' Jewell continued to explain.

Pudner, confused, asked Jewell, 'What the fuck is a Mockey and who in the name of Jaysus are CPA fuckin D?'

'Pudner, I see you're not the brains of the bunch now, are you?' joked Jewell.

'Okay then, listen in; first off, these cunts, the Mockeys, are a Garda undercover operation with a twist. Now get this. They are off fucking duty Garda who use their own personal time to take us on. The Mockey's name came from them mocking or pretending to be addicts so they were christened the Mockeys. They were formed in the North Inner City from Store Street Garda station to take us down.'

'Fuckin hell, Benny, off-duty cunts?' asked a shocked Moran.

'Yes Thomas, unbelievable! Now lads, listen carefully, be wary of the Provo's lads and steer well fucking clear of them, that's all the advice I can give on those lot. Far too organised and powerful to be fucked with plus they hate us, so stay the fuck away.'

'Fuck them IRA lot,' came the arrogant reply from Smyth.

'No! Not the fucking IRA, no! Stay the fuck away from them and do not fucking cross them! Tommy, make sure you fucking stay clear of them.'

'Sound, Benny, we will.'

'Now, moving on, my favourite bunch, the fucking Concerned Parents Against Drugs. Now this lot are a group of people who target drug dealers. Us!' explained Jewell. Benny pointed his finger at all present at the table. 'And they blame us! Because we supply the gear to their fucking kids so their fucking kids can get high and now because they are a bunch of walking fucking zombie junkies, they turn on us! If they were any use as fucking parents, the kids would not be on gear in the first place, fucking cunts the lot of them! So, they and their cunt kids can fuck off!' Laughter broke out among the group.

The CPAD or the group's full title, Concerned Parents Against Drugs, began in Dublin's Inner City around 1983 by ordinary citizens who organised to save their communities from the epidemic of heroin. Not relying on a state to solve their problem as the governments past and present had already failed them miserably, they started to organise themselves within their communities.

The campaigns began when meetings were called by residents in their localities after many concerns were raised about the issue of open drug dealing, including heroin. The genuine fears from residents were that their children could be next to fall into the ill-fated world of the dealers or their children could stand on or fall on dirty syringes, and on certain stairwells in the flat complexes more than often, you could find addicts who had overdosed or laying strung-out where they fell. CPAD was strong in parts of Inner City Dublin and later, suburbs of Dublin like Cabra and Crumlin.

The CPAD groups decided that they had to deal with the problem full on and they needed to adopt some simple but sometimes very dangerous strategies. On many an evening on the streets of Dublin, after an organised mass meeting by CPAD, they marched to a suspected dealer's house, telling him or her to get out of the area. At times, some of the members of the group forcefully evicted suspected dealers while making a direct line of people, physically removing the furniture from the house or flat so that no one person could be charged with any offence. Smaller groups of people, often from other areas to limit the possibility of revenge attacks, called at the houses of suspected dealers, telling them they would have to leave.

Posters with photographs and addresses of dealers were posted around the local areas. The communities mounted permanent vigils at the entries to their estates, preventing any suspected dealer or addict from outside the area from gaining entry. Residents operated the pickets day and night and over a time, they became a permanent fixture of Inner City street life. Heroin was big business, and those standing in the way of that business were selflessly putting themselves in considerable danger. Some of the anti-drug activists were threatened by dealers and a couple even lost their lives; others were shot at but survived.

Word was rife on the street that, officially, the Provisional IRA was not involved in CPAD, but unofficially, IRA volunteers on the ground, and at times against the command of the leadership, were involved in CPAD activity within their own communities. This alone worried Jewell more than anything. Few people within the CPAD had problems with IRA inclusion but the Gardaí were always highly hostile to the anti-drug campaigners; because of this, many of whom faced serious intimidation, were stopped in the street, brought in for questioning, they even had their houses raided or were beaten. It was also widely suspected that some Garda members were very close to major dealers, including strong rumours that heroin was appearing back on the streets in evidence bags.

'Right…' Jewell stood up and called out so all in the bar could hear.

'From here on in, Tommy 'Little Don' Moran and co. work for me and from that they come under my protection. Let it be known: anyone fucks with them fucks with me.'

Jewell then sat back down and put out his hand to Moran. 'Welcome on board, boys.'

'Sound, Benny.' Moran shook hands with his new employer. Moran knew that it was clear to all that Benny Jewell had a personal hatred for the CPAD as they had been a constant thorn in his side for many a year. Moran, even though Benny Jewell had told them, once again warned his young gangsters to steer clear of them and its supporters and not to bring on any unnecessary attention. On top of that, he made it crystal clear that Benny was adamant that the Provisional IRA was an organisation he did not want to be hounded by and under no circumstance were they to go anywhere near them as these were far too dangerous a group to piss off and he knew it. To finish, Moran told his lads to keep their fucking heads down and just get on with their business.

Within days of meeting Benny, Moran was always on call for addicts looking for fix after fix from the young dealer as he had a product with no shortage of customers. Lucky for Moran, the gang was new to the business so they went under the radar of CPAD who targeted the majority of Jewell's more senior gang members, including Jewell himself and his right-hand man, Andy Russell.

In time, the drug problem became so closely intertwined with the fabric of the community it was no longer possible or desirable to adopt the tactics of

CPAD because some people would be targeting members of their own families. There was also a clearer realisation that there was nothing to be gained by just pushing the problem and the addicts from one area to another.

One of the first jobs the Moran Gang had to carry out for Benny on their new patch was to visit a local flat complex in the Inner City to collect a small amount of money from local drug addict, Séan Daly. Daly was known as a fine football player who was scouted by many clubs in England due to his undoubted talent on the pitch. Unfortunately, the sign of the times caught up with Daly and he fell into the world of drug dealing and ended up using more heroin to feed his own habit than he was selling to his customers. Jewell wanted payment and the gang was ordered to collect and let everyone know that they mean business, no matter what it took. One way or another, payment would be made.

On 9 February 1989, Moran arrived at the flat complex with Pudner and Frankie looking for Daly and when they identified him, all they found was a tired, drawn-looking figure with sallow skin, weighing no more than seven stone, sitting at his doorstep.

'Number 27b, Tommy, this is us,' remarked Pudner.

'Here, you. Are you Séan Daly?' questioned McCann.

'Alright lads. Yeah, what ye want?'

Moran challenged him about the money that was owed to his boss. 'We're here to collect Benny's money so Séan, have you got it for him?'

'Tell Benny I'll get it tomorrow for him. Now fuck off,' as he laughed at the young gangsters.

'Oh, I'm funny, am I? Take that cunt onto the roof, lads,' ordered Moran.

And with that, Pudner and Frankie picked the terrified Daly up off the doorstep and dragged him up onto the rooftop, kicking and screaming, tears streaming from his eyes and crying out for help. Nobody took a blind bit of notice as these were Benny Jewell's boys. A furious Moran lashed out with kicks and punches on Daly while Pudner and McCann stood back and laughed as their boss beat the drug addict until he was unable to move.

'Not so fuckin funny now, is it, ye dopey little cunt? Yeah, yeah? Not so fuckin funny now, is it! Now where is Benny's fuckin money, ye little scummy junkie bastard?' demanded Moran.

A terrified Daly cried out, 'I don't have it for fuck sake, please lads, please. I'll get it tomorrow. I'm owed some money and I'll have it tomorrow. Yeah lads? Good? Tomorrow okay?' were the words of a desperate man.

Moran, in a fury, ordered Pudner and Frankie to toss Daly off the flats for not paying a fifty-pound debt. Pudner and Frankie took hold of Daly and swung him back and forwards three times to clear the guttering, Smyth holding his arms and McCann his legs, and then they both released him. All three men watched as Daly fell three storeys onto a grass verge.

'Okay boys, let's get the fuck outta here before the law arrives.'

On hearing the news of Daly's misfortune, the following day, Benny Jewell called his young gangsters to a meeting where a stunned Jewell questioned the actions of his men.

'Why, after I told you to send out a message of intent, didn't you just fucking scare him if he didn't pay? Why did you all decide to go and play fucking Superman with the silly junkie cunt by fucking him off the flats?'

'Let me explain—' began Moran.

'Hold on for a sec there, young Thomas. Now it transpires that he…Mr Junkie is not fucking Superman and he now has two broken legs, two broken fucking arms and wait, now, now wait for this, he also has five broken ribs and, and a fractured fucking skull. The poor bastard is in intensive care. Now please explain what happened?'

Moran responded, 'Well, you wanted a fuckin message sent out, didn't ye? Well, it's fuckin out now, Benny.'

Benny turned to his men and laughingly told them, 'Oh, I like these boys, I fucking like them a lot. You, son, are one dangerous little bastard but more important, you are my dangerous little bastard. Come here, you,' as he hugged Moran. 'Drinks all around!'

Benny walked away giggling and muttering under his breath, 'Mad cunts.'

In a short period of time, Benny was so impressed with his new recruits that he gave the gang an area to control in his lucrative heroin business that had become vacant due to some gang members going out of business having been targeted by the Gardaí and given hefty jail terms.

The large area spanned the south Inner City from Dolphins Barn running across to Clanbrassil Street and from here down to the banks of the Liffey, then continued past the Guinness Brewery up towards Inchicore and back to the Barn. Moran had the world at his feet and the heroin trade was fitting into his life as if it was made for him and him for it.

Moran came up with a deadly but inspirational plan that was put into place with immediate effect. He came up with the idea of giving away the first fix free to unsuspecting clients, coaxing them into the tragic and violent world of drug addiction without a care. Slattery thought Moran was mad but later realised his boss was correct after addicts were flocking to them like lambs to the slaughter. Moran bought from Benny at a certain price and sold it at street level at a greater price, a wholesale-retail system, so to speak, was now in place. In the early 1980s, Dublin had an estimated 550 heroin addicts but later on in that decade, this figure had trebled.

Over time it became obvious that Benny Jewell had garnered a soft spot for the young criminal and Moran would use this to his advantage but he also saw Benny as a father figure. This fondness was tested on the night of 18 April 1989 when Marie Moran, Thomas' mother, being a notoriously heavy drinker got barred from the local pub having caused one of her all too regular drunken outbursts at the bar staff. Long after closing time, the bar manager Pat Callaghan refused to serve Marie any more alcohol after a long day of drinking with friends.

However, Marie told her son that the barman refused her because she was from the flats, not explaining that it was an hour after closing time when she had gotten into this spot of bother. Moran told Benny and a few days later, a couple of Jewell's men paid a visit to the pub and Marie never had a problem getting a drink after closing time again. But Benny was no fool and he quickly told Moran that this sort of thing was his problem in the future.

Nobody else in the gang, except Moran, was ever permitted to deal directly with Benny and under no circumstance would anyone else ever contact Jewell, ever. Benny wanted it this way so he was the only person knowing everything that was going on. Moran had all other gang members report back to him twice a week to keep him updated on every issue, no matter how small the reports were, and he promptly reported back to Benny. Things were now moving very fast for Moran and his gang.

Chapter 6
Street Dealers

The number of heroin users in Dublin during the 1980s continued to grow; a state report found that in certain areas of Dublin, 12% of 15- to 24-year-old males had used heroin and 14% for females of the same age group. The report also confirmed Dublin as the centre for heroin use in Ireland while an additional survey by the Department of Health in the late eighties found that 30% of intravenous drug users were HIV positive, but the dealers did not care about statistics because all they wanted was money, and Moran was about to cash in.

When the summer of 1989 arrived, Moran had just gone up the ladder in the Dublin underworld as he and his young gang had officially crossed the threshold into a world that could bring them everything they ever wanted. At this juncture in life, things could not have been any better for the brazen twenty-one-year-old as the word had spread across the criminal fraternity that he was now officially one of Benny Jewell's crew. Business was very, very lucrative for the gang who were now earning riches beyond their wildest dreams as they quickly settled into their new task of running heroin for Benny Jewell at a very effective rate.

Moran was also growing in stature by the week as he was learning more and more by the day directly from Benny by working close to him as often as he could. It must be said that Benny enjoyed Moran's company and was more than happy to have him tag along on business meetings and with Benny still calling most of the shots across the county, it was good for Moran to be seen with the crime boss. Other gangsters were introduced to him time and time again, meaning that Moran in a way was now officially a 'made' man.

Sitting at home one night, Moran was watching a programme on television explaining that there were huge amounts of monies to be made in the illegal drugs market. Quickly realising that the street dealing was only pittance to what he could be making, he learned that the illegal drug trade accounted for a large percentage of the world's annual economic intake with Europe being one of the major ports for international drug cartels to transfer drugs around the globe with ease. Moran immediately saw Ireland as a prime location to link Europe and this multi-billion-pound industry but what really made him sit up on the edge of his seat and take notice was the presenter saying:

'If you actually break down some of the world's largest industries and put them against the illegal drugs market, the turnover would be equivalent to approximately 8% of the world's total international trade, which is a staggering figure for any legitimate market, never mind an illegal market for that matter.'

Moran had no idea how much the 8% was but he knew it was a hell of a lot of money and all became clear to him as the presenter continued:

'The world financial body's figures estimate that the annual income generated from the illegal drugs industry ranges at somewhere between $400 to $500 billion from sales and all this puts drug smuggling into a frightening perspective.'

'Fuck me! 400-500 fuckin billion!' screeched out Moran in absolute astonishment at the figures. Now kneeling at the edge of his seat, the presenter continued:

'In addition, if you take account of these figures, you will find that they are greater than the annual income of the international trading in the iron and steel sector, the world motor vehicles manufacturing industry and on par with the massive international trade in textiles.'

'Fuckin hell,' quietly whispered Moran to himself while thoughts ran away in his mind of what could be. The young gangster had now found his focus and even though he knew he was only a minor dealer within the bigger picture of the drugs market, he now wanted more, lots more. Understanding that with big money came bigger responsibilities and massive danger, Moran was all too aware of what came with the territory and he was not deterred from making his mark on Ireland's drug trade. In time, these dreams would come with its own pitfalls as they would see friend and foe come and go as the gang strived to become kingpins in Ireland's dark and violent underworld.

That same night while sitting at the kitchen table in his flat at St Christopher's, he devised a plan to run the drug market in Ireland by launching a more profitable and less sporadic industry that was then in place. Moran saw the possibility of getting the smaller dealers to unite under one umbrella, his and Benny's umbrella. However, this was not going to be easy and blood would spill but that was part and parcel of the industry that the Moran gang now found themselves involved in and from that day, Moran put his plan into action.

It may have been on a smaller scale than he wanted but he knew that he had to start somewhere and it was to be the Inner City as the place to build his empire from and with the main core of his gang now in place, he was on his way to the top as things were falling nicely into place. Moran now had the money and the backing to become the biggest dealer in Dublin and with Benny Jewell on his side—he had the perfect supply line to make that a reality.

The gang now included his best friend Noel Slattery, girlfriend Jean O'Shea, leading gang members Danny Moore, Brian 'Pudner' Smyth and Frankie McCann. Other not so senior members included Moran's younger brother Gonzo, St Christopher's residents Joey Flynn, Marko Dunne and heroin addict Tommy Hopkins. Add to this many younger members running errands for him across the Inner City; fact was that Moran had formed probably the most efficient crew in Dublin city.

Each and every one of the members was given a specific job and Moran, as ever, had his gang well drilled and organised right down to the last tiny detail. All of the gang members knew all too well that in Thomas Moran, they had a fussy boss who was an almighty stickler for detail; he made sure everything was done right and then made sure it was done right again. Moran did not tolerate mistakes and this was so evident when on one such occasion, he made sure that Gonzo wore a certain baseball cap to a drop after he told his client what type it was his brother would be wearing.

To Moran's utter annoyance, Gonzo lost the cap; in a fury, he made him go out and buy an identical cap so that everything was 100% correct for the drop and it took Gonzo three days to find an identical cap; he could have changed the item of clothing but not Moran—he was adamant he wanted things done right. All he had to do was contact his client and tell him Gonzo was not going to have the cap but no, not Moran, he never ever left anything to chance. It worked because all the other gang members felt that if he did that to his brother, what would he do to them; mistakes were very few and far between from then on, and once again, Moran was right.

When it came to handing out responsibility in the gang, jobs were divvied out in order of seniority as trusted members got the more important jobs and this trickled right down the line with the smaller and less dangerous jobs going to the lesser gang members.

Nevertheless, for Moran, every job was as important as the next and if one person messed up, no matter how big or small, it would be like a domino effect on his business, knocking everything down piece by piece. That was why he was so hands on with his members, making sure nothing was left to chance.

On deciding the formation of the gang, the first man on the list was Noel Slattery who was given the task of overlooking every aspect of the business with Noel knowing fully that everything went through Moran and Benny. Slattery had to make sure everything was being done the way Moran wanted it and only needed to report to Moran when a major problem occurred. He even had specific times to meet Moran on business and never was business discussed outside of these times, even when having a pint in their local pub because, as Benny had taught Moran, 'The fuckin walls have ears'.

Like the Moran and Benny arrangement, nobody was to contact Moran except Noel, or at times, Frankie; as Benny said, 'He's not very good at doing what we ask in relation to staying away but fuck me, I'm glad he is on our side. I'm not crossing that psychotic bastard'.

Moran agreed with Benny but also explained that it was best if he and Andy Russell were kept apart as 'Frankie can't fuckin stand the ground he walks on'. A nod of agreement as Benny thought this to be the best policy.

Moran was fine with Frankie contacting him; he knew that of all of his gang members, Frankie was one hundred percent committed to him and he would never talk out of place plus he never really listened to orders and nobody was going to challenge him on it.

Danny Moore, aided by Moran's girlfriend, Jean O'Shea, was put in charge of running the Drugs Den that housed the bagging and mixing rooms. They had Jean's two sisters and her auntie Carol working alongside them doing the mixing, knowing they would not rip him off as the money Moran paid was a hell of a lot more than a normal job would pay. Plus, if Moran lost stock or money, Benny still had to be paid and that meant Jean lost too.

Two other members of the Den were lookout, Philly 'Baldy' Cook, who got his name because of his young but balding head. Cook was to keep an eye out for the Drug Squad, CPAD or any other group that would cause problems. The other was Danny Moore's cousin, a young man who also came from the Inner City, Karl Moore, who worked in the bagging area of the Den.

One of the original locations Moran used to house the bagging and mixing of the drugs was in an abandoned flat he found in the Inner City close to where he lived. The flat had been left idle for months after the previous occupiers were evicted for non-payment of rent. However, not long after he moved in, they had to move the factory away from the site when a crew of Dublin Corporation workers tried to gain access to start renovations on the premises to rehouse more Corporation tenants.

Moran, being a cute-minded man, persuaded the workers with a handsome cash payment to ignore what they had seen and told them to return the next day, giving his gang time to move all the gear from the flat. One hour later, the flat was empty but Moran knew well that this had been far too close a call and from that moment on, he decided no premises would be used for more than 3 or 4 days at a time, reducing the chances of their being caught or, as Moran put it, 'The authorities can't stake us out if they can't find us'.

One of the most important jobs in the gang was given to Frankie and Pudner who were both put in charge of the money collections from the streets. The money would be given to either one of the two men at a certain time on a certain day, which changed by the week so that the routine could not be picked up by CPAD or the Garda drug unit. Nobody wanted to owe Moran money due to the frightening fact that the pair had gained a fast-growing reputation for extreme violence. These reputations would grow under Moran as they would sort out any problems that needed urgent attention, no matter what it would take, because McCann and Smyth became very good at enforcing Moran's street law.

Other top jobs in the gang were put in the hands of Joey Flynn, Marko Dunne and Tommy Hopkins who did odd jobs when called upon but their main function was working as street distributors, moving the gear to the street dealers that were, of course, hired by Moran, Jewell and at times Slattery. All three men had been given allocated areas by Slattery to work from and under no circumstances were they to cross over to another dealer's patch.

Over the months, Moran had begun to trust the young men more and more as Flynn, Hopkins and Dunne later got jobs to not only deliver the drugs but also collect the profits from each of the street dealers on a weekly basis.

Money never went astray because the dealers had to set up meetings with Gonzo who became one of the most important links on the streets for his brother. Gonzo worked as the middleman between the collections and delivery of money and drugs. He delivered the drugs across the Inner City to Flynn, Hopkins and Dunne direct from the factory every Wednesday morning.

Like the attack outside the pub many years before, Wednesday was the day people mainly got their dole money so business would be good; again, another one of Thomas Moran's masterminds. Every week, Gonzo would travel around the Inner City area on his pushbike, meeting distributors in cafés, pubs and alleyways while handing out the drugs or collecting money. He also collected the profits from the previous drop on delivery of every new batch from the trio of men each week and as time went by, demand increased and the drugs were delivered up to three times a week. Yes, Gonzo had a small fortune on his person at times but nobody was going to mug him.

After Gonzo collected the money, Frankie and Pudner would organise to meet up but as usual in different places around the city so that they could not be pinpointed by anyone as large amounts of cash changed hands. The rule of law from Moran to all his dealers and collectors was that under no circumstances were any of his drugs to be passed over if the money was not handed over first—simple—and the buck stopped with the person who did not come across with the cash, whatever the level in the gang. If the money or drugs did not change hands when it was supposed to, then someone would pay, whoever messed up.

And messed up someone did when in October 1989, the money did not surface after Gonzo could not find his street distributor, Tommy Hopkins. Not thinking too much of it, Gonzo thought he may have mixed up his times so he decided to head off to the nearby flats complex of St Mary's to the home of local addict, Kevin O'Rourke, who was one of Hopkins' dealers and a close friend.

Gonzo, now a drug addict himself, thought a nice fix of heroin would sort him out before looking for Hopkins but when Gonzo inquired about Hopkins' whereabouts, alarm bells went off when O'Rourke explained that he never received his weekly delivery from Hopkins. On hearing the news, Gonzo was sent into a blind panic and he immediately started fearing the worst but not knowing exactly what was going on, he still gave Hopkins the benefit of the doubt before informing Frankie.

It was now late afternoon and Frankie as usual was expecting to get the money from Gonzo at 5 pm outside the local church next to St Christopher's flat complex. The one thing Frankie liked about Gonzo was that he was never late but as he waited, he did not realise that Gonzo full of fear was quickly making his way to Hopkins' flat in St Christopher's.

When he arrived, Gonzo noticed that the door was open and what he found made him physically sick because what met him inside the flat were Hopkins, two other men and a young woman lying flat out on the floor of the sitting room. On further examination, he noticed that the room was a litter with used needles and discarded pieces of aluminium foil and while he was searching to see if any of the drugs were left, he also spotted the burnt spoons around the room. Gonzo froze as it did not take a genius to realise that Hopkins and his friends had used up a large amount of the supply of heroin he was supposed to give out to the dealers.

'Oh fuck, oh fuck, fuck, fuck, fuck!' panicked Gonzo because he knew that someone was going to pay and pay dear, and he decided right there and then that he was not going to take any of the blame. Immediately, he ran to his meeting place with Frankie where he found him waiting impatiently and explained what had happened to him.

'Where the fuck were you, Gonzo; it's half fuckin five, ye prick. Freezin me bollox off here.'

'Ahh here, Frankie look, it's not my fault right, but look, Hoppo and some junkies are after using loads of the fuckin gear.'

'What! For fuck sakes, where are they?'

'At Hoppo's flat.'

'Okay, okay, Gonzo, leave it to me. You're sound so relax, okay?' Gonzo nodded and breathed out a massive sigh of relief.

'Look, Gonzo, you go find Noel, tell him the story and I'll get Tommy and Pudner. Now fuck off.'

It did not take long until McCann found Moran and Pudner who then gathered together some men who all went to the flat to get the drugs, the money or revenge. Moran wanted something and he was not leaving without it. Unfortunately for Hopkins and his guests, it was the latter; Moran was not in a forgiving humour that day and on that night, Tommy Hopkins, the two men and even the young woman were savagely beaten with hammers and golf clubs and had part of their bodies, including their genitals, burnt with a blowtorch.

The screams were heard around the flat complex but nobody was going to interfere, fearing the same fate as the hapless addicts. Weeks after the attack, Hopkins committed suicide and Moran never had a problem with money again; everyone paid on time.

After that incident, Moran was to become even more careful, trying not to attract too much attention from the watchful eye of the detectives from the drug squad who at the time were leaning on Benny Jewell like never before. Benny was a marked man but Moran's gang was still going under the drug squad's radar, totally unnoticed. Benny took all the heat from the Gardaí, knowing that the money was flowing as his young prodigy was flourishing.

Moran and his gang were now making a very pretty packet from the Dublin heroin trade and could boast to having a steady weekly income of over two thousand pounds a week. Around that time, the average weekly household income was around two hundred and fifty pounds.

With things falling nicely into place in Dublin for Moran and his men, a new craze was beginning to break out across Europe and he really could not have planned the timing any better if he had done it himself.

Chapter 7

'E' Is for Ecstasy

During the late 1980s, a dance phenomenon exploded across Europe introducing a new generation of teenagers to a fresh new underground dance music scene, a scene that was to become known as Rave, with its many styles of dance music genre including Acid House, Electro and House music. Long before the rave scene hit Ireland's shores, its origins began as an underground clubbing fraternity in Chicago, Illinois, and then moving into Europe via English underground dance clubs. As ever with any new organisation, multinational or social fad, a mascot would follow and the rave scene was to be no different, having its very own famous icon—the well-known smiley faced emoji.

In the beginning, underground clubs steered well away from the watchful eye of a society who would not approve of them nor would the authorities who tried to close them down before the scene had ever really begun to find its feet. One of the major reasons for going underground was that during this period, there was an increasing number of chemical synthetic drugs on the market, the most common being amphetamines, LSD and MDMA, more widely known by its clubbing name—Ecstasy. The rave era was to be the breaking dawn for Ecstasy and young Dublin really did open her arms, accepting 'E' as if it was a long-lost relative.

Ecstasy was the ruler of the dance floor because it would intensify pleasurable effects, including an enhanced sense of self-confidence and energy, increased feelings of peacefulness, acceptance and empathy. Ecstasy enabled those people who would normally shy away from the dance floor to find the energy and courage to dance the night away and it was, of course, also a perfect match for those hard-core dancers to stay the distance in an all-night rave.

Now I am most certainly not saying that drugs are fine and of course, there are side effects from Ecstasy, including involuntary teeth clenching, a loss of inhibitions, transfixion on sights and sounds, nausea and blurred vision; does this sound like a good night out? Also, the drug increases heart rate and blood pressure as well as triggering seizures and even at times death.

Medical research also states that repeated use of Ecstasy ultimately may damage the cells that produce serotonin, which has an important role in the regulation of mood, appetite, pain, learning and memory. In the late 1980s and early 1990s, when the clubbers were out on the town in Dublin's underground clubs, none of this mattered and over the years, deaths occurred but the raves continued.

In addition to the underground movement, the rave scene had its own fashions, which included baggy loose-fitting clothing, perfect for dancing the night away to the sound of electronic beats pounding into the night skies. The day of a rave, especially the underground ones in Dublin, was like a secret sect and this would see teens and young adults hanging around the City Centre on a Saturday afternoon, catching the eye of someone similarly clad.

This was where the real magic lay, what created such a massive atmosphere, everyone on the same level, going through that initial birth of the Dublin rave scene together. It was dance, it was freedom of the floor and it was yours and nobody could take it away. The feeling of youth and being free to be who you wanted to be, music was always for the masses but sometimes it was for the few.

The secrecy behind the clubs was vital as they were at first held in places like abandoned warehouses or derelict housing blocks. Just imagine what it was like to walk into a crowd of hundreds of teenagers and young adults, dancing like no one was watching, with laser lights flashing all around you, music from the next century beating through your body and strangers instantly becoming best friends.

Tracing shapes in the air with glow sticks, teddy bears and assorted plastic toys worn as accessories and all through a dense fog of dry ice and retina-frying laser lights—all part of the experience. For many, it was an exhilarating feeling never seen or had before; it was like walking into another dimension and being free from all the woes of everyday life.

The rave scene was thriving in Dublin and it went mainly unnoticed until promoters started staging events in the Mansion House, home of Dublin city's

Lord Mayor. One particular night when a certain government TD and a select committee lined the balconies of the Mansion House to determine just how drug-fuelled these raves were, they actually gave it a clean bill of health.

Unknown to them, the very reason the night was free from any trouble was that the use of Ecstasy had all the clubbers in a buzz of love and energy that burned away on the dance floor of Dublin's first citizen's home; it was a drug-fuelled love-in but to the naked eye, it was a bunch of teenagers having a great night.

Other such clubs like the Olympic Ballroom in Dublin City Centre, which was a very popular and infamous venue for clubbers and the venue where the first 'mainstream' rave was held in April of 1990, the night in question was called Orbit. Just before the ballroom closed down, a new three-level nightclub called the Asylum opened and that is exactly what it was.

It bore witness to the first batch of 'E' casualties with burnt out ravers desperately chasing that initial rush while the dawning realisation that nothing this good lasts forever painted across their jaded faces. The club's eventual downfall was due to its very open display as a drug haven and it was soon shut down.

The Temple of Sound opened its doors in Dublin soon after and was in complete contrast to the Asylum, along with G1, another legendary club based in Phibsborough. An additional two clubs that worked away in the background slowly building from the ground up were McGonagles and UFO.

In 1988, McGonagles started with a mixture of indie, acid house and pop dance under the banner of the Voodoo club, the Dublin club scene was alive and well and the city's youth were lapping it all up. However, danger was lurking in the background unknown to the media and politicians of the time because Ecstasy was big business and Moran was ready to take full advantage as he was about to become very familiar with 'E' over the next few years.

As the 1990s dawned, Ecstasy was to be another of Moran's major source of income because at the beginning of the rave scene, there was a massive market to be tapped and he was more than ready to expand the gang's business. Moran and Slattery could not believe their luck as taking over the raves was reasonably easy due to the lack of understanding of the scene by older and out of touch dealers.

It took a very short time to have all the raves under control with Benny the sole supplier, at a price, of course. So Moran bought 1,000 tabs from Benny for

£2,000 and they would sell them for double or treble the wholesale price, depending on the demand but the demand was always there, simple law of business, and it worked a treat.

Once inside the venues, the gang members would take up strategic positions within the room to do the selling but keeping out of sight of possible Garda drug squad working undercover at the raves when the authorities eventually realised drugs were rampant at these venues. When all was in place, the word was spread around that the tabs were available in certain locations of the venues and business would boom; to combat any members of the drug squad catching them, spotters were put in place as an added security precaution.

Along with the effects of Ecstasy was another major long-term drug problem that grew from the rave scene, known as the deadly 'Party-Packs'. They originated through the rave scene when the realisation by drug dealers that many ravers being so wound up after having taken Ecstasy all night would be worried about going home out of their mind. The big fear was that on arriving home, their parents would see they were hyperactive and figure they were high on something and then stop them going to the raves again. So, Moran and his gang had a solution to this problem.

The Party-Pack was sold at raves with each drug sold to counteract the other, so one of the drugs being Ecstasy and the other heroin; one was to give you the euphoria to dance the night away—Ecstasy—and the other to bring you right back down again—heroin. So if you smoked a bit of gear, it would wind the ravers down before going home and of course, Moran's gang assured users they were safe because smoking a bit of heroin occasionally was not harmful to them in any way.

Of course, this was an absolute lie but to a man like Moran, it was only reaping more regular business because these were not young adults to him, just money so why the hell should he care, it was business and if they wanted the product, he was going to supply it.

In the 1980s, it would be fair to say that not many of the young club-going teens did know or understand any different and more and more young ravers were becoming heroin addicts before they knew what had happened to them. Moran was gathering a small army of clients and nothing was going to stop him. People who were, until then, weekend casual drug users became drug addicts through a popular youth culture being exploited by dealers like Moran who was becoming wealthier by the day.

Nevertheless, not all went to plan for Moran. In November of 1989, when Moran and Pudner were together in the city at a rave, they were approached by a young man in his early twenties.

'You got any Doves, lads?' asked the man.

Moran sensed something and right from the off knew this man was trouble and pushed him away, suspecting him to be too anxious to buy,

'Fuck off, will ye?' snapped Moran, alerting Pudner.

'I'm only here to have a bit of fun, buddy, like everyone else,' the man persisted.

Pudner told the man, 'Fuck off, ye silly cunt, we have nothin here.'

'I hear you're the men to see for some tabs, lads, come on, for fuck sake.'

Pudner then stood into the man closely. 'Did you not hear what I said? Now fuck off, you prick.'

He pushed the man to the ground and as the man got up, he again asked the question, 'Come on, boys, what's up with the aggro? All I want is to have a good time, look, I have money.' He pulled a bundle of notes from his pocket. This worried Moran even more. Moran called to one of the spotters, waving him over to him, and said, 'I think this cunt could be the law. Get everyone onside and get them the fuck outta here with all the tabs, now, just in case!'

At this stage, the man knew he was made and startled, he turned and began to walk off briskly. As the man fled away, Moran and Pudner took off after him. Moran alerted Frankie McCann and Danny Moore by waving his hands to call them over.

'Right boys, let's see who this cunt is.'

As the young gang followed the man into the laneway at the back of the building, he turned and warned, 'Don't be fuckin' stupid, lads; it's not worth the trouble.'

The gang then proceeded to approach him.

'Right, ye cunt, who the fuck are ye?'

'For fuck sake, lads, I'm just a bloke lookin' for a good time, honest.'

'No, no fuckin' way; you're a lying bastard, I think you're a pig and you're trying to land us in it, ye cunt,' replied a furious Moran.

'No lads, no, for fuck sake, not me, a copper? You're jokin me, right?' The man, now very uncomfortable, tried to run when Frankie pulled a knife and stabbed the man in the ribs.

'Aaaaaahhhhhhhhhhhhhhhhhh,' the man screamed in pain.

'Bollox boys, run for it. Come on, boys, come on,' shouted Moran.

Not long after the attack, the club was awash with plainclothes and uniformed members of An Garda Síochána who had lined up everyone in the club against the walls, quizzing each one of them about what had just happened. At that stage, the four gangsters—Moran, McCann, Smyth and Moore—had absconded and were not on the list of people taken by the Gardaí from the club that night.

Those who knew the Moran gang would not grass, no way, it was not worth it, and the vast majority of the club goers had no idea who he was anyway. However, the Gardaí wanted to talk to people again who were in the club that night in case they remembered something. The Gardaí were hoping that a slip of the tongue may point them in the right direction, but every wall was hit with silence.

The following morning, as Moran sat down to a cup of tea and a bowl of cornflakes, the news story on the TV in the background alerted him. The young man from the rave the previous night had died in hospital not long after he was found in the lane. The newsreader read the following report:

'Last night, the nephew of the education Minister, Deputy Eileen Larkin, was brutally murdered in a frenzied attack outside one of Dublin's popular rave clubs. Jeremy Larkin, aged just 22, died after a knife wound that he received punctured his lung; he later died in St James Hospital from his injuries.'

'Gardaí are appealing for any witnesses to come forward or if people have any information that may lead to the capture of the people involved; please contact Pearse Street Garda Station.'

'The Minister and her family are said to be distraught by the news and in a short statement from government buildings, the justice Minister on behalf of the government has said that not one stone will be left unturned until this murderer was found.'

'Oh bollox,' was Moran's nervous reply as he darted out of the flat to round up his gang.

In the meantime, Benny Jewell had heard the news from a member of his gang who had been at the club the night before. He was furious and called in the young men to find out what exactly had happened. As the lads arrived, they sensed that Benny was not happy.

'Right now, can someone please explain to me what the fuck went on in that club last night? Thomas…yes, you Thomas, my good man, enlighten me please to how a fucking Minister's fucking nephew is now fucking dead!'

'He asked if we had any Doves, Benny, I thought he was a copper,' replied a nervous Moran.

'So you fucking kill him! Tell me this, how many other customers have you fucking murdered! Because if you keep doing this, business will be fucking scarce! Oh, and one other thing, he ain't no fucking copper, you stupid fucks!' Trying to calm himself down, Benny again challenged Moran, 'Thomas, you or whichever one of you silly little cunts done it, you fucking killed a fucking Minister's fucking nephew, do you understand the position we are in?'

By now, Benny's temper had gotten the better of him. 'So let us say he was a copper, so instead of getting a minor charge for possession and a slap on the wrist, we now have to cover up the fucking murder of a TD's spoilt brat relation, a fucking Minister's fucking nephew! What were you lot fucking thinking? Do you lot ever think about the fucking consequences?' barked a furious Jewell.

'You stupid cunts, stupid, stupid cunts! Right, we have to get you lot offside for a bit until the heat dies down. So tell me boys, who did him?'

A dead silence came over the gang. Benny nodded with some sort of satisfaction. 'Very good, lads, very, very good indeed, keep it quiet like that, keep it very quiet. Right, I was thinking about this and I have an idea to get you lot offside for the next few months.'

'Where, Benny?' asked Danny Moore.

'Somewhere far from here, where nobody will annoy you or more important, you lot can't annoy anyone. Somewhere you lot will blend in nicely. You like the sun, boys? Because you better get fucking used to it.'

Noel Slattery was confused. 'What you on about, Benny?'

Benny turned to Noel and sarcastically explained, 'You're all going to the Balearic Islands in the Mediterranean Sea, you lucky cunts.'

Pudner was looking lost. 'The what, where now, Benny?'

'Pudner, I always said you were the brains of the group,' sniggered a sarcastic Jewell. 'Ibiza, lads, you're going off to the Islands for a few months. I'll sort your patch while you lot are gone so not to worry.'

'Sound, Benny, but—' Thomas Moran was cut off.

'But nothing; you're all going whether you fucking like it or not, end of fucking conversation. That rave scene will be fucking red-hot for a while because of this fuck-up so get yourselves to the Islands and spend some of that hard-earned cash you all have hidden away. Ride every little slapper with a heartbeat that drops their knickers for you. Just flash some of that cash and they'll be throwing them at you. Noel, I know you like pussy so bring a black sack of Johnnies with ye. Don't want your dick falling off now, do we?'

A cocky Noel Slattery smiling and looking at his friends, sang out, 'Here pussy, pussy, pussy. I'm havin plenty of that. Oh yes, bring it fuckin on.'

The group burst into laughter only for Benny to again interrupt, 'you all got passports, yes?'

Every one of them stood there shaking their heads, not one of them had a passport, as Moore stated, 'I've never been outside of Dublin, Benny, serious like.'

'Oh, for fuck sake. None of you? Fuck me. Okay, I want all your names, dates of birth, addresses. I'll sort it out. I have someone in the passport business.'

'Right, get packed and keep your heads down and stay away from your gaffs as much as possible before you go away just in case some cunt grassed you up. And do not go near each other either; the next time you lot will be together is on the Island of Ibiza. I'll sort the flights so when you receive your passports, get me your passport numbers ASAP, and I mean ASAP. When you arrive in Ibiza, get your own fucking accommodation! I've done enough for you.'

'Fuckin nice one,' replied Pudner.

'Right, fuck off,' was Benny's order. As they all left, Jewell called Moran aside and asked him, 'Tommy, will you more than try and keep this lot in line and trouble-free, for fuck sake, we're in enough shite as it is and we do not need the focus on us right now.' Moran nodded in agreement and both men shook on it.

'No problem, I'll sort them. Look Benny, stick Jean on that list for Ibiza, will ye? Now look, Joey Flynn and Marko Dunne know the story so use them while I'm away.'

'Will do; now get the fuck out of here, kid.'

Chapter 8
The Islands

Following on from the murder of Jeremy Larkin, the Garda investigation unit had not pinpointed anyone for the death. If truth be known, they were nowhere near arresting a suspect but when you had a government Minister looking over the shoulders, the investigation had to continue, and continue it did. For Benny Jewell, not everything was that clear cut and each day the gang were still in Ireland, his mind was racing away because he felt that it was only a matter of time before the Gardaí came knocking on his door.

In his mind, it would not take a rocket scientist to figure out who the leading player in Dublin's Ecstasy trade was. The one and only thing that would give him peace of mind was that his young gang were out of harm's way because as of now, they still had not come onto the radar of the National Drugs Squad and it was good business to keep it that way.

Benny, wasting no time, had within five days of the murder organised to have the gang booked on separate flights to the Balearic Islands—destination, Ibiza. Thomas Moran, Noel Slattery, Jean O'Shea, Danny Moore, Brian Pudner Smyth and Frankie McCann all found themselves on their way to their very own Mediterranean paradise to soak up some sunshine and leave all the troubles of Dublin far behind them.

At 8.30 am on Friday, 1 December 1989, the first of the group to fly out were Danny Moore and Frankie McCann on board Flight Ire202 from Dublin Airport, on-board Aer Lingus Boeing 737 flying direct to Ibiza. Moran had asked both men to seek out appropriate accommodation for the group in private villas, keeping away from the regular tourist crowd; a wise move due to the circumstances of their fleeing Ireland; privacy was going to be everything for the gang.

On their arrival at Ibiza, Danny and Frankie found out quickly that finding rental accommodation was a lot easier than expected as December was the closed season on the island with only natives, full-time staff, bar and restaurant owners and expats living on the island during the winter months.

Three days later, it was Noel and Pudner's turn to fly out to Ibiza, carrying a large amount of traveller cheques to tide the gang over for their extended stay on the island. Benny, for extra precaution and trusting nobody, had arranged for both men to fly out from Cork City airport on the 1.45 pm flight aboard a British Airways Jet, also flying direct to the island. The two young men had taken the Dublin to Cork train the previous night and Benny had booked them into a room in a local B&B close to the terminal they were flying from. Both men arrived on time to meet up with Danny and Frankie on Sunday night, still awaiting their leader, Little Don Moran's arrival to the island.

On the third day, Moran was paired off to travel with his young girlfriend Jean O'Shea as Benny knew this would be seen as nothing more than a young couple heading for the islands for some winter sun. On their arrival to Dublin Airport via taxi, the two young lovebirds could not hide their excitement because neither had ever left Ireland's shores before.

'Keep the change, buddy,' said Moran as he handed the stunned taxi driver a fifty-pound note for a seven-pound fare, a day's work for the man.

'What? This is a fucking fifty, kid!' called out the taxi man who thought this young lad had made a mistake in his excitement to get off on his holiday.

'It's cool, buddy, it's only money,' replied the cocky and excited Moran.

'Fair enough; it's your loss, kid.' The taxi man drove off with a smile from ear to ear, not knowing and not caring where that money had actually come from.

'This should be brilliant, love,' an excited Jean told Moran.

'Yeah Jaysus, I'm living for this, and to get away from this fuckin kip for a few weeks will be the business. The fuckin law will be out of our way too so no worries, Jean.'

'Yeah, it's great, look, I'm starving, Thomas, can we get somethin to eat?'

'Okay, come on then,' replied Moran as they went inside the terminal and feasted on a burger and chips washed down by a coke. In the rush to get away, the young couple had left four and a half hours early so boredom set in quite soon after they arrived and every second of every minute was counted down. Then over the public address system, a crackling noise that was to set hearts racing between the youngsters as this was the one announcement both jetsetters wanted to hear:

'This is the first call for flight number Ire323 to Ibiza, that's Flight number Ire323 to Ibiza so can all passengers please move towards check-in point number 23, that's flight number Ire323 to Ibiza, please report to check-in point number 23.'

A startled Moran jumped in the air. 'Thats us, Jean; come on, move, will ye; thats our bleedin flight. About fuckin time too, here we go, Jean, here we fuckin go,' spoke an excited Moran.

'You have everything, don't you, Thomas?' questioned Jean in a panic as she grabbed the bags of duty-free along with her suitcases.

'Yeah, yeah, I do; here look, passports, tickets and the bags; we're sound, Jean, now come on for fuck sake, let's get up the queue, hurry!'

Thomas Moran was Ibiza bound. Flight Ire323 to Ibiza from Dublin airport took off at 7.37 pm Irish time just 2 minutes later than schedule and was to arrive in Ibiza Airport approximately 2 hours and 30 minutes later at 11.07 pm; Thomas Moran and his gang had finally come together in Ibiza.

The gang's new homes were located on the hillside overlooking the main town of Ibiza after Frankie and Danny had successfully rented three villas between them. Frankie and Pudner were in one with Danny and Noel sharing another while Moran and Jean shared the other. The villas they rented were another world away from the flat complexes in St Christopher's as they all had a private swimming pool, five bedrooms, two living rooms with elegant décor and on top of that, fully fitted kitchens. While at home in Ireland, the flats in St Christopher's had four rooms in total and now they had five bedrooms; life was good right now for the gang but this was nothing compared to what was to come.

What Moran did not know was that Ibiza would become a legendary Mecca for club life; well, not just a mecca but this small part of the Balearic Islands would become one of the most popular club destinations in the world. The island would welcome hundreds of thousands of holidaymakers each year including families, couples and of course, clubbers, who would flock to Ibiza for a week or two of fun in the sun.

The heartbeat of the island centred on its two main areas, one being Ibiza Town where Moran's gang lived and the other was San Antonio. The much more relaxed Ibiza Town sits on the south-eastern shore and is the island's capital while to the west of the Island is the hedonistic town of San Antonio.

Ibiza for a group of 19 to 22-year-olds from Dublin loaded with cash was a perfect match but especially San Antonio; the young Moran gang were going to fit into Ibiza like peas in a pod. San Antonio rapidly fashioned a reputation for alcohol, drugs and sex fuelled all-night parties with dancing and bar hopping catering for an eager nightclub crowd. The town had a clear tolerance towards lavish and outrageous behaviour from tourists and it would be christened the Gomorrah of the Med, and Moran and his friends loved it.

When Moran and Company arrived at Ibiza Airport in December 1989, the party scene was not in full swing due to the closed season of the winter months, so to the young Dubliners, the island just seemed like a small quiet holiday island. But what lay ahead of them was nothing like they had ever expected or ever encountered in the rave clubs back home in Dublin.

Rave was right at the heart of holiday resorts like Ibiza, Cyprus and the Greek Islands and this Balearic paradise had more to offer than just fancy villas, sun and nightlife; much, much more than all these young men could have ever imagined possible. If Benny wanted the gang to keep a low profile, well, he could not have picked a worse destination for this group who were now all residents of the biggest party island on the planet.

The solitude of winter was followed by the calmness of spring; May of 1990 arrived with people from every corner of the globe beginning to arrive on the island to dance their holiday fortnight away. After the rave scene was banned in the UK and further afield, Ibiza was in its heyday in the 1990s after the infamous Summer of Love of 1989, which had seen thousands flock to the island like it was a calling from the gods.

The fact was that Benny had never done his homework about what had happened in Ibiza in 1989 but a little snooping would have told him that a relatively unknown DJ who went on to become a highly acclaimed record producer found a paradise in the Mediterranean Sea and a club culture was born. New music grew from Ibiza in the late 1980s and early 1990s as many DJs travelled to Ibiza during the summer season to establish their own brand of dance music. This style became associated with the island and the more fortunate DJs became world famous and performed to large crowds of more than 3,000 night clubbers.

A short history lesson tells us that it was in Ibiza that acid house was first played by DJs in clubs along with additional new music from all over the world, including Chicago house, German techno, underground disco and anything that made people dance while vibrating across the island like a shockwave. Clubbers danced the night away in such noted clubs like the now world-famous Space, Pacha and of course, Privilege, which is now the largest club in the world.

Amnesia, another club, was known for its famous foam parties; while clubs like Eden and DC10 were all packed to the rafters, well, not exactly as some clubs in those days actually had no roof. Some of the world's most renowned DJs have made their name because of playing on the island.

A typical schedule for clubbers going on the annual pilgrimage to Ibiza included waking up at noon, having a swim and a light lunch, then back to bed for an early evening nap to reserve energy for a long night ahead in many of the aforementioned clubs. Nightclubs in Ibiza stayed open until the early hours of the morning and many people were still up partying when dawn arrived.

On the other hand, perhaps you could just stay up for twenty-four hours straight, listening to house music, sweating like a pig in savage heat and dancing to the non-stop historic sounds of Ibiza. Most clubs did not open up until after 11 pm or even midnight, and when inside, a fog gun blasted jets of frozen air into the crowd, at times to great relief.

All of these partying and fun-loving lifestyles were a world that Moran knew well from his time at the Dublin raves and of course, he was not going to miss an opportunity like this to make money. Ibiza with all its beauty had become an island with a high demand for illegal drugs and Ecstasy was still the drug in demand and Moran was just the man to supply it. It was too good to resist and Ibiza was to become very lucrative for the Moran gang, when in June 1990, Thomas Moran made a phone call to Dublin to a very close confidant.

'Benny, it's the 'Little Don'; you okay to talk?'

'Yes, go on.'

'Well, let me say we could have a business over here that would put the Dublin clubs to shame.'

'Oh yeah, tell me more, young Don,' inquired an interested Jewell.

'Benny, there is no end to how much money could be made on the Islands, a fucking fortune, buddy. In the clubs, Disco Biscuits are being eaten alive and we have a very large home crowd to please.'

'Oh yeah?'

'Come and see for yourself, Benny, for fuck sake.'

'Relax. Okay then, I could do with a break. I'll catch a flight over ASAP so I'll see you soon.'

That short phone call started one of the most lucrative deals in Benny's life and it was not long after that Jewell was on his way to Ibiza to meet his young gang members and see what all the fuss was about. In July 1990, Benny arrived at Ibiza airport where Frankie and Pudner met him off a direct flight from London.

Moran instructed his two boys, 'Collect Benny and bring him straight to the Café del Mar. I'll meet him there first and then we'll bring him to my villa.'

The now world-famous Café del Mar first opened its doors in 1980 and was designed by a very well-known Catalan architect named Lluis Géell and his idea was simple: you relax by the shores of the bay at Calo des Moro in San Antonio and admire the breath-taking sunsets. This was all backed up while the resident DJ played appropriately laidback and atmospheric music. This music was the foundation of the series of Café del Mar chill out albums that followed over the next number of years. Little Don had fallen in love with the place from the moment he set eyes on his first sunset and he wanted Benny to sample its beauty.

After a twenty-minute journey, Frankie, Pudner and Benny arrived at the Café to find the rest of the gang chilling out while looking out over the bay and drinking cocktails.

'Moran, ye little bastard, come on over here and say hello to your Uncle Benny!'

'Benny, my man, how the fuck are ye?' replied Moran.

'I'm fuckin parching for a pint so get me one, will you please, Danny?'

'Sure Benny, yeah anything in mind?'

'For fuck sake, Danny, just make sure it's fuckin cold and there's alcohol in it. I'm sweating like a paedo in a Disney suit. So Tommy, you're here what six fucking months and already you lot are up to no good. Ye call this keeping out of trouble, do ye?' laughed Jewell. 'So what's this business, talk to me?'

'Relax and enjoy the moment, Benny, where else can you see the world-famous Ibiza sunset but in the Café del Mar?' asked Moran, pointing out towards the sun setting.

'Fuck off, will ye! You and your bloody sunset, let's talk business, for fuck sake. I'm only out here for two days so no fucking about. This trip better have been fuckin worth it, Tommy, I swear,' sarcastically threatened Benny, while wiping beads of sweat from his brow. 'Jesus Christ, its fuckin roasting here.'

'Okay, right to it, Benny, the place is full of clubbers and they're taking tabs like nobody's business. The law here don't give a fuck about the clubs or the tabs being sold. The market is ripe as these clubs are hoppin and the punters are certainly buyin. The punters also change by the week and we hear tons of Irish accents too, so they need some home-grown people to buy from. It's a fuckin gold mine, Benny, so all we need is the tabs imported to the islands. So?'

Noel Slattery came in behind his boss. 'Honestly, Benny, its fuckin hoppin here and every cunt under the sun is on tabs at the clubs. And they're payin out with no fuckin questions asked.'

Benny downs half his pint of San Miguel and tells Tommy, 'Okay, let's do it.'

'Yesss, Benny, ye fuckin beauty.'

'But if any of you get stung, I do not exist, understand?' And the group agreed. 'How much do you need?'

Moran looks at Benny. '10,000 tabs will do to start.'

Benny, taking another drink and hearing Moran's answer, nearly choked on his beer. 'How fuckin many!'

'10,000.'

'Fuck me pink. Okay o-fucking-k lads and lady, let's get things moving,' smiled Jewell with a baffled look on his face and muttering under his breath, 'Ten fucking thousand, fuck me!'

Within ten days, Benny began importing the Ecstasy into the islands, always using different avenues. He used couriers, delivering the goods concealed in their luggage portraying themselves as young holiday-goers looking for the sun and club life that Ibiza offered; or he posted the tablets to a safety deposit box in Ibiza Town taken out by Moran under the cheeky name of Mickey Long.

When Moran wanted more tablets, he arranged a call to Benny telling him that Mickey was short and the drugs duly arrived; in no time, the calls became more and more frequent as the summer parties kicked in and the operation was running like clockwork and nobody cared as it was seen as the done thing by the entire club-going patrons on the island.

Prices per tab in the clubs ranged from seven to ten pounds for one Ecstasy tablet and the gang made a small fortune buying their tabs from Benny for two pounds each while servicing the dance-fuelled desires of a generation of Ecstasy users.

Every night, a different club was targeted by the gang and every night the gang came home with pockets of cash and very few tabs. Business was good, in fact, it was very good. Moran, again the clever one, did not become greedy as he rarely strayed away from the little piece of Ireland he found on the Island; in his estimation, he was better off sticking to his own rather than pissing off other drug dealers from Europe and ruining this little gold mine they had encountered.

So the gang continued to sell their product to Irish and British people in the clubs while enjoying the party life they were surrounded by; Moran even became a supplier to some European dealers as he had the product at the right price.

It was 1992 and Moran and his gang had stayed for longer than expected in Ibiza as their venture was booming, while back in Dublin, the profitable South Inner City heroin business was also still going well for them, thanks to Benny who had kept his promise. All this was to change when on Friday, 28 August 1992, all the sunny island living was to come to an end when Moran received a phone call from Benny, explaining to him the situation back home. The call was to let him know that their time in Ibiza was up, it was time for them to come home and home was where they went without question.

To Moran's surprise, not all of his gang wanted to return home. Danny Moore decided that he wanted to stay in Ibiza, realising he had nothing to go home to in Dublin. The gang were sad to leave him behind but Danny was not the fool they took him for back in Dublin; he used his brain and became a bar owner, purchasing a popular nightspot from a local Spaniard he had befriended, along with properties including some prime real estate not only in Ibiza but on mainland Spain from his profitable drug dealing.

Danny named the bar The House of Ecstasy, his own special two-finger salute to the authorities but as stated before, Danny was to become a major part of Moran's plans but for now, he remained Benny's link on the island for drug dealing and trafficking through the Mediterranean. Over the next number of years, Danny was to become very useful for Little Don and his gang as a new chapter was just beginning.

Chapter 9
The Stitch-Up

It was now September of 1992 and just days after the brief telephone conversation with Benny Jewell that Moran and his friends returned home to Dublin, leaving behind two very lucrative and fun-filled years on the Island of Ibiza. More importantly for Moran and most certainly Jewell was that following on from a long investigation into the murder of Jeremy Larkin, the Garda Special Investigations Unit drew blanks and the case was now nothing more than an on-going statistic.

Wasting no time, Moran decided to venture out on his very own research mission to scrutinise Dublin city's club scene to see if much had changed since his Mediterranean sabbatical; it did not take long for him to realise that Dublin still had a very active and flourishing nightlife. On closer examination, what he found was that the old rave clubs had been replaced with more modern trendier bars across the City Centre as the overall club landscape had considerably changed from the one he had left behind him in 1989.

Dublin City Centre had turned into a more mainstream club scene that saw a selection of popular large nightclubs open their doors and at first, he did not like what he was seeing. The raves still continued but they were in rapid decline as Dublin's club life had all but moved away from the dark outdated underground clubs that the gang had previously frequented; most were now either closed down or revamped and under new management.

On returning home that night, he decided it wise to leave well alone for now as Dublin's new nightclubs had more than enough people selling drugs in a very over-supplied market; for the first time in his life, Moran did not have a cash flow problem, but before he considered going back to work, he had more than nightclubs on his mind.

A few weeks later in November of 1992, now aged twenty-four, Moran in a private ceremony married his long-time partner Jean O'Shea. The ceremony took place in the small Roman Catholic Church in Dolphins Barn situated on the edge of the South Inner City at the corner of the South Circular Road and Cork Street.

Following the ceremony, a private reception was held in the Ritz Hotel in Dublin's plush Harcourt Street, right next to the Garda Special Branch Headquarters that was now home to the new Special Drugs Unit set up at Harcourt Terrace. The wedding reception saw a host of Dublin's leading gangland figures show up to celebrate with the newlyweds and also welcome them back from their exile from Ireland's shores. Every gangster worth their salt was at the reception and Moran was now officially reinstated into Dublin's dark world of crime.

Not long after the newlyweds tied the knot, Moran purchased a house in the working-class suburb of Crumlin situated just on the outskirts of South West Inner City in one of the city's sprawling housing estates. Incredibly, Moran paid for the house with cash, totalling £38,550 from his earnings in Dublin and Ibiza but the amazing thing about this was Moran actually received unemployment benefits from the state, a grand weekly total of £82.50.

The average weekly wage in Ireland in 1992 was around £300.00 and the average house price in Dublin £49,785. Therefore, to buy the house outright, you would imagine this would have turned a few heads, especially from a man on welfare payments. No, not at all because nothing happened; it went completely unnoticed by the taxman, the Gardaí and Dublin Corporation.

The taxman was completely unaware of Moran's extra income, the Gardaí in Crumlin were not aware of Moran moving into their area and Dublin Corporation were more than happy to reduce its housing stock. So win-win for the gangster and when Jean made her first visit, she could not believe her luck and was overwhelmed by Moran's fabulous wedding gift to her.

'Fuckin hell, Thomas, it's gorgeous.'

After a few thousand pounds and some serious redeveloping, the house was ready for Moran to move into; along with Jean, he took his mother Marie out of the flats with them as there was plenty of room for her and Jean was not going to argue with her husband—she had everything she ever wanted.

It was a kind gesture taking his mother indeed, but Moran of course, had ulterior motives. You see, the flat in St Christopher's was under his mother's name so he could leave his younger brother Gonzo in the flat to keep it in shape;

as Moran saw it, nobody was stupid enough to inform the Corporation that Marie was gone. In time, the flat would become useful when needed.

Now married and with the new house sorted, it was time to get back to work for Moran and back to work he did. In his absence, thanks to Benny, nothing had changed in the Inner City as he still ran the business for Moran who was handed back all his operations as promised before his departure.

Therefore, with business in good condition and the investigation into the murder put on the back boiler, Moran and his gang were once again free to get on with their dealings. In his absence, Joey Flynn and Marko Dunne had kept things in order for their boss and in no time, Moran and his men were back dealing in the heroin, Ecstasy and marijuana trade around the Inner City just like before. Business was in full flight and everything was falling back into place when on 14 December 1992, Benny called on Moran in his new home.

'Good evenin, Benny, how are ye?'

'I'm great, Thomas, just great, now take a seat. I want to chin wag about something.'

'Okay Benny, let's talk.'

'I have a problem, you see, Thomas. I don't trust that rapist bastard Andy Russell anymore, he's fucking fleecing me. He is taking money from my dealers and keeping it so I need someone who I can trust, someone who will not fuck me about. So I've decided that from now on, you're my new right-hand man and you will run all my operations,' explained Benny.

'What! Are you fuckin takin' the piss, Benny…me?'

'Yes, you, and you cannot say fucking no. Understand?'

A bewildered and stunned Moran replied, 'Okay Benny, yeah fuck him, okay then.' And as simple as that, in an instant, Benny Jewell had just promoted Moran to one of the leading members of his gang, moving him up many rungs of the ladder in the Dublin city underworld.

'What about Andy; he's not gonna be happy, Benny,' asked an anxious Moran.

'You let me deal with that cunt, Thomas, it's not your problem.'

'Okay, okay, Benny but he—'

'But he fuck,' interrupted Jewell. 'I will sort that cunt, okay?'

'Yeah, yeah, Benny, okay.'

Thomas 'Little Don' Moran was now one of Dublin's criminal elite and the future was looking ever so bright for the young gangster but with this new promotion came its own responsibilities, and with responsibility comes its own problems. If one man is promoted, then someone has to take a fall and the fall guy in this case was Jewell's old but unpredictable right-hand man, Andy Russell.

As he left Moran's home, Benny called Andy on his mobile phone to explain the new structure and why this had all come to be. The call was answered by Russell after a few rings, 'All right, Benny, to what do I owe the pleasure?'

'Just a quick call, Andy, to put you straight on a few things,' was Benny's immediate reply.

'Oh yeah and what are they, Benny?'

'You're not my number one from now on, Andy, I've had to make changes and Thomas Moran is stepping into your role from today. New structures, you see. So you now take orders from Thomas. I'll see you later, Andy, and will you let your boys know about the situation.'

Benny hung up his phone and within seconds, his mobile rang and Andy's number came up but Benny elected to ignore the call by putting the phone on silent and sticking it in his pocket as he continued with his day. Andy Russell was furious after the call and he was not taking the news well; there was no way he was letting a little upstart like Moran push him out of Benny's deals.

The word spread like wildfire across the city and Russell began to put out feelers to see how the land lay and who was on his side. Russell was stunned because to his absolute horror and dissatisfaction, all of the top people from around the city welcomed Benny's call. Russell was not liked and was seen as too much of a loose cannon. For Russell, the few members that remained loyal to him were only small-time gangsters and if they went against Benny, they would not be seen as much of a loss to the underworld.

Russell, not taking Benny's demotion well soon got word out to close associates that he was furious about what had gone on. Wanting the backing from these criminals, Russell saw this as a perfect opportunity to gain notoriety in Dublin it irked him that he was always seen as cannon fodder by those at the top; to his delight, not one of his close associates were happy that this young pretender was coming along and taking business away from them; something had to be done and they saw Andy Russell as just the man to do it.

In early January of 1993, a meeting was taking place unknown to Moran and Jewell that saw a group of Andy Russell sympathisers coming together to discuss what was happening in relation to Benny's decision. In a private room in the Oak

86

Tree Pub in Darndale on the outskirts of Dublin's north side, Russell began to organise a plan of action to take down Jewell, Moran, his men or whoever got in their way. Criminals from across Dublin who attended the meeting included Seamus Dempsey, an armed robber from Pearse Street in Dublin's Inner City; Tony Fox, a minor drug dealer from Darndale; Mickey Naughton, a bully boy from Limerick; experienced criminal Tony Dunne from the same area as Russell—Bluebell. In all, a dozen men travelled to the meeting to support Russell.

'Who does this little bastard Benny think he is fuckin with? He just cannot cut me out like that; it's my fuckin money, mine!' screamed a furious Russell.

'Relax, Andy, for fuck sake, do you want everyone to hear you?' came a voice of reason as a member of the Russell gang tried to restore a bit of order in the room.

'Relax, relax, you say? I will relax when Benny fuckin Jewell and that back-stabbin little cunt Moran are dead, fuckin gone, do ye hear me!'

Tony Dunne, who was a close friend of Russell's, stepped in to calm his friend down.

'Andy, Andy mate, he's right, roaring and shouting will get us nowhere. We need a plan and murdering Benny Jewell is not the way forward. If you do that, we'll have every fuckin gang in Ireland on our back. I've put together a plan that'll not involve any of us whatsoever and this'll put Jewell and the Moran cunt out of our way for a long time. And when they're gone…we step in and run the city.'

'Oh yeah?' asked a calmer Russell. 'Go on then, Tony, explain yourself.'

'You just leave it with me, Andy, I've got a plan.'

Still unaware of the Darndale meeting, it was on a cold Saturday morning on 14 January 1993 when Benny Jewell called on Thomas Moran with details of a job he needed him to do.

'Good morning, Thomas, my good man, how are we today?' asked a jolly but obviously freezing Jewell.

'Good, Benny, very good. So you said we need to talk?'

'Yes, we do, but alone,' giving a nod towards Moran's wife and mother who sat beside a big coal fire keeping them warm on the cold winter's day. Immediately, Jean knew she was not wanted around the house; business had to be discussed.

'Okay boys, no need to say nothin, I know. Meself and Marie are goin shoppin so, come on, Marie, let's leave the men alone,' said Jean, kissing Moran on his cheek as both women left for a morning's shopping.

'So Benny, what is it?'

'A job, and I mean a bloody big job. This could be the biggest we have ever done, ever. It really excites me, Thomas.'

'Okay, I'm all ears, go on,' replied Moran.

'It will be a four-man operation, so I want you, Frankie, Noel and Pudner on it, nobody else, okay?' Moran acknowledged his boss with a positive nod of the head.

'Okay, let's get down to it.'

Benny continued to tell Moran about the job, 'I got a call from a close friend who put me onto this deal; it's a fuckin beauty that can make us huge money and it will flood the city for months with gear. Now to do this job, ye'll need to steal a couple of 4x4 jeeps and have all the seats in the back taken out or lying down. So you sort that out as soon as is humanly fuckin possible.'

'I'll get Pudner onto it today, Benny,' replied Moran.

'Good man, Thomas, right, I'll get you the exact detail on the day of the operation so nobody can slip up. All I can tell you is it's goin to be on Friday night running into Saturday morning on 20 January. So Friday 20th not Saturday 21st, okay?'

'Yeah Benny, it's on the Friday night runnin into the Saturday mornin when we have to be there. I get it,' replied Moran.

'Exactly, because I don't want a shipment coming in and men sitting around with a heap of gear waiting with nobody to fucking meet them while they're left scratching their balls all night. So far, we clear?'

'Yes Benny, for fuck sake, it's not fuckin rocket science.' Moran was clearly getting frustrated by his boss's patronising behaviour towards him. Benny continued to outline the procedure of the operation in detail.

'Okay, okay, I just want to get this right, so back to business. There'll be three, maybe four men, I'm not 100% sure just now and they'll have a bunch of packages for you hence the 4x4s, okay?'

'Go on.'

'Now on the night, I'll give you a briefcase, your job, and only you are to give it to the captain of the boat. Simple.'

'Sounds simple enough, Benny, yeah.'

'Right, I'm off now and I want you to get those fucking 4x4s sorted yesterday, Thomas. Understand?'

'For fuck sake, Benny! I hear ye, I hear ye, okay, am I clear now!'

'Right, for fuck sake, Thomas, right. I'm excited and jumpy by this, that's all.'

That afternoon, Moran went to see Noel Slattery about getting Pudner to steal the two jeeps, explaining the importance of why he needed to get them ready for the job. 'Noel, do this right, will ye?'

'Fuck off, Tommy, of course, I'll do it fuckin right.'

'Sorry buddy, it's just that Benny is bein a pain in the hole about the whole fuckin thing.'

Noel quickly understood the importance of this job and how it was equally important for his boss; it was the gang's first major job since Moran's promotion and he wanted to make sure Moran felt better about the jeeps so he immediately called Pudner. Smyth was undoubtedly the man for the job due to the fact he was an accomplished car thief and Slattery knew that if anyone could do it, Pudner was the man as he would know exactly where and how to steal the vehicles needed.

True to form, it was only sixteen hours after Moran's order to find the 4x4 jeeps that Pudner had delivered; one jeep was a red and black 1992 Cherokee Sport and the other, a 1989 silver four-wheel drive Nissan Patrol, perfect for what was needed to carry out Benny's job. Not long after, Smyth had both vehicles stored in a lockup belonging to his cousin, close to the banks of Dublin's River Liffey on St John Rogerson's quay. Two days later, Pudner and his cousin had the two jeeps re-sprayed and fitted with fake licence plates so they would not be sitting ducks for the authorities when they hit the streets and for now, Moran had his part of the plan in place.

Friday, 20 January 1993, arrived and early that day, Benny Jewell met with Moran in the upper ground level carpark of the Square Town Centre in Tallaght. Benny gave Moran the details of where the drop-off point was to be and exactly where the goods had to be delivered afterwards. Benny explained to Moran that, 'In the County Louth village of Carlingford, you're to meet a fishing boat down at the Lough at 3 am Saturday morning. The name of the boat you have to meet is called 'The Lady of the Lough' and it will arrive at the main fishing depot where you'll find her moored and this is where you start unloading from the boat.

You meet the captain hand over the briefcase and unload the packages to the jeeps aided by your men and the crew of the boat. Simple.'

'Sound, Benny, I'll be in touch.'

The destination for the drugs haul was the picturesque town of Carlingford, a small fishing town in County Louth with a large Loch that forms part of the international border between Northern Ireland to the north and the Republic of Ireland to the south. The Loch is bordered by the coastal towns of Warrenpoint and Rostrevor residing in County Down and are backed by the Mountains of Mourne on the northern side, while on the southern side are Omeath, Carlingford and Greenore, which are all part of the Cooley peninsula in County Louth. So for residents to see fishing boats arriving in the early morning was nothing strange to a busy fishing town.

But unknown to the locals, this ship's cargo did not contain fish or the popular cockles that lived in the Lough but it was carrying numerous amounts of packets in its hull that held over one million pounds worth of class-A drugs that included heroin, hash and tablets ready for the Dublin market. The money invested in this shipment was everything Benny had and understandably the reason why he was pushing Moran so hard to make sure nothing went wrong.

On the night in question, sitting at home in his Dublin home, a very edgy Benny sat beside the phone as he most of all wanted nothing to go wrong and the call he wanted was that the operation was officially in full swing. The call came from his men not long after collecting the jeeps on Sir John Rogerson's Quay at 11 pm as Moran and his three accomplices—Noel Slattery, Frankie McCann and Brian Smyth—started out from Dublin City to meet their 3 am deadline in Carlingford. Frankie drove the Nissan Patrol with Noel Slattery riding along while in the other jeep were Smyth the driver and Moran.

Heading northbound from the City Centre, the men travelled towards Dublin Airport and out onto the Swords Road heading for Rush, Skerries and onto Balbriggan and from here, they headed out of Dublin towards Carlingford via Drogheda, County Louth. An hour and a half into the drive, the men stopped in Castlebellingham, County Louth, because Slattery needed to have a pit stop for 'a coffee and a piss' so with this, Moran took the opportunity to finalise all the details before making the final stage of their journey through Dundalk.

After a thirty-minute pit stop and two and a half hours of driving, the jeeps reached the town of Carlingford at 2.05 am leaving the men with fifty-five minutes to spare and all they could do now was wait. It was, as expected, quiet that morning around the Lough as just a handful of local fishermen were coming and going, plying their trade on the Lough as the men sat waiting patiently; well, bar Frankie, who could not sit easy.

Frankie was now out of his jeep, standing on the edge of the pier looking out over the peaceful Lough. By now, Noel Slattery had joined Moran in his jeep and again was going over the plan with him to make sure everything was correct; the conversation between Moran and Slattery was interrupted briefly, startling both men, when Frankie knocked on the car window.

'Fuck ye, Frankie, ye frightened the shite outta me.'

'Come on, for fuck sake, Tommy boy, we're up; the Lady of the Lough has arrived.'

'Okay, nice one, Frankie, okay, boys, heads into this and we can get the fuck outta here as soon as we can so no acting the bollox, okay,' was Moran's order.

As the boat moored, a man jumped onto the walkway and asked, 'You lot Benny's boys?'

'Well, we're here to collect some packages if that's what you mean,' replied Moran.

'Sound, lads, well, before we go any further, have you got something for me?' asked the man.

Noel Slattery came from behind one of the jeeps and handed Moran a briefcase that had one million punts in bank drafts inside. After a close investigation of the drafts, the man returned to chat to another man and in seconds returned to Moran and agreed to start unloading the goods from the boat.

'Okay, we're good to go,' explained the man.

'Right, let's get a move on, start unloading the boat, men,' ordered Moran.

After about twenty-five minutes, the two jeeps were fully loaded and the boat empty. Moran turned to the man and told him, 'Okay boys, we are outta here. Good luck, lads, take it handy.'

'We will have this on the street in days, boys,' gloated Slattery.

However, in the background, a voice called out, 'Nice haul, Tommy.' Was the call from one of the men on the boat?

'Yeah, yeah, it is,' replied Moran with caution in his voice as he glanced backwards over his shoulder to see who was on the boat; Moran was spooked as the man had a strange tone in his voice. Moreover, how did he know his name, and how right he was because as he looked the stranger in the eye, he told him the words that would knock him for six, 'Got ye, Tommy.'

Moran knew something was very, very wrong and once again, the man spoke but this time he had a more cocky edge in his voice. 'You're all mine now, you little bastards.'

On hearing these words, Moran's head dropped and he whispered under his breath, 'Oh bollox, fucking hell, you shower of cunts! How the fuck?'

Within seconds, the four men were surrounded by members of the National Drug Squad and local Gardaí with flashing blue lights blinding the men.

'Freeze, freeze, do not move a fucking inch!' were the words that rang out in the County Louth skies that put all four men into a blind panic.

'Tommy, what the fuck is goin on here, were we set up or what? Who the fuck set us up, Tommy, who done us?' shouted Slattery.

'Shut the fuck up, Noel, I have no idea what the fuck is up and not a fuckin word to anyone, boys, okay, say fuck all.'

Within seconds, all four men were handcuffed and led towards individual cars sitting on the banks of Carlingford Lough.

'I do not fucking believe this. I do not fucking believe this!' muttered Moran as he was bundled into the car.

'Thomas Moran, I am Detective Inspector Liam Kiernan of the National Drugs Unit. It is finally not a pleasure to meet a little scumbag like you. Thomas Moran, I am arresting you under Section 23 of the Misuse of Drugs Act 1977-1984, you fucking dirty scumbag. This is part of the Drugs Trafficking Act that falls under the Irish Legislation. The fucking law, Thomas! Do you understand, you dirty little bastard?'

'Fuck you.'

'No, fuck you, Thomas, fuck you, you filthy drug dealing bastard, have you any idea what you and your gang have done to many a family in Dublin with that filth you deal, you fucking scumbag! Oh, now wait, wait now. Look at me, how rude, I forget my manners, Thomas.' And in a sarcastic manner, Kiernan told Moran, 'Please Thomas, go fuck yourself.' Detective Inspector Kiernan smiled as he slammed the car door shut in Moran's face, delighted with his night's work.

Thomas 'Little Don' Moran along with his three gang members were caught up in a Garda National Drug Unit sting operation and they knew they were done. Moran's mind was running at one hundred miles per hour trying to figure who set them up, who it could be that wanted them out of the way. *Surely not Benny?* thought Moran.

After all the commotion on the pier, the four men were taken away in separate Garda cars to different Garda stations around County Louth with Moran taken to Drogheda, Frankie to Ardee, Slattery to Dundalk and Smyth to Castlebellingham. In each case, not one man opened their mouth even under intense interrogation by the Drug Squad. To Moran, rules were rules and this most certainly included top criminals not talking to the Gardaí; this was an unwritten rule in the criminal fraternity, you did not grass out your friends as it was certain death or, if you were lucky, you just got a severe beating from your peers.

This did not surprise Detective Inspector Kiernan, knowing all too well that these were hardened criminals and not some group of little low-level scum that they had picked up on a silly little possession charge. Kiernan had encountered this sort of behaviour many times before but the long-serving detective inspector did not care if they talked or not as his case was one hundred percent solid and here, he had one of the most active drug gangs in Dublin in the palm of his hand. 'Little Don' was done for.

The next morning, Benny heard the news for the first time when he got a phone call from one of his men telling him to turn on the radio to listen to the early morning news. When the newscaster read out the report, Benny turned pale and his heart was beating like a racehorse after the Grand National.

'Four men in their twenties have been arrested by the Garda National Drug Unit in an early morning sting operation at Carlingford Lough in County Louth. Sources say that the Gardaí were tipped off about a well-known Dublin gang who were purchasing illegal drugs for sale and supply on the streets of the capital city. All four men were charged under Section 23 of the Misuse of Drugs Act 1977-1984.'

Benny, head in hands, screamed, 'Oh fuck! Fuck! Fuck!'

The news reporter continued:

'All four men reportedly had been on the radar of the Garda Drug Unit and are part of a major Inner City crime gang in Dublin. Thomas Moran, Noel Slattery, Brian Smyth and Francis McCann were all remanded in custody and will appear in court next week on drug trafficking and supply charges.'

Benny was in a blind panic and did not know what to do or where to turn as he had invested heavily in the shipment and he was awaiting a knock on the door from the Drug Unit to take him into custody,

'Oh, fucking hell, oh fucking hell, bollix, fuck, what am I going to fucking do? Tipped off…what the fuck?'

Seven days since the sting, that knock never came on Benny's door but he did get a welcome visit. John Donegan, one of Benny's gang, arrived with news telling him that the four men had recently been given bail under condition that they did not mix with each other and that they surrendered their passports to the local Garda stations. Donegan further explained that Thomas Moran wanted to meet up that afternoon and Benny agreed to meet later that day.

It was 3 pm when Benny met up with Moran in the Red Lizard pub in the safety of the South Inner City, away from prying eyes; on his arrival, a very uneasy Jewell was sitting at the bar, drinking whiskey and shaking like a leaf.

'Thomas, Thomas, what the fuck is going on, son? What the fuck is happening here?'

'I was hoping you could tell me, Benny. They stung us big time and got us red-handed, the cunts, they have us by the bollix, Benny, and we're fuckin going down.'

'Thomas, it was nothin to do with me!' fretted Benny.

'I know, I know, for fuck sake. Why would you, for fuck sake, it was all your money that was invested but I'll tell you someone done us and we have to find out who so let's think about who it is that wants us out of the way.'

'I have no idea, Thomas; I really do not know who would set us up. It was Tony Dunne who put me onto the deal so I could go see him when the heat dies down a bit.'

'Okay Benny, do that. I'll fuckin kill the cunt who set us up, I swear on it, Benny. The coppers knew every fuckin thing; I mean, everything.'

'I know, son, I know, leave it with me, Thomas, now please, come sit down and tell me what happened in court.'

'The trial date hasn't been set yet but we're fucked. We were given bail on a number of conditions—we're not to associate with each other and not to drive any vehicle and other shite like that.'

'I heard; John Donegan told me. The fuckin BASTARDS!' a clearly annoyed Jewell cried.

'They told us we've to surrender our passports and sign on in Garda stations every day; and we've to stay away from known criminals. Like you, ye little bollox.' Laughed Moran.

'How can you fucking laugh at a time like this, for Christ sake, Thomas? Fucking hell, this is a mess. Right, I'm off. I'll be in touch when I hear anything. Take this phone and do not share the number; it's just me and you, so any calls is me.'

'Sound, Benny, talk later.'

Up until the time of the court case, Benny had no news on who had grassed the gang then the date was given and on Friday, 5 March 1993, Thomas Moran, Frankie McCann, Pudner Smyth and Noel Slattery all stood trial in Dublin's Central Criminal Court on drug trafficking charges. Benny was not at the court but members of his gang gave him daily reports.

The Central Criminal Court tries the most serious criminal offences and the judge residing this case was hard-line veteran, Judge Seamus McArdle, who was known as a man who did not tolerate drug trafficking in any way, shape or form, and he was going to hand out the longest term he possibly could to Moran and his gang.

The four men used the same solicitor, Séan Coleman, a man known for his defence of Ireland's criminal underworld and detested by his fellow solicitors for the simple reason that he was never out of work and was paid very, very well by many of his clients.

Taking the case for the state was the Attorney General Alan Carson, a right-wing lawyer who stuck to the book of law as if it was his Bible. A jury of nine men and three women were sworn in and the court was officially in session; Moran and company knew all too well they were in for a very rough time in court. The state was ready to pounce and at 10 am on 5 March, courtroom number one was awash with activity with press people, Gardaí, courtroom staff, family and general onlookers.

'All rise for the Right Honourable Judge Seamus McArdle,' was the call from the bailiff as Judge McArdle entered the room shortly after the accused.

The case evidence was so strong against the men that not even plea-bargaining was going to help them but Coleman knew that the gang was never going to speak to the Gardaí under any circumstances, no matter how bad things got, so it was all about how much time was coming.

As the gang sat in court, they heard witness after witness condemn them to time in prison and there was absolutely nothing they or anyone else could do. They just took it on the chin and knew that one day they would be free men and that kept them sane through the whole trial. After only 3 days, the trial came to an end due to the strong evidence put in front of the jury by the state. When the guilty verdict was read out, none of the men batted an eyelid as it was a foregone conclusion they were going down but the only outstanding matter was, for how long?

Two days later, on Wednesday, 10 March, the sentencing by Judge Seamus McArdle came in: 'Drugs are the scourge of our nation and men like you bring nothing but heartache and despair to Irelands citizens and if I could, I would sentence each one of you for a very long time but the law restricts me. So under Section 23 of the Misuse of Drugs Act 1977-1984, Thomas Moran, Francis McCann, Brian Smyth and Noel Slattery, this court is sentencing you each to five years imprisonment for the importation of illegal substances to Ireland with intent to sell on the open market for profit. Bailiff, take them down.'

As the verdict was read out, inside the courtroom suddenly cheers and clapping rang out by local Inner City residents and Gardaí alike. All four men were sentenced to serve their time in Portlaoise Prison, Ireland's maximum-security prison in County Laois, the heart of the Irish midlands. Portlaoise Prison was built in the 1830s, making it one of the oldest in the Irish prison system and has housed and still houses Ireland's most violent and ruthless gangsters along with members of the IRA and other such paramilitary organisations.

The prison has a capacity for 203 prisoners, but because of the security-sensitive nature of its inmates, it operates below this capacity. A large number of well-armed Irish defence forces soldiers guard the prison 24 hours a day, making it one of the most secure prisons in Europe. The security features include a detachment of 120 troops, armed with rifles and anti-aircraft machine guns, which patrol the perimeter, the rooftops and operate the watchtowers. An air exclusion zone operates over the entire complex while the perimeter consists of high walls, cameras, sensors and acres of tank traps.

This was not a summer camp for the four gangsters who, on their arrival at Portlaoise, were met by mounting grey walls that gave away little skyline as the prison had a dull murky feel. Among the grey interior of the prison, Moran swore he would never get set up again and he was never going to go down without a fight, as prison was really not for him.

'Okay, move it, come on, fucking move this way,' was the cry from a prison warden. Prisoner K93467 was to be Thomas Moran's identity for his duration as a guest of the Irish state. The first night in a prison cell is the hardest; the air of loneliness can be tough even on the hardest of men; as the steel grey door slammed behind him, the stark reality hit Moran while the light angled in through the prison bars, showing hazy streams of dust shifting lazily around in the air and Moran settled into his new surroundings. It was a long lonely night.

The next day, all the rules were set out by the chief officer who explained, 'Normal family visits are allowed Monday to Saturday between the hours of 10 am to 12 noon and 2 pm to 4 pm, but inmates are entitled to just one thirty-minute visit per week although you may make an application to have a special visit, which is of a fifteen-minute duration. Visitors must report to the visitors waiting area beside the main gate at Portlaoise where a visitor's pass must be booked. Visitors are required to present identification and only three adults are allowed per visit but we have no restriction on the number of children. This can all be explained in your one and only weekly phone call.'

The months passed as Moran and his gang gained a reputation in the criminal fraternity inside the walls of Portlaoise as a vicious quartet who would take no nonsense from anyone, but when in prison, this kind of behaviour does not go unnoticed and the Moran gang were about to be taken under the wing of crime kingpin, Billy Gallagher.

Gallagher was a criminal powerhouse, who ran everything in Ireland; nothing happened without his knowledge or go-ahead. He was serving his ninth year of a thirty-year stretch; he inquired about the young men and when the news came back that these were top people who could be trusted, Moran got the call from Gallagher.

'Alright Billy, ye want to see me?'

'Sit down, Tommy.'

'Yeah, what's up?'

'I'm told you and your boys are solid so I want you to come under my control in here; you work for me, I look after you, it's that simple. When you get out, I may call on ye every now and again to help me with some business but you get the run of whatever you need, ye know?'

'Sound, Billy, but I work for Benny Jewell.'

'It's okay, I've sorted it with him so it's done, welcome on board, Tommy.'

Nobody turned down Billy Gallagher so it was a wise move by Benny allowing the four men to get tight to him; on the outside, if they were known as Gallagher's men, it was a blessing and a warning all in one. Like Benny Jewell previously in the South Inner City, Gallagher was so impressed by the gang that he took them into his world of crime and guided Moran through the Irish underworld, teaching him who to trust and, more importantly, who not to trust, names of the crooked members of the Gardaí, judges and important contacts for when he would eventually get out.

Moran was given a free run of Ireland with Gallagher's blessing; this was like being given the Holy Grail of crime. You see, Gallagher was sixty-seven years of age and with about an additional fifteen years at least to go inside, he had to pass the reigns over to someone new because his old gang members were just as old, so young fresh blood was needed. With new contacts on the outside, it was through Gallagher that Moran was introduced to other gangsters who would play a major role in Moran's rise to the top of Ireland's criminal tree.

The first of the men was a drug dealer from Bootle in Liverpool, Charlie 'The Scouser' Butterfield, who had ended up in Portlaoise on drug smuggling charges when the 24-year-old was caught importing four kilos of heroin into Ireland by customs officers at Cork Airport in 1992. He would be released from Portlaoise after serving every day of a five-year sentence in November of 1997.

Another of the soon-to-be new gang members was 52-year-old Tony 'The Fairy' Rothwell from Castleblaney, County Monaghan, who had ended up in Portlaoise for embezzlement and fraud on a massive scale. Rothwell got his nickname due to his sexual preferences and was released from Portlaoise in late 1996 having served just four years of his seven-year term. Rothwell, a highly intelligent man with a fantastic business brain, would come to full use in years to come.

Next was 38-year-old George Mayweather who hailed from Omagh in County Tyrone; he had ended up in Portlaoise after being caught up in a botched drug smuggling deal on the border between Fermanagh and Monaghan. Mayweather was caught when selling two undercover detectives a kilo of hash but his main downfall came later in a further operation when the Gardaí raided his home and found an additional fifteen kilos. He was released in March of 1997 after six years.

The next new member of the gang was 44-year-old Phil Mackey from Sallynoggin, County Dublin, who had ended up in Portlaoise for multiple armed robberies, extortion, racketeering and political affiliation. Mackey was released from Portlaoise in late 1996 having served nine years inside. An extremely intelligent man, Mackey had a long line of criminal behaviour and was involved in many gangs and organisations. Mackey was a category 'A' prisoner and what the State would class as a menace to society.

Finally, there was Dean 'Deano' Coyle, a 24-year-old born and bred Dubliner from Tallaght who had also ended up in Portlaoise for drug dealing. Coyle was released in March 1997 having served only eighteen months of a four-year sentence.

With things going well inside the walls of Portlaoise, all was not well on the outside and this became evident when a visitor of Gallagher's passed on information that was to infuriate Thomas Moran. In April of 1996, Billy Gallagher called Moran to a private meeting in his cell to pass on some startling information he had received about an old friend.

'Alright Thomas, come in and have a seat. Look, I'll get right to the point, I've just heard info that Benny Jewell has discovered by chance that Andy Russell and Tony Dunne worked with the Gardaí on the operation at Carlingford Lough.'

'Are you fuckin kidding me, Billy?' asked Moran as the colour ran from his face to a pale white.

'Yes, and that's not all.'

Gallagher continued to explain that on 29 March 1996, Benny went to confront Andy Russell about the allegations made about him and Dunne. Gallagher explained that Benny entered O'Dwyer's bar that Russell regularly frequented in Dublin City Centre.

'Word has it that Russell was furious at Benny's questioning and he took him into a back room of the bar out of sight.'

'Go on, Billy.'

'Russell beat Benny to death with a wooden pole and warned the barman not to open his mouth or he would get the same treatment.'

'I'll kill that cunt, I fuckin swear, Billy, I'll fuckin kill him,' quietly spoke a calm Moran.

Unknown to Andy Russell, the young barman working in the bar that night was the nephew to a Davy Egan who just happened to be one of Billy Gallagher's men. After the murder, the young man told Davy Egan what had happened. Gallagher had never liked or trusted Russell and did not accept him back like others did after the rape of his fifteen-year-old daughter; that episode had sickened him. When Davy Egan passed on the information to Gallagher, he ordered his nephew to come straight to Portlaoise to inform Gallagher of what exactly happened. Egan's nephew explained that he had heard the full conversation between the two men and versed off detail-by-detail what was said between them, including Russell admitting to Jewell that it was he who had set up the four men.

Even after Gallagher told Moran all about what had happened, he stayed calm but inside a rage was burning. Egan also told Billy Gallagher that Andy Russell had beaten Moran's brother, Patrick Gonzo Moran, for dipping into the profits he made from selling hash for him and these revelations just enraged Moran more.

Gallagher continued, 'Russell got what he wanted by murdering Benny and getting rid of you and your men; he now has control over Benny's patches in the city. All your lads have been dropped by him too; well, that's how your brother ended up working for him. You know that you need to take control back, Thomas.'

'Oh, I understand that, Billy, I fully understand.'

Moran from then on had only one thing on his mind and that was Andy Russell; the one thing he had was time on his side to plot his downfall.

In 1997, all four members of the Moran gang were released from Portlaoise within four months of each other, having only served three years of their five-year sentence. Noel Slattery was released on New Year's Day, 1997; McCann on 10 March; Smyth on 28 March; then Moran a week later.

It was now time to get organised and payback was on the cards.

Chapter 10
Cash in Transit

In 1997, just before Moran left prison, it was, of course, thanks to Billy Gallagher that he found out Andy Russell was running the drug trade across Dublin and on hearing this, he decided that his old patch was out of reach, not knowing who was on his or Russell's side. So it was wise to stay away, not forever but for just enough time to see who was friend or foe and until he got some cash together to regain what Benny had worked so hard to build.

Moran knew that for this to happen, he had to put a proper plan in place and take back his inheritance from what he viewed as a small-time scumbag like Russell. After a brief call to Noel Slattery, a meeting was organised with his men to discuss ways to raise cash so that they could once again get involved in Dublin's drug trade. On 16 June 1997, Moran, Slattery, Smyth and McCann held that meeting in Moran's Crumlin home.

'Okay boys, the heat is off us now so it's time to go back to work,' explained Moran.

'About time, Tommy, I'm fucking skint,' replied a relieved Smyth.

'I know, I know, lads. Right, we can't do anything with the smack or the hash for now because we're undermanned and as Pudner said, we're fuckin broke. So what do we do?'

Moran scanned the room looking for suggestions, any suggestions, because right now, the men were desperate to make money and he would consider anything that was put to the floor.

'Old-fashioned blaggs, that's what we should do,' was the suggestion from confident Frankie McCann?

'You taking the piss, Frankie, you want us to do armed robberies, do you know how risky that is?' spoke Slattery with an edge of nervous caution in his voice.

On hearing his friend's reaction, Frankie coldly stared directly into Noel's eyes, then he calmly explained his plan, 'Noel, the risk isn't as bad as yis fuckin think, right, RIGHT!'

All three men jumped at Frankie's commanding tone, nodding to indicate that they were listening.

'Now look, lads, none of the post offices and building societies have armed guards and no real security, so fuck it, why not, boys? Ye might get a hero guard every now and again but a good fuckin slap in the mouth will sort that easy enough, ye know.'

A sniggering Moran questioned Frankie more about his plan, 'Okay, talk to me, Frankie, what you got in mind?'

'Tommy, it's like takin candy from a cuntin baby, ye know. We make a plan to get away and stick to the fuckin thing unless we can't, and if not, then we turn to plan B.'

'Plan B, Frankie?' asked Noel Slattery with a puzzled look on his face.

'Yeah, fuckin plan B, Noel, but only if the shite hits the fan, then we change to Plan B. Firstly right, we hit them fast and hard early in the mornin, catchin them off guard. A driver will be waitin with the engine runnin in a stolen car and then someone will meet us at a certain place and we swap cars into a working van or something, ye know?'

'Okay, okay, Frankie, what about guns?' asked Pudner.

'I can get them, Pudner, not a problem,' replied McCann with a sarcastic voice.

'Fucking hell, buddy, you've been busy.'

'No shit, Pudner, I've been planning this stuff since I got out from me three fuckin years' holiday, thanks to Judge Seamus McArdle the cunt.'

'And this Plan B would be what exactly, Frankie?' asked Slattery.

'Ahh, we just open the guns up and whoever gets in the way, ye know… fuck em!'

McCann with a massive grin from ear to ear asked his friends, 'What d'ye think, a fuckin savage plan or what?'

'You're a mad cunt, McCann, a mad cunt!' joked Moran.

All four men then burst into laughter; possibly the first time each of the men had had reason to in many years. From that moment, the gang agreed to start planning some serious armed robberies and as usual with Moran, immediately, the gang was ready to go to work. In an instant, the laughter was broken when

Moran changed the tone in the room, 'Right lads, enough of this bollox; let's get fuckin sorted now! Frankie, get the guns; Pudner, sort us out a car and a builder's van. Noel, we've got some investigation to do. Right boys, fuckin do it.' With that, the house was emptied and all four went about their assigned duties.

On the morning of Friday, 24 June, the gang's first job was an armed robbery on a small local post office on the outskirts of Navan, County Meath. Frankie was armed with a handgun and Moran with a sawn-off shotgun when at 9 am, as the manager of the post office opened its doors, Frankie and Moran entered the small narrow hall; Frankie dragged the manager into the office screaming out threats and Moran kept a watchful eye as they proceeded to carry out the robbery.

The getaway driver was Pudner Smyth who waited outside with the engine running and he did not have to wait long as the two men were in and out in just minutes and they got away with an admirable amount on their first outing, a total of £8,000. As planned, a carefully detailed route of escape was put in place and waiting for the men in a builder's van in a wooded area along the Navan to Dublin Road was Noel Slattery who had four sets of overalls to make them look like legitimate workers just in case they were stopped by any Garda checkpoints. The plan worked to precision as per usual and the Moran gang was again back in business.

Later that night, as Moran relaxed with his wife, a Garda report was read out on a news bulletin stating that, 'Fortunately, no shots were fired and no persons were injured in the robbery.'

According to the Navan Garda Inspector Matt Divine, the culprits who had planned the robbery 'were professionals and armed and dangerous. The silver getaway car with false plates registration number 95WW 1724 was found abandoned and burned out a short time later in a wooded area along the Navan to Dublin Road. We are appealing for anyone who may have seen this car or has any information to please contact us here at Navan Garda Station.'

Inspector Divine's claim that the robbers were professionals was far from the truth, they were a bunch of amateur first-timers who were just good at doing things right. With a taste of success in the air, Moran wasted no time and the next outing for the gang was the robbery of a building society in Rathmines, Dublin, quickly followed up by another post office robbery in Leixlip, County Kildare, earning the gang a mere £33,000 pounds for both jobs.

Moran was not happy as the windfalls were not in keeping with the risk of getting caught in an armed robbery because possession of firearms carried a very heavy prison sentence, so things had to change and bigger targets were needed. With this nagging feeling in the back of his mind that the jobs could be bigger, Moran met Noel Slattery in the Black Horse on Cork Street.

'Hey buddy, what's so urgent?' asked Slattery.

'You know, this was Benny's favourite pub, Noel.' The memory of Benny never left Moran and he had a sense of loss inside like never before.

'Yeah, I do, mate, I do,' replied a sympathetic Slattery.

'That Benny business isn't forgotten, Noel, and it'll be sorted. Billy Gallagher is sortin a meeting.'

'Good Tommy, good; the sooner the better, mate.'

'Fuckin hell, Noel, look at me gettin all bleedin sentimental. Look, never mind me shittin on, just forget about this Benny business for now, we have other things to work on.'

'No problem, Tommy, what's on your mind so?'

'Okay, the reason I called on ye is I'm not happy with where we are. I'm sick of this fuckin hay penny shite!' explained Moran.

'What the fuck do ye mean, Tommy?'

'All this hassle for fuck all reward! Right okay, we are making a few bob, I'll admit, but nothin like we should with all this risk we're takin. You do know it's twelve fuckin years straight up for armed robbery, don't ye, Noel? So I'm thinkin, why not do it big time?'

'Go on.'

'We have to aim higher, we need more and I have an idea. Call the boys. I want another meetin.'

Moran decided that a new wave of specialist armed robberies was to be carried out and the main targets where to be ATM heists. The opportunities posed by unarmed security men making big cash deliveries to ATMs were too good to ignore and it was a lot more cash than post offices and building societies.

At the next meeting, all three men agreed with Moran without hesitation that this was the way forward. Pudner Smyth had news that was to prove invaluable to the gang's new line of work. As it turned out, Smyth's cousin was a bass controller for one of the biggest cash-in-transit companies in the country and he was happy to give the gang information of the routes taken by the vans, for a price. Moran was ecstatic because he finally had some good luck after all the problems he and his men had encountered over the last few years.

The background work had been done, the men put in place and the operations gone over repeatedly—Moran and his men were ready. The workings of the operation began when Smyth received information from his inside man then Moran would carefully select what van to hit under a strict set of rules.

'Listen up, the area must have more than one possible getaway route, and it must not be within touching distance of a Garda station, if at all possible. any wannabe hero gets taken out first; the ATM machines are our only targets. The source does not meet any of the group, bar Smyth.'

After the first handover of the pinpoint cash-in-transit routes from the inside man, Moran studied the routes with precision and care so as not to put any of his gang in any unnecessary danger. After a couple of hours' deliberation, the selection for their first job was to be the ATM at a bank in Rathfarnham village, a nice quiet leafy suburb of Dublin. The area was perfect, the suburb was a prime location for the job due to its many getaway routes and also Moran did not expect any of the middle to upper class residents to play the hero. The heist was to be carried out on the Main Street at around 9.15 am on the morning of 10 September 1997.

That morning, Pudner sat in wait as ever with the engine running while the security van approached to carry out its regular cash delivery to the local ATM. As the passenger got out of the van, Moran and Frankie sprang out of the awaiting car, wielding handguns, and held up the security guard as he approached the doors of the bank.

'Drop the bags, drop the fuckin bags or I'll blow your fuckin head off, ye bastard!' came the roar from McCann.

The guard froze on the spot, he had never before been held up and he did not put up any resistance to the men, the operation was over in a matter of seconds. Startled onlookers ran for cover as the car screamed off towards Nutgrove and up to the foot of the Dublin Mountains to meet up with Noel in the gang's preferred getaway vehicle—a builder's van. It was a good day's work and the men had their first success with that one job, getting them just under £100,000 in cash.

A fortnight later, the next job was in Tullamore, County Offaly, at an ATM machine at the local shopping centre.

'Okay boys, shoot first, ask questions later. Better them than us,' warned Moran.

'Tommy, what if somebody gets in the way, normal shoppers like?'

'Fuck em, it's their fault for bein there.'

'No fucking problem, boss,' replied the psychotic Frankie McCann.

Like in Rathfarnham, the job was to be carried out in the same way, as Moran told his men, 'if it ain't broke, don't try and fix it'. Again, like the first job and after a couple of minutes of shouting and swearing, the men made off with a bag of cash containing £70,000.

Next up was an extremely high-risk operation right in the heart of Dublin city, the hijacking of a security van at the main ATM on O'Connell Street. Christmas shopping was starting to get into full swing so the city was packed with shoppers looking for a bargain; when on 17 November 1997, Moran, McCann and Slattery armed with sawn-off shotguns and wearing dark balaclavas surrounded a security van while Pudner waited in the getaway car, a stolen BMW.

After the security guards surrendered the cash, the men bolted into the car and it immediately sped northbound on O'Connell Street towards Dorset Street and then onwards to a warehouse located in a Dublin airport industrial estate. The robbery was the third major cash-in-transit raid in six weeks by the gang and made them in excess of two hundred thousand pounds.

On 7 December 1997, the gang, now full of cautious confidence, forced a security van into a lay-by off the Howth Road while armed with sawn-off shotguns. Within minutes, they had stolen a grand total of one hundred thousand pounds from the security van, which had been making its way down the coast road towards Clontarf to make its routine drop. The men inside were taken completely by surprise and put up no defence at all.

Two weeks later, the gang carried out a similar raid on a security van in the Town Centre of Maynooth, County Kildare, as they made off with six hundred and thirty thousand pounds. The machines were being loaded up for the Christmas period; Moran could not believe his luck—this was the jackpot. This raid could not have come at a better time because he and his gang were to find out some news in the New Year.

At the turn of 1998, the government passed legislation under severe pressure from opposition parties and public dissatisfaction at their failure to counteract Ireland's rapidly growing armed crime. An announcement from the Minister for Justice caught Moran's attention:

'Armed gangs are easily getting away with daylight robberies and there is a public fear that some innocent victim could be hurt or even killed in a shootout while out doing a day's shopping. It is time to fight back and fight back we will.'

On 5 February 1998, as he drove home, Moran listened ever more closely to the RTE News bulletin as the newsreader announced something that would steer his gang in a new direction:

'Breaking news this time from Garda headquarters, Garda Commissioner Gerry Daly announced, "Today at Government Buildings, a new law has been passed by the Joint Oireachtais Committee on crime, which has increased armed robbery or possession of an illegal weapon to an automatic twelve-year prison term without bail or early release. 'Operation Clean Sweep' is being launched to tackle the fight against these armed crime gangs. A fulltime specialist unit has been set up to tackle gang-related crime with additional funding from the Department of Justice, Equality and Law Reform to fund the operation."'

Moran pulled over to the side of the road to give his full attention; the news reader continued:

'The Organised Crime Unit will have over fifteen full-time officers and will target armed gangs and their criminal activity in cash-in-transit robberies. The man to head 'Operation Clean Sweep' is to be Chief Superintendent Francie O'Leary. Chief Superintendent O'Leary and the unit will be based in Harcourt Square, Dublin. The unit is investigating the possible involvement of up to ten criminals believed to be involved in robberies in Dublin, Kildare, Meath and Wexford.'

During the news broadcast, Moran rang Slattery. 'Ye listenin to the news?'

'No, what's up?'

'I'll tell ye later, Noel.' Hanging up his mobile, Moran continued to listen with great interest.

'Direct Allied, one of the major providers of cash-in-transit security in Ireland, have been hit eight times in the last year and have agreed to partly fund the operation. In addition, all the security companies will have to introduce new measures to combat cash-in-transit robberies, including the use of sealed boxes with dye packs inside, which explode if tampered with, rendering the cash unusable.'

'Bollox' was Moran's reply to the news and from then on, he knew it was time to get out of the armed robbery business as the robberies were far too risky. The chances of being caught now increased tenfold, and the risk of doing a twelve-year stretch did not appeal to him. The armed robberies they carried out had served their purpose, netting them £1.5 million, so it was now time to concentrate on far more serious matters back in Dublin.

Chapter 11
Redser Daly

Moran now turned the gang's full attention back to the fight for control of Dublin's booming drug trade and that fight was about to come to the streets. The Celtic Tiger had now passed its fledgling years and it was clear that the next few years in Ireland would have vast amounts of cash available with staggering opportunities to come, beyond even Moran's wildest dreams.

With the armed robberies over, Moran quickly put the wheels in motion to get back into the drug trade and word was sent out that he was looking for a meeting with Andy Russell; it was no surprise that not long after, he heard word back from him.

Russell arranged a meeting and the venue was to infuriate Moran even more as it was in O'Dwyer's Pub, the scene of Benny's murder. As ever, Moran being Moran, he never let his guard down and never disclosed the information he had found out about Russell when in prison to anyone outside of his closest allies.

At 8.30 pm on the night of 15 February 1998, the night after St Valentine's Day, Moran went to meet Russell at the proposed destination. O'Dwyer's is a typical inner-city pub with its own sense of local ownership by the punters who all have their favourite seats aligned with each of their preferred drinking patterns. At the bar, the male locals relaxed over a newspaper, taking a break from family life before heading home to get ready to bring the wife out later that night.

Also seated along the bar were the typical male conservationists, holding up the counter talking about world affairs and how they should be solved, occasionally including predictions of the forthcoming weekend sporting calendar, recent football results and the daily horseracing winners and losses. These debates and conversations at times got very heated as each and every one of the debaters believed that they were always right. The couples and the younger crowd frequented the seats at the back of the pub so they could have their own conversations about cars, music and the goings-on of the local area while visiting the pub's toilets to take their nightly intake of their preferred drug.

Not taking any risks, Moran had Noel, Frankie and Pudner enter O'Dwyer's a short time before him, ensuring none of them were seated together so as not to arouse suspicion. Russell had not seen the men in four years so the hope was that he would not recognise them. Noel Slattery sat at the bar reading the evening newspaper while Frankie sat just inside the door watching a match that was on the television, donning the jersey of Manchester United and blending into the pub's busy football-watching crowd. Pudner sat at the far end of the pub and joined in a game of Don that was going on when he arrived.

As Thomas Moran entered the busy bar, Russell greeted him with a friendly handshake and a warm smile as if they were lifelong friends and nothing had ever come between them.

'Thomas, my man, what's the fucking story with ye?'

'Not much, Andy, not much.'

'So Thomas, what'll ye have to drink?'

'A Bud will do.'

'Sound; Pat, two Buds yeah and bring them over here, will ye? Now Thomas, the word from the streets tells me that you were lookin for me so what can I do for ye?'

'Well, I need work, Andy, and I want my patch back and I thought you…'

With that statement, the air changed and Andy Russell got annoyed with Moran. 'Work, you fuckin takin the piss, Thomas, from what I hear, you're makin serious money from blaggs. Now this patch you speak of is not your fuckin patch, the neck of ye, your fuckin patch, ye cheeky little cunt. I own this city now. And don't you fuckin forget it, ye little cunt!'

In the middle of the conversation, before Moran could respond to Russell's outburst, Terry Dunne entered the bar and leaned over the table to Moran. 'Evening Tommy, how you keepin, son?'

'Who the fuck is this, Andy?' asked Moran as he went to stand up. Dunne introduced himself as a friend of Russell's and then continued to explain that he had some very important news he would be interested in.

'I have information on the murder of Benny Jewell.'

'What!' This was not what he expected, this was not what he was told in prison, and a stunned Moran was set back as this hit him like a freight train.

Moran thought to himself, *What the hell is going on, what the fuck is this pair playing at?*

'We were shocked and sad to hear of Benny's death, Tommy, it was a fuckin terrible thing to happen.'

'Yes, it was a terrible thing; Benny was a good man and like a father to me,' Moran replied, playing along to see what this man had to say.

'Indeed, Thomas, but anyway, more important is who killed him,' was Russell's reply.

'Okay, continue Andy, I'm all ears.'

'A fella known as Redser Daly is the man who murdered Benny. He's a Northside criminal working out of the North Inner City. He's a dangerous cunt if ever there was.'

'Redser Daly, you say; never heard of him. Anyway, why the fuck would he want to kill Benny?'

Russell asked Dunne to continue to tell Moran their story of Benny's downfall.

'He killed Benny to get control of the Southside drug trade so he could have complete control of the city; word has it he's out after all of us now as he sees us as threats to his plans.'

'Really?'

'Yes Tommy, the bastard called Benny out to a meetin and from what I hear, Benny told him to go fuck himself after he tried to muscle his way into his patch and you know what happened next. We have to sort this cunt, Thomas. We have got to take him out!' stated Russell.

'We, or do you mean me, Andy?'

'Look Tommy, he does not trust me but he will trust you so who better? If you do this for me, I'll set you up with a patch in Ballyer and Clondalkin. Well, you interested?'

'It's tempting, Andy, very tempting and after all he did do Benny. Look, give me a few days to mull over the offer.'

'Sound, Thomas, I'll find ye when I need to see ye, okay?'

'No problem, Andy, I'll talk to ye later. Terry, I'm sure we'll meet again.'

'Indeed, Tommy, indeed.'

'Goodnight gentlemen, see ye both soon.'

Of course, Russell thought if Moran was to take out Daly, he would be doing half his work for him and then with Daly out of the way, his men could pounce on the Moran gang and from there on, Dublin would be his. Elements within the Russell gang had been plotting to have Moran taken out of the equation because Dublin's underworld was Russell's dream but he feared that with Moran back on the scene now, he was not to be trusted and he had to be taken care of.

After the meeting in O'Dwyer's, Moran met with his men to explain what went down and having told the full story, tempers were fuelled even more within the Moran crew.

'So what do we do now, Tommy?' asked Frankie.

'Lads, you're not going to like this but I got to tell yis, Russell and this fella Dunne came out and blamed a bloke called Redser for doin Benny.'

'What!' screamed a furious Frankie McCann.

'You're fuckin jokin, mate?' asked a gobsmacked Slattery.

'No Noel, in O'Dwyer's, the cheeky cunts even said they were shocked and sad to hear of his death.'

Smyth joined in with absolute disgust at the blatant cheek of Russell.

'I know, Pudner, I know, but their time will come.'

'You better fuckin' believe it, Tommy,' cried Frankie.

A few days later, not to be outdone, Moran added another twist to the tale and it was to be the turning point in the whole saga of Moran vs Russell. What Andy Russell, Terry Dunne and not even Moran's own men were aware of was that Moran had been put in contact with Redser Daly after visiting an old friend in prison, none other than crime kingpin, Billy Gallagher.

Moran filled Gallagher in on the conversation that had taken place in O'Dwyer's and soon after, Gallagher got word to Daly. Days later, Moran was informed that Daly was now aware of the discussion in O'Dwyer's and Gallagher had since organised a meeting for both men in Athlone, County Westmeath. Moran told his men something was in the works but he did not let anyone know what exactly was going on until they needed to know.

'Okay boys, Noel and meself will be going to Athlone to meet up with some people so stand by for a call.'

'No problem, boss, who yis meetin?' questioned an inquisitive Smyth.

'People; that's all ye need to know right now.'

'Okay, Tommy, okay.'

'Sound, in time, mate, okay?'

A couple of days later, an associate of Redser Daly contacted Moran about the meeting in Athlone and it was set for 5 March 1998 in a hotel in the Town

Centre at noon. The man that Moran and Slattery were to meet was 36-year-old Redser Daly, a born and bred Dubliner from the North Inner City and a key figure on the Northside of the city and in the Irish underworld. Daly had learned his trade growing up in the flats on Gardiner Street and he got his nickname due to his burning head of red hair and his fiery temper to match. Redser had been in and out of prison all his life and thanks to prison life, he became a hardened criminal with an extreme taste for violence and just the man Moran could work with.

On the morning of 5 March 1998, Thomas Moran and Noel Slattery travelled to Athlone on the 9.15 train to meet Redser at the arranged meeting place at twelve noon and he went straight to business.

'Thanks for meetin me so soon, boys. Right, I'm a really busy man, I won't keep yis long, I gotta be outta here in half an hour and I'm sorry for draggin yis up here but the law are all over me at the moment.'

'Not at all, Redser, not at all.'

'Nice one, Tommy. Okay, this business, I have news for you from a friend in common and he asked me to help you out with a problem we now both have.'

Daly continued to explain, 'Terry Dunne was involved in the full setup in Carlingford and when he told Russell the plan, Russell gave the order to set yis up to get yis outta the way so they could sort Benny.'

With a wry smile on his face, Daly spoke, 'I liked that little bollix, I have to admit, didn't trust the little cunt but I liked him.'

Moran coughed, trying to hide his laughter. 'Yeah, he was a good bloke, Redser, anyway, when I was at the meeting in O'Dwyer's, Russell and Dunne said that it was you who killed Benny to get control of the Southside drug trade and best of all, they want me to take you out.'

'Hold on now, boys, I did NOT—'

'No, no, for fuck sake, Redser, I'm not sayin that I believed them, I'm just lettin ye know what this pair of cunts is up to,' explained Moran.

'These cheeky bastards, okay, right, we got to sort these out once and for all, lads.' And Daly was the man to do just that.

'This can get messy, lads, or it can be done without any fucking problems, I'm not a fan of problems. Tommy, do you trust me to sort it, will you follow me for now?'

'Without a doubt, Redser, without a doubt. It's your call.'

'Okay, I have some information on a job that Russell and his men are about to pull so I'm goin to give this info to another source to do whatever they want to do with it. I'll let you know what this is in time, Tommy. Okay?'

'Yeah, no problem, Redser.'

'I want you to sort Russell; I'll take care of that little cunt Dunne and the rest of his fuckin gang. Right, I have to split. I'll be in touch.'

'It'll be a pleasure. Keep in touch.'

After only twenty-five minutes, all three men went their own way and the fight to take down Russell and his gang had just begun. It would not be long after the meeting in Athlone that a deal would be brokered to split Dublin in two. Moran was to get the Southside and Redser the Northside of the city and for now, only Russell stood in the way.

Noel Slattery was stunned by the brilliant work of his boss. 'You, Little Don, are one calculated and smart little bollix with balls of steel.'

Moran just gave Slattery a smile and continued towards the train station. Smyth and Frankie McCann were waiting patiently in Crumlin for Moran to return home with some news and when Moran told his men that the stakes had just risen and if anyone wanted out, now was the time to go—to Moran's delight, nobody moved. It was time to avenge Benny.

Also that night across Dublin City, Redser Daly was passing on the information to his source about the job that Russell had planned. You see, word had gotten back to Gallagher in prison about Russell's next job and he then swiftly passed the information onto Redser Daly, Daly subsequently passed this information to a known grass that, for cash, passed it onto Chief Superintendent Francie O'Leary, the head of Operation Clean Sweep.

The night before a certain armed heist was to take place, an anonymous phone call was made to the unit in charge of Operation Clean Sweep in Harcourt Terrace, providing information regarding when and where details of an armed robbery due to take place. From this information, the Garda Special Branch moved in and arrested all the members involved at the scene and Garda Commissioner Gerry Daly announced he and his special unit, Operation Clean Sweep, had taken down the main gang responsible for the wave of armed robberies carried out across Leinster.

Russell's men were refused bail and remanded in custody following strenuous objections by the Special Branch to allow them be released. Moran laughed in private at the brazen neck of Gallagher but he was only too happy to see the Russell crew take the blame for his work and once again, Moran had been lucky; Redser had now done his bit and Moran still had to take care of Russell. Now was the time for the final play in the Redser/Moran joint operation while the iron was hot and in September of 1998, Moran acquired a handgun, which was collected by Smyth in Finglas on Dublin's Northside of the city.

Moran was informed that Russell was playing with a darts team in his local Inner City pub and they played regularly on a Thursday night without fail. Frankie got his hands on the fixture list after paying a visit to the pub and it was decided that on Thursday, 20 September 1998, Andy Russell was to be taken out once and for all.

Both Frankie and Moran arrived at the bar on a high-power motorbike at 9.45 pm and after parking the bike in a laneway near to the bar, Frankie entered and went straight to the toilets to see if and where Russell was in the bar. As Frankie came back to Moran, he explained, 'He's in there alright. Top of the bar at the darts area, it's pretty empty with about forty people in the place but I didn't recognise anyone in there so it looks as if he is on his own with no bodyguards and hopefully no fuckin wannabe heroes. If so, Tommy, plug them too.'

'Sound, Frankie,' were the stuttering words from a nervous Moran.

'Look Tommy, do you want me...'

'No, no, buddy, I have to do this.'

Moran checked the gun before he crossed the road and Frankie gave some words of help to his boss. 'Look Tommy, squeeze the trigger, don't force it. Two shots, bang, bang in the head and then get out. Don't panic; just keep your head and remember, I'm just outside. In, bang, bang, calmly turn and walk out, the punters will fuckin cream themselves so you stay calm while they panic, okay.'

Moran took a deep breath. 'Right, let's fucking do this.'

As Moran entered the bar still wearing his motorbike helmet, his heart was racing like never before, sweat ran down his face but he quickly spotted Russell joking with some people at the end of the bar. As Moran approached his target, he pulled his gun from his pocket and as Russell turned towards him, Moran shot Andy Russell twice in the head. Screams rang out as Russell hit the ground and Moran turned and headed towards the door and out onto the footpath where Frankie was waiting.

'Go, go, go, Frankie; drive, let's get the fuck out of here!'

And Andy Russell was no more. The next day, the word on the street was all about the murder of Dublin crime lord Andy Russell; Jean came into the bedroom to wake her husband to tell him the news.

'Thomas, I was down the shop and people were sayin that someone had been shot in town. I didn't find out exactly who it was but some people were sayin it was some fella called Russell.'

Moran was half-asleep. 'I know the cunt, Jean, and I can't say I'll shed any tears; I don't imagine that many others will either. So fuck him, Jean, here, turn on the news, will ye?'

Moran caught the tail end of the news bulletin:

'The man wearing a motorbike helmet shot down Russell in cold blood at approximately 9.45 pm last night in O'Dwyer's bar. Reaction in the area from the public was fear of violence and everyone here said that this is not the end. Gardaí are appealing to any people with any information to come forward.'

Moran lay back in his bed and smiled while whispering, 'Now you can rest in peace, Benny, mate.'

A couple of weeks later, Terry Dunne was suspiciously mugged coming home from his local and died later in hospital from his injuries. The Gardaí said it was not gang-related but Redser Daly would think differently.

Chapter 12
The Builder's Yard

During the mid to late 1990s, Ireland was experiencing an economic boom that transformed the country from one of Europe's weaker economies into one of its wealthiest under a new era of fiscal growth that was to become known as 'The Celtic Tiger'. This rapid economic growth was due to many reasons, but the credit has been primarily given to low corporate taxation, a low-cost labour market and Ireland's EU membership, which provided transfer payments and export access to the Single Market. In addition, many economists also credited this growth to an over-exposed housing market backed by reckless lending by its banking system. As a result, the price of accommodation both in the sale and rental sector rose sharply in a very short period of time.

The fact of the matter was that many customers were given anywhere from 80% to 100% mortgage loans by the banks and this resulted in too many Greenfield sites situated in and around Dublin and further afield being developed. The knock-on effect of this reckless lending saw a building boom not seen in Ireland for decades, driving the construction industry out of control with housing estates appearing almost overnight, but the difference between this and previous building projects was that these estates were not part of a national social housing project but the development of many overpriced private homes entering the market.

As a result of Dublin's boom, a commuter belt was formed outside the county boundaries as young couples bought homes outside of the capital due to ever increasing price and rent. Property developers were firmly in the pockets of a cohort of crooked elected representatives who personally approved many of these building programmes at local area level through city and county councils. Ireland was prospering and Moran was about to join in.

It was 1999 and Thomas Moran had just turned thirty-one years of age and now had a solid vision of his future and exactly how he was going to achieve it. Achieving this dream was not going to be easy and he understood this all too well, but not even the most determined, experienced and ambitious of gangsters could have foreseen what was about to come down the line.

One thing that Benny had taught Moran was that not even the most level-headed gangster from Dublin could control every instant or every person in a world of deceit and murder, and how true those words would be. Yes, the good times lay ahead for Moran but they were not pathways paved with gold but pathways full of cracks that were just waiting for a chance to trip him up; he had to take the good with the bad, that was a given in his line of work.

The murder of Andy Russell some months previous had left Dublin City in gangland limbo with the once powerful Russell gang now in absolute turmoil and its remaining members not knowing where to turn or who to turn to. Most had left Ireland and others just disappeared off the gangland radar, fearing the same fate as Russell; Ireland's gangland encountered a massive void within its higher ranks and for the first time since his release from prison, Moran felt that the time was right to take the opportunity he had been waiting for and regain the Inner City streets.

Along with his closest confidants, he called on some newfound friends who had been introduced to him by Billy Gallagher in Portlaoise prison, and they were Charlie 'The Scouser' Butterfield, Tony 'The Fairy' Rothwell, George Mayweather, Phil Mackey and Deano Coyle. It was early February when Moran sent out word to all that they were to meet in the small town of Blarney, the home of the famous Blarney Stone, just outside of Cork City.

The scenic little town was, for now, the meeting point for a newly formed gang who was about to put plans together, which would change the face of the Irish underworld forever. Blarney was ideal for the meeting as it was away from the watchful eye of An Garda Síochána back in Dublin who would have alarm bells ringing if this group was seen together but as ever, Moran made sure all nine men registered into separate hotels and B&Bs in the locality under false names so as not to arouse any unwanted suspicion.

The meeting was taking place in a conference room Moran had booked at the main hotel in the town just a couple of weeks before the meet. Jokingly, he had Jean as his secretary book the room under the name of 'Genco Oil', which was near enough the name of the company Vito Corleone opened in Moran's favourite movie *The Godfather*. To add to his high-jinx, Moran booked the room using the name Michael Corlon, short for Corleone. Again not wanting to arouse any suspicion, he made sure that all the men looked and acted like legitimate businessmen, making sure they were all dressed in business attire to give the impression that this was a meeting of the company's executive body.

It was at 10 am on 11 February 1999, when Moran arrived into the main reception area of the hotel and after a brief chat with the receptionist, he was politely directed down a hall towards the Oak Leaf Conference room where the meeting was to take place. What caught his attention above everything else was the overpowering aroma of fresh coffee wafting throughout the hotel and he quickly asked a passing waitress to have five pots delivered to the conference room. As he entered the room, he found all eight members of the gang inside waiting for him and as he closed the door behind him, he went straight into business.

As Moran made his way to the top of the table, he told his men, 'Okay, listen up, we have a lot of work to get through but most important, this is quite possibly the last time that this group of people will be in the same room again so listen fuckin closely. One rule is that not one person is to take any fuckin notes. I do not want any evidence about our discussions that we are about to have here.'

He continued as he sat down, 'Right lads, we all know why we are here so let's hear what you have all got to add. As you all are quite aware, a certain gentleman pointed you all out to me due to your very own personal expertise, so let's hear what you got.'

The doors were locked and the curtains pulled, blocking out not just the natural sunlight but also unwanted eyes that just might be watching. All nine men gave their own input to how and where the gang should go and after hours of discussion and debate, it was overwhelmingly agreed by all that the illegal drug market was going to be their place of business. This was the start of a drug operation like never seen before in Europe, never mind Ireland. From that moment, a prison meeting was to lead to the setting up of a gang that would run one of Irish state's most profitable and sophisticated drug operations ever seen and they had the contacts around the world and the money to do so.

Everyone, of course, had a job and Moran handed out the positions. 'Noel will become the gang's head of operations, that means he is the link to hold everyone together and reporting every last-minute detail directly to me. Nobody else comes near me unless I clear it through Noel. Is that clear?'

Nods of agreement came from all eight men as Moran continued. To no surprise, Pudner Smyth and the ruthless Frankie McCann were given the job of Moran's enforcers, along with transporting the goods and taking care of local financial issues like before. Of the new members, Charlie Butterfield would become Moran's contact for smuggling drugs through Britain and Ireland via Spain while working alongside another of the original St Christopher's gang, Danny Moore. Moran had not seen Danny since he had left Ibiza but in time, he would look after Southern Europe and North Africa while working alongside Butterfield as the two men would traffic drugs through Spain and Africa to Ireland's shores while also supplying England and Wales.

Tony Rothwell, a numbers genius, was given the role to look after all the financial aspects that included laundering money from the gang's dealings plus he was to pay off members of the Gardaí, customs, foreign gangs and anyone else who needed paying. In time, Rothwell would set up a finance network so sophisticated that not even the Gardaí or Interpol could break into it. Even judges and businessmen were going to be paid off. Rothwell was to become Moran's mister fix-it.

Next was George Mayweather hailing from County Tyrone in Northern Ireland, an expert smuggler; he was to become Moran's main importer of weapons and drugs. Mayweather would work out of Amsterdam and take care of Northern Europe and the Eastern gateway and just like Butterfield and Moore, he was going to be the main importer in his region of Northern Ireland, the rest of Ulster and Scotland.

Another member of the gang, Phil Mackey, would be Moran's intelligence operator and it would be his job to gather as much information as humanly possible on rival gangs and police forces, all the while locating gangs to deal with across the European and African market. Finally, Dean Coyle would be the Irish drugs link, moving the drugs from base to base and onto the street dealers across Britain and Ireland.

Thanks to Butterfield's British connections, Moran—through him and directing Mackey in that direction—was able to organise four gangs from north, south, east and west of the British mainland to take care of his business; he had the money and the product to hire the biggest and best gangs in Britain and they took care of business as Moran paid them very, very well indeed.

With everyone now in place, Moran then decided that the gang needed a secure base where they could organise all their business without coming under suspicion and Tony Rothwell came up with the idea that a legitimate business was the way to go.

'I have a thought, Thomas.'

'Go on, Tony.'

'How about something like a builder's yard, cement, sand, blocks and all that stuff?'

'Yes, they're building materials, so the fuck what?'

'Excellent, I'm happy to see you have grasped the concept, young Thomas, can I finish?' Moran knew he had been premature with his interruption, grinned, put out his hands to indicate that Rothwell had the room.

'Right, as I was saying, as we all know right now Ireland is in the middle of a building frenzy so what better to have as cover, a builder's yard! Now when back in Dublin, take a good look around, you gentlemen, with all this building going on, the yard is a perfect cover. Two birds with one stone, so to speak, laundering money and having a base to work from. So what do ye all think?'

Noel Slattery jumped up and spoke, 'What do I think? Well, Tony, I think it's a fuckin deadly idea.'

Moran sat in his chair and with a wry smile on his face, looked at Rothwell and expressed his opinion, 'Good stuff from you, Tony. Okay, let's sort it. Noel, you're over this now but Tony, as you're our moneyman, I want you to look out for sites around the area as near to Crumlin as possible. Noel, I'll introduce ye to a couple of the lads I think will be perfect for this. So we'll talk later.'

'Will do, Thomas.'

Moran, now fastening his jacket, approached Rothwell and placing his hands on his shoulders told him, 'Tony, you're my fuckin man; well done, nice one.'

Not long after the Blarney meeting, Dean Coyle contacted Slattery having noticed an advertisement for a possible site in the window of a prominent estate agent in the city. The cost was £350,000 and the site sat on 3.56 acres and just as importantly, it was perfectly located close to the Harold's Cross Road just outside Crumlin.

Slattery rang Rothwell and a couple of days later, Moran and Rothwell looked at the property and immediately contacted the estate agent for a meeting. Rothwell purchased the property under a Marie Conroy, Moran's mother's maiden name, and then he opened a legitimate bank account also under the same name.

On the day of purchase, Slattery had one of his many girlfriends, a Debbie Cox, go along with Rothwell to impersonate the would-be property developer to open the bank account and also register the business legitimately with the Revenue Commissioners. For someone like Rothwell, simple false paperwork like a social security card and a driver's licence was child's play for him and not an eyelid was blinked, paperwork was seen as above board in the eyes of everyone involved, plus Cox got a pretty payment for her endeavours that day.

On 22 April 1999, Tony Rothwell contacted Moran about the yard. 'Thomas, I looked into changing the yard structure and because it has no buildings on it, what I found out was that we need to apply for planning permission from Dublin Corporation for any new development. So this has to be signed off before you're allowed to start development work in the city, we have to get permission; it has to be done. These planning people are normally fussy as fuck when it comes to these things; we do this right, we get no unwanted visits.'

'Nice one, Tony, I would never have known. Will you sort it because I want this done right on all accounts because this has to be 100% legit, ye know?'

'I'm on it, Thomas.'

Moran wanted everything sorted by the book as much as he could because if he was going to open a builder's yard, it had to be right. Rothwell had good news after a fourteen-week wait as the planning went through and the trucks began to roll into the site. So the name Moran came up with was 'The Builder's Yard', nice and simple you think, but Moran being Moran, nothing was that simple because the logo read 'Everything we stock is a steal'—smart and cheeky.

For five days, trucks arrived with sand, cement, blocks, bricks, plaster boards, bags of plaster and every type of wood imaginable plus all types of builder's tools, manual and electric, along with boxes and boxes of screws, accessories and glues. The yard had everything a tradesman needed and was possibly one of the best around Dublin. Now Moran needed staff to run the yard so he employed his uncle, Seamus Conroy, who was to be the yard manager, making sure everything ran properly, including keeping an eye on stock, making sure stock was delivered and bills were paid.

Seamus Conroy was always Moran's favourite uncle and unlike his other uncles, he had never neglected his mother Marie after his father left for England. Conroy, a career criminal, came from the old-school Dublin criminal world that had the unwritten rule of take what you can and keep your mouth shut at all times but he knew where his bread was buttered and Moran was that butter.

The other staff members included Dean Coyle, four youngsters from the area who were known by him or were recommended to Moran by close friends in the underworld. The young recruits were 19-year-old Brian 'Nailor' O'Neill from Crumlin, known for his violent history and had found himself in and out of homes and prisons all of his young life. He would in time be close to Moran.

Next was 18-year-old Mark 'Bubbles' Fahey who was, let's just say, not the brightest spark in the world. Bubbles was loud, had a big mouth and always spoke before thinking but the only reason Moran took him on board was because of his father—a well-known criminal from St Christopher's who was shot in a robbery some years gone by. Now, if you had to sum Bubbles up, all you had to know was what happened on the opening day of the yard. Seamus Conroy was doing the stock check in the back office when Bubbles came in and interrupted him, explaining that there was someone outside.

Conroy, looking confused, asked him, 'What does he want, Bubbles?'

'He said wants to buy some sand and cement. What the fuck will I do?'

'Sell it to him, ye fuckin thick, after all you do know this is a fuckin' builder's yard.'

'Oh right, yeah sound, what is it and how much is it, Seamus?'

'Oh, for fuck sake, I'll be out in a minute.'

The third member of staff was Aaron 'Packey' Young, the elder of the four at 20 years of age. Young was a slimy character and a chronic thief who was one of Moran's top street dealers. Young even sold heroin to his younger sisters and their friends so that he could make a profit. A real gem, this one.

Finally, there was Paul Price from Drimnagh, or better known to his friends as 'Slug', but he was, like O'Neill, unknown to Moran. The 19-year-old was a clever young man who could achieve anything he put his mind to and unlike the other three, he had excelled at school but chose to take the life of crime.

With the Builder's Yard functioning quite well, Moran was now in a position to start organising the importation of illegal drugs and high on his list were marijuana and heroin. In the meantime, Smyth had made contacts with two former members of the Benny Jewell crew in Dublin a couple of weeks before the opening of the yard after he accidentally bumped into them on Cork Street. John Deans and Cyril Gilmartin told Smyth that they had smuggled shipments of cannabis for Benny from Morocco to the Netherlands and then onto the Irish market in the past.

After a closer background check on the two men, Moran got positive feedback so wasting no more time, he sent Tony Rothwell and Noel Slattery to meet up with Deans and Gilmartin in Amsterdam to organise the possible importation of cannabis and heroin to Ireland. Both men had already organised a shipment of drugs they had bought from a Moroccan dealer, Mohammad El Zhar, in Amsterdam but soon after purchasing the drugs, it transpired they could not move the gear back to Ireland.

During the background check on the men, Moran had been informed that their contact in London—a one Terry Bridge—had been arrested after he stabbed a bouncer to death during a bar brawl. Bridge was their man in Heathrow airport who moved the drugs through customs and with Moran now knowing what went on, he was going to play it smart as he knew that both men were stuck with the drugs.

On 11 May 1999, after driving to Belfast Airport, both men boarded the 7.45 am flight to Amsterdam's Schiphol Airport on-board Flight KLF23 but just before Rothwell and Slattery left Dublin, Moran had sent word with his men that the price that Deans and Gilmartin were asking per kilo was too much. The original price they quoted was £7,500 per kilo of heroin and the cannabis was priced at £5,500 per kilo. Their hands were tied and Moran knew it, with the drugs just sitting in Amsterdam making no profit, he was only going to offer £6,000 per kilo for the heroin and £5,000 per kilo of cannabis and it was a take it or leave it offer.

On their arrival at the airport, Noel was in a buoyant mood because even though Amsterdam was the home of such world-famous artists like Rembrandt, they were not the only reason why people flocked to the city and Slattery knew this all too well.

'Ahh here, Tony, I'm going to sample all of what Amsterdam has to offer, if ye know what I mean.'

'Oh Noel, I know exactly what you mean, you dirty git.'

Amsterdam has its many attractions and those attractions include Amsterdam's renowned red-light district known as De Wallen. The area of De Wallen is set out in a network of alleys servicing hundreds of tiny one-room apartments rented by male and female prostitutes behind a window or glass door, typically illuminated with red lights or the less visible blue light for men.

Another of the main attractions in Amsterdam are its world-famous coffee shops, but these are not just any old coffee shops because in Amsterdam, cannabis is openly sold and smoked so they tend to be popular with tourists. The coffee shops can legally store up to 500g of marijuana and general rules require owners and staff to abide by a customer ruling of a minimum age of eighteen years, and it was in one of Amsterdam's coffee shops where the four men would meet.

Deans had sent word to Moran to make sure one of his men was wearing a cap with a small red ribbon on it so he knew who to look for. In addition, Deans also explained the details of how his men should travel to the meeting place. At the airport, Rothwell and Slattery were to take the Dutch Direct Rail Link, which connects Schiphol International Airport to Amsterdam's city centre, and from there, they were to take the city trams to the meeting, getting off in Dam Square and only having a short stroll to the coffee shop.

The meeting time was set for twelve noon in the Abacus coffee shop situated in the heart of Amsterdam's red-light district overlooking a canal. At twelve-fifteen, both men arrived at the coffee shop and as they made their way inside, the two men found the bar decorated with beautiful ceramic mosaics with a menu of brownies, muffins, cakes and shakes all mixed with that special Amsterdam ingredient. Slattery and Rothwell had ordered coffee from the waitress and as she put the cups on the table, two men entered the Abacus and approached them.

'You pair Tommy's men?' asked one of the men.

'Yeah, I'm Tony, this is Noel,' answered Rothwell who was wearing the cap with a red ribbon attached to it.

'Sound, lads, I'm John and this is Cyril,' spoke Deans as both men sat down.

Deans, standing only five feet five inches tall, was a short but blocky man who had a bad limp on his left side; he had wild grey hair and a dirty beard, giving the impression that he had just gotten out of a bin truck. On top of his appearance, Deans had terrible breath, bad grammar and regularly swore as if he had Tourette's. Rothwell realised straight away that Deans was no businessman.

Gilmartin, on the other hand, was a much taller man, standing around six foot four inches and well turned out with not a hair out of place; he was dressed in a fine pinstriped suit and spoke like a man who knew his business.

'Okay, gentlemen, we know why we are all here so let's talk business,' started Gilmartin.

'Right then, lads, let's talk, our orders are from Thomas Moran and these are his own words. He said we're only going to offer six grand a kilo of heroin and five grand a kilo for the cannabis and it is a take it or leave it offer.'

But even before Slattery finished his sentence, the smaller and more aggressive Deans stood up and ranted, 'Well, you can tell Moran he can go fuck himself. Fuck off, you cheeky cunts!' And he started to leave the bar.

'Hold on, hold on,' replied Gilmartin, holding Deans' arm while calming his friend, 'John, sit down, my good man, and relax. Okay, young Thomas has done his homework, I see. I remember when he first met us in the Black Horse many years ago now, my oh my, how things have changed,' openly sniggered Gilmartin to Slattery's hidden annoyance.

'Well, are we in business?' quizzed Slattery.

'Yes, we are, Noel, yes, we are.'

'Excellent; so as I stated, it's six grand a kilo of heroin and five a kilo for the cannabis.'

Gilmartin reached out his arm and shook hands with the two men. 'Yes, yes, all agreed, lads.'

'We will transport the goods to Cork via cargo plane leaving Rotterdam next Wednesday. You pair transport the goods to the holding bay for us,' explained Rothwell.

'Perfect, that is not a problem.'

Rothwell continued to explain, 'I'll forward all the details in the next twenty-four hours. It will include the proper documents and the number of the freight.'

As Gilmartin handed Rothwell an envelope with all the details, he told him. 'Fine and this is the address to post the documents to and the account number to transfer the cash. That's three hundred and fifty grand in total.'

'Yes, yes, give it here; I'll sort that out later today.'

Slattery cut across Rothwell and the tone changed, 'Right, let me tell you one thing, if you pair fuck us about, we will find yis no matter how fuckin long it takes and I promise yis this, we will slit your fuckin throats and put a blowtorch to your fuckin eyes. Do I make myself fuckin clear?'

Deans' temper changed, the colour ran from his skin as he realised that he was not dealing with any old fools and Gilmartin stepped in to calm things down.

'For fuck sake, lads, what the hell do you think we are?' replied an edgy Gilmartin.

'Good to hear, right, so gentlemen, a good day to you both and take heed of what I said. Right Tony, let's go.'

Rothwell and Slattery left the coffee shop as the Moran gang had just done a very decent drug deal; at 5.30 pm the following day, both men were on a plane out of Amsterdam and back to Belfast after a very good day's work. This was to be their first visit to the city of Amsterdam but would certainly not be their last. Moran did not worry about the £350,000 price tag he was paying out, he knew that as soon as the drugs hit the streets, he would see a profit of around £800,000 and from that, he would invest in a larger shipment of drugs.

Days after the meeting in Amsterdam, the cannabis and heroin arrived in four wooden boxes to a warehouse at Cork City airport as previously arranged. With all the paperwork in place, McCann and Smyth travelled to Cork on 17 May in a rented van to collect the boxes from the airport storage facilities.

From there, it was transferred to a builder's truck that was waiting to the rear of a nearby derelict site where Deano Coyle drove it to Dublin to a warehouse Rothwell rented on Dublin's docklands.

Within days, the cannabis and heroin were cut, bagged and then dispersed out to a number of dealers that included Bubbles Fahey, Aaron Packey Young, Paul Slug Price and Brian Nailor O'Neill, who would all sell it around Dublin city to waiting customers on the street. The complex network of supply meant that only a small number of people knew the identity of Moran so if one of the street dealers was caught, Moran and his drugs gang was protected.

In September of 1999, Moran had George Mayweather and Charlie Butterfield import a quantity of cannabis and heroin from Deans and Gilmartin from their base in Holland. The shipment was on board a flight between Amsterdam's Schiphol and Belfast International airport. The ground crew had loaded the cargo on 19 September in Schiphol Airport but the flight was delayed due to bad storms over Holland and two days later, the plane was still in Amsterdam. This sent panic into both men because the delay had increased their chances of losing the cargo due to the possibility of additional security checks plus the main worry was the fact that the street value for this cargo would net the gang a tidy one million in profit.

The drugs were put in small packets and were very well concealed inside the numerous pallets stacked with boxes of building material that included shovels, spades, rakes, small hand-trowels and other such materials that were destined for the Builder's Yard in Dublin. But the most important stock item next to the drugs was the dozen bottles of white spirits intentionally left beside the drugs so that the sniffer dogs could not get past the smell of spirits and would then move on straight away to the next pallet. To Moran's relief, after the delay, the pallets arrived in the builder's yard on 22 September and the drugs hit the streets within two days of arrival.

The gang's next job was coming from Morocco, which included a major heroin shipment totalling more than one million in value and cannabis valuing eight hundred thousand before it hit the streets, and the deal was once again through Deans and Gilmartin. From this, George Mayweather set up a courier business beside his home in county Tyrone as a cover for his illegal gains and later established a national transport business, putting several lorries and vans on the road plus some continental journeys that were to become a new importing avenue for Moran.

With everything moving along, Jean dropped a bomb on Moran when on 3 October, she arrived home after a night out with friends and asked Moran a question that was to put him on the back foot.

'Thomas, now I'm only askin so don't go fuckin ape-shite on me, okay? I'm only fuckin askin, right?'

'Askin what, Jean?' questioned Moran, interested to see what his wife had to say.

'Tonight when I was out with the girls, I was told by Wendy Burke that you murdered Andy Russell?' Moran went berserk on hearing this but did not take it out on his wife.

'Are you fuckin havin a laugh, holy fuckin Christ, the mouthy cunt! I'll kill that cunt, the cheeky cunt. I could get ten fuckin years for that shite, Jean, serious, if a copper heard that, I'd be rightly fucked. The big-mouth cunt! Where does she live, Jean? Where does she fuckin live, Jean, where!'

'On the avenue, Thomas, now stop shouting. It's number 212; why, Thomas?' fretted Jean.

'I just want to put her straight about a few things, love, that's all.'

'Oh right, then I'll tell her—'

'You'll tell her nothin. I'll see her meself.'

Of course, Moran was going to have more than words and this became clear when he sent both Smyth and Frankie down to have a 'word' with the 24-year-old unmarried mother of three, Wendy Burke. You see, Thomas Moran's way of having a word was by having Smyth and Frankie putting her in hospital for three weeks after they both handed out a severe beating to the young woman. Frankie wore a pair of steel-toed builder's boots and he put full force of the boots into Wendy Burke's body and head while Smyth punched her around the head and ribs as he donned a knuckle-duster, taking no notice of the young mother's screams.

Wendy Burke's young children aged one, four and six years sat and roared the house down as they witnessed their mother getting battered by these two giant men. Frankie McCann told her, he would kill her if she opened her mouth again. When the word hit the streets, it sent a harsh warning to anyone who dared to open their mouth against their gang, even if it was so innocently like Wendy Burke. That night, both men arrived in their local pub to inform Moran of the business they had attended to.

'That's sorted, Tommy,' explained Frankie.

'Good man, so no more problems?'

'You must be fuckin joking, Tommy, not a chance.'

'Ahh good auld Frankie, you and Pudner are so persuasive, a pint, lads?' laughed Moran.

Chapter 13
Sam the Turk

It was now early January 2000 and the big hullabaloo surrounding the new millennium had come and gone while the so-called millennium bug that scientists and computer geeks alike had warned the world about never came to fruition. In reality, it was just another year for the vast majority of people as life continued on as before. Life for Moran also moved on when on a very wet January evening, Charlie Butterfield arrived at Moran's Crumlin home with a proposal.

'Tommy, how the hell are you, mate?'

'Good Charlie, very good but what the fuck are you doin here?'

Butterfield explained in his undeniable Scouse accent, 'We got to get involved in the cocaine market, Tommy, you know, coke, nose candy, snow, dust?'

'I fuckin know what it is, Charlie!'

'Look Tommy, mate, we are missing out big-time on this coke market.'

Moran dismissed this claim and told Butterfield, 'It's a fuckin rich man yuppie drug, Charlie.'

'Tommy, mate, I know what you're saying but coke is outselling every other fucking drug out on the streets, cunts are snorting it in parliament, so are fuckin doctors, solicitors and right down the line to the fucking clubbers at the weekend. It's fucking snowing out there and we are missing out big-style, Tommy lad.'

'Look Charlie, George Mayweather contacted me not so long ago about a huge trafficker he had in mind and that this contact has already asked about us moving coke shipments from him.'

'Well, I can get it for seven and a half grand a kilo off my bloke and we can sell it at a profit of around one hundred per cent, a hundred fucking per cent. A gram will cost you around fifty to sixty quid like for a paper wrap, d'ye know what I mean, like.'

'Okay, okay, leave it with me, Charlie, and I'll contact ye soon.'

'Sound, Tommy, mate.'

'And Charlie, don't you ever come near this fuckin house again, never.'

'Okay, right mate, sorry like.'

'Right then, now fuck off.'

When Butterfield left, Moran pondered a little because this was now two of his men who had put the idea of cocaine to him and he thought it was about time he did some research on it and his findings were more than enough to get him interested. On examination of the cocaine industry via a relatively new search engine called Google on the Internet, Moran sat and read all about Columbia being the world's largest supplier of the cocoa crop, a key ingredient of cocaine. On further examination, he found out that ninety percent of the planet's cocoa is actually grown in the Amazonian Rain Forests of Putumayo in Columbia, which sits high in the Andes Mountains. Moran was completely transfixed to his computer screen as he discovered:

'The breakdown of the cocoa leaf is turned into cocaine base and it then has cement added to break the leaves down. After this action, some gasoline is then poured to clean it followed by sulphuric acid to turn the leaf into a crystallised form so later it would be easier to make into cocaine.'

'Cement, gasoline and fucking acid! What the fuck?' The next piece was to completely enthral the gangster:

'In 1989, at the height of Pablo Escobar's power empire, Forbes magazine estimated Escobar to be the seventh-richest man in the world; the Medellín cartel was taking in up to $30 billion annually and controlled eighty percent of the global cocaine market.'

'Thirty fuckin billion dollars, fuckin what, thirty fuckin billion!' screamed Moran out loud as he then paused and pulled away from his computer. 'Holy bollix!'

Jean, on hearing his outburst, ran into the room. 'Everything okay, Thomas?'

'Yeah, sound, Jean. I was just reading something, it's grand; go on.'

These figures had Moran's heart racing at the thought of the kind of potential income that could be generated in the pubs and clubs across Ireland.

The next day, Moran contacted George Mayweather who only a few weeks earlier had explained to him that cocaine was the future and that he was in contact with a European drug smuggler that made Deans and Gilmartin look like primary school kids. Moran knew he had to act.

Two days later, Moran met up with Mayweather who explained that his contact was a 33-year-old Dutch native named Dirk Van Der Beek, who was a seasoned smuggler from the province of Groningen in the Netherlands and was widely believed by European police forces to be the mastermind behind a 25-million-pound shipment of pure cocaine into Britain back in 1997. During their meeting, Mayweather also explained to Moran that Van Der Beek would be able to get them a meeting with a man known simply as Sam 'The Turk' and this was the man everyone wanted to work with but nobody wanted to cross.

When Moran inquired further about Sam, he found that Sâmîzâde Altintop, otherwise known as Sam 'The Turk', was born in 1950 in the popular Turkish tourist resort of Bodrum in the scenic South Aegean's. Moran's intel also told him that Altintop had been at the summit of Europe's criminal underworld for over twenty years and he was one of the most senior figures in Europe's vast drug smuggling operations while amassing a multi-million-pound criminal empire that had begun some years earlier.

Altintop got involved in drug trafficking in the early 1980s when he first sowed the seeds for this empire in the coastal town of Bodrum through his then tiny boating company that sailed tourists on daytrips along the magnificent Turkish coastline while also transporting his product at the same time. It really was plain sailing, Altintop being a local, he did not look out of place; nobody took any notice of his comings and goings as he ran daytrips while shipping his drug cargo undetected by the authorities.

In time, those small boat trips would be nothing compared to what was to come for the Turk when during the early 90s, developments in Eastern Europe saw the region experience major geopolitical changes that would alter the face of European drug trafficking forever.

The collapse of the Soviet Union signalled the end of the post Second World War bipolar system and transformed the European landscape dramatically with the largest and most rapid changes taking place in Central and Eastern Europe. First of all, there was the bloody war in former Yugoslavia and the second was the falling of the Iron Curtain, both were significant not only politically but would open up new borders for major European drug smugglers to move their bounty with a lot less chance of detection.

Before the Eastern European war, most heroin on the Balkan route was passing through former Yugoslavia but the war resulted in a diversification of the trafficking routes, both in Northern Europe and Southern Europe.

The Mediterranean Sea was now being used for the transportation of heroin, enabling traffickers to reach countries like France and Spain directly while in the northern direction, new trafficking routes were also found in part facilitated by the falling of the Iron Curtain, which opened up possibilities to reach the European countries on the eastern side.

Drugs could be transported via the Black Sea into Bulgaria and Romania from where it could reach countries like Slovakia, Poland, Italy and Germany. All of Europe was open for business. Europe became an open market for drug smugglers and they were certainly capitalising on the heroin business.

This was where Sam stepped up and understanding that Europe now had many men with certain qualities, he began recruiting from within ex-military circles and using their expert knowledge, he was able to smuggle large quantities of cocaine and heroin with a lot more precision and expertise.

The figures did not lie because world opium base production doubled since the collapse of the Soviet Union and heroin dealing exploded, generating vast amounts of hard currency while giving Sam and his small army immense power. His highly sophisticated networks began trafficking heroin and cocaine across Europe, becoming known as the most violent and murderous gang in Europe, and Moran wanted in.

It was on St Patrick's Day when Moran contacted George Mayweather, asking him to persuade Van Der Beek to organise a meeting with Altintop to talk business. Moran explained to Mayweather that he wanted to do direct business with Sam as soon as possible but he understood that getting time with him was going to be difficult.

Within days of Moran's request, Mayweather was contacted by Van Der Beek while in Edinburgh and to his absolute disbelief, the Dutchman informed him that Altintop was very excited by the news and agreed to a meeting with Moran and an associate. On hearing this, Moran carried on like a giddy child on Christmas morning and was unbearable to be around right up to the time to actually travel for the meeting.

On 23 March 2000, the business deal was to be discussed in Switzerland and Moran decided that it was to be Noel Slattery who would travel with him to meet Altintop in the Swiss city of Geneva.

It was no coincidence Altintop chose Geneva for this meeting as it is a major international financial centre that encounters the layering and integration stages of money laundering by major criminal organisations despite significant legislation and reporting requirements. Non-residents are permitted to conduct business through offshore entities and various intermediaries, thus making Swiss bank accounts a haven for criminal proceeds to be hidden away from Interpol and other such agencies.

On 23 March at 7 am, Central European time, on a direct flight from Dublin, both Thomas Moran and Noel Slattery arrived at Geneva International Airport. Altintop had organised to meet the two Dubliners by the scenic Lake Geneva at 11.45 am on the well-known Lake Cruise boat under orders that both men would be donning black suits with red neckties to make identification easy.

As their taxi arrived at Lake Geneva, the men were astounded by the lake's beauty as the crescent-shaped lake formed a breath-taking visual display, which made both Dubliners stop and take a second to admire its beauty. On the opposite side of the lake to where the men stood, they could do nothing but stare at the fabulous scenic view embraced by the climbing vineyards of the City of Lava and the steep cliffs complemented by Geneva's castles, parks and old medieval churches that sat proudly upon the banks of the lake as if they were there since time itself began.

After their brief moment of tranquillity, both Moran and Slattery got on with their business at hand and purchased the tickets for their arranged 11.45 am Lake Cruise and the meeting with Sam. The boats were old paddle steamers that have for years serviced locals and tourists alike with the red and white steamer displaying a plaque on its side that said it was launched on 24 September 1934 and was two hundred feet long by thirty-three feet wide.

A smart-witted Slattery pointed out to Moran, 'Nineteen fuckin thirty-four! I hope this old bastard doesn't sink.' Moran just sniggered and started to board the boat.

On-board, Moran stood looking out over the lake in a brief moment of solitude as the fresh air blew gently across his face and as it filled his lungs, he let out a large breath of air that came deep from his lungs.

'Fuck me, Noel, this is a beautiful spot.'

They were approached by a man who had the look of an eastern ethnic nationality, dressed in a tee-shirt and a pair of denim jeans; he asked in broken English, 'Are you Tomas and Noel?'

'Yeah, yeah, I'm Thomas and this is Noel. Are you—'

And just as Moran was about to put his question, the man interrupted while pointing to where both men stood, 'You two stay, my man will come here so stay.'

'It's on, Noel, it's fucking on,' remarked a clearly excited Moran.

'I feel sick, Tommy, and it's not from fuckin sailing either.'

'Just relax, Noel, it's cool.'

'Well, you can do all the fuckin talking, Tommy,' suggested the very nervous Slattery when across the boat coming out of the crowd of tourists, a man began towards them.

'Is this Sam 'The Turk?'

'I'm fucked if I know, Noel, but he's coming our way.'

What Moran noticed was just like the previous man, he had the look of an eastern ethnic nationality but what made him different was he held his posture as if he was royalty; he was impeccably dressed in a designer made-to-measure suit with slick, combed back jet-black hair while donning a pair of designer sunglasses. He had on his person a gold crucifix around his neck and wrists full of bracelets and a ring for near enough every finger on both hands. If this was not Sam, it was someone very important.

'Gentlemen, I am Sam,' spoke the well-dressed man with excellent English. He then turned to Moran and greeted him, 'Thomas, good to see you, my brother,' wrapping his arms around Moran and patting him on the back as if these were two old friends meeting up after a long absence.

'Good to finally meet you,' replied a stunned Moran.

'And Noel, my good friend, how are you?'

'Good, Sam, good thanks', answered a now visibly shaken Slattery.

'Oh Noel, relax, you are with friends,' replied a jolly Sam.

'Okay, let us get down to business, Thomas, yes, which is why we have come such a long way today. Now from what I hear about you and your people through Dirk, I am thinking we can do much business together, Thomas, would you like this?'

'Very much so!' replied Moran with an excited tone to his voice.

'So you want my heroin, marijuana and cocaine, Thomas,' stated Altintop.

'Well, I was here for Coke but—'

'But nothing, let me explain something to you, Thomas, and of course, you too, Noel. Now you both listen to Sam for a minute, the facts are simple now, because after a massive crackdown on drug manufacturing and transportation by the governments in the South East Asian area known as the Golden Triangle, they have seriously damaged the business in the region.'

'So they are cracking down big time?'

'Precisely Noel, therefore, to get heroin from South East Asia is very difficult at present as it is now produced in the Golden Triangle of Burma, Laos and Thailand, way too many problems with this for me. They like to give the areas stupid names but ahh well, we carry on.'

'So what d'ye mean, Sam?' questioned a confused Moran.

'Okay, with South East Asia out of bounds, that leaves the so-called Golden Crescent of Afghanistan, Iran and Pakistan—see, more fucking names. Anyway, this is where Sam comes in; you see, Afghanistan supplies much of the global heroin market, which I and only I can distribute an annual product of one and a half thousand tons of opium every year from this region to Europe, now you can include marijuana and cocaine to that.'

Sam continued to explain, 'Around seventy percent of the heroin on the European market is made of Afghan opium and it is in laboratories where it undergoes a second transformation to become heroin. Eighty percent of the heroin on the European market is being processed in Turkish laboratories or, in other words, gentlemen, by me! Sam the Turk!'

Sam burst into a fit of laughter and Moran and Slattery just grinned to show support for this not so funny statement. When the laughter finished, Sam continued to explain, 'With regard to the hashish, Morocco is the world's largest cannabis producer and I am in with leading politicians, so no problems. Since Morocco is Europe's main supplier, it comes, as no surprise, through me!' Again, Altintop burst into a loud burst of laughter.

'So look, gentlemen, I have people from the Kurdish communities in Germany, Sweden, Holland and other European countries that help in moving my product across Europe. They will smuggle huge amounts of heroin, marijuana and cocaine through Europe into the hands of you, the Irish gang, and then you take it into Ireland. My prices are fair and the more you buy, the less the price, okay?'

'Okay Thomas. Okay, we will do this. Yes, yes! Welcome to my world.' Laughed Altintop and both he and Moran shook hands on a deal that was to see the Moran gang take a step into a new world bigger than any of them could ever imagine.

'So we will deal in cocaine, hashish and heroin. Okay? Okay. Good, that is sorted.'

'I guess so, Sam,' answered a bewildered Moran who was spinning from Sam's lesson in drugs in such a short time-frame; in all, Moran did not get to say a word. Well, it was not like the two Dubliners had a choice but it was a clever choice as this man could make them both very, very wealthy but just as both men were about to leave, Altintop was not finished and gave both men a cold stare as he waved his finger in their direction.

'Oh, just to let you know, Thomas. I do not like problems and where they do arise, they are never my problems; they are the individual or individuals' problem and they must be sorted immediately. You do not want me to sort your problems, Thomas, because that would be very bad, very, very bad. Are we clear?'

'Understood, Sam,' replied Moran with a cautious tone to his voice and with that, the meeting was over as Altintop turned and looked out over the lake with the look of a man in deep thought. Without looking at the two men, Sam told them, 'You can get off here and we will do business soon, good day, gentlemen', and that was it. From that moment on, Moran was a wholesale cocaine, cannabis and heroin smuggler through Sam the Turk, thus cutting out the intermediaries that were Deans and Gilmartin.

'Jesus fucking Christ, Tommy, I think I creamed meself,' fretted Slattery.

'Calm down, Noel, Sam is sound once we don't fuck him about. We will be fine and rich so it's all good,' joked Moran. 'Right, let's get the fuck outta here and get our plane home,' suggested Moran and Slattery was not going to argue.

On arrival back in Dublin, Moran immediately put the wheels in motion and had George Mayweather and Dirk Van Der Beek installed as his main drug traffickers in Northern and Eastern Europe. Tony the Fairy Rothwell was now to be the gang's only direct contact with himself or Sam as Moran sent out word that under no circumstances was anyone to contact or try and make contact with Sam or himself and if they needed anything, they had to speak directly to Tony. Southern Europe and North Africa were now to be taken over by Charlie the Scouser Butterfield while dealing with one of Sam's top men—a South African national named Marcel Kromkampp.

The son of South African schoolteacher, 41-year-old bachelor Marcel Kromkampp grew up in Pretoria, located in the northern part of South Africa with his parents and two siblings. It became apparent to all that he would never follow in his parents' footsteps because of his regular encounters with the South African police.

Over the years, Kromkampp made a name for himself for being a very elusive and intelligent criminal and excelled at moving anything the South African underworld would need moved. His reputation did not go unnoticed when in 1993, one Sâmîzâde Altintop took him under his wing because he had become a renowned smuggler for hire and was revered by all in the smuggling world as one of, if not the, best in the business.

At the time of the meeting in Geneva, Kromkampp was living in Bloemfontein but had to flee South Africa because of an outstanding arrest warrant. The South African authorities wanted Kromkampp for his part in a major drug trafficking operation that went wrong when one of the crew spoke openly to undercover agents in a local bar in Cape Town only days before the drugs were to be moved. His fellow members were all caught but he managed to get away before he was arrested so the timing of this new Sâmîzâde Altintop partnership was perfect.

Altintop got word to Marcel Kromkampp about the meeting with Moran just days before he left South Africa and he then quickly proceeded to Spain where he discovered that he was now going to work directly with Charlie Butterfield.

Butterfield was then living on the Costa del Sol on the Spanish south coast when he met Kromkampp for the first time and both men set out to work straight away. The area is particularly famous for its towns like Marbella, which provides the Costa del Sol with its reputation for being a playground for many gangsters along with the famous and super rich. The most perfect place from which to run a drug smuggling empire. There were so many deliveries coming and going in Southern Spain, you could never spot anything untoward in these idyllic surroundings, especially for both Kromkampp and Butterfield who knew this all too well.

Back in Dublin, things were beginning to run like clockwork with Moran working directly from the builder's yard, organising everyone in Ireland and across Europe. The young yard workers were finding their feet in the building trade while at night, they were running drugs around the city. McCann and Smyth also ran operations around the city for Moran when needed while also moving drugs from the yard to the warehouse on the Dublin Docks.

Marcel Kromkampp and Charlie Butterfield were working closely together along the Mediterranean, making contacts and organising drug shipments to

Ireland and Britain as were George Mayweather and Dirk Van Der Beek in the Northern and Eastern parts of Europe.

Tony Rothwell was looking for more constructive ways to transport drugs and forever meeting new contacts while paying off people in the right places, such as police, customs officers, border guards and even politicians in some cases. Phil Mackey was keeping a close eye on everyone and everything as he put together a list of people for Moran or Rothwell to visit if he thought they could make things work a lot easier or if they stepped out of line and needed sorting.

Danny Moore was left to sort out other business in the region and beyond when called upon while Dean Coyle worked from the yard transporting the drugs in the builder's van from location to location on request from Moran. Big things lay ahead for Moran and his gang of professional smugglers and only one thing was missing, but Moran was about to sort that little problem out.

Chapter 14
The Spirit of St Christopher

With Sam now on board, Moran had an endless supply of cocaine, heroin and marijuana at his disposal and it was time to start moving large quantities of the Turk's product to the streets he once again controlled. Following the meeting in Geneva, things began to move; during the summer of 2000, Tony Rothwell had a meeting with one of Sam's Turkish associates at a hotel located just off East Berlin's famous Potsdamer Platz in relation to moving drugs to Ireland.

At this meeting on 19 August, Rothwell was informed about a large shipment of cocaine that was located in a secure lockup stored in a private boathouse situated on the banks of Amsterdam's Emperor's Canal, close to the Central Station area of the city. Rothwell was also informed that the keys to gain entrance to the boathouse were left in an envelope in the lobby of a small local hotel named The Canal View.

The Turk continued to tell Rothwell that on his arrival at the hotel, 'Sam is the owner so no problems. At reception, ask for Gini and tell him you're Franz Schroeder and you need the key; when you have the key, head to the canal and find the boathouse marked JA-2 close to the section of the canal where the tourist barges are docked. It's a boathouse that we own and it is very rarely used but if you are questioned by anyone, the lockup again is under the name Franz Schroeder. You should have no problems.'

'Perfect. I will get on it as soon as I get the details I need.' From here, Rothwell would lodge the exact amount of cash needed for the purchase of the drugs directly into a Swiss bank account through the account number he duly received from Sam's accountant a day later.

Only five days later, two of Moran's men, George Mayweather and Dirk Van Der Beek, met up with Tony Rothwell in Amsterdam and they gained access to the boathouse where indeed, they found their white gold, some twenty kilos of pure cocaine at £70,000 a kilo. It was only a small shipment in comparison to what Moran wanted but this was a feeler to see if he was good on his word and of course, to see if Sam was good to his. On inspection of the goods, Rothwell began counting and weighing the cocaine to make sure that the correct amount was there, he then tested its purity and not long after, he was happy and gave the men the key and headed back to Dublin.

'Okay lads, it's all yours. Get it packed up and ready for delivery.'

'What will we pack it in?'

'I could not give a flying fuck, gentlemen, it is your fucking problem as of now, not mine, now good day to you both.'

After Rothwell departed, Mayweather noticed that there were some boxes stacked in the corner of the room and when he went across to see what was in them, he found ten boxes of porcelain dolls and with that, he had a brainwave.

'Dirk, I have a fucking great idea.'

'Oh yah, George, what is that then?' asked a curious Van Der Beek in his very distinctive Dutch accent.

'Here, take these boxes, we can smuggle the cocaine inside the fuckin dolls.'

Van Der Beek's eyes lit up. 'Oh yah, George, great idea, great!'

The two men then proceeded to pack the cocaine into a total of fifty-five hollow dolls then wrapped them in plastic and sprayed each one individually with white spirits to throw the scent away from the sniffer dogs. After a couple of hours, all the dolls were packed and the men then sent the cargo to Amsterdam's Schiphol Airport by couriers where they had previously booked a shipment by airmail via Paris' Charles De Gaulle Airport then onto Dublin.

That way, if the cocaine was located, nobody was going to be arrested for the transportation as the delivery address on the crates was an old abandoned warehouse on Dublin's Docklands where a large percentage of the units were now dilapidated and nobody would be the wiser as to who owned the goods if intercepted.

The drugs were never going to that address; as per usual, this was Moran leaving nothing to chance. When he had Rothwell organise it so that Dean Coyle could lawfully collect the goods from the airport thanks to some passing over of cash to those who could organise Coyle's easy access to Dublin Airport's cargo holdings and of course, tip them off if customs and the drug squad wanted to set up an operation to arrest those responsible for the importation of drugs to Ireland.

Three days later, the drugs in crates marked 'FRAGILE' were collected and Coyle got in and out of the airport holding area without any problems and within a week, the cocaine was on the streets. Moran's first piece of business with Sam was a roaring success and there was going to be more, a lot more to come. It was time for an even bigger job.

Moran knew his gang was ready to move large shipments but he realised that the airports were becoming far too risky due to the increased security along with modern technology that was now able to locate drugs without the use of sniffer dogs. So from then on, he left all of his small shipments in the hands of his 'mules' and if one got caught by security, it would only be a small amount rather than the full shipment. Fact was that Moran really did not care much for the mules who were normally hired drug addicts from his locality or at times just some people who were down on their luck and needed ready-made cash.

Nevertheless, Moran made sure none of them would 'rat him out' by threatening family members including their children and/or parents. But as time went by, the mules would have run their course, and Moran would get rid of them for good as he had an idea in mind; to carry it out, he had to pay a visit to an old friend; it was time to visit Danny Moore in Ibiza.

Without delay, Moran immediately contacted Danny and explained that Noel Slattery and he would be flying out in early September to have a chat about an idea he had. Following the phone call, Moore was very excited that his old friends would be paying a visit but nervous as he had not seen them since they had returned home to Ireland in 1992.

In that time, Moore's success on the island grew rapidly after he began to cleverly invest the money he made from the sale of the Ecstasy tablets they had imported from Benny Jewell. Moore's first purchase in 1993, as previously stated, had become a popular mid-sized bar in San Antonio, the heart of Ibiza's club land, which he aptly named The House of Ecstasy.

The so-called dopey lad from the Dublin flats had done very well for himself and from his first purchase, Moore never looked back. Moore was actually a very shrewd businessman and he was ready to show his friends all of his progress since they had left him. On arrival in Ibiza, Moran and Slattery found the very busy terminal filled with excited holidaymakers coming and going in the midst of the holiday season.

'Jaysus Tommy, it's like it was in 1992, nothing fuckin changed at all.'

Moran just nodded and both men started for the exit when Slattery noticed what looked like a local man holding their names aloft on a piece of corrie board. Slattery tapped Moran on the arm and pointed towards the man.

'Yeah, I'm Tommy Moran and this is Noel Slattery; who the fuck are you?'

The local man explained in broken English that Danny had sent him to collect them and bring them to his house. When they reached the car, Moran decided he wanted to sit in the back seat to work on the final details of his idea so he told Slattery to go sit in the front seat and keep the driver busy, he wanted no disruptions from, as he told Slattery, 'A fuckin chatterbox'.

Not long into the journey, Moran could not sit easy as the midday sun was beating down on the black Mercedes with its dark leather interior that had been roasting in the warm Balearic sun.

'Noel, open those fuckin windows, will ye, I'm fuckin roastin back here.'

On request, Slattery opened the electric windows to allow in some much needed fresh-air but for Moran, this was a pain as he could not keep his paperwork in place as it blew in the wind.

'Ahh, for fuck sake,' moaned Moran.

'What?'

'Nothin; just get him to fuckin hurry up, will ye, Noel.'

Slattery just laughed to himself and after a fifteen-minute car ride, the men arrived at a villa on the western coast of Ibiza, with a breath-taking view, located right on the edge of the mountainside overlooking the bay at Sant Antoni de Portmany, or commonly known as San Antonio.

'We are just about here, Senor Moran.'

'Nice one, right Noel, let's get out of this poxy fuckin oven before I fuckin roast to death.'

When the car reached the gates, the driver spoke to someone inside in Spanish and the gates slowly opened, to Moran's annoyance.

'For fuck sake, hurry the fuck up, ye cuntin gates!'

All Noel could do was laugh at his red-faced stressed boss but that soon stopped when he saw the house. 'Fuck me, is this Danny's gaff?'

Moran's agitation was soon silenced as the car drove up a long driveway to reveal a luxury villa with a swimming pool set in large sun terraces, both open and covered for shade, along with a built-in barbecue and a poolside shower and changing room. When they got out of the car, both men were in awe of this absolutely outstanding property and its jaw-dropping view of San Antonio and its bay.

'Alright boys, what's the fuckin story?' came a voice from behind both men.

They turned to see Danny and a stunning-looking woman on the doorstep. To the men's amazement, the once dull and shy Danny had changed his life around and he looked good, really, really good. His hair was now dyed blonde and he had grown a goatee; his appearance had changed so much he looked like a high-rolling player who oozed confidence and charm. A shocked Moran at the sight of Danny questioned his friend's new look, 'Danny, my good man, is that you?'

'Noel, Tommy, how the fuck are yis keepin, boys? I take it ye like my new look, Tommy.'

'Fuckin hell, Danny, are ye a surfer or something?'

On hearing his old friend's description, Moore laughed as he answered, 'Not quite, Tommy, no but an image change is never a bad thing.'

Danny explained briefly to his friends that over the years, he had become a very successful businessman on the Island, telling them both that he now had sole ownership of three bars, a nightclub, three villas and ten apartments and on top of all this, he had made some very interesting contacts. In the few years that Danny Moore had lived on the Island, he had become a popular figure amongst locals and holidaymakers alike and he had ended up marrying a local politician's daughter.

Maria De Souza, aged 23, was a stunning woman standing five foot eight. She had long black hair and deep brown eyes and to the two men's amazement, she was crazy about this bumbling but likeable Irishman.

'Gentlemen, please meet my wife, Maria; Maria, Tommy and Noel. Watch Noel dear, he thinks with his dick,' sarcastically joked Moore but knowing all too well that Slattery would sleep with his wife without hesitation if he got the opportunity.

'Fuck off Danny, but I'll give ye this buddy she is gorgeous,' replied Noel quietly in Danny's ear.

'Very, very nice to meet you, Maria,' said Moran, visibly in awe of this beauty.

'And nice to finally meet you both and thank you for your compliments, gentlemen,' was the answer from Maria's soft velvet voice.

'Okay, let's go inside, lads.'

They entered the house through a large hallway; the villa had a split-level dining room and lounge with lovely high ceilings with a large separate kitchen and a breakfast room where glass doors led out onto the pool area. The villa boasted five bedrooms with two double bedrooms, both with bathrooms en-suite, lava walls and a sunken bath; the three twin bedrooms shared the third bathroom.

Later that night, over dinner, Moran mentioned to Danny that he was over on business, but Danny immediately cut him short and explained, 'Not now, Thomas, I have an office for that. Tonight, we talk of days gone by.'

Moran knew right away that Maria was not safe to talk around and the next morning, the three men headed into San Antonio to talk business.

'I'll tell you something, Danny, you've done very fuckin well for yourself and that wife, I'd burst her—'

'Touch her, Noel, and I'll have you shot.' Slattery went silent and Danny and Moran looked at each other and burst into laughter.

'Very funny, ye pair of cunts, but she is a fucking fine thing, Danny.'

'She is that,' added Moran.

'Oh, I know, lads, right this way.'

Danny had an office in the heart of San Antonio only a short journey from his villa so the walk was short and welcomed by the men who needed to stretch their legs. When they arrived at the building, Moore went in first and told his staff to take an early and long lunch and return back at the normal time, giving the men a couple of hours to chat. After telling of how things came about and the dealings across Europe, Danny got to the point of Moran's visit.

'Okay, you're Mr Big Balls now, are you?'

'Funny cunt, you.'

'Yeah, hilarious but enough bollox, Tommy, what can I do for you?'

'Look Danny, you know my trade but I cannot move what I actually need to move.'

'Go on, Tommy.'

'For me to bring in big shipments, the airports are far too fuckin risky these days so I need to find a good-sized boat for sale.'

Danny leaned back in his chair with a thoughtful look on his face and explained, 'Well, I might know of someone on the Island but I need the details of what exactly you're lookin for.'

'Sound, Danny, I need a big boat ye know, like those big fishin ones and the price is no problem. But as you're well aware, I'm no fuckin Popeye so that's as much as I can give ye.'

Grinning, Moore told Moran and Slattery, 'Okay lads, leave this with me and for now, you pair go and relax and enjoy the Island. I've got a few calls to make.'

Moran's mobile phone rang; it was Sam the Turk.

'Sam, how are you keepin?' asked Moran.

A conversation continued for about a minute then Moran finished the conversation, 'Yeah I'll ask them, leave it with me. Okay Sam, bye, bye. What the fuck is up with him?' a puzzled look on his face.

'Everything okay with Sam, Tommy?' quizzed a curious Slattery.

'He's rantin on over some fuckin dolls that have gone missin from a lockup in Amsterdam.'

'Fuckin dolls!' answered a dumbstruck Slattery.

'Yeah, seemingly he had 55 porcelain dolls in that lockup when our lads collected some gear and the fuckin things are now on the missing list so he wants me to ask George and Dirk did they see the fuckin things.'

'Dolls?'

'Yeah! They belong to his fuckin missus, she collects the things. He's sayin they're collector's items or somethin and are worth a small fortune and she is losin the fuckin plot over them gone missin. Fuckin dolls, for Jaysus sake, I have better things to be fuckin doin than worryin about some fuckin dolls.'

A bemused Slattery shook his head and jokingly told Moran, 'They better not be playin with fuckin dolls when they're supposed to be workin.'

All three men burst into laughter. 'Fuckin dolls, Thomas, holy Jaysus.'

Luckily for Moran, he had more luck finding a boat than he had with the missing dolls because not long after Moran's inquiry, Danny Moore came up trumps.

'Interesting news, Tommy. I may have found a boat but we have to fly out to Málaga to view it.'

'Sound, Danny, sort the flights.'

On arrival in Málaga, wasting no time, Moran, Slattery and Moore met up with Tony Rothwell and the owner of the trawler, one Jose Marie Perez, a good friend of Moore who he had met while on a family holiday in Ibiza. Moore had arranged to meet Perez at 5 pm at the port so that Moran could physically see the boat.

Perez greeted Moore with a friendly smile and a welcome handshake. 'Danny, my friend!'

'Lads, I would like you to meet Jose Marie Perez.'

'Hello everyone, so you want my boat?'

'Yes, yes please, may we have a look?' asked Rothwell.

'This way please' as Perez led the men to a dry dock situated at the back of the wharf.

'Okay come, come this way please.' As the men turned the corner of the workshop at the lower end of the dock, a blue and a white striped fishing trawler appeared in front of them and what was apparent was that Danny had done a fine job because on first looks, it looked in pristine condition. Perez began to explain, 'This is Anna, my trawler. Anna was my mother's name.'

'Oh right, lovely,' replied Slattery, giving Moran a look as if to say, *I really could not give a fuck, mate.*

Perez continued, 'This trawler was manufactured by a local Malaga ship builder in 1976 and is 24 metres or 79 feet long with a beam standing 6.9 metres or 22 feet high. She is fully equipped with fishing nets, JRC Radar, JRC GPS, Ray VHF, Compass, 25 Kw generator, quarters for 6 crew and captain; it also has two baths, a galley, hydraulic steering, mechanical trawl winch, 9,000 litre fuel engine and container space for 7,000 litres of fresh water.'

Absolutely baffled by all the information, Moran and his men just listened and nodded as if they knew what Perez was actually on about; out of nowhere, Noel Slattery asked the most ridiculous question Moran had ever heard in his entire life.

'Ahh Jaysus, that's great, Jose, so it floats then?'

Baffled by this obviously stupid question, Perez replied, pointing towards the boat, 'Well, yes senor, it's a trawler.'

Moran, Moore and Rothwell were speechless at Noel's idiotic question and to put things back on track, Moran began looking around the boat in great detail. 35 minutes later, he agreed to buy from Perez and left Rothwell to finalise all the financial dealings and a price of £380,000 was agreed. Rothwell would transfer the funds the next morning into Perez's account but before they left, Moran had to ask Noel Slattery a question.

'Does it float? Ye silly bastard, Noel!'

'I had to fucking ask him something to let him think we knew our stuff, didn't I? You all stood there like a bunch of dopey cunts when he was yappin on about the cuntin boat.'

'Yes, but not "does it float", for fuck sake, of course, it floats, that's what fuckin boats do, ye dozy bastard. Ye made us look like a bunch of fuckin eejits and you came across as a special kinda stupid.' Moran laughed and muttered to himself, 'Mother of Jaysus, does it float.'

'Ahh fuck off, will ye.'

Later that night, all three men flew back to Ibiza while reminding Slattery all the way back that the plane will fly and cars stay on the ground, all to Slattery's embarrassment. When back in Moore's villa, three things were playing on Moran's mind; first, he had to make the trawler seaworthy and he also needed a crew that he could trust with millions of pounds worth of drugs. Time was against him, he needed to get the crew sorted and quick as the trawler had only eight weeks left in the dry dock before it had to be sailed out of Málaga.

Secondly, he needed to change the name of the boat; finally, he had to get it registered so if spotted by Coast Guards, it would register as legal. The day after he purchased the trawler, Moran sent word out to all his men that he needed experienced sailors who could be trusted, and if possible to be known by underworld figures so they would not have to be checked out because the one thing he did not have was time. Tony Rothwell as usual was sorting the business end of things and began the legal proceeding for the registering of the licence for the trawler in Spain and Ireland.

After many weeks of searching for a crew, five names came to Moran's attention all through his own people. The five men where Mark Lowe, Edmund Baxter, Casper Von Bommell, Danny Higgins and Terry McLaughlin. These five men would all become the newly formed crew on Thomas Moran's cocaine trawler.

Mark Lowe was at the time a 29-year-old ex-British Royal Navy Acting Sub-Lieutenant and hailed from Swansea in Wales. Lowe was discharged from the Royal Navy for importing cocaine to the troops via the navy fleet and was introduced to Moran through his very close friend, Charlie Butterfield. Lowe came with vast sailing experience and he would be handed the job of Captain due to his expertise in maritime law and understanding the international sailing handbook like the back of his hand.

The youngest member of the crew was 21-year-old Edmund 'Eddie' Baxter from Derbyshire in England. Baxter, a petty thief, had done time for drug possession and after his release from prison, he moved to Ibiza where he befriended Moore while searching for work and Moore gave him a job as a bartender in one of his bars. Baxter was given the job on board Moran's trawler as a deckhand.

Next came 46-year-old Casper Von Bommell from Cape Town, South Africa, a professional smuggler and associate of Marcel Kromkampp. Von Bommell would be the trawler's engineer due to his experience serving in the South African Navy for fourteen years as a marine engineer. He had met Kromkampp in Pretoria a number of years earlier having left the Navy and joining Kromkampp's gang running drugs and guns across Africa.

Like Kromkampp, Von Bommell was wanted by the South African authorities for charges that included drugs and weapons smuggling but he was also wanted for questioning in relation to the murder of a 23-year-old security man who was shot dead during a drug deal that he had interrupted in Cape Town.

Another crewmember was Terry McLaughlin, a 32-year-old father of six from Cobh, County Cork. McLaughlin, a vastly experienced sea fisherman, was hired due to his superior knowledge of the fishing industry, which Moran thought essential if the boat was ever stopped by the Coast Guard; he felt at least someone could talk the talk on the fishing industry.

However, equally important for Moran was McLaughlin's knowledge of the layout of Ireland's southern coastal shores. Over the years, McLaughlin had gotten to know every landing point and hideaway that ran from Wexford to Kerry when he was smuggling contraband for a number of well-known Irish gangsters. It was in 1996 when he was imprisoned that he met up with George Mayweather and he then happily informed Moran of his skills.

The final member was Danny Higgins, a 40-year-old from Dublin City who was in every aspect the perfect man for the job as it was widely known in the underground that he was the best drug smuggler in Europe. Higgins had very close ties to Moran's old friend, Benny Jewell, and he was to be Moran's personal choice; he dearly wanted him on board his trawler but he knew if he was to get him, it would be at a very high asking price. As Moran saw it, 'you get what you pay for' and how right he was, Higgins was to be a jewel in the crown on the trawler. In time, he would prove his worth by outfoxing the authorities on numerous occasions in a deadly game of cat and mouse on the high seas.

Moran's drugs crew was in place.

The renaming of the trawler was the easy part; Moran had only one name in mind–'The Spirit of St Christopher'—after the flat complex where he grew up in Dublin.

With everything in place, Moran returned to Málaga to meet with Perez to finalise everything and when he told him the name of the trawler, he turned to Moran and commented, 'I like the name, St Christopher. St Christopher is the patron saint of travellers, my friend.'

'Really! That's good because we will need all the fuckin help we can get, Jose.'

Chapter 15
Maiden Voyage

It was early morning on 31 September 2000, when Mark Lowe arrived at the harbour in Málaga to meet up with Tony Rothwell to get all the details of where *The Spirit of St Christopher* would set sail for.

'Sail directly to Ibiza into Puerto de Ibiza and when you arrive, moor her at IBZ12, one of Thomas' men has sorted an official permit to moor and fish the area so all is good.'

'Will do.'

'Good. Now look here, after you arrive and the boat is tied up, we have an account set up with a local building and maritime trader named El Maritimo Talamanca to purchase the equipment and tools needed so the work can begin to convert her into a smuggling vessel.'

'What is the account name?'

'Jesus yes, good question, it's under the trawler name. It is all on account so no need to pay for anything.'

'Perfect.'

'Look, you'll be fine there under the disguise of a working fishing trawler so just make it look as if you're a fishing crew and take her out every now and again for a few hours to give the feel you are all actually doing some fishing.'

'Okay, I'll get the lads here ASAP and get her to Ibiza soon after.'

'One more thing, Mark, you will have her permanently moored in Ibiza when in the Mediterranean and when in Ireland, she is to be moored in the fishing port of Kinsale, County Cork. I will get the Irish details and send them to you.'

And that was that; the Spirit was soon to make waves when Capitan Mark Lowe gave the order for his crew to make their way to Spain and four days later, on 4 October, the boat set sail on the short journey from Malaga to Ibiza where after only ten weeks of intensive work, the trawler had been made seaworthy and in a position to carry large amounts of drugs.

The trawler modifications included numerous hidden compartments for the movement of drugs in hollowed walls, false roofs, cargo holds, voids between decks, ballast tanks, fuel tanks, oil tanks, engine room pipes and hidden within the cargo itself, all areas of the boat could carry huge quantities on board. Not only was the boat modified but weeks and weeks of training followed as the crew were made shipshape and ready for when Moran was ready to move drugs.

At 4 am on 22 January 2001, the crew were given orders to set sail on course for North Africa and into the Port of Al Hoceima, Morocco, to collect a large shipment of Moroccan hashish, Columbian cocaine and Afghan heroin. As Mark Lowe set sail out of Ibiza, he stood at the top of the trawler looking out over the ocean and took in the crisp breath of fresh sea air and instructed his crew, 'Right gentlemen, let's open her up. We have a long journey ahead of us and we have a deadline so let's make it.'

The Port of Al Hoceima on Morocco's Northern Coast on the Mediterranean Sea serves the many fishing vessels that fish locally, which was just perfect for smuggling as the trawler would again not look out of place. The instructions given to Lowe were clear: the trawler was to be loaded two days later at 6 am after docking at loading area 7B. There, they would be met by a local crew of Sam's people who would load 80 kilos of hash, 55 kilos of heroin and 90 kilos of cocaine onto the trawler.

Back in Ireland, Moran was not too worried due to the fact that there were only eight operational Irish Naval Service patrol boats in the Irish navy and they had to cover a huge area to the south and west of the country of around 250,000 square kilometres in size.

The Service is tasked with patrolling all Irish waters from the shoreline to the outer limits of the Exclusive Fishery Limits, approximately 200 miles offshore and covering an area of 132,000 nautical square miles; fact was it would be like looking for a needle in a haystack.

Under maritime law, the Coast Guard's mandate includes arresting traffickers even if they are on the high seas that are far outside any country's territorial boundaries. Defence personnel are prohibited from directly engaging in law enforcement activities but the ship can put on a Coast Guard law enforcement detachment when a suspicious vessel is identified at sea, the Coast

Guard will then notify its own State Department, which then gets permission from the vessel's flag nation for the Coast Guard to board.

In the rare instances when permission is denied, the Coast Guard will generally monitor the vessel as it approaches the country's territory. In this case, the Coast Guard could board the vessel and spend days searching for drugs, which they eventually might discover in the space below the fishing holds.

Under Irish law, the responsibility for the prevention of drug trafficking rests primarily with An Garda Síochána and the Revenue Commissioners. However, the Irish Naval Service and the Air Corps do assist and support the civil authorities in their extensive work. The Air Corps provide air support and, on occasion carry the Customs National Drugs Team in an observational capacity for the purpose of monitoring vessels suspected of drug trafficking and other illegal activities.

However, the gang knew that if they stayed clear of the Irish authorities, the Spanish waters did not serve such a risk as Spain's criminal organisations also benefit from the country's massive 4,900 kilometres of coastline from which drugs shipments can be received from South America via Morocco or Algeria to the south and launched into northern Europe with little fear of detection by police or coastguard patrol boats. Criminals and law enforcement agencies regard Spain as the premier continental European base for organising drugs shipments via South America, Eastern Europe and Asia as the Spanish police are ill equipped and basically uninterested in tackling non-Spanish criminals.

The crew knew this all too well.

As the sun rose over North Africa, *The Spirit of St Christopher* arrived into Al Hoceima and began loading the drugs on board. Twelve hours later with new supplies and a full tank, Lowe once again gave his orders that the trawler was to head to the Irish south coast where they would rendezvous with Moran's Irish crew in approximately five days' time and along with the instructions were the radio frequencies to contact the land crew when in Irish waters. After their brief stopover in Morocco, Mark Lowe set sail for Ireland with Danny Higgins getting ready to begin monitoring Garda emergency radio frequencies and monitoring activity at major West Cork, Waterford and Wexford Garda stations for signs of increased drug squad presence when close to Ireland's shores.

On 25 January 2001, the crew of *The Spirit of St Christopher* set sail from Morocco and headed for the Irish south coast taking a route via Ibiza and Malaga up through the Strait of Gibraltar directly off the south coast of Portugal, viewing the city of Lisbon by night in the distance while heading to the north passing the city of Porto. The second half of the journey would have them sail right through the Bay of Biscay past Roscoff in France around Plymouth on England's South Coast and finally onto Ireland.

Within five days, a trawler flying an Irish flag named *The Spirit of St Christopher* set anchor two miles off County Wexford on the Irish South Coast where they met Butterfield, Mayweather, McCann and Smyth who were in two small twelve-foot cruiser boats. The crew then unloaded a cargo of £5,500,000, which included the eighty kilos of hash, fifty-five kilos of heroin and ninety kilos of cocaine into the two boats and after three hours, the men parted ways. Before leaving, Mayweather told Lowe to dock in Kinsale in a rented dry-dock in the harbour.

Waiting on a beach near Ballytra, Wexford, was Dean Coyle with a rented van, ready to move the gear to the Docklands warehouse to be cut and shipped out to the streets.

The next job was a deal that was originally organised in Istanbul by Kromkampp and Sam and it was to smuggle eighty kilos of cocaine into southern Ireland. The drugs were moved to Ibiza and loaded onto the trawler and the crew set sail and soon anchored two miles from the Irish coast off Kilmore quay, Wexford, at 2 am on 13 April 2001.

Once again, the voyage went without detection and on their arrival at their exact rendezvous point, McCann, Slattery, Nailor O'Neill and Paul Slug Price boarded two speedboats and made their way to the trawler as Dean Coyle stayed on the beach ready to move the drugs. The cargo was moved into the boats and over to the awaiting Coyle on the beach in little more than an hour and all were on their way by 3.15 am and back in Dublin by 5 am. It was yet another success for the gang who were all now making big money. The systems put in place around Europe were working fine and Moran had the world at his feet.

Chapter 16
A Day at the Races

At the turn of the 21st century, Ireland was encountering a massive increase in cocaine intake with the white powder becoming a regular fixture in the lifestyles of many of the nation's weekend party-going population. Of course, what comes with any demand, you need a supply and the supply of drugs was hitting the Irish streets quicker than the Garda National Drugs Unit were physically able to control. Cocaine addiction took its hold as the drug spiralled out of control across all sections of society; cocaine had no social demographic.

Like any addiction, not everyone could admit they had a problem as they thought it was best to ignore it by saying, 'I have it under control and I only take it at weekends.' The question is though, when does cocaine become more than just a recreational drug? Cocaine was no longer the drug of the wealthy as the massive demand rapidly dragged the prices downwards, which saw the drug become an affordable addiction for many people in Ireland; whether they were a doctor or factory worker, coke began to control their everyday lives, and Moran did not complain.

The very successful summer and autumn months of 2001 had swiftly passed by with relative ease while Moran and his gang were finally establishing themselves as one of the most lucrative and notorious gangs in the Irish underworld. The crew of St Christopher along with Charlie Butterfield and Marcel Kromkampp had sailed a number of very successful cargos out of their Ibiza base. Meanwhile, George Mayweather and Dirk Van Der Beek were moving large shipments of heroin and cocaine out of Northern Europe via Amsterdam into Ireland, Britain and Scandinavia—times were good, really good.

Of course, some Irish gangs envied his success while others applauded his monumental rise and his growing reputation on the European mainland. Even many European gangs were acknowledging his crew as one of the biggest and most efficient drug smuggling rings across the European Union as cocaine was fast becoming the overwhelming drug of choice for many on Ireland's very active social scene.

The Irish market, through Moran's network, saw drugs become more widely available outside the more traditional markets of Dublin, Cork and Limerick as his products had now seeped into every city, town and village across the country.

Unknown to the buyers, the cocaine they were snorting was less than twenty per cent pure after it had been cut and mixed in the warehouse before it hit the street dealers. Various inert white powders are used as fillers, including talc, flour, corn-starch and various sugars. Other fake ingredients that aren't toxic but simply weaken the drug include baking soda, vitamin C powder, glucose, and baby milk powder.

Cocaine became available to the cash-laden Celtic Tiger generation in near enough every bar, club or even in some cases the daily workplace to keep the mind focussed. As Moran was told, it was snowing and his coke was not only available at the highest levels of society, his product spread right across the sprawling working-class housing estates of Ireland and further afield. So much was the demand on dealers to supply cocaine that the gang members had to work around the clock when shipments arrived from either Spain or Amsterdam, which saw the warehouse become close to a 24-hour mixing factory.

The gang was expanding as much as the demand but to be a successful crew, the network needed to grow and grow it did. At the heart of this whole Irish operation was Moran's main distributor, Dean Coyle—he was the man who would transport the drugs between Cork, Limerick and Dublin working between Moran's Irish links, John Joe Daly from Cork and his Limerick contact, 'Tinker' McFadden.

Hailing from Patrickswell, County Limerick, not too far from the Limerick city boundaries, 43-year-old 'Tinker' McFadden was a champion bare-knuckle fighter and those who knew him would always say he was 'one tough bastard' and a man with an extremely violent past. The father of thirteen children and a career criminal, McFadden met Moran while serving time in Portlaoise prison for armed robbery and both men had kept in contact over the years since their release.

Well known across Southern Ireland, McFadden had plenty of contacts in the criminal underworld, especially around the southern province of Munster so

Moran knew Tinker could be trusted to run operations for him and it was because of this trust that he was given the job to operate the southern area of Ireland taking in counties Waterford, Cork, Kerry, Limerick, Clare, Tipperary and Wexford.

Another Munster man, John Joe Daly from Mallow, County Cork, came to Moran's attention when he was working at the Cork docklands and was recommended to him by St Christopher crewmember, Terry McLaughlin. Daly, unlike McFadden, had not done time but it was on McLaughlin's recommendation that Moran went to see him and from the very first moment he met him, he knew Daly was okay.

Following a period of time taking on odd jobs and being closely scrutinised, Daly was to become the main supplier in the north and northwest area of the country covering such counties as Leitrim, Longford, Roscommon, Galway, Mayo, Sligo, Donegal, Cavan and Monaghan. With the original crew covering Dublin and the rest of Leinster, Ireland was now covered and the drugs were moving out of the warehouse at an extreme pace.

Northern Ireland was left alone due to the fact that Loyalist paramilitaries ran the trade there and it was thought to leave well alone. The British end of the business was supply only as Moran knew he had a good thing with this arrangement so why mess with it.

With the importation of such a large quantity of drugs, Moran and his gang had amassed a significant amount of capital that at first could not be numerated precisely, but it can be safely assumed that it reached quite a few million over the first year or so. So much cash came in so quickly that at times, Moran had wads of cash in his home as he struggled to hide hundreds of thousands of pounds from the eye of the authorities so he knew that something had to be done and Tony Rothwell found out exactly how to sort this problem out.

To hide some of their income, Rothwell was purchasing a number of properties and investing in merchant companies but he and Moran knew that eventually this criminal capital would without doubt have to be laundered through some kind of legal system.

Rothwell being a financial genius understood well that the European banking system would not allow for such a massive breach of its regulations, not a chance. He knew it would bring way too much unwanted interest in the gang's income, so he decided that the only way to bank money was by laundering it; this became a necessity for the gang.

Rothwell discovered that filtering cash through European-based casinos was a fantastic opportunity for the gang to launder dirty money into the system. This was a perfect avenue for the gang because money goes in and out of casinos with such speed and in such quantities, regulators and cashiers struggle to track it efficiently; as an added bonus, Rothwell, Moran and Slattery enjoyed the nights out in Amsterdam's casino life. In one night, Tony Rothwell had actually laundered £200,000 in a single sitting, completely undetected. It was a case of lose a lot but gain a small fortune, lose half a million to gain a clean two hundred grand, simple.

Rothwell also worked out a scheme that had millions illegally flowing annually into Ireland's exchequer by many simple and sophisticated ways of laundering their ill-gotten gains. One of the less sophisticated but blindingly simple way of turning the money into legal tender was to get members of the gang to pay a visit to the races or betting shops where between them, they would bet on every dog or horse in every race. So on any one race, Moran would bet from £1,000 up to £5,000 on every dog and horse but even if he lost thousands in a race, he could gain a nice profit when obviously, he had a winner in every race.

Therefore, in simple terms, Moran could bet ten grand on a race with ten horses and lose nine but would win four grand if his horse came in at say, 4/1, generating him a legal five grand on that race. Overall on a day if the race card had seven races, Moran could walk away with a very hefty profit from that meeting and of course, he would always hold onto the betting slips to prove how he got the money legally if the taxman ever called upon him.

If you multiply that by possibly six or seven different race meetings across Ireland and Britain, average thirty-five races with winnings of four grand per race, a nice day's work. In time, Moran hired a team of people to do his betting on a daily basis and paying them ten percent of the winnings when the dockets were handed over; it kept them in line making good money and giving Moran a fortune in clean money.

Another more sophisticated way Tony Rothwell laundered money was to transfer vast amounts of cash through a number of financial institutions by way of multiple but much smaller accounts to finance illicit transactions, a perfect way to legalise these funds within legal associations. The use of multiple personal and business accounts to collect and then funnel funds to a number of foreign accounts with numerous deposits followed within a short period by wire transfers of funds. In time, Rothwell became an expert and demonstrated a great creativity in combining traditional money laundering techniques into complex money laundering schemes designed to stop or stall the ability of authorities to prevent, detect and prosecute money laundering.

With this newfound wealth, his gang splashed out on designer clothes, expensive cars, high-end prostitutes and exotic foreign holidays. Despite being at the top of a very lucrative drug empire, unlike his gang Moran was not flashy but instead preferred to adopt a more low profile. He carried out this low profile by wearing casual clothes and tracksuits while driving around Dublin in a three-year-old Toyota Corolla while surrounded by modest circumstances. He did not want any unwanted attention on him by the Gardaí as he still lived in the house he had purchased in Crumlin on his release from Portlaoise prison back in the early nineties and he still worked out of his Builder's Yard while running his business.

Even though the business was flowing, Moran, as ever, was not one hundred percent happy with the overall situation in his own backyard of Dublin; he wanted to tighten his control on the city by controlling the doors to the main bars and clubs. In November of 2001, Moran decided to call on Tony Rothwell in an effort to secure as many of the contracts that controlled the bouncers and security guards to dozens of the pubs and clubs around Dublin.

'Do whatever it takes to get these poxy contracts, whether they fuckin like it or not. Use Frankie and Pudner if you need to; they can be pretty persuasive,' he told Rothwell.

On one occasion, when a bar owner refused to take on the gang's doormen, Moran dealt with the situation like he always did. The Ha' Penny Place bar located on the west side of Dublin city was a popular haunt with the younger locals and at weekends, it was packed full of potential customers for Moran and his people to exploit. After the owner, Martin Nelson's, refusal to deal with Rothwell, Moran got in contact with his main intelligence officer Phil Mackey to gather as much information as possible on the owner and what Mackey came back to him with was more than enough detail on the owner and his family.

At 9.35 pm on 26 November 2001, McCann and Smyth paid Martin Nelson a visit. When both men entered the bar, they noticed that there were only around a dozen or so punters inside watching a football game on the TV and a solitary barman was tending to their needs. That barman was Martin Nelson but it was no surprise to them because Phil Mackey had already given both men his shift times so when both men took a seat at the bar, they knew exactly who the barman standing behind the counter was going to be. Nelson spotted the new customers coming in and as they sat down, he walked towards the men in an open and friendly manner asking, 'What will it be, lads?'

Both McCann and Smyth looked at each other than McCann turned to Nelson and asked, 'Is Martin Nelson about; we need to speak to him about something?'

The barman answered in an interested voice, 'That would be me, gentlemen, what can I do to help you?'

Frankie, speaking softly across the counter so that the patrons could not hear him, explained to Nelson, 'A certain person inquired about the doormen for this—'

Nelson cut off McCann, 'Look, you can tell your boss I said fucking no. I have my men already.'

With that outburst, Frankie, not caring who saw or heard him this time, reached across the counter, got a hold of Nelson by his shirt and dragged him outside into the carpark.

'Come out here, you stupid little cunt.'

Two customers got up to see what the commotion was about and Smyth pulled back his jacket and showed them a gun that was in his belt and told them, 'No heroes needed, lads, so sit fuckin down. It wouldn't be very healthy to call the pigs either, lads, so shush now and enjoy your match.'

Outside, Nelson was petrified as these two huge men started knocking him about, punch after punch connecting with his head and body.

'Now ye little cunt, you fuckin listen and listen well,' warned the hugely intimidating McCann. 'We are taking over the doors here whether you fuckin like it or not and if you rat us out, well, let me just say…'

Then the information they had received from Mackey was used to frighten the already terrified Nelson into submission as Frankie, now leaning over Nelson who was slumped in a ball on the ground, continued, 'We know that Aoife and Sinéad go to the Holy Ghost school in Celbridge, when they get on and off the school bus, when they have lunch and when they go for a fuckin piss! They're 14 and16 years old, if I'm not mistaken, now let me tell you this, Daddy, imagine one of my big cocked lads who like a bit of young fresh meat, if you know what I mean?' grinned the psychotic McCann.

Nelson was slumped in a ball on the ground. 'Okay, for fuck sake, okay, okay, just don't touch my girls please, you can have the fuckin doors,' cried a terrified father. After that night, Nelson never gave any more grief to Moran as his men moved in on the doors.

Having warned off many of Dublin's most respected and well-established security companies, Moran had taken control of some of the best security contracts in the city. Gang members collected monthly charges on the premises for the services they supplied and then they got additional payments from sanctioned drug dealers in order to let them operate free from threats and intimidation in the premises under their control.

In all, Moran had nine nightclubs and over forty bars around the county in his control and with the contracts in place, Moran needed someone to keep the staff for the clubs and bars in line, so as per usual, he shopped around the criminal underworld for his man.

After his search for a man to run all the doors in Dublin, Noel Slattery hired 35-year-old Stephen 'Rocky' Farley, who was once an amateur boxer and eight-time Irish heavyweight champion. Farley, who came from the North Inner City, stood over six feet tall and was more than able to look after himself. However, it was not Farley's art of pugilism that interested Moran as he had more than enough tough men on his books.

Moran's interest was that Farley had run a firm of professional nightclub bouncers for a long time and this was exactly what Moran needed. Plus, Farley had form and was known to be a good skin and on deeper investigation from Mackey, Moran discovered that 'Rocky' had taken over the firm when his father retired two years previous. He was not just your usual muscle-clad bouncer pumped up on steroids who normally hits first then asks questions later. No, Moran noticed that Farley was a clever businessman with a clear head and he would later become Moran's ears on the ground in and around the town.

Dublin was firmly in Moran's control.

Chapter 17
Slug

Moran's control over Dublin was about to be challenged when on Wednesday, 26 December 2001, an altercation would bring a period of untold violence that would change the face of Irish gangland forever.

It was 10.40 pm when Paul Slug Price, Nailor O'Neill and Packey Young were out celebrating the Christmas festivities in a bar located close to the South Inner City when two young men entered the bar and approached the table where they were seated.

'Heads up, boys, it looks like we have company,' warned O'Neill.

'All right Slug, how's tricks?' asked a stocky man. Price stood up, greeted them and made it apparent that he knew the two men, releasing some of the tension from Packey and Nailor.

'It's all good, you know, same shite, different day and all that. Anyway, lads, this is Nailor and over here is Packey. Boys, these are me mates, Terry and Derek.'

'Yeah, sound,' replied O'Neill, nodding his head but still cautious. Accompanying Slug's friendly introduction, Nailor reached out his hand in friendship.

'Nice to meet yis, lads.'

'Yeah whatever,' replied the stranger Terry, looking at O'Neill's hand, then looking into his eyes and laughing in his face then followed by looking at Price and Derek with a grin on his face.

'Fuck you, ye prick,' replied an annoyed Nailor, standing up from his chair.

'Here, relax for fuck sake, Nailor, will ye, he's only takin the piss. It is Christmas after all, ye know,' laughed Price.

'Come on, let's get the gargle in, boys,' said Price as he tried to calm down the situation.

After a few more vodka and Red Bulls mixed with cocaine, the atmosphere did not change; if anything, the alcohol and drugs made it more and more edgy and to add fuel to an already paranoid fire, the atmosphere intensified when three more unknown young men arrived into the bar and joined their company.

Terry called Slug Price aside and after a couple of minutes, he returned to the table and called his two friends outside, saying it was important that he had to speak to them,

'Nailor, Packey, a word.'

When outside, O'Neill questioned why so much secrecy. 'What the fuck is up, Slug?'

'Look, these boys are here on business and you pair are not our favourite people right now, okay? I didn't know they would be here tonight but fuck it, they are here now.' explained Price.

'What the fuck you on about?' asked a panicked Packey.

'Look, we are involved with people who do not like 'Little Don' fuckin Moran.'

'What are you fuckin on about?' questioned a now extremely irritated O'Neill.

'That cunt killed our boss,' explained Price.

'Hold on there now, Slug, what the fuck are you on about with all this, us and we hating Tommy Moran business?' asked a confused but clearly annoyed O'Neill.

'What does he mean, Nailor?' stressed Packey.

'Well, Packey mate, I'm guessing,' answered a furious Nailor, pointing his finger into Slug's face in an aggressive tone. 'Now Slug, you put me straight here if I'm wrong.'

'Go on,' answered Slug.

'Well, Packey, he said their boss so this cunt is, was, working for Andy Russell's old gang now. They think Tommy shot Russell, now if he did fair fuckin play to him because he was only a child-raping cunt.'

'Fuck you, Nailor, ye cunt!'

'Ahh, I always thought you were the stupid little cunt but I guess I was wrong, because you are a little cunt.'

Nevertheless, Price was not finished and he asked a question with a more condescending but serious tone, putting the two young men on the spot. 'So tell me this, are you for or against us, boys?' With a look in his eye that gave the indication that something bad was about to happen there and then.

O'Neill, furious with Price, grabbed hold of him and pinned him against the wall of the pub. 'You can go fuck yourself, I guess once a Slug, always a fuckin slug, ye scumbag! Answer me this, Slug, why?' asked O'Neill.

Price shouted in O'Neill's face, 'Why? I'll fuckin tell ye why! Andy Russell's men paid me a fuckin fortune to get as much detail out of that cunt Moran as I could and now we have enough to take over his areas with or fuckin without yis. So fuck you and fuck Thomas 'Little Cuntin Don' Moran.'

The five men exited the bar and walked over to the group as Price shouted, 'Over here, over here, get them, boys.'

'Bollix, run, Packey run and don't fuckin stop till ye get home, go!' screamed O'Neill.

Nailor and Packey made a run for it but the gang of six easily caught up on the two due to the much weaker Packey who was at this stage well inebriated. Nailor stayed by his side, urging him to run faster but to no avail and a mass fight broke out in the middle of the street. Nailor was more than able to protect himself against his two attackers who soon realised that they had picked on the wrong man when he beat them both up and down the street after they could not take down the excellent street fighter.

On the other side of the street, Packey Young was overwhelmed by his four attackers as he was nowhere near the strength or calibre a fighter as his friend and he was easily knocked to the ground. As Packey lay on the ground, the young men kicked and beat him until Terry burst into the middle of the group, pushing them away while pulling out a knife.

'Stand back, boys, this cunt is mine,' and he then jabbed the knife repeatedly into Packey's throat while the rest looked on.

Packey lay on the ground covered in blood trying to catch his breath when a call came out, 'Leg it, boys, let's get the fuck out of here now, come on move, fuckin move!' screamed Price as he realised what had just happened.

The fights took a total of three to four minutes when O'Neill made his way over to help his timid friend. Lifting him in his arms, a blood-soaked Packey looked up at him, took his last breath and died in his arms.

'No, fuck no, Packey, ahhh Jaysus fuckin hell, no Packey!' were the screams from O'Neill as his long-time friend lay dead in his arms. By now, a crowd had gathered having heard the ruckus in the street. One of the locals had called an ambulance and the Gardaí who on arrival found O'Neill holding the dead body of his friend in his arms.

Before the Gardaí arrived, O'Neill warned them all, 'Nobody opens their fuckin mouths, nobody. These cunts are mine, fuckin mine! This ain't over by a long shot, Price, you cunt!'

Nobody was going to say a word as it soon became apparent exactly who O'Neill was. Later that night, when O'Neill was questioned by the Gardaí, he denied knowing who murdered Packey Young or why someone would want to, telling them it must have been a drunken argument that went horribly wrong. The Gardaí knew all too well that this was going to be settled on the streets and to criminals, the law had no reason to interfere in the revenge.

The next morning, Moran got a visit from Noel Slattery and Frankie McCann explaining that Packey was dead but no reason was given and the only information they had was that O'Neill had been there too. Moran demanded to know who was behind this and exactly why it had happened.

'What a fuckin mess, a fuckin mess, Nailor didn't do it, that's for sure, he loved that little fucker. Find Nailor and bring him to meet me at the yard now! Not fuckin later, fuckin now, Noel! I want to know who done it and why this happened and not some fuckin hearsay story, Noel. Now fuckin go! Frankie, you fuckin go with him!'

It did not take the two gangsters long to find O'Neill who was at home asleep in bed. When O'Neill came outside, both men were waiting in a car and right away the two men could see that O'Neill had had a long night, 'You okay, kid?' asked Frankie.

A clearly exhausted O'Neill softly answered, 'Just about, Frankie, just about.'

'Look, we know ye had a long and hard night but Tommy wants to see ye and he's fuckin well pissed off over this and wants to know what the fuck went on last night, Packey is dead, for fuck sake.'

'You fuckin think I don't know that, Noel, fuckin hell!'

'Yeah, yeah sorry Nailor, anyway, Tommy is waitin so you up for it?'

'Sound, yeah lads, yeah, come on then, let's go.'

At the yard, O'Neill told the gangsters everything that had happened from the first moment the two men, Terry and Derek, had entered the bar until the interview in the Garda station.

'Did you tell the law anything, Nailor?' asked Slattery.

'What? Of course, I fuckin didn't, Noel, what do ye take me for, fuck sake!' replied an irritated O'Neill.

Moran stepped in, 'For fuck sake, Noel, of course, he didn't, look son, go home and get a kip and I'll see ye later.'

'Sound, Tommy, I need a few hours. I'm bollixed. Look, if anything is goin down, I want in. Packey was me mate, ye know?'

'Okay Nailor, okay, give us five and we will get you off home. And get some fuckin sleep.'

'Will do, Tommy.'

Not long after O'Neill left the office, an even more furious Moran told Slattery, 'Noel, we have a big problem here and people are goin to die, you do understand this?'

'Yeah Tommy, I know that, we have to be careful and watch our people,' warned a cautious Slattery.

'Oh, I know, we always knew this kinda thing was comin but I tell ye this, Noel, it ain't gonna be us who go down. I fuckin promise it ain't gonna be us.'

Moran, with a look of intense anger in his eyes, told Noel, 'Round up the men for a meetin in The Black Horse at 9 pm. I'll sort out the room upstairs later today so tell them all I don't want any fuckin excuses, okay?' Slattery nodded his head in acknowledgement to his leader's order.

'Now go on and sort the men and I'll see ye later. Drop the kid home too.'

'Will do, boss,' acknowledged Slattery as he left the builder's yard with orders on board.

'Frankie, you stay with me. I want to talk about how this can be sorted.'

'Sure Tommy.'

Later that night, when Moran arrived in The Black Horse with Noel Slattery as ever by his side, he was met by a large number of his gang and close friends including Pudner Smyth and Frankie McCann. Sitting beside them were the new young gangsters, Brian 'Nailor' O'Neill and Mark 'Bubbles' Fahey. Across the room were Stephen 'Rocky' Farley who was sitting next to Moran's very own mister fix-it Tony Rothwell along with Phil Mackey and Dean Coyle. Arriving just behind Moran were Limerick's Tinker McFadden and Corkman John Joe Daly while other members present from the crew included Moran's Uncle Seamus Conroy and hired help, Paddy D'Arcy, a career criminal who came from the South West Inner City and was a close friend of Conroy's.

Three more members present were 25-year-old Noel Brady, a barman from The Black Horse, another Inner City man, another was Gerry Dunne, an old-school gangster and as streetwise as they came. Dunne had served numerous years in prison for armed robbery, assault with a deadly weapon, drug offences, arson and extortion. Also present were Moran's younger brother Patrick 'Gonzo' Moran who sat next to another new member, Dennis Scully who came from Coolock on Dublin's Northside.

Scully was an Irish Army deserter who went absent without leave two years into his 4-year term. In time, Scully eventually would be given the role of teaching the Moran gang about the art of weaponry. Apart from his men from the trawler and his European gang, this was the nucleus of Moran's ruthless and murderous gang.

'Okay, shut the fuck up, lads, Tommy has important news to tell ye all so listen,' shouted Slattery.

'Thanks Noel, right lads, I've had a meetin with some of ye before and I said that many in this group would never meet again but we have a problem. And by problem, I mean a big fuckin problem.'

Although the Moran crew were now the most dominant gang in Ireland, they were not the only gang looking for the domination of what was now an extremely lucrative drug trade but deep down, Moran always knew something like this was going to come to pass.

'What is it, Tommy?' asked Gonzo.

'For fuck sake, Gonzo, if ye shut fuckin' up, ye'll find out, ye fuckin thick,' blasted Frankie.

'Okay come on, lads, listen, I'm not too sure if ye've all heard that Packey Young was murdered the other night?'

'The young fella in town, yeah, what of him, Tommy?' asked a curious Dean Coyle.

'Well, Deano…' Moran then continued to explain what had happened with Paul Slug Price and warned his gang of the problem in hand. As the room echoed with words of revenge from all the gang, a roar rocked the room.

'The dirty little fuckin scummy cunt,' came from Smyth.

'Relax, we'll get the little bastard, we'll get him.'

'Why would that little cunt do this?'

'Price is in Russell's fucking gang's pocket. Ex-members of the Andy Russell gang sanctioned the murder and now they want us out of the way. It's now clear that these cunts want to take over from where Russell failed.' warned Moran in a forceful tone.

'We'll sort those cunts, Tommy,' warned Frankie.

'Yes, we fuckin will, Frankie. But listen, I want info back about what members of Russell's crew are knockin about Dublin but more importantly who are still loyal to him.'

The gang was then told to keep their heads down, their eyes open and keep their ears to the ground. Moran told everyone to report back anything big or small to his intelligence operator, Phil Mackey. Not long after the meeting, Mackey was given specific details to find out as much as he possibly could on the gang they were going up against, plus who was now running the Russell gang. But with Mackey, nothing ever took time and Moran was made aware of at least one meeting in which Paul Slug Price met with the head of a young gang led by a one Karl Brown.

Mackey told Moran that this meeting took place in a popular café in the Inner City a few days before the murder of Aaron Packey Young. The information came from a Janice Stacy who lived in the same block of flats as Moran in St Christopher's and she told Mackey all about the conversation she overheard between the two young men. She explained that Brown wanted Moran and his gang done and he was to start by taking them down one by one but he also wanted to see who would come on board with them. This made sense as it fitted in perfectly with Nailor's account of what had happened outside the bar.

Following on from more digging by Mackey, he found out that the young rival gang came from all across the city and they were indeed led by Karl 'Brownr' Brown who was a cousin of none other than Paul Slug Price. Brown led a young vicious gang of over twenty members who had no respect for anyone or anything as they ran riot in the housing estates in their own areas until they came to the attention of some more senior gangsters. The leading members of Karl 'Brownr' Brown's gang were, of course, Brown, a 22-year-old from Tallaght in West Dublin who was a professional car thief and a known bully who was always in trouble with the Gardaí.

The gang also included both of the men in the bar the night Packey Young was murdered. The first name that came up was 20-year-old Terry O'Keeffe, the man responsible for Young's death and a youngster who had been in and out of prison for all types of crimes, including mugging, car theft and robbery. O'Keeffe lived in Pimlico in the South Inner City, a mere stone's throw from where Moran had lived in his early years. The other man in the pub that night was Derek O'Neill, a drunken thug and housebreaker from Walkinstown on the outskirts of the Inner City neighbouring Crumlin and the other man was, of course, Slug Price.

The other three members in the pub the night of Packey's murder were leading members within the gang, first was 18-year-old Freddie McDonald from Blanchardstown on Dublin's Northside who already was a career criminal. He had been in and out of custody since he was 12 years of age for assault and robbery. Next was Jason 'Clarkie' Clarke, 20 years old with a reputation as a vicious gangster with a temper to match while 22-year-old Peter 'Nikey' Jordan from New Street on Dublin's Southside was known as a fine footballer but chose crime instead of going to England for trials with a top club. He got his nickname due to the fact he was always in sportswear. Another name that kept popping up was coke addict and joyrider William 'Willow' Ryan, another Walkinstown man who became a career criminal to feed his heroin habit.

Phil Mackey, through an old prison mate Dommo Nolan, was able to make contact with Brown and organise a meeting between Moran and his rival gang members. On 2 January 2002 at 10.30 am, a meeting was organised in a public place, the Ha' Penny Bridge that sits on the river Liffey linking Dublin's Northside and Southside of the city.

Moran was happy enough with the public meeting place but had his men in place in case Brown and his gang tried anything. When Moran and Frankie arrived on the bridge, to his surprise they were met by four old members of the Andy Russell gang and not the youngsters who had murdered one of his gang. They were Tony Fox from Darndale, Mickey Naughton from Limerick and Tony Dunne from Bluebell and the quartet also included the now leading member of the gang, Seamus Delaney.

Delaney was another one of the old-school Dublin gangsters, an only child when it was even more taboo to be an only child in Ireland, born to his mother Esther on 13 July 1950 in the St Bridget's Gardens flat complex on Sherriff Street in Dublin's North Inner City.

The area known as Sheriff Street lies only a quarter of a mile from Dublin's City Centre, and lies between the East Wall and North Wall close to Connolly Station and depending where you live on the street, often considered if you came from Upper or Lower Sheriff Street. The area was once a notoriously run-down part of Dublin with a high crime rate and low employment that brought poverty and crime along with a serious heroin epidemic in the 1980s and 1990s. It was here Delaney learned his trade including a stint behind bars in Britain.

As a young boy, Delaney started his life of crime as a runner for various organised crime figures in his area, earning a lot more money than he could have done doing a legitimate job. In the 1970s and 80s, Delaney ran many different types of rackets such as street enforcer for hire, drug dealing and loan sharking, even charging his own mother a 25% interest repayment on a loan he gave her for Christmas. Delaney was a hated figure in the Dublin underworld and was given his unwanted nickname by his fellow gangsters in the city of 'Ungentlemanly Jim', after the popular boxer from New York, 'Gentleman Jim Corbett'.

Yes, Delaney was hated and to be hated by the criminal underworld makes a statement about a man. He had a major disrespect for everyone around him but especially women who he saw as objects and over the years, he had gathered numerous charges for wife beating and assault on prostitutes and many other women he came across.

Infamously in 1989, a prostitute named Carrie McDonald, who knew Delaney, refused to have sex with him due to his ongoing aggressive behaviour. Delaney, it is told, lost all reason and in a drunken rage broke her neck but he was never convicted for her murder. The reason why Delaney was hated so much was when drunk, he would tell the story and brag to his friends and tag-alongs about it.

Delaney was scum of the earth and pure evil, not many wanted to run with him until he found a gang of young tearaways who fell for his stories of bravado of bygone days and combined with the hatred of Moran, this was just the tonic for both groups to join together.

As Moran reached Delaney, he found Paul Price and Karl Brown lurking in the background with him and the meeting was fiery from the first word.

'You horrible little bastard, Moran, I'm takin you and your gang down then I'm gonna rape your cunt of a wife in your bed, and she'll like it too,' Delaney laughed.

Moran lunged at Delaney only to be held back by, of all people, Frankie McCann. 'No, not here, boss, we'll see them again but especially you, Price, ye little bastard,' said Frankie, pointing his finger in Price's face.

'Fuck off, Frankie, ye prick. Do ye think I'm afraid of you, ye wanker?' replied Price in an extremely cocky and arrogant manner.

'So it's a war ye want then, Delaney? I'll give ye your fuckin war, ye cunt.'

'So it begins. All rules go out the fuckin window from the minute we leave this bridge, Thomas, all the fuckin rules, ye scummy cunt.'

The passing crowd had started to take notice of what was happening and so as not to have the Gardaí all over them, the two rival factions decided to leave. 'See you soon,' remarked Frankie as they left.

'Looking forward,' replied Slug as Moran and Frankie turned and walked away.

'Okay Frankie, will ye go and get Noel and let him know what happened and tell him to tell all the boys. I want you, Noel, Pudner and Tony in my gaff as soon as humanly fuckin possible.'

As they reached the Temple Bar area just across the Liffey on Dublin's Southside, Dean Coyle was sitting at the back of the Central Bank and Moran ordered him to 'get the fuck out of here fast' as the car sped away, heading for Moran's Crumlin home.

Frankie hailed a taxi and headed for Noel Slattery's newly opened brothel that was situated close by Heuston Station in Dublin, only a short trip up the Liffey from O'Connell Street and just across the river from the famous Guinness Brewery. On the way, Frankie rang Noel on his mobile phone and told him, 'Put your fucking dick away and meet me at the door in five minutes; we have business to take care of.'

Moran knew he had to take down Delaney before he did it to him and he had to disseminate his gang. With this in mind, he warned his men who were present at his house 'to prepare for a bloodbath'.

Moran explained to Rothwell, 'Tony, I thought the shit might hit the fan but this is a whole lot worse than I expected so a couple of days back, I contacted the lads in Holland just in case and put in an order so I want you to go over and make sure it's sorted. You're on a plane to Amsterdam in the morning at eight. Ring George when ye land; he'll be waiting for ye.'

'Sound, Tommy, will do.'

Moran, through Sam the Turk, knew about the availability of a large number of high-quality military-style weapons that were going on the cheap via the newly independent states of the former Soviet Union and the deal was too good to miss out on. And with the happenings in Dublin, he was going to take full advantage of this opportunity, these weapons were going to come in very handy indeed. As ordered, Rothwell went to Amsterdam the next morning to organise the payment and transportation of the cocaine and weapons that Mayweather and Van Der Beek had put together.

On 20 January 2002, direct from Amsterdam, Holland, by Airfreight to Liverpool's newly named John Lennon Airport, George Mayweather and Dirk Van Der Beek were shipping out thirty kilos of pure uncut cocaine in crates of specialised roof slates in the hollow cut-out bases of the pallets that were reinforced by metal plates so as to hold the weight.

From there, the paperwork was again sent to the builder's yard where Dean Coyle collected it, caught the ferry from Dublin Port to Holyhead in Wales and then drove up to John Lennon Airport, Liverpool. Coyle was to then collect the pallets, head back to the ferry and on arrival in Dublin, he would then take the cargo to the newly rented warehouse close by Dublin Airport. On leaving the ferry in Dublin, Coyle was stopped by a Customs Officer on a routine check.

'What you importing in the crates, mate?' asked the Customs agent in Dublin Port.

'Specialised roof slates, officer, expensive fuckin things too. Me boss is buildin his own gaff, ye know, and he wasn't takin the risk of sendin them by plane again after they took a bit of a bashing in transit from Europe, can't say I blame him, to be honest.'

'Nice to have that money to waste.'

'Who ye tellin, mate.'

'Okay, buddy, go on.'

On arrival at the warehouse, the pallets were stripped clean by a crew who flung the so-called expensive slates across the room; to their excitement, they found the guns. The stock included nine AK-47s, seventeen Glock automatic pistols and five Heckler assault rifles plus thousands of rounds of ammunition to suit the weapons.

It was with this shipment that army man Dennis Scully would earn his keep by teaching the gang members how to handle a gun with military precision.

'Right, let's go to fuckin war,' screamed Frankie as he pointed an AK-47, otherwise known as a Kalashnikov, in the air; the Moran gang was now ready to bring the fight to the streets.

Chapter 18
Turf War

February 2002 arrived under a huge media spotlight when in Frankfurt, Germany, the European Union member states were welcoming into circulation the introduction of the new European currency, the Euro. In Dublin, hundreds of miles away from the Euro circus, Dublin city was on the verge of a vicious gangland war, a war that would attract its very own media attention over the following months as Seamus Delaney and Thomas Moran would go head-to-head in an all-out bloody gangland feud. Like Moran following the meeting at the Ha' Penny Bridge, Delaney was organising his men to make moves to take sole control of the very lucrative multimillion-Euro cocaine industry and Thomas Moran was more than ready to meet violence with violence when the war came to him.

After the murder of Packey Young, everyone knew that it would only take the slightest incident to ignite the fuse on this ticking time bomb that would finally bring this gangland war to Dublin's streets. At the outset, members of both gangs were being assaulted in a series of minor incidents that broke out across the city, albeit many of the incidents included an occasional fist fight in a bar or minor criminal damage to housing and vehicles. The local Gardaí and their hierarchy took little notice at first because criminal damage did not register too high on their priority listings but this mindset was to take a dramatic change when the stakes were raised with the feud escalating over a four-week period starting on St Patrick's Day.

On 17 March 2002, Seamus Conroy was out socialising with a friend in the North Inner City when not long after closing, full of Guinness, he got up from the barstool and said his goodnights and soon after two members of the Delaney gang spotted him leaving the premises. As he staggered on his way home just past midnight, Tony Fox and Mickey Naughton were driving home and Fox noticed the inebriated Conroy struggling along the pavement.

'Holy fuck, I don't believe it, that's Moran's fuckin uncle Seamy! In here, Mickey, pull up in here. I'm fuckin positive that's Seamy Conroy.'

Fox told Naughton to park the car up in a nearby laneway along the Royal Canal close to the GAA headquarters at Croke Park. As Conroy headed towards Dorset Street, jumping out of the car, Fox confronted Conroy by calling out to him from behind, 'Alright there now, Seamy?'

Conroy, barely able to stand, stumbled forward as he tried to turn around. 'What, who the fuck who is that, I'm locked, buddy,' said the drunken Conroy, finding it difficult to hold his stance while wobbling around the footpath.

'Give my best to Tommy, ye cunt,' said Fox as he reached inside his pocket, pulled out a Stanley Blade and cut a line down Conroy's face. Falling to his knees, he screamed as he was dragged into the lane out of sight of passers-by. Down the narrow laneway, both men beat Seamus Conroy unconscious with heavy planks of wood they found lying against a wall, putting him in hospital for fifteen days.

Conroy received twelve facial stitches and suffered two broken ribs, a broken hand and heavy bruising to the body along with concussion from the blows he received. Hours after the attack on Conroy, word had gotten to Moran who at the time was out of Ireland on a business trip in Marbella. The attack on his favourite uncle certainly infuriated Moran but the straw that broke the camel's back came soon after when another attack occurred and this time it was at the home of Nailor O'Neill.

It was 7 pm on 3 April 2002 while O'Neill's mother Dolores was feeding her young grandchild, two-year-old Emily, at the family home on Captains Rd, Crumlin, when her evening was violently interrupted as a number of shots were indiscriminately fired into her house from a passing car. Dolores O'Neill, a woman in her fifties, was hit in the shoulder only inches away from where the infant's head was lying as she fell asleep on her granny's shoulder. This was the moment that would see the start of a bloody war that would escalate to a new level as Moran and his gang now had had enough of Delaney and his men; something had to be done.

On 4 April 2002, Moran called on Noel Slattery, 'It's fuckin open season, Noel, so give the lads the green light to take that cunt Seamus Delaney and that shower of bastards that run with him down, fuckin do it now, Noel!'

'Will do, Tommy, but will ye relax, mate, I'll sort it.'

'Relax fuckin nothing, Noel, fuckin do it now, take them down!'

Moran gave the order to take the guns onto the streets of Dublin and on Easter Monday, 2002, revenge arrived. Frankie McCann got a call from Moran informing him that one of the men they wanted was drinking in his local bar in Drimnagh, enjoying the last of the weekend's festivities. That man was 19-year-old Paul Slug Price. Moran was told by a close associate who was drinking in the bar at the time that Price was inside drinking vodka and Red Bull like it was going out of fashion and Moran told McCann that 'he needed to erase the problem' that night. Paul Price's death warrant was signed and Frankie McCann was bringing it to him in person.

'Understood, boss.'

McCann lay in wait in a car parked in the driveway of an abandoned house directly across from the pub so that he could see all the comings and goings when at 1.30 am, he spotted Price leaving the premises. McCann got out of the car, pulled up his hood and walked towards his target as Price started home. Frankie, only feet from Price, called out, 'Is that you, Slug?'

As Price was close to his home patch, he thought nothing of this and he figured it had to be a friend or neighbour who had spotted him as he left the bar. Price replied in a drunken slur, 'Yeah, it's me alright, who's that then?'

As the man got closer, Price noticed that he was concealing something inside his jacket and as he came into eye contact, he froze on the spot and the blood drained from Price's face, realising it was Moran's cold-blooded enforcer, Frankie McCann. Clearly terrified of the presence of the unstable thug, Price nervously said to McCann, 'Fuckin hell, Frankie, fancy meeting you, buddy.'

Without blinking, McCann from under his jacket calmly produced a Glock pistol and said to Price, 'Not such a smart cunt now, are ye, I bet when ye left your house tonight, ye didn't think ye were goin to die so say hello to Russell in hell for me, ye cunt.'

'Please no, Frankie no, fuckin hell no!'

'This is for Packey.'

From close range, McCann without remorse put two bullets into his head, turned and calmly walked away, got into the car and drove to Slattery's brothel, where he took two young prostitutes to his private room for the night.

Back at his house in Crumlin, Moran listened to the early morning news on the radio as the Garda spokesperson read a statement:

'Early this morning in the Drimnagh area of Dublin, at approximately 1 am, a man in his late teens was gunned down in a mindless attack. The victim, a 19-year-old local man, was known to the Gardaí. Initial investigations show that this incident points towards a gangland-style execution. CCTV footage shows a lone gunman approaching the victim outside a local bar and in cold blood fired two bullets to the victim's head. This new era in gangland violence has sunk to an extremely low standard.'

With a wry smile on his face, Moran muttered his reaction to the news bulletin, 'Fuck you, Price, ye cunt' and continued to eat his breakfast.

In the North Inner City, Delaney was in a panic having heard of Price's murder and to protect himself from assassination, he began to put the wheels in motion to seek revenge on Moran and organised his men for an all-out war. It was in May of 2002 that Delaney called in a favour from an old friend in Belfast, Anton Ferguson, whom he had met while serving time in an English prison for armed robbery during the mid-1980s.

59-year-old Anton Ferguson, a Belfast man born and bred of Protestant descent and a man who staunchly supported the Loyalist cause in Northern Ireland. It was during the 1980s that Ferguson had become the officer in command of the North Belfast Brigade of the Ulster Defence Army, otherwise known as the UDA.

Ferguson's rise through the Loyalist ranks began when he had begun supplying the Loyalist UDA with weapons from Africa during the height of the Northern Irish Troubles through a contact he had made in the South African Secret Service in the late 1970s. From this, he became a prime target for the Provisional IRA's Belfast Brigade but after the IRA ceasefire in the 1990s, Ferguson realised that the paramilitary life was no longer for him so he started to network drugs through his Loyalist contacts in Belfast and further afield.

Ferguson was known in certain circles around the six counties of Northern Ireland and Glasgow, Scotland, as he ran a successful drug and arms trade operation and it was through him that Delaney purchased weapons from Loyalist paramilitaries in Belfast.

Members of the Delaney gang knew that dealing with these paramilitaries was a risky business due to the fact that if the republican dissidents found out that Delaney was dealing with them, they were all as good as dead. But Delaney was not political and the way he saw it, he and the Loyalists were conducting business and any possible threat from IRA dissidents did not perturb him, in his own words, 'The IRA can go and fuck themselves'. Not everyone followed this line of thought and members of the gang began to distance themselves from Delaney with fear of reprisal from the IRA.

Early in the morning of 5 May 2002, Tony Dunne and Seamus Delaney drove north out of Dublin heading towards County Antrim. After two hours and thirty-five minutes the men arrived into the Loyalist conclave of Belfast known as Tiger's Bay to meet up with Ferguson and his associates. Tiger's Bay is a working-class Loyalist community in North Belfast and commonly regarded as one of the staunchest strongholds of the Ulster Defence Association; this became apparent to Delaney and Dunne as they arrived and were met by murals of King Billy perched upon his white horse with the flag of the Union draped around him.

Not only was Billy looking down from his white horse on the men but also vast amounts of military-style murals surrounded them that read 2nd Battalion, B Coy, North Belfast Brigade, including paintings of dead Loyalist volunteers from Tiger's Bay and across Belfast. After twenty minutes waiting in Tiger's Bay as arranged, a blocky man approached the car and told Delaney in a hard Belfast accent to follow him; after a short journey, the men arrived at a local city centre hall and both men were led into what seemed to be the main meeting room of the local Orange Order. In the hall, a single table sat in the middle of the room surrounded by four chairs and nothing else as the room echoed at the slightest movement.

'Welcome to Belfast, James, how the hell are you keeping?' roared a thunderous voice that echoed throughout the room as Ferguson entered, calling him by his English name while refusing to use his native Irish given name.

'Good, well, not great, to be honest, Anton, I've got big fuckin problems in Dublin.'

'Ahh, Dublin the city on what the rock of Irish Republicanism sits, never been and I never want to either. They say it's the city that defeated an empire or some fucking shite like that. Anyway James, trouble you say, well, what do you expect from a bunch of dirty fucking Taigs who don't know their rightful place beside their Queen.'

'Yeah whatever, ye can have your politics, Anton, I just want your guns to sort my gang trouble down south.'

'Gang trouble, sounds bad,' with that, Ferguson laughed out loud and then in an instant he stopped and told both men, 'Okay, let's talk, big man! Guns you want? Well, I think I can sort you out, here Ian, go get me my brochure like a good chap!'

The blocky man left the room only to return seconds later carrying a large suitcase and after a small struggle, he placed it on the table with a loud thump that once again sent an echo throughout the room. When the suitcase was opened, Delaney made his choice of weapons as he purchased five handguns, four sawn-off shotguns, two rifles and ammunition to suit all.

Delaney and Ferguson knew that transporting the guns across the border was not going to be a problem as the checkpoints that so clearly hampered any guns going north or south during the Troubles in Northern Ireland from the early 1970s until the late 1990s to enforce border controls had now disappeared so no security checks, no problems.

Delaney also acquired the services of Ferguson's right-hand man: a professional hitman from Belfast called Ian Bouncer Howe. Howe, like Ferguson, was born in Belfast and had spent time in the H-Blocks for his part in paramilitary activities he carried out on behalf of the UDA during the 1980s and early 1990s. Like Ferguson, Howe never forgave the Catholics for, as he put it, 'Poisoning the air in his beautiful Belfast'.

Howe swore to protect the Union in every way he could until he had no breath left in his body. But the added incentive for Howe now was that he would be paid to take out Taigs and that was too good an offer to turn down as one less Catholic in Ireland was a step closer to the perfect Union he yearned for all his life.

Now that the Delaney gang had Howe, he was to be for Delaney what Frankie McCann was to Moran. Yes, another complete and utter psychopath and a man who would not think twice about putting a bullet in a man, woman or child to help the cause he was fighting or being paid for.

Within weeks of agreeing to work for Delaney, Howe travelled to Dublin by train on the Dublin express early on 12 June 2002, with clear orders and the details of an address in the apartment complex at Citywest on the Mid-West side of Dublin city. The address was that of Phil Mackey, Moran's intelligence officer. At 8.35 am on the morning of 14 June, as Mackey left his apartment in Citywest, he did not take any notice of the maintenance man who was working on the Emergency Exit lights on the floor of his apartment.

Howe was dressed in worker's overalls and when he saw a man leave apartment 345, he realised that his man was on the move. Howe cautiously followed Mackey into the underground carpark and increasing his pace, approached Mackey as he was about to get into his car.

'Hey Phil?' called out Howe and a startled Mackey turned and looked into the eyes of his assailant. Howe pulled out his gun and fired two bullets into Mackey's chest and one into his forehead. Mackey fell to the ground and died instantly as the gang war had now taken its 3rd victim in a very short period of time.

On hearing of Mackey's murder, Moran sent his mother Marie and wife Jean over to stay with Danny Moore in Ibiza, out of harm's way as things were now out of control.

Only two weeks had passed after the murder of Phil Mackey when Moran would again be given reason to put his gang on high alert when information was passed onto Delaney about another of his men. It was a warm fresh night in Dublin when Frankie McCann was out on the town with friends and like clockwork, he did his normal routine after a few drinks by spending some time in Noel Slattery's brothel.

In the early hours of 26 June, as McCann exited the building, he hailed down a taxi and like the Mackey murder, just as he was getting ready to step into the taxi, a man with a Northern accent echoed from behind him, yelling, 'All right there, Frankie; this is for you, a little present from Seamy D,'

The man then fired two shots from less than ten feet away at McCann's head but the normally ruthless Howe slipped up and missed and as Frankie dived for cover; Howe let off another shot and this time he hit McCann in the arm and he then turned around and ran off to a waiting car.

'Fuckin hell, mate, are you okay?' asked the panicking taxi driver.

Frankie, who was clearly distressed from his gunshot wound, screamed out, 'Yeah, yeah, just get me to fuckin St James' Hospital quickly.'

Two days after the shooting, Frankie eventually got out of the hospital and he was like a demon and immediately went to see his boss, Thomas Moran.

'Frankie, you okay?'

'I'm fuckin fine but I want this cunt and soon. The pigs were at me asking questions but I told them to fuck off.'

'Okay, okay, Frankie.'

All he could think of was that he wanted the man involved in his shooting or take his temper out on any of the Delaney gang as soon as possible, and he wanted Moran to set it up. Moran had to act because Frankie was not taking no for an answer and he knew it. On top of the McCann attempted murder, Moran knew he had to react to Phil Mackey's murder with ultimate results and they did not have to wait long. He could get revenge and keep Frankie happy, so win-win.

Slattery was told that on 22 July 2002, two of Seamus Delaney's younger gang members, Freddie McDonald and Jason 'Clarkie' Clarke, would be renting a cottage on the South East Coast of Ireland in Wexford close to Cairn beach to impress their new young girlfriends. On the night, the two young men had brought Tanya Maxwell aged nineteen and Laura Keating aged eighteen who were both from Tallaght and after drinking and snorting cocaine, all four were highly intoxicated when they were startled by a dog barking outside.

'What the fuck is that poxy dog barking about?' muttered Clarke.

'Don't fuckin mind it, Clarkie, for fuck sake. Right, I'm going to bed, you comin in for a ride or what, Tanya?' asked the very drug-dozy McDonald.

'Yeah of course, I am and if you're good, I'll suck your cock clean off.'

'Tanya, ye bleedin slapper ye,' giggled Keating at her friend's brazen behaviour.

'Fuck this, come on then,' rushed the randy McDonald as he took the more than willing teen to the bedroom.

'So Laura, me and you gonna ride or what?' asked Clarke, hoping to get the same reaction that his friend had gotten.

'Yeah, in a minute, I just need a piss first.'

'Bit more detail than I needed there now, love, but I'll wait here for ye.'

Again the dog barked and Clarke went to the window and looked outside to see what was up. He saw a car parked on the roadside but thought nothing of it as his mind was distracted when the young girl returned from the bathroom. Unknown to the two men, Frankie McCann had received a phone call from Noel Slattery with the address of where they were staying after being contacted by Stephen Farley who overheard a conversation between Maxwell and Keating while working a pub door in Tallaght a few days earlier and now himself and Smyth where about to pay them an unwanted visit.

It was 3 am when McCann arrived with Smyth at the beach house to find the party still in full flight. Smyth sat in the car as Frankie walked towards the rear of the house, screwing the silencer onto his Glock, and cheekily knocked on the back door.

'What the fuck?' was the reaction of a half-drunk and stoned Clarke who without thinking opened the door only to be met by a bullet to the head that dropped him to the ground instantly. Laura Keating, on hearing a commotion, walked out towards the back door and found Frankie standing over Clarke but before she could scream, he fired a bullet that passed straight through the young girl's head, killing her where she stood. As he made his way into the sitting room, McCann heard the groans coming from the bedroom to his left, he walked over and opened the door only to find Tanya Maxwell performing oral sex on Freddie McDonald as he sat on the side of the bed with the young girl knelt down in front of him.

'That's the last cock you're gonna suck, you little slut.'

Frankie put a bullet into the chest of the young teenager and then turned his gun on McDonald, shooting him in his penis. McCann stood over him as he screamed and calmly continued to put two more bullets into his head. The screaming then stopped and McCann, still standing over his victim, looked down on the naked body of 19-year-old Tanya Maxwell lying in a pool of her own blood when he noticed that she was still breathing. McCann bent over and whispered to the teenager as she wept in a blind panic, 'Shush now, little girl, it will be all over soon.'

He opened another round into the youngster's head; in that moment, a young girl out for some fun would never breathe again. Over the next couple of weeks, the public outrage following the murder of the two young girls went all the way to the Dáil as the politicians ran for cover. The Minister for Justice John O'Connor TD met with the Garda Commissioner Gerry Daly about the problem at hand where in a meeting with senior officers of An Garda Síochaina, the Minister demanded answers as to why gangsters were being blown away on his streets.

'In five months, we have now seen men gunned down along with drive-bys, attempted murders and to make things fucking worse, two young innocent girls were murdered and things are not looking like getting any better right now! So will someone please explain to me what the fuck is going on?'

'Well, Minister, we are following all lines of inquiry—'

'Inquiries my bollox, Gerry. It's a fucking bloodbath out there and I am getting it in the neck from all directions. So tell me what information do you have on this feud and not your fucking inquiries?'

'Well, Minister, we believe that two rival gangs on the Southside of the City are fighting to control the drug trade in the city. We are gathering as much information as we can at—'

A clearly under pressure and very agitated Minister ran his hand over his head in frustration. 'So what I am hearing from you here is that you know fuck all about these gangs?

'Well, Minister—'

'Well, my hole, Gerry, okay, look, I will do everything in my power to get you all the resources you need and by this, I mean that it will also include funding for possible overtime if need be. But let me be crystal clear. I want some fucking results and quick.'

'We need to set up a task force to tackle this outburst, feet on the ground, information gathering, Minister.'

'Right then, right. Look, come back to me with details of what you want and who these people are. I'm sure you have people in mind?'

'Yes Sir.' The fact was they knew little to nothing about the two feuding gangs but there was not a chance in hell the Minister was going to be told this information, and this was just about the only information they had right then.

'Okay, do it ASAP. Sort this fucking out or it's your head on the block, Commissioner.'

'Yes Minister, we will get on it right away.'

In November 2002, not long after the meeting between the Minister and the Garda Commissioner, things were not going to get any better for the head of the Gardaí when two of Delaney's men, Jimmy Cox and Michael Gaynor, were sent by Karl Brown under orders from Delaney to collect a five-kilo load of cocaine and a number of weapons in Spain.

The shipment was to be smuggled from Southern Spain to Madrid where Cox and Gaynor were to collect the shipment and deliver it to Ireland. Cox was a trusted operator who had built his fortune by keeping his word and not behaving like your normal gangster. An only child, Cox kept himself to himself on Dublin's Northside in Swords where nobody knew him or anything about him. His neighbours thought he was just the strange man on the block and did not realise that he was a master forfeiter of banks notes who plied his trade all over the world to customers from all types of business ranging from gangland to corrupt governments.

Cox, a quiet bachelor, had never worked with anyone in his life until now, as he trusted no-one but himself and as he saw it, he could never turn himself in so it was a win-win situation for everyone. After meeting up with Delaney in

London, he was coaxed into taking Gaynor to Madrid on this business venture but only after a long discussion and only under duress.

Michael Gaynor, on the other hand, was what was known in Dublin as a waster, he had never worked in his life but pulled scams to feed his drinking habits while his wife Mags did all the working to keep a roof over their heads and food on the table.

It was 10 November 2002 at 9.23 pm Spanish local time that Cox and Gaynor on board Flight MAD/5346 from Dublin to Madrid's Barajas International Airport touched down for the meeting. Not long after leaving the airport, Cox and Gaynor arrived at the Internationale Hotel located in Madrid's city centre on the well-known street of Gran via Madrid. What Jimmy Cox and Michael Gaynor didn't know was that they were not alone in Madrid and neither would ever see the five-kilo load of cocaine and the cache of weapons.

On 27 October, Sam the Turk got wind of the transaction from one of his Spanish sources who claimed that two Irishmen were about to arrive in Madrid to do a deal with a known Turkish drug trafficker named Arda Boral, one of Sam's men who, to Sam's annoyance, was working alone without his permission. Sam already knew that relations between the Delaney gang and Moran had boiled over to a gangland feud and when he investigated the claims, he quickly found out that the men were working for Moran's rivals.

The Turk sent out word and warned Moran of what was going down and it was from this that George Mayweather and Dirk Van Der Beek were ordered to Madrid to make sure that the shipment never made it to Irish shores, no matter what.

On the night of 14 November, Jimmy Cox and Michael Gaynor were about to leave their Madrid hotel to meet up with Arda Boral to finalise the deal when to Gaynor's annoyance, Cox forgot to bring the details of the meeting with him. Gaynor decided to go and relieve himself in the hotel bar toilet while Cox went back to the room to get the details they needed.

As Gaynor stood at the urinal, George Mayweather with a false moustache and wig came up behind him and fired a single shot to the back of his head, spraying his brains all over the urinal wall. Gaynor dropped to the floor, dying instantly while Dirk Van Der Beek followed Cox into the long hallway on the second floor of the hotel; he waited for Cox to come back out and as he left his room, shot him at point-blank range but instead of puncturing his head and entering his brain, the bullet tore into the skin behind his right ear. It then ricocheted around the nape of his neck, slammed into a wall behind him and landed spent on the floor.

Cox staggered and fell back; Van Der Beek stood over him and fired three more rounds into his head, spreading his brains all over the floor and walls. As Van Der Beek walked away, he wiped the fragments of Cox's brain from his face and shot Cox once more in the body just for good measure. It was all in a night's work and before the police knew what had happened, George Mayweather and Dirk Van Der Beek were long gone and heading back to Holland.

Later that week, reports in the Spanish press claimed that on 14 November, as well as the two murders of Cox and Gaynor, a well-known Turkish drug trafficker was found with his throat cut and his hands bound behind his back in a gangland-style murder—Arda Boral. No witnesses were found for any of the three murders in Madrid that day.

On hearing the news from Spain, Commissioner Gerry Daly placed Inspector Niall D'Arcy in full control of a new taskforce set up within the National Drugs Unit to combat the gangland feud and the taskforce would be called 'Operation Gangland'.

Chapter 19
Inspector D'Arcy

Inspector Niall D'Arcy, born in Leitrim in 1950, had joined An Garda Síochána in 1973 and quickly rose through the ranks due to his impressive record. Over the years, he became known as a man who went by the book when his superiors were watching but was not so clean when they were not around; he was well known by the country's criminal elite as 'one tough bastard' and a man who would do anything to take out any criminal when he got onto their scent. He was like a dog with a bone when he got his teeth into something and Thomas Moran was about to find out all about the aptly named 'Super Kop' sooner than he thought.

After his meeting with the Minister, the following day Daly paid a visit to see his good friend, who was only too happy to lend his expertise. 'Niall, a word.'

'Niall, is it? Well, fuck me, Gerry, what is it you're after?'

'Not now. I really do not have time for any fucking jokes today. Look, I have a job for you. I need—'

'You need me to get the Minister for Justice out from deep up your hole, Gerry.'

'So you know then?'

'Of course, I do; it's my job to know.'

'Well, that's just fine and fucking dandy because I want to find out everything about this fucking mess in Dublin. And I want it soon.'

'Jaysus. O'Connor has you rattled,' joked D'Arcy.

'For fuck sake, just…just…'

'Yes, I understand; leave it with me.'

'Okay, I have his backing so whatever you need, just ask.'

'Yes Commissioner.' He gave a sarcastic salute to Daly.

'Fuck off, D'Arcy.'

It did not take D'Arcy long to get things in motion as he picked three trusted men to hit the streets and gather as much information as possible. While that was happening, he had ideas of his own and one such idea lay in Portlaoise prison; that idea was one of Ireland's most senior criminals, a man named Paddy Bourke, otherwise known as 'Mr Heroin'.

D'Arcy had put Bourke away and he was serving his seventh year of a 25-year stretch for major drug running in the late seventies, eighties and nineties.

'You have got to be fuckin kidding me, D'Arcy, they said it was a family member visiting.'

'Are we not brothers, Paddy?' joked D'Arcy.

'Fuck off; guard, take me back.'

'How's that grandson of yours getting on, Paddy?' Bourke turned and gave D'Arcy a look as if he wanted to kill him.

'You bastard, D'Arcy.' Bourke's grandson had been caught with five guns and drugs worth over a half a million Euro a few weeks previous to this meeting and both men knew it was leverage.

'I can make things a lot easier for him with the judge, Paddy.'

'What is it you want?'

'Information.'

'Info, from me? What the fuck would I know locked up in here, for fuck sake?'

'This drug war in Dublin.'

'Fuck off; guard!' again ordered Bourke, turning to leave.

'It's okay, guard, I've got this.' And with that, the guard left.

'Ye bastard, okay, this one is goin to get messy so I hope you're up for it, D'Arcy. From what I'm told, this is linked all the way back to the Benny Jewell murder; Andy Russell murdered him and Jewell's child prodigy murdered him. The Christmas murder and the Drimnagh murder are all linked.'

'We fucking get that part, who are the players?'

'Jewell's man is a top operator named Thomas Moran from Crumlin and he runs a fucking serious outfit. More than I could have ever done.'

'Okay, go on.'

'Russell's man is that tramp, Seamus Delaney.'

'You have got to be fucking joking me, that two-bit scumbag?'

'Yep, now fuck off.'

With the information he received, D'Arcy headed back to Dublin and held a meeting with his men who all had additional links to Moran and Delaney from their respective street touts. The same names popped up all the time and they were Moran, Delaney and Slattery.

The first port of call was to the Commissioner to get permission to gather information from the National Drugs Unit who estimated that between €7m and €8m worth of cocaine, based on street values, had been seized in the past eighteen months and the retail price to users had remained at a steady €70 a gram. With statistics estimating that only 10% of imported drugs were seized, D'Arcy knew that a major player was in play and he knew it had to be Moran as Delaney did not have the manpower or capability to organise such shipments into Ireland.

D'Arcy met with the Commissioner and explained his findings; the Commissioner told the Minister and wheels were quickly put in motion to set up a taskforce. On 28 December 2002, under the office of the National Bureau of Criminal Investigation, D'Arcy briefed his new 24-strong squad of nineteen men and five women on the men they were about to go up against.

'Okay, everyone, settle down, settle down,' ordered Sergeant Donald King who would be D'Arcy's assistant in the National Drug Unit's newly formed taskforce. D'Arcy then began to give his outline on the situation.

'Good morning, everyone, I would like to take this opportunity to welcome one and all to this taskforce with the aim of taking down the people behind Dublin's and Ireland's out-of-control drug trade. This operation will be known as 'Operation Gangland'. I am not a fan of these stupid fucking names but I guess we will have to call it something, so Operation Gangland it is, fucking ingenious whoever came up with that one, I must admit.'

This caused a small giggle in the room as D'Arcy continued:

'Following on from the activities of those involved in organised crime, particularly the spate of gangland murders in Dublin and related murders to this feud in the last months, we will be taking on some of Ireland's most experienced and extremely dangerous criminals. Now this is important, these people are no fools and yes, they are extremely dangerous and yes, they do not like you, but we will stand firm against these people.

'Make no mistake; this will get very, very fucking messy, this I can guarantee. Remember these things and we will get them. So commencing Monday, the taskforce will be in full operation and it will be run by myself, Inspector Niall D'Arcy, and I will be aided by Sergeant Donald King standing right here to my left. We make the decisions around here and we play by my fucking rules. Yes?'

D'Arcy got the nods of approval from his team.

'Good. Okay, then. Let me quickly elaborate exactly what it is we will be doing here. Extra funding will be allocated to this Organised Crime Unit at the National Bureau of Criminal Investigation in conjunction with the Drugs Unit to support our gallant efforts to take down these scumbags, all thanks to our most gracious Minister for Justice, John O'Connor, such a nice man,' received with muffled laughter around the room.

'We will do everything in our power to bring down these gangs and bring their leaders to justice. We will get them, mark my words, we will get them. 'Operation Gangland' will be in place to stop its activities and curb the current levels of organised crime in Ireland, and this taskforce will be focussing on well-known individuals who are involved in organised crime, which includes the trafficking of illegal drugs and firearms. Clear so far, yes, yes, so let us move on.

'Now ladies and gentlemen, we are fully confident that there is a large number of people who know these people and that they are all too aware of their illicit wrongdoings. We also know that the public has information that could and should be passed on to the Gardaí and it is up to us to find it. There are people who do not like this scum so let's find them and find out what they know.

'You have all been selected because you have excelled in the field and now we want nothing less than one hundred and ten percent from this group. You were all brought together to bring the men I am about to tell you about to justice, no matter how long or tough it gets, let me once again make it crystal fucking clear.

'We will take them down!

'Now, the gang members, oh yes, do not write this stuff down; memorise it please as I'm sure none of you would leave your notes in a public place for it to get into the wrong hands, but just to be safe, let's not write it down. Thank you.

'Again, the gang members…'

Sergeant Donald King pulled away a white sheet from a large board to reveal a prison mug shot photo gallery of Ireland's gangland's top people. D'Arcy started by pointing out Moran.

'The man believed to be at the top of the drug trafficking operations across Ireland is the one and only Thomas 'Little Don' Moran, who is now believed to be among the top drug traffickers in Europe and it is estimated that he could be worth in the region of €25m due to figures we have gathered. Not bad for a little prick who grew up in the Inner City slums, aye?

'From our sources, we are told that this scumbag has flooded the Irish market with vast amounts of cocaine, heroin and hash from Turkey, South America and Africa. Moran does not run his operations alone so enter his right-hand man and best friend, the dashing-looking Mr Noel Slattery. Wherever you find Moran, you will find Slattery so he is another prime target.

'Another close associate of Moran and the man who organises the whole operation is a man known as The Fairy, we think; a work in progress, this one. Word is The Fairy travels across Europe sorting deals, laundering hundreds of thousands of euros and organising drug shipments for the gang through their many, many European contacts. We don't have too much information about The Fairy or even a picture of him or these European contacts but Europol and Interpol are updating us by the day so as soon as we have anything new, you will.

'Apart from Slattery and The Fairy, Thomas Moran's other close Irish associates who have been lifelong friends and have done time together are, first of all, Francis 'Frankie' McCann from Dublin's South Inner City. Now ladies and gentlemen, take my word on what I am about to tell you. Frankie McCann is one of the most dangerous and out-of-control gangsters you will ever encounter. This man in short is a fucking psychopath and is suspected of murder so approach with extreme caution.

'Another member of this bunch of scum is this fat heap of shite called Brian 'Pudner' Smyth, also from Dublin's South Inner City and is known in the criminal fraternity as 'Pudner'. Again, he is one of Moran's enforcers and this fella is certainly not in the league of McCann but again, an extremely dangerous man.

'It is because of Moran and his gang that the cocaine market has exploded in this great country and his empire is still expanding. Again, we will stop him.

'Now, on the other side of this argument, Mr Moran's nemesis is this scumbag little bastard, Seamus Delaney. Delaney is from Sherriff Street in Dublin's North Inner City, a right fucker this one. He and his gang are also the people we will take down but again apart from Delaney, we do not have much about them but we are working on it and so will you.

'I like you all for now so please remember that these people are the dregs of society and they will do everything in their power to stop us taking them down.

Okay, enjoy your weekend and I will see you all here at 7.00 am on Monday; good day.'

As D'Arcy was not a man to be pushed around, he went straight to the lion's den to confront his new, as he told King, 'friend' when information came across his desk of Moran's whereabouts. On 4 January 2003, D'Arcy paid him a visit, and where better to visit than in Moran's local pub, The Black Horse bar on Cork Street. To Moran, this was the one place where he was surrounded by, as he put it, 'his own people who he could always trust'.

In The Black Horse Bar, Moran even had a personal barstool that was strategically situated so that it was backed against a wall that faced the main door to keep an eye on those coming and going from the bar. Even when the bar was packed and Moran wasn't there, nobody would ever sit on that stool in case he came in for a pint. That rule was always adhered to until one night sitting in the seat was a strange man and Moran was called upon to see who it was.

'Ahhh, the great 'Little Don' Moran, I'm humbled by your presence, I mean, fucking hell, I'm blessed to meet the great man himself. I'm Inspector Niall D'Arcy of the National Bureau of Criminal Investigation.'

'You're not wanted here, D'Arcy.'

'Come on now, Thomas, that's not very hospitable of you now, is it?'

'Cut out this bollox, D'Arcy, what the fuck do you want?'

'Just to say I'm going to fucking nail you and the cunts under your command, you scumbag bastard. That is all, Thomas, just to make it clear like, you know?'

'Is that right? Well, as I see it, D'Arcy, you have got to be very careful out on those streets these days, very dangerous, you know.'

D'Arcy stood up to Moran and both men were now literally toe to toe with each other.

'Don't you dare threaten me because I'm watching you and I'll get you. I fucking promise you that, Thomas, so have a nice day and say hello to that drunk you call a mother for me.'

'You fucking cunt—'

'No boss, he ain't worth it,' was Frankie's warning as he held Moran back.

'Let's go, Inspector, the smell around here is sickening,' suggested King.

'Okay then, let's go.'

As the men left the bar, Frankie asked Moran, 'Do you want me to get rid of him, Tommy?'

'No Frankie, no, as much as I would like to but no because that is far too much heat right there and we don't need that much on our heads with the business going so well but we need to be more careful, that's all. So fuck him, he's full of hot air and he knows they have nothing and they will get nothing. Send out the word across the country that if I hear of anyone speaking to D'Arcy or any of his fucking taskforce, they will answer to me and they do not want that.'

'Sound, will do, Tommy.'

'And I mean anyone, Frankie.'

Chapter 20
Tit for Tat

The dawn of 2003 brought a very quiet and peaceful January, thanks to immeasurable public pressure in a government that had seen increased funding for the taskforce put in place to keep the gangs at bay. Not only were the public vocal but both government and opposition representatives pressed hard on the Minister for Justice who in turn leaned on the Garda Commissioner to keep the wheels in motion on Operation Gangland. The extra funding meant that extra hours were put in place to keep Inspector D'Arcy's unit not one but ten steps ahead of both the Moran and Delaney gangs as the violent gang war was stopped in its tracks and residents saw life on the streets of Ireland's capital once again become more relaxed.

Following intensive investigations by the taskforce, names of gang members on both sides were coming in fast from informers, enabling them to come down heavy on all those involved in organised crime in Dublin and beyond. The pressure on the rival gangs got so intense that the Gardaí where arresting gang members on sight and raiding houses across Dublin, Cork and Limerick like never seen before.

A lull had indeed come across the city but Inspector D'Arcy was still on edge as he knew all too well that what was happening now was only a containment operation they had in place and as the old saying goes, 'Nothing lasts forever'.

It was late February when the Minister for Justice called Inspector D'Arcy to Leinster House for an update.

'Great work, Inspector, not one murder in an age!'

'Thank you, Minister, but we must not stop what we are doing as these gangs are not finished.'

'We have had nothing happen in months, Inspector, not one singular incident, so relax, it's all under control and you and your taskforce are all over them.'

'Well, yes but—'

'But nothing, the public is happy, government is happy, for fuck sake, even the opposition is happy. We are winning.'

'If you say so, Minister, but again, we need to keep the taskforce going.'

'We will, Inspector, but maybe in time when this all settles, we can disband it. Public money saved and the Minister for Justice along with the Gardaí save the day, great headlines.'

'In fairness, Minister, these gangs are still here and are just waiting to go off again, I am serious.'

'Well, let me be serious, do not let it fucking happen, Inspector, have a good day.'

'Yes sir.'

All of D'Arcy's fears were realised when unknown to the taskforce, a meeting was held in the North Inner City on 14 March 2003, which saw Seamus Delaney organise Tony Fox and William 'Willow' Ryan to carry out a retaliation hit to make amends for the slaying of his two men, Cox and Gaynor, in Madrid some months before. If the Minister for Justice and the Garda Commissioner needed a serious wake-up call, well, they were just about to get one.

It was 8 am on Saturday, 23 March 2003, when Tony Fox and his driver 'Willow' Ryan collected a high-powered Glock semi-automatic handgun from the letterbox of an old abandoned factory on the Belgard Road, Tallaght. It was a typically calm bright spring morning and nothing felt any different when a man in his late thirties reversed his car out of his driveway as he and his wife started out towards the local shopping area in Tallaght's Killanarden Estate.

That man was Ian Smyth, the older brother of Thomas Moran's friend and fellow gangster, Pudner Smyth.

Unlike his brother, Ian Smyth was a family man who had three children: a son Jordan aged eleven, daughter Martina eight and his youngest daughter Edel aged five. Smyth did small deals from drugs he got from his brother but only selling to his friends for the extra pocket money.

Pulling into the carpark of the shops, a conversation continued as Smyth and his wife spoke of the wedding they had been invited to by a neighbour the following week, all the while never noticing the blue 4x4 jeep that had followed since they left their home. On arrival at the shops, Willow Ryan pulled up and parked closely to Smyth's car with the engine still running when he noticed that their man remained sitting in his black Toyota Carina E, listening to the team news for the football that day while he waited for his wife, Gracie, who had gone to the hairdressers to organise an appointment for the morning of the wedding.

'He's a sitting duck; you're up, Foxy.'

As the sun shone brightly through the windscreen of the car, Smyth had to squint his eyes as he was blinded by its fierce light while he leaned forward, pulling down the sun visor. As Smyth leaned forward, he never saw Tony Fox walking alongside his car until he tapped on the window with the butt of the gun. Smyth with his hand shielding the bright light turned to see who it was and as he did, Fox stepped back, stood about three feet from the driver's side of the car and opened fire, killing Smyth instantly. The radio still on, Smyth fell over onto his wife's seat having been hit four times—twice in the head, once in the neck and once in the shoulder.

Within an hour of Ian Smyth's murder, the news had reached Moran who, out of respect, called Pudner to his home to explain what had happened. When Smyth arrived, he had already heard the news and to Moran's amazement, Smyth did not bat an eyelid and commented, 'Ah well, Tommy, shit happens. So what next then?' And that was it, nothing from the cold-blooded gangster, absolutely nothing. Moran, stunned by his reaction, was not happy to just forget like Smyth and to add insult to injury, what happened next was to serve a massive blow not just at the gang but directly into the heart of Moran himself.

Only days after the murder of Ian Smyth, it was on 30 March 2003 that Delaney and his men were to strike once again; at nine that morning, a high-powered Honda Fireblade motorbike was driving around the Inner City area, watching for the victim to come into sight. The driver was Karl 'Brownr' Brown and the passenger was Peter 'Nikey' Jordan and when they drove down the South Circular Road for a second time, Jordan spotted their target and pointed him out to Brown.

'There's the little cunt, Brownr.'

The target was Moran's brother, Gonzo, who was very uneasy and tense that morning as he stood waiting for a bus suffering from severe heroin withdrawal symptoms while taking no notice of the motorbike pulling up alongside him. Dismounting the bike, Jordan pulled his gun and four shots rang out, echoing across the busy morning traffic; three of the bullets hit Gonzo with one hitting him in the head and another two hit him in the chest.

The fourth shot went astray and hit a 24-year-old mother, Breda O'Rourke, in the chest while she was passing by with her young baby in a pram. O'Rourke did not die from her wound but the feud had now taken on a new direction of absolute recklessness and the public were once again agitated at the government and Gardaí for their inadequate way of dealing with these gangs.

D'Arcy had warned the Minister not long ago and it was now coming home to roost when he once again came under fierce pressure from the public, demanding that the gangsters be taken out of business once and for all; the shooting of an innocent mother brought outrage not just from the public but also from across the parliament chambers.

To make matters worse, Minister O'Connor then received a hammering from members within his own government and he knew that he had to once again act. Fighting back, he put it to the government and opposition that the taskforce needed an extension of the funding and after a night's debate, O'Connor was given all the money needed with the full backing from Cabinet to continue the crackdown on the movement of the Dublin gangs.

Without any delay, O'Connor quickly ordered the Garda Commissioner Gerry Daly to put the taskforce on high alert as he feared that the murders of Ian Smyth and Gonzo Moran were going to spark an increase in gangland activity on the street.

And how right he was.

After hearing all about the Dáil debate and the imminent pressure that was about to come down heavy from the taskforce, Moran knew he had to play it safe, knowing all too well that he and his men were going to be under the watchful eye of Inspector Niall D'Arcy and his men. The authorities were going to be even more active in the fight against organised crime and with the government giving its full backing, D'Arcy would have every means available to him and he would put it to good effect. Moran once again was spot on when under orders from D'Arcy, members of the National Drugs Unit placed surveillance on Moran's office at the builder's yard and taskforce members were watching every movement of both gangs as Dublin city was in lockdown, but business had to continue.

Following the murder of Gonzo, Tony Rothwell was given the name of the man responsible for his murder after it was overheard by 'a friend of Tommy

Moran's' in a city pub when one of Delaney's members were overheard mouthing off about the assassination. With things still under lockdown in Dublin, Thomas Moran, Noel Slattery and Frankie McCann under a tarpaulin in the back of a van from the builder's yard sneaked out of the city where they were met in Naas, County Kildare, by John Dean, a friend of Rothwell. Dean passed over a set of keys to a BMW car in which the three men made their way to Limerick City to pay a visit to a close friend.

That friend was Tinker McFadden; Moran and Limerick man Tinker McFadden had formed close associations with each other and it was now time to call in a favour.

At 8.45 pm on 22 July 2003, Moran and his men arrived at an old Community Centre that sat right in the heart of the Moyross Estate, a notorious working-class area of Limerick city. As the three men entered the building, they were met by a number of men seated around the hall and sitting in the background was the city's most infamous son, Tinker McFadden. McFadden called out to the visitors in his thick Limerick accent, reaching out his huge hand in friendship to the men.

'Howya lads, welcome to Limerick.'

'Alright Tinker, what's the fuckin' story with ye?'

'Fuckin great, Thomas, my good man, just sound.'

Taking a small step backwards, McFadden looked his friend from head to toe. 'Jaysus, now would ye have a look at you; you're lookin great.' But then, Tinker's welcoming tone changed as he remembered Moran's sad news.

'Look, my good man, I'm terribly sorry about your brother Gonzo. Shockin stuff and those fuckin' cunts that done this, ye know, it was just fuckin wrong like.'

'Thanks Tinker.'

'So, Thomas, you said you need to talk business with me so?'

'Are we okay to talk here?'

'Yes, yes, my good man, but we cannot stay too long, ye know, cause them fuckin' cunts from the Drug Squad are all fuckin over us. Okay, lads, fuck off outside now; leave us be for a few minutes, will yis?' With the order, Tinker's men left the room and took watch outside.

'Right now, Thomas, what can I do for ye?'

'Lads, you three go on out as well.'

'No problem, Tommy.'

'It's about the bastards who done my brother and another of our men.'

'I thought as much, so Thomas?'

'A little cunt named Peter 'Nikey' Jordan was the man who pulled the trigger that killed my brother and the heat is far too hot for us to take him down. So I'm asking—'

'Stop there now, Thomas, stop. It's done, say no more, all I need is details of the cunt and it's done.'

'Thanks Tinker.'

'Look it here now, Thomas, I promise ye that I will personally carry out the job on the fucker who murdered your brother. We'll say no more. Get the detail to me, done.'

And on that note, McFadden put his hand out and shook on his word. When back inside, Noel Slattery passed over an envelope to McFadden that contained all the information that he needed on Jordan.

'Jaysus, ye have all the info, no fuckin messin with you lads. Good stuff, right, so goodnight. Okay, boys, we have to go.'

Within three and a half hours of the meeting, Thomas Moran, Noel Slattery and Frankie McCann were once again back on familiar soil as the gangland war in Dublin was about to see blood spill on the capital's streets once again.

On the night of 31 August 2003, a Mercedes car with two men inside pulled into Long Lane on the corner of Clanbrassil Street just minutes from Dublin's famous Christ Church. As the car was parked on the curb outside a known bar, the driver got out and entered the lounge. Two minutes later, the same man exited and got back into the car and told the passenger that the man he was looking for was sitting just inside the door in a small snug where two other men accompanied him. The passenger pulled out a pistol and began to load the bullets into the chamber.

'This is for Gonzo; may he rest in fuckin peace, boy.'

That passenger was Tinker McFadden and as he left the car, he made his way towards the door of the lounge, fully pulling on his balaclava as he entered just before 10 pm. With Jordan's location pointed out, McFadden walked straight over to where he sat and without blinking an eye, Tinker shot Jordan twice in the head at point-blank range; he watched his victim die and then as cool as ice, while the bar was in absolute panic, turned and walked to the car and drove away in the direction of Limerick city.

Another tit for tat murder had just been carried out on Peter 'Nikey' Jordan who was assassinated as he sat sipping a pint in his local as a revenge for Gonzo Moran.

Minister O'Connor and Garda Commissioner Gerry Daly's fears were to be realised as the gangland feud was about to go into full swing and The Black Pool was to witness more blood spilled on her streets as the Moran gang were ready to take the war to Delaney.

The following morning at 6 am, members from the taskforce raided Moran's Crumlin home and took him into custody for questioning in relation to the murder of Peter 'Nikey' Jordan but Moran refused to answer any of the questions put to him until his solicitor was present at the interrogation. Moran's solicitor was Diarmuid Corrigan QC, a young hotshot who had risen through the ranks of his firm with remarkable pace and style. Corrigan was known in the ranks of the legal world as a pompous little bastard but red-hot when he got into a courtroom. Corrigan arrived at Crumlin Garda Station to find out that it was actually D'Arcy who was ready to interview Moran.

'Jesus Inspector, the Minister must want my client bad.'

'Fuck off, Corrigan,' D'Arcy barked as he hated Corrigan for aiding the criminal elements. Inside the interview room, Moran sat motionless as D'Arcy began his interrogation.

'Okay, Thomas, where were you last night at the time of the murder?' questioned Inspector Niall D'Arcy.

'At home, I told you already, for fuck sake, this is a load of bollix, this.'

'Come on, Thomas, you can do better than that,' replied Sergeant King who was assisting the Inspector.

'I fuckin told ye I was at home, didn't I, ye thick culchie bollix. Are we done here now or what?'

'We will finish when I say so, Thomas.'

'Jaysus, D'Arcy, come on for fuck sake, this cunt charges a grand an hour.' Moran pointed towards Corrigan.

'Okay, enough of this, Inspector. Do you have any solid evidence that my client was involved in this awful crime? Because if not, this is bordering on harassment.'

'I know you fucking done this—'

'So what proof have you?'

'Look, get out, get the fuck out!'

'About fuckin time too, D'Arcy.'

'We will get you, Moran, we will. Now get out of here; you're stinking the place up,' snapped D'Arcy but before Corrigan left, he challenged his motives.

'Corrigan, how do you sleep at night working for these scumbags?' asked Inspector D'Arcy.

'Well, I can sleep well at night with excellent Gardaí like you on the street, Inspector, and to be honest, they do pay well, you know,' answered the smug solicitor.

'See yis now, lads, you have a good day,' remarked the now cocky Moran and as they left the station, he asked Corrigan a question, 'Why did you take us on, Diarmuid?'

'You and your associates are my best customers, Thomas, and you all pay well and up front. Money is money.'

'You're a bigger fuckin' crook than me.' And the crime boss began to laugh at Corrigan's blatant greedy remark.

'Okay, anymore hassle from these, give me a call.'

'Sound, Diarmuid, talk to ye.'

When the Gardaí drew blanks on the murder of Jordan, things did not go well for Moran; if anything, it got worse. One such circumstance that was to put the crime boss on the back foot was on Sunday, 6 October 2003, when George Mayweather was arrested at Heathrow Airport as he was about to board KAM flight 34576 to Amsterdam. Unknown to Mayweather, he had been tracked by British customs officers after they had spotted him meeting in a London hotel with notorious British drug smuggler, Ali Hasan, who at the time himself had been under extensive British customs surveillance.

Mayweather entered the airport at Heathrow with a briefcase full of money totalling £330,000 and two kilos of pure Columbian cocaine that he carried by hand in an aluminium briefcase onto the plane. He was arrested by British Customs and Excise as he left the departure lounge to board his flight and charged under the British Drug Trafficking Act 1994 and taken to Belmarsh Magistrate's court the following morning for his committal hearing. He was now facing a possible sentence of up to ten years in prison.

On top of George Mayweather getting arrested, Frankie had more bad news for Moran. It was a dull damp evening when Frankie called to see his boss. It was 8 pm on 20 October 2003 when Frankie arrived at Moran's home.

'What the fuck are you doing here, Frankie?'

'Tommy, mate, word has come my way that you've been ripped off in a drug deal for about €2,000 by Bubbles.'

'What! You're fuckin' takin the piss? He's too fuckin thick to come up with an idea.'

'Yeah, ye would think that. No look, Tommy, what I was told is that Bubbles was on a bender with some mates of his and they all ended up down in Noel's place with some dirty fuckin brazzers. He had a load of our coke on him and the fat cunt blew it all that night. But there's more, he fuckin told the slut he was ridin all about the business and I think all about the Slug shooting too.'

Moran's faced dropped and his stomach churned at the thought of being caught because of a fat loudmouth like Bubbles.

'Oh, that silly little cunt. That stupid silly cunt! I'll fuckin kill him, Frankie, I will fuckin kill him when I get me fuckin hands on him!'

'Relax, Tommy.'

'Relax? Frankie, go get Pudner and the pair of yis find Bubbles for me and hold onto him. And find out who the slut he was ridin was off Noel. We need to have a word with her too.'

'Sound, boss, will do.'

After Frankie left Moran's house, he phoned Nailor to see if he had seen Bubbles and Nailor told him that he had called on him earlier that day asking him to go on a bender down in Gaffney's Pub. Within seconds of hanging up, Moran then called Frankie and told him to call into Gaffney's and see if Bubbles was there. When both Frankie and Pudner arrived at the pub, they spotted Bubbles who was half-drunk staggering against a wall in front of Gaffney's pub trying to urinate. Frankie got out of the car and approached him and called out to the bumbling teen.

'Bubbles, ye fat bastard, Tommy wants a word with ye,' as he grabbed hold of him by the jacket and pushed him towards the car.

Confused and drunk, Bubbles shouted out while stumbling towards the car, 'For fuck sake, Frankie, I'm after pissin' all over me leg.'

'Shut your fat fuckin mouth, Bubbles, and get into the fuckin car,' ordered Frankie as he called Moran on his mobile phone. 'Got him, boss.'

'Okay, good stuff, Frankie, bring him down to the wasteland at the old church in the village right fuckin now. And I fuckin mean now!'

'Okay, Tommy, we'll see you there.' As Frankie hung up his mobile phone, he whispered to himself, *Fuck me, he is in one poxy humour.*

On arrival at the wasteland, Moran was met by Frankie who had a hold of the dim-witted Bubbles as Smyth was standing in the background.

'Well, now Bubbles, what am I going to do with you?'

'For fuck sake, Tommy, what did I do?'

'Now from what I hear, Bubbles, is that you are taking more of my drugs than you are selling and along with that fat fuckin belly of yours, I'm told that you also have a fuckin big fat mouth.'

'No, not me, Tommy, for fuck sake, I wouldn't do that to you.' The now terrified youngster physically broke down as the tears began to roll down his face.

'You are a fuckin liar and you're a fuckin liability, Bubbles. So what do you think I should do, fat boy?'

'Jesus Tommy, I'll get your money, we were only on a bender, ye know?'

'Now there you go. After saying you'd never do that to me, you did just fuckin lie to me, Bubbles. So I have just now decided that I must deal with this so nobody will ever try and fucking rip me off again. I can't be seen as a soft touch now, can I, Bubbles?'

'Ahh Jaysus, Tommy, please no.' The tears were now flooding from the helpless Bubbles.

'Okay, Bubbles, kneel down here,' was the order given by Moran, as Frankie pushed him to his knees.

'Tommy please, please, I'm sorry,' cried Bubbles as a cold hard rain began to fall on the men and then in an instant, Moran pulled out a gun from his jacket and all his recent frustrations came out in a moment as he fired a single shot into Bubbles' forehead and Bubbles cried no more.

As the rain fell, an eerie silence came across the wasteland; all that was left was the body of another dead man who was taken before he could enter the prime of his life, just for a mere €2,000. Another serious letter of intent was sent out and Thomas Moran was not going to be taken lightly anymore by friend or foe after the word of Bubbles' death hit the streets.

'Here Frankie, get rid of all these phones now before they track them back to us.'

The following morning at 8 am, local man Paddy Doyle who worked in the church on its rejuvenation project was heading into work to open up the premises as he did every morning when he spotted what he thought was a person lying on the ground. As Doyle approached the body, he thought it was just a homeless person who had taken shelter from the heavy rain the previous night under the large canopy that hung from the church roof but as he got closer, he realised that he was away from the canopy so he approached with a bit more caution; when he got close to the body, he recognised that it was Mark Bubbles Fahey.

'Mark, son, are ye okay there?'

Within seconds, Doyle had noticed the wound to Bubbles' head and with fright, he fell backwards over one of the nearby gravestones. Stumbling to his feet, Doyle ran to the home of the Fahey family, which was only a five-minute walk from where Bubbles lay. In a blind panic, Doyle knocked frantically on the door of the house when Bubbles' mother Annie answered as his sister Tina looked on from behind her mother. Annie Fahey, only just home from her cleaning job that had her up at four every morning, was still wearing her uniform as the tired woman was standing in front of her panicking neighbour.

'For fuck sake, Paddy, what are ye doing, trying to knock me door off the hinges?' demanded Annie.

'No Annie, it's Mark, he's been shot in the church yard.'

'What! What you on about, Paddy, this is not funny.' Annie's face turned pale and the heart of a mother sank as a look of disbelief came across her weary face.

'Ma, what's Paddy on about, what does he mean, Ma, Ma, what's wrong with Mark?' asked Tina Fahey in a hysterical voice.

'I'm sorry, love. He's over at the old church. Annie, come on, come on, love.'

'Ahh Paddy no, not me baby Mark, please no, Paddy.'

As a shaking Annie Fahey's heart broke into a million pieces, the jaded mother took her daughter by the hand and ran as fast as her exhausted body could take her. Three women who neighboured the Faheys heard the commotion and came to the side of their stricken friend. As Annie arrived, her worse nightmare came true as she found her only son lying still in a heap on the ground, having been shot in the head.

'No, no, no! My baby, my little boy, no.'

The cries of a heartbroken mother rang through a community like a chill that shook people to the bone as she held her baby in her arms for the last time.

'No Ma no, Mark!' cried Tina at the sight of her brother lying in the arms of her mother, lifeless, dead and gone forever.

'Ahh Jaysus, poor Mark.' Annie's friend, Maureen Cloake, put her arms around her friend for comfort.

The Gardaí arrived on the scene and immediately, a murder inquiry was launched. As the news spread of Bubbles' murder, the whole community was numb to know that this could happen on their doorstep, and to rub salt into the wound, Moran, Noel and Frankie arrived at the funeral, unknown to the distraught mother that these were the animals who had taken her son's life away. There were about thirty Gardaí investigating the Mark 'Bubbles' Fahey murder but again, the Gardaí found no links to the murder. However, the local community had the rumour mill in circulation about who had done the crime and it all pointed towards the Moran gang and Inspector D'Arcy had the same suspicions.

Five days after the murder of Bubbles, Moran left Ireland and headed off to one of his luxury homes in Spain's Costa del Sol with wife Jean and his mother Marie as per usual until things had died down in Dublin over the murder. While Moran was away in Spain, the taskforce team found a bin full of shredded documents at the builder's yard and managed to put them back together after two weeks of painstaking work, to Moran's amusement; they were all legitimate documents from builders' transactions.

In his absence, Diarmuid Corrigan fought a case for wrongful entry to his premises and won it in the high court—another kick in the face for D'Arcy and his taskforce.

Once again, Moran had won yet another round.

Chapter 21
The Sting

Spain's Costa del Sol is certainly no stranger to Europe's criminal elite walking its streets on a daily basis, and Moran was no exception to that rule. The added bonus for him was that he knew D'Arcy could not touch him or any of his men when they were on Spanish soil due to Spanish law that stated:

Extradition is not possible for citizens located in Spain for a conduct that is not a crime in Spain. No one can be extradited unless the offense is a crime in both countries and carries a prison sentence of at least 1 year.

So Moran knew he was fine as he had not broken any laws in Spain and he could sit easy until the Bubbles case died down. As ever, his gang continued its money laundering exploits that also included their new venture of purchasing property on a large scale while also acting as a financial services agent for many local and European criminal gangs, all thanks to Tony Rothwell.

Although D'Arcy now had his hands tied, he took some comfort in that the Moran gang was now firmly on the radar of the major European police forces, with Interpol and Europol keeping a very close eye on their dealings. Reports sent to Garda headquarters in Ireland from Interpol estimated that the gang had amassed high-end properties estimated at a value of over €500 million in some of the most expensive real estates across the planet. Under an intense and microscopic investigation, these properties were traced back to Ireland, England, Spain and Holland and further afield to Cyprus, South Africa, Turkey, South America and Dubai, all thanks to D'Arcy tipping off the authorities in Interpol's headquarters in the Hague, Holland.

These investigations found that in the whole, the properties purchased were in the residential market but the portfolio included some business interests such as pubs, restaurants, clubs and retail businesses, which were all organised by a major international network of solicitors and accountants under the watch of Tony Rothwell.

A plan was to be put in place to try take down the Moran cartel that included both bodies within the Hague, the Gardaí and other police forces across Europe; as ever, when investigations began, they had some parts of this massive jigsaw but it was going to take time to break a very sophisticated network across Europe and beyond.

Unknown to all agencies, in December of 2003, the Costa Del Sol would see Moran organise a meeting with the crew of *The Spirit of St Christopher* and the leading members of his European gang to outline the gang's future plans. The crew was still the same five men who had set sail from Ibiza to Morocco on 22 February 2001. Also present were Charlie Butterfield, Dirk Van Der Beek, Marcel Kromkampp and Tony Rothwell.

Newer members included 29-year-old Fergus Bellew from County Fermanagh who came to Moran's attention having done a few small jobs and impressed his new boss. Bellew was a small-time gangster but the thing that Moran liked about him was he had a canny knack of getting drugs through Customs. Another new man was 45-year-old Gerry Dunne hailing from Bray in County Wicklow, an old-time gangster and known as muscle-for-hire; he fitted right into Moran's gang with ease.

Next was Jimmy Greg who came into the gang after Moran met him while on holiday in Spain and like Bellew, he impressed Moran right away due to the fact he was an expert in forgery and this was more than helpful in the world of drug smuggling. Last was Dennis Scully, a Glasgow native, who had some contacts on the British mainland, especially in Liverpool and Edinburgh that Moran found useful.

Previous to this meeting in Spain, Moran and Tony Rothwell had organised through Sam the Turk a massive shipment to Ireland that included ten semi-automatic rifles, seven handguns and boxes of ammunition, a cocaine-pressing machine along with a haul of heroin, cocaine and cannabis and other such drug paraphernalia. This was no ordinary shipment as everyone present that day was about to find out—this shipment was to be the biggest ever to be imported into Ireland.

At the meeting, Rothwell explained to the gang, 'These fuckin counter-narcotics officers are now able to monitor emails and telephone conversations so we must not talk business on the phone, ever. You must only relay messages and instructions in code or if very important, deliver the news in person, but that is an extreme last resort. These codes are vital to our business so from now on, coke will be known as Jack. Hash is known as Mr Black, heroin as Harry and tabs as Mr Smart. Thomas, please continue.'

'Right, back on track, the crew of the St, Mark, when the shipment is ready to load and set sail, you'll be contacted with the codeword 'Mother wants you home today', but if you receive another codeword, 'Mother cannot make it home today', you do not set sail until the word is given again.'

'Perfect, Tommy, I'll use that when contacting the crew also, okay lads.' And all crew members acknowledged the Captain.

'Sound, Mark, now these codes can and will change but not everyone will be privy to them,' stated Rothwell as once again everyone in the room nodded in agreement. 'Now Tommy wants a few last words, lads.'

'Nice one, Tony. Everybody in this room right now are the only people on this planet who knows these codes so if they get leaked to the Gardaí or any other Force, you're all fuckin dead.'

Silence once again came over the room as Moran put it plain and simple; make sure nobody opened their mouth. Rothwell continued, 'Okay, gentlemen, back to the business at hand, the Irish government have launched a major operation against us and they have now got a full-time special detective unit working out of Harcourt Terrace. Leading the operation is a right cunt called Inspector Niall D'Arcy and his personal arse licker is the wanker Detective Sergeant Donald King. The pair of them are a pain in the hole and to make things worse, they have now teamed up with the Criminal Assets Bureau to try bringing us down. Gentlemen, we have got to be careful because they are very fucking proficient at what they do. Remember that well.'

Moran cut in, 'They are tracking us and we must not, and I fuckin mean NOT, speak to anyone who is not associated with us; now again, I am fucking warning you all. This operation is too fuckin big to fuck about so if I hear of anyone opening their mouths, I will put a bullet in their head and kill their fucking families and I mean, all of them. This is very important to me so take fucking heed of what I say. Tony will explain the operation to you now. I'm going out with me Ma and wife for dinner, so good luck, lads. Tony, it's all yours.'

And with those words ringing around the room, Moran left and Rothwell once again took control of the meeting.

'Right gentlemen, as you've all just heard, Thomas is very serious about this one so no fuck-ups; again, nobody takes notes, this will all be done by memory. The drugs will arrive in Ibiza via Morocco and Turkey. *The Spirit* will be carrying weapons and cocaine with a street value of €50,000,000, heroin worth €10,000,000 and €15,000,000 worth of cannabis.'

'What!' barked Eddie Baxter.

'Yes Eddie, a grand total of €75,000,000; you got a problem with that?' questioned a clearly anxious Rothwell.

'No Tony, mate no, it's just some fucking haul.'

'It is and it's costing Thomas a fucking fortune so listen and learn the route off. Okay, now may I continue?'

The operation was simple; the crew of *The Spirit of St Christopher* would load the heroin, hash, cocaine, weapons and supplies onto the boat in Ibiza from a number of smaller Moroccan boats in stages over a five-day period and then they were to set sail for Ireland.

Danny Moore had already rented out a warehouse for the crew in Ibiza harbour where they could load the boat away from prying eyes. As normal, the instructions were given to the crew with the exact radio frequencies and meeting point where they were to meet up when in Irish waters off the Irish South coast. Here, they were to rendezvous with the gang's Irish crew who would be waiting.

On 14 January 2004, Mark Lowe received the codeword, 'Mother wants you home today', and they set sail for Wexford's coast with the largest ever cargo to be smuggled into Ireland on board. Again, the crew left Ibiza, sailing out past Malaga up through the Strait of Gibraltar and off the South coast of Portugal. Later that night, the crew were called to action as they passed Plymouth on England's South Coast; Plymouth was Lowe's point to have the crew in place as the next stop was Wexford.

It was on 17 January 2004, when *The Spirit of St Christopher* once again set anchor two miles off the Irish South Coast as they were met by Gerry Dunne, Dennis Scully, Frankie McCann and Pudner, who were waiting in two twelve-foot cruiser boats. On a beach near Cairn, Wexford, was Dean Coyle and Brian Nailor O'Neill waiting in a van and ready to move the gear to the Docklands warehouse to be cut and shipped out onto the streets—Moran had hit the jackpot.

Even though Moran was out of the country, business had to continue as he directed operations by sending out orders from his base in Spain including the order to dispose of a woman called Kelly Dillon, the prostitute Bubbles had seemingly told about the murder of Paul Slug Price. 22-year-old Dillon, who lived in Cabra on the Northside of Dublin city, was an attractive young woman who had met up with Noel Slattery a year previous.

After a quick fling with Slattery, Dillon, after falling on hard times, was put to work in his brothel. It did not seem odd to Dillon when Frankie McCann arrived at 2.25 am as he normally came into the brothel after a night on the town.

'Hi ye Frankie, have a good night out then?' asked the ever-cheerful Dillon.

'Yeah great, now get your knickers off, Kelly, and turn around,' demanded McCann.

'Oh, up the arse tonight, is it, Frankie?' Dillon cheekily replied.

'Yeah, yeah, now come on.'

Unknown to the young woman, Frankie was there to take care of business but not the sort she was thinking of. Kelly Dillon turned her back and got on all fours while McCann pulled out a sharp fishing knife from his belt; he then grabbed hold of the much weaker woman and slit her throat from ear to ear; she died within seconds. Kelly Dillon's crime was that Bubbles had opened his mouth on that night in Slattery's brothel, she possibly knew too much and knowing too much was very dangerous in Thomas Moran's world so she had to go. No human trail meant that there would not be any evidence and it was unfortunate that Dillon had heard what she did from a drunken stupid loudmouth like Bubbles. Her body was taken out to sea by Frankie and Deano Coyle and dumped into the Dublin Bay in a bag filled with rocks; the body would never be found.

On his return home to Ireland, Moran was briefly questioned about the murder of Bubbles Fahey and Peter Jordan but no charges were brought as his solicitor Diarmuid Corrigan QC once again filed a complaint to the Garda Complaints Board about D'Arcy. For Inspector D'Arcy, the main problems were far from the pending investigation by the Garda Complaints Board as he was once again to have another murder on his hands as another member of the Moran gang was about to meet his maker on the streets of Dublin.

On 16 February 2004, another life was to be taken in the vicious feud in the fight for control of Dublin's booming underworld. This time it was Stephen Farley, the man who ran the doors around the city for the crime kingpin and he was, like many before him, to become just another statistic in this never-ending bloodbath. Farley was supposed to be off duty when at 5.35 pm, he got a call from Derek Finnegan telling him that he could not make it to work due to a death in the family. Farley did not have the time to organise another doorman so he did something he had not done in a long time—stood in for Finnegan himself.

His wife was upstairs getting ready for an arranged night out with her husband when Farley shouted up to her, 'Paula love, Paula!'

'Yeah Stevie?'

'I've got to do a door tonight. Derek Finnegan can't make it; someone in his family died.'

'Ahh, fuck off now, Steven, will ye; you promised me that we would go out later. For fuck sakes, he's a lying bastard, that Finnegan fella.'

'I'll make it up to ye, promise.'

'Fuckin' hell, I suppose ye have to fuckin go then. Okay, I'm going over to Betty to see if she fancies a few drinks.'

'Okay, I have to get ready; I promise I'll make it up to ye.'

'Ye fuckin better, Steven.'

On any given Saturday night in Dublin City Centre, the bars around Temple Bar area are awash with young and old of all demographics, stags' nights, hen nights from Ireland and across the channel mixed with international tourists and the locals looking for a good night to give the city that special blend of unbeatable excitement unlike anywhere else in the country; this was Ireland's nightlife hotspot. The area of Temple Bar sits right in the heart of Dublin city surrounded by the south quays of the River Liffey, Dame Street, Fishamble Street and Westmoreland Street and is where Handel's *Messiah* is said to have been first performed in 1742; where Farley was to work on that night.

So when Steven Farley left his house to go to work, he expected nothing more than the party-going fun-loving people he remembered from his time on the doors, but he was wrong. As Farley and experienced doorman Joshua Kimbenga, a very well-respected and trusted doorman, stood and chatted about the normal everyday life, all was quite as expected before the massive late-night rush. Kimbenga hailed from the Democratic Republic of the Congo and stood a massive six foot six inches tall; to add to his height, he was built like a freight train—a huge figure of a man who gave a feeling of comfort to those who worked alongside him.

With the time passing, both men had gathered themselves to get ready for the now visible larger crowds that had begun to gather just shortly after ten o'clock when out of the crowd came a high-powered motorcycle at speed that pulled up outside the bar with a screech. Not taking much notice of the bike,

Farley fobbed it off, calling the driver a fuckin eejit, and continued watching the crowd when the passenger, one Stewie Carroll, drew a semi-automatic machine gun from his jacket and sprayed the bullets across the doors of the bar, hitting Kimbenga twice in the body as Farley got hit five times. The one bullet that ended Farley's life hit him right in the heart leaving him in a seated position at the door to the bar with his head hanging to his left, lifeless.

With panic breaking out all over the street as party-goers ran for cover from the hail of bullets, the driver, Robbie Kennedy, then sped off towards the city quays and out past Fairview where the bike was later found burnt out on a plot of land on Howth Head.

Even on that very busy night with a large number of witnesses, not one person could give any clear evidence on Dublin's latest gangland shooting. Joshua Kimbenga survived but Farley's murder went unsolved like many before it and again the next morning, a furious Justice Minister John O'Connor had to face a public and press core, baying for answers, and again, he had none.

'The gangland killing of a major player in Dublin's South Inner City may have been over a drug deal gone wrong or a row over territory, sources within the National Drugs Unit have informed me. At this present moment in time, we are still looking for information on this murder and if anyone has details, please contact my office or the National Drugs Unit in Harcourt Terrace.'

With such a lack of information, the newspaper headlines on the Monday morning trounced the Minister, chief superintendent and the operation and challenged them to combat the out-of-control gangland feud in the capital city.

O'Connor must resign post as Justice Minister
Gangland 5.0 Government
Gun crime is the Law of the Street

At Minister O'Connor's office, Commissioner Gerry Daly and Inspector Niall D'Arcy felt the full wrath of his fury after yet another murder on the streets while innocent bystanders ran for their lives.

'If I go down, you two are coming with me! Now go get this fucking sorted, I have given you everything you have asked for and I have nothing! Absolutely fucking nothing! Well, when I say nothing, I mean I have a public outcry because a bunch of fucking gun-toting scum are running my streets like it was the Wild! FUCKING! West! Now get fucking out and do something now!'

'Yes Minister,' softly spoke Commissioner Daly.

Outside of Dáil Éireann, Commissioner Daly pulled D'Arcy aside and told him, 'Whatever it takes, I want you to bring these bastards down. They are making us look like a bunch of fucking idiots. You deal directly with me and only me. Do whatever it fucking takes, okay?'

'I hear you, Commissioner.'

'I hope so; again, I'll say it. Whatever it fucking takes.'

The same day that the Minister for Justice was lashing out at D'Arcy and the Commissioner, Thomas Moran was holding his own meeting in the large warehouse they worked out of on Dublin's Docklands. This meeting was arranged to discuss the large shipment they had just imported into the country. Moran decided that the drugs were to be cut and mixed as soon as possible and moved to the dealers across the country because he knew D'Arcy was going to come down heavy on them as a result of the press they were now getting. The order was given and Noel Slattery and Tony Rothwell were to oversee the full operation.

Seamus Conroy, Paddy D'Arcy and Noel Brady worked in the warehouse preparing the drugs for the streets that were then quickly moved onto Pudner Smyth, Frankie McCann, Brian Nailor O'Neill, Gerry Dunne and Dennis Scully, who then supplied the Dublin street dealers as they delivered their product.

The drugs were delivered to houses, flats, apartments, street corners and various other secret destinations across the city to eagerly awaiting dealers to supply a public with a huge demand for their product. Dean Coyle was to supply Limerick's Tinker McFadden and Corkman John Joe Daly by moving the drugs across country and getting Little Don's product onto the streets of Munster.

Fergus Bellew and Jimmy Greg were given the job of dealing with the supply and demand of Leinster's and Connaught's main towns and cities, a large amount of uncut was also couriered to Britain. Within days of the cocaine and cannabis hitting the streets, Moran and his men were making huge money as the demand for more coke became a 24-hour job for the gang. The consumption of cocaine in Irish cities became such that the demand was starting to overtake the supply, with *The Spirit of St Christopher* soon readied for yet another shipment.

But one thing was still nagging on Moran's mind and he called Noel Slattery, 'Oh yes, before I forget, Noel, I want to talk to Derek Finnegan.'

'I'll sort that, boss.'

In March of 2004, Noel Slattery sat with Derek Finnegan in his car, a blue Nissan Primera outside the Nibbles Café on the banks of the River Liffey on the Southside of Dublin city, looking out across Dublin Bay. Slattery had contacted Finnegan through a close friend of both men, one Dermot Maxwell, after telling Maxwell he needed to see Finnegan about some work he wanted to run by him.

Finnegan on hearing about the request from Slattery quickly agreed to meet but what he did not know was that Moran, after digging, had found out that he had taken a ten-thousand-euro payoff from Seamus Delaney to lure Steven Farley to work on the night of 16 January.

'So Noel, what is this job then?'

'The job, like the one you did not turn up to the night Steven died? Ye fuckin backstabbing cunt.'

'What you on about, Noel? You think I...no, no way, Noel, I never,' Finnegan continued but now with a terrified tone in his voice.

'Well, we got told you set him up for ten grand, Derek. Now that was not very nice, was it?'

'Fucking hell, no way would I get mixed up in that shite, Noel, do you think I'm fucking mad or what? Crossing Tommy Moran, fuck no.' Finnegan was now in a blind panic.

'Don't fucking lie to me, Derek, I know you set Stevie up.'

'Ahh for fuck sake, Noel, I had to. I fucking had to; they said they would shoot me kids; what else could I fucking do?'

'Who made you do it?'

'That little cunt 'Brownr' Karl Brown he came to me one night a few weeks back and told me what I had to do.' By this time, Derek Finnegan was in tears and pleading to Slattery not to kill him.

'Gimme your keys, Derek, I need a piss.'

'I won't fuck off on ye, Noel, I promise.'

'The fucking keys, Derek.'

Finnegan handed over the keys to Slattery who got out of the car and walked to the edge of the river and sent a text message to another mobile phone. Within two minutes, a black car pulled up next to Finnegan's Primera and Frankie McCann got out of the passenger's seat, walked to the driver's side where Finnegan was sitting and blasted away, emptying a magazine into Finnegan while Slattery and Moran looked on. Finnegan died instantly and lay slumped out of the driver's side.

'Okay, lads, go back and get some brazzers and tell them you lot were there all night. I'll call you in the morning, Noel.'

'Sound, Tommy, now let's get the fuck out of here.'

Weeks had passed and the Finnegan murder was classed as a botched robbery gone wrong; as he had no gangland connections, the Gardaí presumed he was a victim of a desperate mugger but in reality, D'Arcy covered it up from the Minister for Justice and press, knowing all too well that a spray of bullets was no botched robbery. But the tide was about to turn on Moran when on the morning of 3 June as he drove to the builder's yard, a story on the radio caught his attention:

'Two men have been arrested following the seizure of 100 kgs of cannabis resin and uncut cocaine at Dublin Airport. The drugs, with an estimated street value of one million Euros, were intercepted during a Garda Special Investigation Unit sting at the back roads of the airport this morning.

Detectives believe a well-known Dublin-based criminal gang is responsible for bringing the drugs into Ireland.'

What the fuck? I wonder who that is? As Moran questioned the bulletin, confused to who it could be, he continued to listen.

'This morning's seizure is the result of a European investigation into the activities of Irish and European drug traffickers that involved both members of the Garda Drugs Unit and Irish customs officers.

The Garda Drugs Unit monitored the truck containing the drugs as it left St Margaret's Road close to Dublin Airport this morning after customs officials had tipped them off and the van was stopped on the Ballymount Road, Walkinstown, at around 8.45 am when Gardaí moved in on the van. Two men aged in their thirties were arrested at the scene and are now being detained at Crumlin and Ballyfermot Garda stations.

'Dean Coyle, who is well known to the Gardaí, and Gerrard Coleman, both with addresses in Dublin's South Inner City, were arrested and charged under Section 23 of the Misuse of Drugs Act 1977-1984.'

What! Deano! How the fuck! Moran continued to listen.

'Both men deny the charges of possession with intent to sell or supply, and having drugs for sale or supply. Detective Inspector Niall D'Arcy said that this was a major bust in the fight against Ireland's biggest drugs gang.'

Moran panicked as he had no idea who Gerrard Coleman was and if he could be trusted not to open his mouth about their operation or how much he actually knew. Moran called Noel Slattery and told him to meet at the yard without delay and cancel everything for the time being. What Moran did not know was Inspector D'Arcy had targeted Coyle as the weak link of the gang and had him put under 24-hour surveillance since his last meeting with the Justice Minister. On the night of 2 June 2004, Inspector D'Arcy got hold of information from one of his street touts who told him, 'Alright Inspector, now you never heard this from me, right? Now you'll sort me if I get pinched soon yeah?'

'Okay, yes, go on.'

'Coyle asked me to move some gear with him that was supposed to be done weeks ago like. He's in a fuckin panic that Thomas Moran would find out he still had the fuckin drugs, ye know like yeah, but I told him to go fuck himself.'

'You did fucking what!'

'Relax, Inspector, for fuck sake. I told him to fuck off because I'm in deep shite as it is but he got his mate Gerry Coleman to tag along. He's paying him two grand for it and they're moving it in the morning at six bells from his fuckin private lockup beside the Airport. Ye know, the big one in Dublin.'

'Yes, I'm familiar with it.'

'It's in St Margaret's Industrial Estate. Right, I'm off.'

'Good man.'

'You better fucking sort me, yeah?'

'Yes, of course.'

Within an hour, D'Arcy had organised a unit led by Sergeant Donald King following a briefing at Garda Headquarters in the Phoenix Park where D'Arcy outlined the plan of attack on Coyle and told members not to move in until he gave the word.

'Okay, lads, the man we are after is Dean Coyle. Coyle is a big player for Thomas Moran and we have it on good authority that he is going to move a lot of gear in the morning. If we can get this fucker, I think we can break him and help bring down the Moran gang so you all know how important this is.'

King then pointed to a photograph of Dean Coyle. 'Okay everybody, this is Dean Coyle. Memorise the face, lads. We will be in three separate cars and will observe from a distance but we must never lose sight of our target. Our source tells us that he and an accomplice will collect cannabis and cocaine at a lockup in the St Margaret's Industrial Estate area of Dublin at 6 am. Now, the traffic should be quite light at that hour but we want to know where he is taking the gear so we will swoop at the point of delivery but if we need to move beforehand, the word to go is 'Go, Go, Go', three times, and only from myself and nobody else. If things do not go well, I will call 'Abort, Abort' twice and we return to base in Harcourt Terrace.

'We must keep in close contact with each other and not give it away that we are onto them. Traffic may get heavy as the morning gets on so try to stay together as much as we can. Do not and I fucking mean do not use sirens because we will be spotted immediately. Any questions?

'No? Okay men, we will travel in three cars as I said—Garda Murphy, Rogers and Dean in the front car. Those in car two will be myself, Garda Keane and Spillane and the rear is taken up by our armed response unit of Detectives Kelly, O'Reilly and McFadden. Okay lads, get some tea and toast into you; we move out at 5.00 am. Best of luck and stay focussed.'

The unit was mobilised, the cars were in place and to King's delight, Coyle arrived after an anxious wait at 6.43 am with an unknown man to the exact lockup in the industrial estate the tout had told them. At 7.27 am, Coyle and Coleman then set off.

'Okay lads, it's a red Ford Transit van 97D 17396 so let them move and follow with caution,' ordered King.

When they reached Ballymount, King feared that Coyle had noticed the Garda tail as they circled the industrial estate three times; he ordered his men to move in at 8.35 am.

'Go, go, go!'

Coyle did notice something was not right and gave up without any fuss, knowing he was done for as one car pulled in front of the van and the other across the back of the van as the armed response unit held back, seeing the men surrender without any sort of confrontation. After a quick investigation of the van, it was clear that the unit had uncovered a large quantity of cannabis resin and cocaine.

'Dean Coyle, I am arresting you under Section 4 of the Misuse of Drugs Act 1977-1984.'

King continued to read both men their rights after it was made clear that the passenger in the van was a Gerrard Coleman who was not on the Dugs Unit's watchlist. Coleman was never in trouble before and he now faced up to a ten-year sentence for drug smuggling. Unfortunately for D'Arcy, Coleman had no idea about the full operation that Coyle was involved in but Coyle was still there to be worked on. Not long after Moran heard the news, he arrived at the yard to find an anxious Noel Slattery already waiting for him.

'Well, what's so fuckin important, Tommy?'

'Get inside now and I'll explain this fucking mess.'

'Mess? What you on about?'

'Get fucking in, Noel!' barked Moran as the worry had gotten the better of him.

Inside, Moran explained to Slattery what had happened and both men agreed to cancel all operations until they knew what way Coyle was going to fall while in custody.

'What fucking gear was he carrying on board, the silly cunt, and who the fuck is this Gerry fuckin Coleman?'

'I have no idea, Noel, but what I do know is we have to get moving just in case he does open his fuckin mouth.'

Moran, leaving nothing to chance, had every piece of paperwork destroyed but before that it was all broken down and put to code in a number of small notebooks so only himself, Tony Rothwell and Noel Slattery could read them; these were the codes that organised the whole European operation so they needed to be safe. Rothwell took the notebooks and stored them away out of Ireland under safekeeping in a small cottage he had bought on the edge of the Alps, close to Salzburg in Austria.

Numerous calls were made, again using strict codes that the gang had devised that would be used under different circumstances such as this and when Seamus Conroy heard on the other end of the phone from Tony Rothwell that 'There's a rat in me kitchen', he knew that someone in the know had been arrested and his first order from this was to empty the Airport and Docklands warehouses of everything, leaving behind no evidence.

Pudner Smyth, Frankie McCann, Brian O'Neill, Seamus Conroy, Paddy D'Arcy, Noel Brady, Fergus Bellew, Jimmy Greg, Gerry Dunne and Dennis Scully were all called in to help move the gear and within two hours, both of the warehouses were completely emptied with military precision. Taking no chances, Conroy torched the warehouse on the docks, which was going to be torn down to be replaced with luxury apartments anyway.

It took four units of the Dublin Fire Brigade three hours to put out the fire; everything was burnt to ashes and any evidence that could be used against the gang was well and truly gone by that stage. All the contents of the warehouses used by the gang were moved to a single private warehouse purchased by Rothwell close to Celbridge, County Kildare, that lay two miles outside the town and well out of sight from any other industry or residential areas; Moran did not want any unwanted visitors.

Coyle and Coleman were released on 7 June but Moran did not try to make contact for two weeks, fearing that the eye of the Special Investigation Unit would be on him 24/7, so he decided to meet him in Limerick in a safe house owned by the Tinker McFadden gang.

The word was sent out but Coyle never showed to the Limerick meeting. Not long after, Tony Rothwell got news that Coyle had been put under the newly established Irish Witness Protection Programme by the state, sounding off alarms that Coyle had turned on his leader. As soon as Moran was told about Coyle, the order was sent out that Dean Coyle had a price on his head and the man who got him would make a cool one million euro for the job.

The one essential factor in this entire debacle was that Moran would never find out that Coyle had never uttered a single word to the Gardaí about the gang's operations. Equally important was that he was never contacted about the meeting in Limerick; instead, he went to Galway on a short break with his girlfriend Mandy O'Leary to get away from the troubles he had in Dublin. Crossed wires and people not carrying out their duties drove Coyle into the arms of D'Arcy but unlike Moran, D'Arcy had heard of the mix-up and he was going to use it to his own advantage.

Moran would never find out how sloppy the operation involving Dean Coyle was from his own end, only thinking his man had turned; problems like this needed to be sorted and Moran was not going to sit back and let him take down the empire he was building; Coyle had to be taken out.

D'Arcy had finally won a round.

Chapter 22
The Scouser

It was on 12 September 2004 when at a meeting in Dáil Éireann, Inspector D'Arcy was told by Justice Minister O'Connor that Moran and his rival gangster Seamus Delaney had been the sole reasons for a massive thirty percent increase in reported crime figures for the greater Dublin area alone. The justice Minister was not shy about pointing out that these figures included gun offences, serious assault and drug seizures.

'Good morning, Minister, how are you today?'

'Well, it's Sunday, I'm in Dublin and I have not had a day off in two full weeks, so have a fucking wild guess if I'm okay, Inspector?'

'Point well taken, Minister.'

'You were once told by your boss to do whatever it takes to take these scumbags down, well, it is now coming from the top, fucking sort this shite out now, Inspector, and do not let Coyle slip through your fingers, nail these bastards once and for all.'

D'Arcy just sat and listened as the Minister vented all his anger at the shortcomings of his team, knowing all too well he could only do what he could as no easy solutions were available to put a complete stop to this gangland problem. As the Minister was pointing out the obvious to D'Arcy, another meeting was taking place in Dublin that saw Seamus Delaney and his top gang members discussing how they needed to get tougher with Moran and his gang. The outcome was to pick targets, bide their time and wait until the time was right to hit them but these plans went on hold as not long after the meeting with D'Arcy and the justice Minister, the city of Dublin once again went into lockdown.

Like Delaney, Moran was also not in the mindset of letting sleeping dogs lie as he had far too much to lose if Delaney got control of Dublin, but for now, he was going to take the opportunity of this welcome break. Moran even got time out to visit Jean and his mother in their new apartment on the Costa del Sol but as ever, in his line of work, nothing lasted; he once again got interrupted with a visit from Tony Rothwell that would infuriate him to the core.

Just two days previous to Rothwell contacting Moran in Spain, a member of the Turkish mafia had gotten word to him while in Ireland, saying that he had some very important news and a meeting was arranged in Berlin. Within hours, Rothwell was on a flight to Germany to meet up with one Hamza Serif, a native of Istanbul and a well-known foot solider for Sam the Turk.

It was 10 pm on the evening of 20 October at the Central Bar in the heart of Berlin, Tony Rothwell met Serif and the Turk began to explain to Rothwell the news he needed to pass onto Moran. To Rothwell's amazement, Sam had found out that not only was Charlie Butterfield running Moran's lucrative cocaine deals out of the Southern part of Europe, he was also pocketing hundreds of thousands of euros for himself through his own contact that he had spoken of to Moran in his home in Crumlin some years previously.

'You have got to be fucking joking.'

'No, I wish I was. And just let me say Sam was not too happy to find this out, Tony, not happy at all. Our English friend has been adding his own coke to our shipments and moving it through our contacts around Europe on the undertaking that it was our goods being shipped. Now your people moving the goods, they took no notice of this but why should they, nothing to do with them, but Charlie, no, he fucked up.'

'Yes, indeed he did, but he is smart, I'll give him that, the cheeky scouse bastard.'

'Tony, you do remember Sam told your boss he does not like problems, yes?'

'Of course.'

'Well, let me tell you, my friend, that this is a problem, so tell Tomas he knows what to do. Sam's words, not mine.'

'I hear you. What about Charlie's contact?'

'He is not your problem, Tony, so you just concentrate on your problem, okay?'

'Okay, that is done.'

'I am leaving now. I must be in Istanbul tomorrow morning so I bid you a good evening, Tony.'

After a phone call from Berlin explaining that he needed to meet up, Rothwell arrived at Moran's apartment on 22 October 2004 to inform him of the meeting with Serif. On hearing the news, Moran was furious.

'Are you taking the fucking piss! Where is that scouse cunt?'

'Monaco; I'm told he has a fucking beautiful apartment there.'

'Of course, he does, the cheeky bastard. Right, look Tony, this is not something we can ignore, sort it now, not later, not tomorrow but fucking now!'

'That will not be a problem, Thomas; I'll get on it as soon as I leave you.'

'Good man, Tony, now I tell ye what, I want you to send Frankie to Monaco and make sure he takes care of this problem personally but also tell my uncle Seamy to go along with him as his driver and back-up.'

'No better man than our Frankie.' Rothwell grinned.

'Exactly Tony, now I need you to go and get two false passports sorted as soon as possible and have them both on flights shortly after, make sure they have every fuckin detail sorted that they need before they move on Butterfield. But listen to me, Tony; I do not want them flying in and out of the same airports, okay?'

'Gotcha, boss.'

As Rothwell left the apartment, he got on the phone and started putting the wheels in motion to carry out yet another gangland hit. In Monaco, the unsuspecting Butterfield did not know his days were now well and truly numbered as he had signed his death warrant and Frankie was coming to get him.

Now the thing was if Moran thought this was to be his only bad news, he was very, very wrong; to make matters even worse the next day, Sam had a verbal message sent with one of his couriers to Moran at his apartment in Spain.

The man began explaining, 'Thomas, not only was Butterfield selling coke from his own supplier but the drugs and cash that George Mayweather was carrying when arrested in London were also from that same contact. Nothing to do with him as he actually had no idea as he went on with his everyday routine, thinking he was working his regular job.'

This infuriated him even more but Moran was about to get some redemption as his men were soon on their way to see Charlie Butterfield. Unknown to Butterfield, McCann and Conroy arrived into Marseille Provence Airport from Cork on the 02.18 pm flight, where they met Hans Krieger, a bagman for Jan Kromkampp who then supplied them with a car and a Glock handgun in order to carry out the assassination.

The false passports and driving licence that Moran had told Rothwell to organise were cheekily under the names of Gerry Daly, after the Garda Commissioner, and Niall D'Arcy, after Moran's favourite Garda inspector.

On Sunday, 18 November 2004, McCann and Conroy arrived in Monaco where they had only to travel a short distance to where Butterfield was living. When they got to their destination, McCann had to look at the address again because what he found astounded him as the Scouser was living in the absolute lap of luxury. McCann could not believe his eyes as the apartment complex was situated in very plush surroundings with a staggering monthly rent of €19,000.

As Frankie looked up at the apartments, he spoke out loud to Conroy, 'Fuck me, this is some fuckin pad, this scouse cunt is livin the life. Okay, Seamy, you just keep that fuckin engine running; I'll be back in a bit.'

Leaving Conroy in the car, Frankie began to make his way up a small flight of steps and while he was screwing the silencer to his gun, instinct took over and he turned slightly to his left just enough so that he could see over his shoulder. When he turned, the killer was met by the breath-taking view of Monaco when he spotted a familiar area of the principality. Speaking to himself, *Oh, look at that the fuckin racetrack, Jaysus.* The bit that caught his eye was part of the world-famous Grand Prix strip in the city of Monaco but McCann shrugged it off and made his way to Butterfield's place.

The tiny principality had attracted the rich and famous from across the world but now a ruthless killer was in town to take care of one of her residents. In one of the world's hottest resorts, Butterfield was dining in the best restaurants, driving a top of the range Mercedes, BMW and Porsche, while spending weeks on end in St Tropez living in the lap of luxury. He had the money, the cars, plenty of women and gambled big, but his biggest gamble yet was about to come back and haunt him.

It was 8.30 pm; Charlie Butterfield was spending the evening at home with his Dutch girlfriend, Anna Van Der Veldt, and as they were just about to sit down to dinner, the doorbell rang. Butterfield, unperturbed, turned and asked if Anna was expecting anyone. Anna shaking her head calmly replied, 'No Charlie, not tonight. Possibly, it could be just a neighbour looking for something.'

'In Monaco?' Butterfield joked as he started towards the door. When Butterfield answered the door, a set of alarm bells went off in his head as Frankie McCann was not the person you wanted calling at your door.

'Frankie, alright mate, and to what do I owe the pleasure?' was the clearly shaken words from Butterfield as he was faced by this psychopathic killer standing in front of him.

'You have been a bold boy, Charlie, a very bold boy.'

'What do you mean, Frankie?'

'I have come to give you a present from Tommy.'

'A present, Frankie?'

'Yes Charlie, you see, Thomas does not like people who shaft him. You have been shipping gear into Ireland and Britain and that is not good, Charlie, not good at all.'

'For fuck sake, Frankie, it was just an extra cash-making opportunity, a bit on the side like, I was harming nobody, mate.'

'Not good enough, Charlie, you got Mayweather caught for bein fuckin careless and Tommy doesn't like that. So take care now, you silly little bastard. Oh, and who the fuck are you calling mate, ye scouse cunt?'

The cool and calm McCann pulled out the gun from behind his back and pointed it at Butterfield. As Butterfield spotted the gun, he forcefully tried shutting the door but Frankie quickly reacted and jammed his foot between the door and its frame. As the stronger man, Frankie easily pushed the door open, knocking Butterfield to the ground; standing over him, McCann shot Butterfield three times, two in the head and one to the heart, killing him where he lay.

During the ruction, Butterfield's girlfriend Anna came to see what was going on and as she reached the hallway, she quickly realised what had happened. Spotting Frankie, Van Der Veldt looked him in the eyes and then turned to run when McCann shot her with a single bullet to the back of the head. She dropped to the floor, lifeless.

Frankie quickly got to the car and told Seamy Conroy, 'Right, get the fuck out of here.' Within seven hours of the hit, both men were back in Dublin having taken a flight direct to Dublin Airport out of Milan, Italy.

Moran knew he had to respond to Butterfields's treachery in the most deadly of ways and that the message needed to be clear so that in the future, nobody else would think about crossing Moran again. For the unfortunate Butterfield, he was the example of what happened when someone did and the next day when Frankie reported to Moran about the job, Moran asked, 'Frankie, was the bird necessary?'

'She had seen me face, Tommy.'

'Ahh right, fuck her so. Good work.'

And that was that; Butterfield and his innocent girlfriend had been disposed of. It was just another day's work for the gang as life moved on and Thomas Moran had to move on as he had bigger fish to fry. Within days of Butterfield's assassination, the skipper on *The Spirit of St Christopher*, Mark Lowe, had now become the new Southern European contact for the Moran gang.

As the last days of a violent and volatile 2004 were coming to a close, things were not going to get any easier for the gang boss because a New Year comes with new problems and for Thomas Moran, 2005 was ready to go off with a massive, massive bang.

Chapter 23
St Valentine's Day

In February of 2005, McCann and Smyth were to have an altercation at a bar that would escalate the feud to an even higher level than ever before and put D'Arcy and his men on full-blown high alert while putting Moran firmly on the back foot.

The altercation was at The Rambler, a West Dublin pub, on St Valentine's Day, 2005, when the celebrations were in full swing. During the early part of the night, one of the doormen had spotted five men sitting together, which he thought strange on that night. What caught his attention even more was not only were these five men sitting together but two of the men were regularly approaching punters, moving to a more remote corner of the bar and at times, customers following them into the toilets, away from watchful eyes.

The doorman, uneasy by what he had seen, inquired with some well-known regulars as to what exactly was going on with these men and it was explained to him that the men were dealing cocaine. He immediately rang Noel Slattery, who thus informed Moran, who subsequently told Slattery to contact McCann and Smyth to head over to the bar and find out who these men were and why they were selling coke on his patch.

'Frankie, Tommy wants you and Pudner to head over to The Rambler as he was told someone is selling coke there right now.'

'Serious, okay, I'm on me way.'

McCann and Smyth arrived at the bar just after 10.15 pm where they were greeted by the two doormen, John O'Reilly and Dominick Grace, who then quickly pointed out the men in question. As McCann and Smyth entered the bar, they found it bustling with couples full of love as the bar was covered head to toe with hearts, balloons and pink decorations but love and happiness was the last thing on their minds.

'That's them, your man at the bar and the rest at that table there, Frankie.' Grace nodded towards where the men were sitting.

'Sound, lads, we have men on the way if we need more bodies. You two keep an eye out for them and when they arrive, get them to watch our backs,' ordered Frankie.

'Will do,' replied Grace.

'Okay, let's have a look, Pudner.'

As they approached, Pudner saw as clear as day that these were indeed dealing at the bar.

'Ahh here, Frankie, would ye have a look at these cheeky cunts!'

'I see them, I fuckin see them, enough looking, let's go have a chat.'

Both men made their approach towards the table to find only two of the men sitting in an alcove facing the main door, just left of the men's toilets; the other three men ran errands in and out of the toilet with more than enough willing customers. As McCann and Smyth got closer, one of the men noticed them and nodded towards them, alerting the group leader who at the time had his back to both men. With a quick wave of his hand, all three men had returned to their seats as the leader spoke, 'Ahh Frankie, my man, what's the fuckin story?' asked the man in a very strong Dublin accent.

'Not too sure; for one, you know my name and well, I have no idea who the fuck you are,' replied Frankie with an annoyed tone in his voice.

'Come on now, have a seat?' asked the Dubliner.

Frankie, running his eyes across the gang of men, turned his focus towards the Dublin man and asked, 'Can I have a word in private?' nodding towards a free corner in the bar, out of harm's way.

'No, fuck off!' was the abrupt reply from another of the men.

Frankie continued in a more sarcastic tone, 'That's not very nice now, is it, have you no control over your children, dickhead?' as he pointed at the Dubliner.

'Frankie, I'll tell you what. Why don't you and your fat girlfriend fuck off before you get hurt?' threatened the Dublin man, the tone of his voice changing.

Frankie, who had stayed calm up to this point, became his normal aggressive self and turned to Pudner and said, 'I've enough of this shite', then turned his head and asked the Dublin man, 'Why don't you make me fuck off, you ugly cunt?'

Within a second, the Dublin man jumped at Frankie but as he leaped forward, Frankie hit the man a head butt, instantly knocking him to the ground. As blood poured down his face and all over his white cotton shirt, he shouted, 'Me fuckin nose, Frankie, ye fuckin bastard!'

As this was going on, Nailor O'Neill, Seamy Conroy, Gerry Dunne, Dennis Scully, Fergus Bellew and Jimmy Greg all entered the bar and before the Dubliners gang could get off their seats, a vicious brawl broke out. Frightened punters ran for cover as glasses were smashed and tables got overturned. The fight had quickly moved into the carpark as Moran's men dragged the men through the bar and overpowered the five strangers who were handed out a savage beating. As the five were being severely battered, the sirens of approaching Garda cars stopped the fight and the two groups broke and went their separate ways.

'This ain't over, Frankie, you cunt,' screamed a man with a northern accent. 'Not by a fucking long shot. You're all fucking dead.'

Out of breath, Frankie told the strange men, 'Go fuck yourself, ye cunt, and stay the fuck out of our town. Right boys, leg it before the law arrives.'

Not long after the brawl, Frankie received a call on his mobile phone from bouncer John O'Reilly, 'Yeah John, what's up now?'

Clearly nervous, O'Reilly explained, 'You're not gonna fuckin believe this, Frankie, but those cunts are paramilitaries.'

'What! You're fucking takin the piss!'

'Yeah, one of the punters here is a close friend of mine and knows one of them and he tells me he's a fuckin Republican hardliner. Your man you loafed is called Timmy Kelly, he's from up the road here in Clondalkin and a deffo paramilitary.'

'Bollix! Right, you lot, get in and clear the bar and tell nobody to open their fuckin mouths because if they fuckin do, I will kill them.'

'Will do, Frankie, talk to ye.'

Hanging up his phone, McCann could not hide his dismay. 'Fuck, fuck, fuck! Right pal, we better tell Tommy.'

'Tell him what?'

'Those cunts are paramilitaries.'

'What! Fuck off, Frankie, you fuckin jokin or what?' asked Smyth and McCann turned and looked at Smyth; without saying a word, he gave him a look that told a story.

'Fuck, oh fuckin fuck! You're positive that's who they are?'

'Yeah Pudner, I am, for fuck sake, well, one of them anyway, called Timmy Kelly from Clondalkin, is, so John was told.'

'Oh Frankie, what have we done. Bollix, fuck, bollix!'

Without delay, Frankie told Pudner to head straight for Moran's house so they could inform their boss of what had happened and explain to him who the men were. On hearing the news, Moran could not believe his ears.

'You're tellin me that this lot are a bunch of fuckin paramilitaries? Well, that's just fuckin great now, isn't it, lads, why could they not be a fuckin chess club? No, of course not, they have to be fuckin Para fuckin headcase militaries. Why are fuckin Republicans sellin fuckin coke?'

'I've no fuckin idea, Tommy.'

'Of course, ye don't, Frankie, of course, ye don't, look, I gotta make a call.'

Moran promptly got Tony Rothwell to dig deep and find out everything about the men he possibly could and when the word came back that they were actual members of the IRPP a dissident group, Moran—in fear of reprisal—got Rothwell to contact them in Belfast for a sit-down meeting. The last thing Moran and his gang needed were paramilitaries chasing them down as he remembered well what Benny Jewell had told him about staying clear of the IRA when they had first met.

On deeper investigation, Moran found out that these were a breakaway Republican group named the Irish Republican Peoples Party or IRPP, who described itself as a republican socialist party like many political parties in Ireland. The IRPP opposed the Good Friday Agreement and the Irish Peace Process, viewing both as simply cementing British rule in Ireland but many believe that this was only a front for its criminal dealings and their paths had now crossed with Moran's crew.

What would help their case more was that later in the year of 2005, the Provisional IRA would decommission after the announcement to the end of its armed campaign in July followed in September when Canadian General John de Chastelain would make the announcement at a news conference accompanied by the two churchmen who witnessed the process, Rev Harold Good and Fr Alec Reid, who bore witness to the arms being 'Put beyond use'.

Within hours, the word that Moran wanted a meeting had reached the IRPP organisation and they contacted Rothwell and told him that they would meet in the IRPP offices in Belfast, situated on the now infamous Falls Road.

Moran sent Noel Slattery and Frankie McCann to Belfast to find out as he told Slattery, 'What the hell was going on and why the IRPP wanted to take him on in Dublin?'

On 22 February 2005, Noel Slattery and Frankie McCann travelled to Belfast and on arrival at the office, they were met outside by the Tricolour flying alongside the Starry Plough flag. As both men entered the building, they found Republican memorabilia that included prints of the 1916 Proclamation of Irish Independence and photos of all ten men who had died in the 1981 H-Block Hunger Strikes.

'What the fuck are we getting into here, Noel, this lot are fuckin nutters,' giggled McCann.

'Will you shut the fuck up; these cunts are fuckin mad about all this shite.'

After a short time, Jackie Keenan, an old-school IRA man from Armagh City, came out to greet the men. Keenan had served a total of 19 years in prison for membership of an illegal organisation in the 1970s and 80s and still lived under the beliefs he had as a young man that 'Ireland Unfree shall never be at Peace'.

'What are yee finding so funny, lads?'

'Nothing, nothing at all, just a personal joke,' muttered Slattery.

'Okay, so in here, gentlemen,' as Keenan pointed to a door that was situated down a narrow corridor to the left of the reception area.

'Right, I know why you're here and people in the IRPP do not have any affiliation with these men you have fallen out with.'

'Ahh, come on—'

Keenan, clearly annoyed, looked right through Slattery and told him, 'Don't you ever fucking interrupt me again, is that clear.'

'What the fuck?' asked Frankie with a slightly pissed off tone to his voice but that quickly changed.

'Shut up and fucking listen to me, it's for the best, Mr McCann. Now I do not like you and your fucking drug dealing boss but the IRPP have told me that the men you have dealings with, let's say, were fucked out of the organisation for being bold boys, very bold boys as it stands. Now, what I am about to tell you is not for public consumption. This conversation never happened. Understand?'

'Yes, yes, I understand,' spoke Slattery.

'The IRPP have washed their hands of these men completely, you get me?'

'Go on,' replied Slattery.

'In the next few days, at your little builder's yard, you will receive in the post a letter for an 'Esther Lawler' and I recommend that you give it to your boss, quite interesting what you can find in letters, Mr Slattery. You lot can sort this problem out yourselves. Fuck all got to do with us now. Okay, gentlemen, you can go.'

The meeting ended and both men headed south back to Dublin. Two days later, as good as his word, Keenan's letter arrived at the builder's yard addressed to 'Esther Lawler' and when Moran opened it up, to his amazement he found the names and addresses of seven leading ex-IRPP men who were trying to push their way onto his patch.

Well, fuck me, he thought to himself.

Timmy Kelly, the man correctly spotted in the pub brawl by one of the doorman's friends; 29-year-old Kelly was the leader of the group and a well-established gangster from Clondalkin with a history of violence who had spent time in prison for membership of the dissident IRA. Next on the list were 32-year-old Micky Donnelly and his younger brother, Gary Donnelly, aged 28, who both hailed from County Cavan, both men living in Swords on Dublin's Northside, close to Dublin airport. Micky, a giant of a man, was a hardened Republican who turned his back on the Republican movement citing his displeasure with the Good Friday Agreement but that was just the excuse he needed as he turned his time to the more lucrative drug trade.

Next was Paddy Gallagher, a 28-year-old criminal from Tallaght in Southwest Dublin, who had served time for armed robbery under orders from the dissident IRA's Dublin leadership. The eldest of the group was Martin Fagan from Finglas on Dublin's Northside; Fagan was a 40-year-old career criminal who had served time in prison in England under the terrorism act for his part in a botched bombing of a police car in London during the eighties aged only 18.

Finally, from Dublin's North Inner City were 36-year-old John McDaid and 35-year-old Billy Masterson. Both men had been at the heart of operations for the dissident Republican groups for the best part of a decade until they decided to get into the drug trade, turning their backs on their beliefs.

Fact was that the IRPP leadership were not happy with the workings of the organisation in Dublin and expelled all seven men under a military trial some months previous to the Belfast meeting. Even though Moran had now collected all of the information he needed to take care of the rogue gang, something did not sit right about the whole thing. He knew all too well that these men had friends and very powerful ones at that, who may not take kindly to his murdering them, no matter what Keenan had told them.

Moran was correct because the IRPP leadership had now seen an opportunity for Moran to sort out the dirty work they had previously not finished but he did not know that they also gave the order that none of the IRPP members were to interfere with what they hoped was about to go down in Dublin. When Slattery met up with Moran later that week on 29 February 2005, he was full of caution.

'Noel, I don't trust this cunt Keenan or his fuckin revolutionary nut jobs so we have to be very fuckin careful how we sort this out. It all sounds a bit too fuckin simple but we need to sort out our patch so let's be fuckin clever about it.'

'Yeah Tommy, I know, but you know we can't have this lot takin over our areas.'

'Yeah, but I don't want those fuckin lunatics from up north on our backs, Noel; look, we have enough fuckin problems at the moment with Delaney and that silly cunt Dean Coyle in custody so what the fuck can we do, Noel?'

'I don't know, Tommy.'

'Okay, right, look, go and tell Tony, Frankie and Pudner what's up so they know where we are with this and tell them that nothing is to be done until they hear more from me. Nothing, tell Frankie, fuck all nothin.'

'I'll tell them, Tommy, especially Frankie.'

'Fuckin hell, what next?'

'I know, Tommy, I fuckin know.'

After talking to Moran, Slattery met up with and explained to the men that Moran was not worried about the news in regard to the ex-paramilitary but he was cautious as they needed to be on standby and at the ready if they had to go to war with the rogue gang. Slattery also aired his own caution to his men that the possibility could arise that they could get a backlash from their comrades in Belfast.

Things were now very, very complicated and problems needed to be taken care of but just how they were going to be sorted was a problem.

Chapter 24
Streets of Fear

Inspector D'Arcy feared he was about to see the lull in Dublin's gangland violence come to a dramatic and violent end after he received intelligence reports from the Garda's special gang unit, informing him that the fight in the Rambler bar on St Valentine's night had not just been any regular bar fight on any given night in Dublin.

'So why are you coming to me about some random fight in a bar, detective?'

'Intelligence tells us that the fight was involving the Moran gang with a group of Republican dissidents.' The report from head of the Garda intelligence unit, Detective Danny Bean.

'Tell me you're fucking joking.'

'Afraid not, sir, my worry is that this incident is by no means going to be an isolated one.'

'And you know this, Detective, because…?'

'Inspector, we have it on good intel that Timmy Kelly contacted Seamus Delaney about both gangs joining forces and the Rambler bar was a deliberate attempt to spark off tensions that would bring an all-out gang war to Dublin.'

'Fuck me, seriously; oh, this is all we need.' D'Arcy began rubbing his hands on his face, trying to relieve some of the stress this information gave him.

'But tell me this, why are these Republican dissidents looking to get into bed with Delaney, surely their leaders won't have that, I just don't get it.'

'Indeed Inspector, it is a strange one but what I have heard is that Seamus Delaney and Timmy Kelly formed an alliance after the pair met up in the town of Ardee, County Louth, in November of 2004. This is strong intel, Sir.'

'Okay, okay. So what are we doing now?'

'Well, we have armed units who will be patrolling selected areas of Dublin from tomorrow. There are fears that either gang could use the fight as an attempt to attack one another. Areas of Crumlin, Clondalkin, Tallaght, areas of the South and North Inner City and Ballyfermot will all be patrolled.'

'Good, good.'

'But the thing is, as well as being involved in the dissident Republican end, investigating officers believe that the Republican gang have offered to supply guns along with manpower to the Delaney gang.'

'Fucking hell, detective, okay, thank you and well done. Keep me posted if you hear anything more in relation to any of this, no matter how big or small it is.'

'Will do, sir.'

Wanting to find out more in relation to the intelligence he had just received, D'Arcy followed this information up by contacting colleagues in Northern Ireland who indeed had a file on Kelly and confirmed that he had actually met with one Seamus Delaney. The additional information told him that in addition to the Ardee meeting, both men had met on the Bogside of Derry City that same year but the question of why Republicans were involved with Delaney still baffled D'Arcy. Of course, the Garda intel did not tell him that the Kelly unit was disbanded from the dissident IRA group as this would, of course, have made a lot more sense to him.

To confound matters even more because as far as the PSNI (Police Service of Northern Ireland) understood, the Dublin brigade of this branch of the IRA was still very much an active unit so the gangs joining forces to control Dublin or even the drug trade made no sense at all. D'Arcy would have to dig just that little bit deeper to get his answers but for now, he needed to try to control the Delaney gang and a group of paramilitaries as well as the Moran gang.

The original intel from the Garda unit and the PSNI was spot on because during those meetings in Ardee and Derry City, it was clear from the outset that two things stood in the way of Kelly and Delaney controlling Dublin and they were Thomas Moran and Redser Daly. During the meeting in Derry, it was decided that they would go into business to take control of Ireland but especially the very lucrative Moran business.

It was to be in January of 2005 that Delaney and Kelly would meet again but this time in the small seaside town of Ardglass, County Down. At 4 pm, both men met in its small picturesque marina to discuss their next steps.

'This cunt Moran and his gang are armed to the bollox, Timmy, plus he has major contacts across Europe and he can call on a small army of men to back him up.'

'Fuck him, Seamus, we have weapons and together, we can match him for manpower too. We take him and Daly out, we take Dublin.'

'Let's fuckin do it then.'

It was at that exact meeting that the incident on Valentine's night was planned but so was the idea to take out the first of Dublin's gang leaders, Redser Daly.

On the night of 3 April 2005, Redser Daly was contacted by one of his men when an anonymous caller visited his house in Dublin's North Inner City. The caller informed Daly's man about a deal his boss may be interested in, explaining that his own boss had arranged to move a large amount of cocaine to Dublin via Morocco at a very cheap price but complications arose and they needed his help to move the drugs.

'Is he with you now?' enquired Daly.

'Yeah, he is with me alright.'

'Okay, bring him here but make sure he is fuckin clean first.'

'Will do, Redser.'

When both men arrived at Daly's home, the man began to explain that his boss had no money to move the drugs due to the fact his moneyman was arrested in Malaga after a police sting caught him in possession of a large quantity of drugs and cash as he tried to leave the country.

'My boss told me to explain to you that if you help him out, he would cut you in for a very handsome price per kilo.'

'Your boss has a lot to say, my friend.'

The man continued to explain, 'He has a lot to say as he has a lot to lose; look, my boss is still in Morocco trying to organise the shipment but the main problem is he needs €100,000 to shift the goods by cargo plane to a private Dublin airstrip. He has 25 kilos and he will give you back your 100K plus 20% on street value per kilo.'

But of course, this was all a fabricated story to lure out the crime lord as Daly committed a cardinal sin and never checked the information he received to be true or who was sitting in front of him in his home; the young man who had called at his door was Stewie Carroll.

'Look, ye want it or not because we know plenty out there who will.'

Daly sat back in his chair, rubbed his chin and thought that he could not look a gift horse in the mouth and duly accepted the man's offer. Redser, an experienced gangster, let his greed blur his judgement and he agreed to meet up with a man he had never even set eyes on before—Daly was hooked.

Timmy Kelly and Seamus Delaney organised to murder Daly by arranging a meeting luring him out of his safety zone away from the Northside territory of Dublin. On 21 April 2005, Redser Daly and Dominic Ward set out from their Inner City headquarters at 8 pm to meet up with this unknown man who was going to make them a cool three million euro for just a simple €100,000 investment.

The meeting place was in the carpark of the Seven Towers Hotel in Ballymun on the outskirts of Dublin's Northside, close to Dublin Airport. As Daly and Ward sat in their jeep, Daly noticed a metallic blue 2002 BMW 330i SE approach them and a man in a hooded top pulled up close to where they were parked and gave them a wave.

'Okay, we're up, Dommo.'

Seconds later, the man got into the car as he opened the back door and slid in. 'Evening, lads.'

'Evening, so who the fuck are you then?' questioned a curious but cautious Redser Daly.

The man quickly pulled a gun and shot Daly point-blank in the head and then without blinking an eye, the gunman turned to the terrified Ward and put another two bullets into his head. As both men lay slumped in the car, the cold-blooded assassin spoke, 'I'm the fuckin Grim Reaper, you cunt.'

He then stepped out of the car as a high-powered Kawasaki ZX-12R motorbike pulled up alongside him and the gunman jumped on the back of the bike and sped away. The gunman was Timmy Kelly and one half of Dublin's leading criminal underworld figures lay dead in a cold-blooded attack that would send shockwaves out across the city and further afield.

Not long after the killing, Moran got a phone call from Noel Slattery informing him of what had happened to Redser Daly and Dommo Ward in Ballymun. Moran, stunned by the news, told Slattery that he wanted everyone on the ground to not leave one stone unturned until they found out exactly who it was that carried out and ordered the murders.

Around the same time Moran found out about the murders, word had hit Garda headquarters as Inspector D'Arcy was attending a meeting with the Garda

Commissioner only to be interrupted by a knock on the door as one of the Garda unit gave him the news, 'Inspector, Redser Daly and one of his men have been taken out.'

It sent a chill down his spine as right away he knew that not only was this the biggest double murder in recent gangland history but Dublin was without doubt about to explode into mayhem once again. The meeting with the Garda Commissioner had now taken on a very different agenda.

All D'Arcy's fears were realised when another brutal gangland killing occurred on 20 June 2005. It was a typical Monday night as Karl Brownr Brown was drinking in O'Neill's Bar in Blanchardstown with his new girlfriend, 20-year-old Debbie Moore. It had just turned 10.05 pm, a masked man entered the bar and quickly walked towards him, stopped, pulled a Smith and Wesson gun and shot him in the head at point-blank range. As the man stood over the body, he spoke, 'That's for Redser, you cunt.'

'No Karl, Karl!' screamed his young girlfriend cowered into a ball on the floor, screaming uncontrollably. The gangster life that excited her so much had now clearly demonstrated that the harsh and brutal reality was a lot more than the youngster had bargained for. The bullet to the head was now a clear assassination trademark in the ruthless Dublin underworld after another man lay dead as Ireland's latest murder was carried out by Brian Nailor O'Neill under orders from Moran.

For Inspector D'Arcy, things were not going to improve when only five weeks later, while Moran was in Spain meeting with Sam the Turk and Tony Rothwell to organise another large shipment of cocaine to Ireland, two more gangland figures were about to meet their end.

On Friday, 5 August 2005, as the bank holiday weekend opened to a blazing hot summer's day, Frankie McCann received the phone call he was waiting for from his boss, which had been organised before he left for Spain.

'Take out the rubbish.'

Frankie McCann hung up his mobile and the following morning called at the home of Jimmy Greg.

'Jimmy, my good man, we're on; let's go.'

'Okay, who is it we've got then?

'Kennedy the pox who drove the bike the night Stevie Farley was murdered. He's been bragging around town about it.'

'Well, he should have learnt to keep his fuckin mouth shut then. Fair enough, let's do the cunt.'

'Dennis and Pudner are stakin out the gaff where Kennedy lives over in Mulhuddart and they just told me he is not home so they are sittin on the gaff.'

'Sound.'

Over in North County, Dublin, Pudner spotted Kennedy arriving back home at eleven on the Saturday morning with another man. As both men sat talking outside Kennedy's home, Smyth quickly rang Frankie who had already made his way to Mulhuddart.

'All yours, buddy, he's back. Sittin outside his gaff.'

Soon after the call, Frankie McCann and Jimmy Greg arrived on a motorbike at the house and pulled up about twenty feet away from where Kennedy was in conversation with the other man. McCann dismounted the bike and approached the victims as they sat; as ever, the cool and calm McCann walked out in front of the men and began to open fire. Within seconds, McCann shot Kennedy in the head; turning slightly towards the second man, he then shot him twice in the head before fleeing the scene on the back of the motorbike.

As Scully drove away at speed, McCann emptied the magazine into the air from the back of the bike. The bodies of Robbie Kennedy and Martin O'Neill lay dead in the hot summer sun as screams rang out when the local children who played in the street ran over to find out what had happened.

The news of these new murders reached the Justice Minister John O'Connor on the Sunday morning of 7 August as he had been on a weekend break with his wife Esther. That day, he quickly returned to Dublin and called the Garda Commissioner Gerry Daly to Dáil Éireann. Daly, not wanting to feel the wrath of the Minister on his own, summonsed D'Arcy to the meeting to find out what exactly was going on in his capital city. In the Minister's office, D'Arcy told O'Connor that one of the victims, Robbie Kennedy, was associated with the Delaney gang.

'And what about this other victim, Inspector?'

D'Arcy paused and swallowed before passing a file containing the pertinent information:

Reading aloud, the Minister began,

'Martin O'Neill was a member of a gang of IRPP men who specialised in the importation of guns to Republican dissidents and was also wanted for questioning in relation to a gang who carried out armed robberies across the country.'

'Well, isn't this this just fucking great, Inspector.'

'It looks as if the IRPP boys and Delaney have joined forces to take down Moran, Minister. I fear an all-out gang war will spill onto the streets to take full control of Ireland's drug trade. It's all specul—'

'Fucking hell, hang on here now, so you're telling me that these few recent murders are only a starting point, is it?' replied a now visibly annoyed and frustrated Minister.

D'Arcy continued to tell the Minister, 'It's looking very, very likely that the IRPP men and Delaney are in this side by side versus Moran. We have received information from the PSNI telling us that two of Moran's men were spotted at the IRPP HQ in Belfast earlier this year after an incident in a Dublin bar, Minister.'

'Oh, and why was that?'

'Additional information now tells us that the Dublin Brigade was disbanded and they are now rogue, it's looking like they washed their hands of Kelly and his men so I guess the meeting after the bar incident was a clear-the-air with Moran and the IRPP men.'

'Ohhh, you guess, that is very reassuring, Inspector, I must admit. I'm glad to hear you're on top of things. I mean, look at the heroin business, it is as rampant as it ever was, the cocaine market is thriving and despite the maimings and killings, there seems to be a self-replenishing pool of ambitious young thugs willing to risk all for a piece of the action. But you guess that one is working with the other, or maybe the IRA lads are doing a bit of fucking moonlighting, is it? Well, that's just fucking great! We must have them shitting themselves, Inspector.

The Minister sat with his head in his hands as Inspector D'Arcy and Commissioner Daly stood silent, waiting for him to say something,

'Well, gentlemen, don't just stand there, what the hell are we going to do?'

'Well—'

The Minister immediately cut down the Commissioner. 'Well, my fucking hole, Commissioner, okay, sit, both of you tell me, come on now what next, where do we take this? Okay, Commissioner, Gerry.' The Minister stood and placed his hand on his shoulder.

'Gerry, I need this to work. I'm getting it in the fucking neck from everywhere, especially after the operations in the past, let's be honest, failed miserably.'

D'Arcy jumped in, 'I have an idea, Minister.'

'I'm all ears, Inspector, let's have it.'

'I want to round up the best of the best from across the country but to be honest, it's going to take extra funds. Like in the past operations, what I want to do is put a 24-hour surveillance on the Moran and Delaney gangs' top people.'

'You mean like Tango Squad?'

'Indeed, Minister. It worked before so why not again.'

'Okay, leave that with me; the Minister for finance owes me one, I'll get the funding and you get me Moran and Delaney.'

'Yes Sir, I'll get on it right away,' answered a seriously under pressure Commissioner.

'And finally, Commissioner, do not release the information about the second man being an IRPP man because all we fucking need is a bunch of have-a-go-hero Republicans looking to avenge their falling comrade's honour.'

'Yes Minister.'

A week later, in the Dáil Chambers during the Government's Order of Business, Justice Minister John O'Connor got what he and Commissioner Daly wanted as the funding was once again given the green light to take down Moran and Delaney. 'Operation Downfall' was the name given to the taskforce to bring down the capital's main gangs. The funding that parliament had passed saw D'Arcy's new unit lock down Dublin city as an extensive series of checkpoints, patrols and surveillance began to take on the gangs on their own streets. One of the biggest operations ever carried out by the Irish state since the North of Ireland Troubles involved local Gardaí and a number of national Garda squads, including the organised crime unit, to take the fight to the streets.

D'Arcy knew that Moran was in charge of a gang of up to thirty associates but he had the upper hand for once when he was lucky enough to receive intelligence that included addresses of business and homes in Drimnagh, Bluebell, Dublin's South Inner City, Crumlin, Walkinstown, Ballyfermot and other areas of the city. Garda intelligence now had a good indication of who was in the Irish section of the Moran gang and what roles each person played in the organisation. The Delaney gang, on the other hand, was much easier to pinpoint as they were far less organised than Moran.

On Wednesday morning, 14 September 2005, the new Garda unit swooped in one major operation like never seen before against organised crime, as over forty raids were carried out by over 150 uniformed Gardaí and forty Special Investigation Unit members who raided houses and premises across Dublin. More than a dozen houses were raided as factories and storage facilities were searched and many a successful seizure included everything from cars, phones, laptops, weapons, drugs and cash.

Additional raids occurred in Limerick, Carlow, Cork, Westmeath, Longford, Louth and Wexford over the following days as D'Arcy and his new team wreaked havoc on Delaney and Moran.

D'Arcy was now fighting back and Moran was on the back foot for the first time in a long time as 'Operation Downfall' hit him, and hit him hard.

Chapter 25
Stephen Trimble

The criminal fraternity right across Ireland was hurting as the full effect of Operation Downfall had a substantial effect on all gangland activity with just about every corner of the Island being hit considerably hard. The word on the street clearly rang out that all drug dealers were suffering from a severe shortage of stock, especially cocaine and cannabis, as for the first time in a long time, the demand could not be met, leading to prices soaring and punters searching high and low for a hit.

However, not everyone was suffering because at that moment in time and for the first time in a long while, D'Arcy was in control of his streets and just about everything was running smoothly in the city of Dublin and further afield. Even the justice Minister could afford a smile as he sat over his morning coffee with nothing but good headlines in the Sunday tabloids and broadsheets about his department's work to take down the country's gangs. All was good for Minister O'Connor as the citizens of Dublin city became witness to some sense of normality on their streets for the first time in a very long time.

Despite this new-found political solitude, what the papers and the public were kept in the dark about was that several individual officers from Operation Downfall had been threatened and at times assaulted by criminals affiliated to Moran and Delaney. Reacting to these incidents, caution was the order of the day from the Commissioner who informed all uniformed Gardaí across Dublin 'to take special precautions when stopping and searching cars in certain areas of the city at day or night'.

For a time the checkpoints worked but the intimidation was escalated by Moran who hoped it would scare off the ordinary street Garda but it went too far one night when Garda Geraldine Power was threatened by gunpoint when arriving home from her shift. On hearing the news, the justice Minister was furious and ordered the Garda special armed unit known as the 'Emergency Response Unit' to be deployed to the streets of Dublin during operations.

This special unit was formed on 15 December 1977 following an agreement on international terrorism at the European Council meeting in Brussels and was based out of Harcourt Street, Dublin. Many of the unit's first challenges were in combating the increasing threat of the Provisional IRA during The Troubles and in 1984, its members underwent training with the Army Ranger Wing forming the Anti-Terrorist Unit. The Anti-Terrorist Unit was later renamed the Emergency Response Unit in 1987 to better reflect its role in modern society and it was now time to deploy them on Dublin's streets.

Speaking to reporters on the steps of Dáil Éireann, a clearly annoyed Minister explained, 'Enough is enough from these thugs, I'm done playing nice and the men and women of An Garda Síochána will not be intimidated by gangsters, not on my watch. From tomorrow, after a meeting at Garda HQ with full support from the Garda Commissioner, I'm deploying the Emergency Response Unit to support our uniformed members, so write what you like in the papers; this is my stance, good day.'

The following day, the news outlets looked to have gotten the message when the front pages gave full support to the Minister and his actions. Even though the criminals were still working, albeit under the shadows of the night, the new Special Investigative Units stood strong against the gangsters and their intimidation soon stopped; the Minister's words were clearly heard this time and not just by the media.

With growing confidence, the citizens of Dublin were getting on with their everyday lives but Inspector D'Arcy did not share in this air of optimism; as ever, he had something niggling away at the back of his mind. He knew all too well, more than anyone, that the peace and quiet was not going to last forever as bad blood ran very deep within the two gangs and like in the past, this would no doubt all come crashing down in the most dramatic of fashions.

It was only a matter of time before something would reignite the flame; D'Arcy was right when a sequence of events would put him firmly on the back foot once again and send out a deadly message that this feud was far from over.

It was on 4 November 2005 that the first snows of winter began to fall in a blissful silence, the flakes began to cover the ground like a great white blanket that cushioned the feet of the early morning church-goers who were attending a funeral Mass at St Malachy's Catholic Church in Swords, North County, Dublin.

It was just after the service when mourners, which included Pudner Smyth, began heading towards the local graveyard that was only walking distance from the church. Smyth was attending the funeral of his uncle, Bertie Smyth, who had died aged 87 just three days previous. Along with all the other mourners, Smyth exited the church grounds as the funeral cortège moved across the perfectly laid white blanket of snow.

As Smyth made his way to the graveyard, the sound of the church bell ringing caught his attention and it was at that moment, as he passed by the main gates of St Malachy's, he raised his head and stared up at the bell tower and was blinded by the midday sun by a momentary break in the clouds. Putting his hand up to cover his eyes, a single gunshot echoed out in the calm fresh air and Brian 'Pudner' Smyth fell to the ground and the white blanket beneath him turned a crimson red as the blood spilled around him.

Smyth never heard the screams that bellowed out all around him just as he never saw his assailant coming from behind the overgrown shrubbery that ran along the church grounds. The gunman was ex-IRPP man Micky Donnelly and that moment signalled the end of the fractured peace.

Another major gangland figure was now taken down but this was now one of Moran's closest friends, original gang members had fallen. Someone was going to pay and pay dearly. With Redser Daly and now Smyth murdered, Moran was hurting inside but he would never show it to anyone; he wanted things sorted and quickly called in all the men he had available to organise them to get even.

As ever, the gang never stood still as Moran recruited new additions to his crew and these were five members of Redser Daly's gang that included Redser's brother, 33-year-old Joe Daly, a career criminal who specialised in robbery. Joe Daly brought along 24-year-old Ken Fox, a drug dealer from Artane and long-time criminal Dermot Behan, a 35-year-old armed robber from Clondalkin. Finally, there was 27-year-old Philippe Garrone, a member of Naples' notorious 'Camorra' gang, or 'Camorrista'. The Camorra itself is the oldest organised criminal organisation in Italy.

Garrone met Daly after he had fled to Dublin when he was named in the murder of a local priest, Father Benedict Capello, in Naples due to him exposing a sex trafficking ring in the city. Daly explained to Moran that his brother was very fond of Garrone because he swore by the 'Omertà' or, in English, a code of silence, and Moran was to take him in under his wing on that recommendation alone. The thing that must be remembered is that criminal gangs are a business and just like many, many businesses across the world, criminals also network and this was a perfect opportunity for Moran to expand his contacts within Europe and this was the perfect man to aid him.

The fifth new member was Stephen Trimble but this was not just any member of the gang as Stephen Trimble was covered in secrecy and deceit. For this, we must go back to 16 August 2005 when all hell was breaking loose across Dublin and shortly after the murders of Robbie Kennedy and Martin O'Neill, Justice Minister O'Connor contacted D'Arcy privately on his mobile phone. At eight o' clock that evening, Inspector D'Arcy went to the Dáil for a meeting in the Minister's private chambers.

'Inspector D'Arcy, thank you for coming on such short notice, please do come in.'

'Thank you, Minister, so what can I do for you, sir?'

'Okay, this Moran thing—'

D'Arcy interrupted, 'Look Sir, we are on it—'

'Hold on, Inspector, will you just listen to me, just listen to me please. The reason I called you in is that I want a man on the inside and I feel the time is right to try and infiltrate the gang.'

D'Arcy was caught off guard and did not agree with the Minister as it was not only going to be difficult to get a man on the inside but it was also a danger to the life of the person sent in.

'Look Minister, do you really think this is a good idea? No offence meant, Sir, but you sit behind a desk and do constituency cases and sign bills, this is real life and these gangsters take no messing, Sir!'

'Point taken and I completely take on-board your concerns, do you honestly think I made a snap decision on this, Inspector?'

'No Sir, of course not, but—'

'I respect the loyalty you have to all your men but it's going to happen so find my man, Inspector, oh and one thing, I want a single man with no ties.'

'Okay, okay, but there is one thing I must insist on, Sir.'

'And that is, Inspector?'

'That for this to work properly, we need to keep this information within this room, nobody and Sir, I mean nobody else can now about this, it's for the best. I mean, Minister, just the two of us in this room, not even the Comm—nobody, it's for the best and the absolute safety of our man.'

O'Connor duly agreed and under orders from the Minister, D'Arcy combed through the service and family records of Gardaí from the length and breadth of the country for a number of days. D'Arcy genuinely did worry about his men and he was not just going to put some undercover agent in the field to keep the Minister for Justice happy, he was going to take his time to make the correct decision. Over the next few weeks, D'Arcy travelled across the country interviewing a total of five members of the Gardaí, telling them the position was as a researcher within Harcourt Terrace, the Garda Special Investigation Unit's headquarters so as not to stir any unwanted suspicion.

After weeks of painstaking research, D'Arcy felt that he had found the right man and that man was 25-year-old Garda Shaun Ryan. Ryan came from a quiet farming background in the small village of Gweedore in County Donegal in the far most corner of North West Ireland and had graduated from the Garda College in Templemore, County Tipperary, in October 2002, qualifying with an average score, nothing exceptional.

From Templemore, Ryan was stationed to a small rural community station in County Mayo where he remained until the day that Inspector D'Arcy came looking for him. It was not his average Garda records or family life that caught D'Arcy's eye but it was his painstaking work carried out in the quiet West of Ireland Garda station that interested the wily inspector.

After a brief meeting and saying no more than needed to the young Garda, D'Arcy returned to Dublin for a meeting with the Minister for Justice. Moran explained to Minister O'Connor that Ryan was the ideal man to infiltrate the Moran gang.

'He is no Super Cop, that's for sure but he has a perfect record so I firmly believe he can be trusted, but the really interesting thing about Garda Ryan is that he has also been part of a research unit for our special gang surveillance team that tracked the Moran gang. All this before Operation Downfall had even come into effect, he had been tracking them.'

'Go on, Inspector.'

'Yes, it's true, Minister, Ryan did all of his research from his post in Mayo while never meeting any of the other members of my team, he knows the Moran gang inside out and another bonus for us is that he is also unknown to the Operation Downfall members, so he is ideal. I mean, he knows everything about this gang and he could spot each and every one of them without actually meeting them in person. This lad even knows what they drink, he has done so much background on them. For fuck sakes, we actually got some of our intel from this fella.'

'Holy shit, Inspector, we have our man, we have our man. Okay, so let's do it. Thank fuck for quiet rural stations.'

On 9 November 2005, Inspector D'Arcy once again contacted Garda Shaun Ryan at his Mayo Station, telling him he wanted to meet up while making it abundantly clear he was to tell nobody where he was going or who he was meeting with. Ryan agreed and a few days after the contact, a meeting was arranged for 14 November.

D'Arcy asked Ryan to meet him in the Cork Arms hotel located in Cork City Centre on the banks of the River Lee at 6 pm. D'Arcy explained that he need not worry as everything had been sorted with his superiors who had been contacted from the Commissioner's office telling them that he was called to Dublin to give a briefing on the data he had gathered in relation to the Moran gang. D'Arcy continued to explain that on arrival in Cork, he would explain everything to him but again also cautiously said that he was not to mention the meeting in Cork City to anyone, including his family, friends or Garda superiors; again, Ryan agreed.

On the morning of 14 November 2005, Shaun Ryan took a plane from Knock airport in Mayo directly into Cork City. It was just an hour before he left Mayo that D'Arcy once again contacted Ryan, explaining that he was to find room 214 on the second floor of the hotel. At 6.03 pm, full of apprehension and nerves, Garda Shaun Ryan knocked on the door of Room 214 and D'Arcy opened it and welcomed him in. In the hotel room, D'Arcy went straight to the point and explained to Ryan why he asked to see him in Cork.

'We need you to work as an undercover officer to infiltrate the Thomas Moran gang. Are you the man for this job, Shaun?'

'Who me, Inspector?'

'Look, I understand that this is completely out of the blue but we need to act and act fast, if you want time…' questioned D'Arcy, full of hope that the answer he wanted to hear was about to come his way.

After a momentary pause, Ryan with his head bowing to the floor in deep thought, looked D'Arcy in the eye. 'This is not going to be a problem, Inspector.

'Excellent, Shaun, excellent,' replied a delighted Inspector as he shook the young Garda's hand. 'Right, so let's get down to business, shall we? We have a lot of work and detail to get through so have a seat, Shaun. We have carefully arranged your cover, you got yourself involved in a weapons smuggling ring with Republican paramilitaries in 2000, the Real IRA, in fact, so you're anti-Good Friday Agreement and everything that goes with that.'

'Not a problem, sir.'

'So your story is that the operation went wrong and you got yourself arrested and because of this, you were locked up in England for four and a half years in Belmarsh Prison. You were released in May of this year, so you are not long out and looking for work.

'Perfect, Sir.'

'Now we have also got you in contact with an informant of ours named Paddy Bird who works in the North Inner City close to members of the old Redser Daly crew. He is your way in as Daly's men are, as we have gathered, now working with the Moran gang. Bird cannot be fully trusted but he is our only inlet to the Moran gang.'

'Sounds good, Inspector.'

'I have done a lot of background work on this so your path has already been laid into the Daly crew; it's up to you to make that final step to earn their trust, Shaun.'

'Understand, Sir.'

'Okay, now Bird has already been briefed and he will get you in contact with members of the Redser Daly gang and from here, we hope that you can infiltrate them. But make no mistake; your aim is to get information back to me on Thomas Moran when possible but your main aim is to get into the circles that Moran hangs out in.'

'Got you, Sir.'

'Good man, I want you to report to me and only me; is that clear, nobody and I fucking mean nobody, knows anything about this.'

'Crystal clear, Inspector, I'll say nothing.'

'I've noticed already you are a man of few words,' joked D'Arcy at the young man's quick but short replies.

'Look, I understand fully that you know the workings of this group inside out, Shaun, but do not get cocky around them and do not tell them things you should not know or slip up with your name, remember you don't know any of them to see, so don't call them by name until introduced, you must stay focussed all the time and never relax around these scumbags. Again, I must state this that

Bird is an informant so he cannot be trusted, he would sell his own granny for a few quid.'

'No problem, Sir, I understand fully.'

'Okay, good man, now you're meeting with Paddy Bird in the Stork Bar on Dorset Street on Dublin's Northside in four days' time; that's 18 November at 5 pm. You will be going under the alias Stephen Trimble and, we have rented a two-bed apartment for you on Ardee Street right in the heart of the Liberties. Now I have also provided a false profile for you on the Garda system that includes your membership of an illegal organisation, time spent inside on weapons charges and other charges added to your criminal record, so if the Moran crew come looking, you are officially in the system. Right, so that's it from me, I think.'

With those words, D'Arcy handed over an envelope to Ryan. 'Okay son, make sure you read the contents of this envelope as it contains all your new details along with your key for the apartment, the address, of course, a new driver's licence, passport and mobile phone. You also have bank account details in there with the bank card, pin number and account number. Now you have twenty grand in it so do not go fucking mad on it, okay?'

'Yes Sir, I understand.'

'Buy clothes but nothing flashy; you're only just out, remember; also, I am in the phone under the alias of Uncle Jimmy and finally, you have a photo of Paddy Bird, memorise the face and burn the photo, you do not want it left about if any of the gang visit you at home. So best of luck, son, and be careful. Remember, report to me and only me. Oh, one more thing, we are not sure if Moran knows about Delaney working with the dissident group, so say fuck all about that but keep an ear open if it's mentioned.'

'Will do, sir, lucky you said that as I only got that report very recently so was in the dark about that part.'

'Jesus, lucky I said it, fuck, have I given you everything? I'm sure I have but remember, play dumb; you know fuck all.' D'Arcy turned and started to leave the room when he called out, 'Stephen!'

'Yes, my man, do I know you?'

'Good lad.' D'Arcy then shut the door behind him, leaving Stephen Trimble to work out his plan.

Chapter 26
Milan

It had just turned 5 pm on a cool dark November night when Paddy Bird met with Stephen Trimble at The Stork Pub on Dorset Street as previously planned. Once inside the bar, Trimble began scanning the room, noticing many familiar faces from his days in the research unit. Bird introduced him to many of Dublin's hardened gangsters but his heart skipped a beat when Bird introduced him to none other than the cold-blooded killer, Frankie McCann.

'Frankie, this is my man, Stephen.'

'So you're the man Paddy tells me about?'

'I guess I am and you are?'

'Frankie, Frankie McCann. So culchie, do you want a gargle or what?'

'Culchie?'

'Well, ye fuckin are, aren't ye?'

'Well, no, I'm a Donegal man.'

'Yeah, a culchie.'

'Well, yes, I guess I am. Okay, so go on then, Frankie I'll have a Carlsberg.'

And it was as easy as that; Trimble was now in the circle as the word of any friend was good enough. Trimble's first outing with the gang came days after the shooting of 'Pudner' Smyth as he was invited to the funeral that took place in Mount Jerome Cemetery in Harold's Cross. The South Inner City came to a standstill such was the security that surrounded the day as the funeral party was joined by a very heavy Garda presence.

After the burial, the funeral party headed back to Moran's local, The Black Horse on Cork Street, which was still under the watchful eye of An Garda Síochána. Trimble wanted to get close to Moran to introduce himself but such was the security around him that it was next to impossible.

As the day wore on, Moran was about to receive news that would both interest and worry him when an Inner City heroin addict named Marko Diugnan wanted to talk.

'Tommy, this junkie scum wants to talk to you about something important so he tells me.'

'Not interested, Frankie. Fuck off!'

'No Tommy, serious, I have sometin to tell ye. It's really important.'

'Will you get that junkie cunt out of here!'

As Frankie dragged Diugnan away, he called out, 'Tommy, I know who shot Pudner and Redser!'

'What did you fuckin say! Frankie, bring that cunt out here to me.'

Once out of the bar and in the confines of his office, Moran questioned Duignan, 'Now tell me where did you hear this, ye junkie cunt?'

'On the streets, Tommy, on the streets, cause ye know how it is, I heard these boys talkin, ye know, so I came straight here, yeah? Ye know what I mean, Tommy? It was Micky Donnelly who done them both. Delaney got him to do it.'

Moran stood silent for a moment and then turned to Diugnan and said, 'Okay, fuck off.'

'Sound, Tommy, see ye right. Remember I told ye so if ye need me again yeah. Here, Tommy, any gear on ye?'

'Get the fuck out!'

What Moran or Delaney did not know was that Diugnan had been given heroin for passing over the information having had a chance meeting with one of Delaney's gang members, Stewie Carroll. Diugnan had met him in the north Inner City when Carroll was visiting a local prostitute who owed him some money. Carroll had it in his head that he could someday take over the city and felt that if he could stir up some more bad blood between Delaney and Moran, both gangs would continue to take each other out, so with both gang leaders gone, he could have an easy path to becoming top man.

After Diugnan left the bar, Moran called Frankie McCann, Noel Slattery, Tony Rothwell and Joe Daly into the back room to inform them that both Delaney and Donnelly were working together and it was them who had murdered Redser and Pudner.

'It kinda makes sense, now look lads, we fuckin knew Delaney done both Redser and Pudner, we knew that, but Donnelly involved? Ye know, does it make sense that those two cunts would be working together?' half-questioned a clearly irritated Moran.

'It certainly makes sense, Tommy, it certainly does, remember Valentine's and being told by that fella in Belfast they were fucked out of the IRPP?' remarked Rothwell as Moran, hands on hips looking to the ground, nodded in acknowledgement.

'So what do we do now?' asked Slattery.

'We stay on plan and we now take both of these cunts down. But we play dumb as if we know nothing about them working with each other. Frankie, I need you to go make sure our junkie friend never tells a soul that we know what's going on with Delaney and Donnelly.'

'Understand, Tommy.' And it was at that moment that innocent heroin addict Marko Diugnan's death warrant had just been signed for the passing on of information for a few scores of heroin.

Following on from the information Moran received from Diugnan, he and his top men agreed to arrange a meeting with Seamus Delaney but keeping the information they now had close to their chests. The reasoning behind the meeting was that Moran wanted Delaney to believe he was citing peace talks. Moran had spoken in private with Noel Slattery and Tony Rothwell about the proposed meeting and they all agreed to arrange it but due to the massive Garda crackdown, Dublin or anywhere in Ireland was not safe to meet.

It was to be three weeks later on 6 December 2005, both gang leaders agreed that they would meet up in the Italian city of Milan. But for Moran, a truce was far from what he wanted out of the meet and the famous Italian city was about to meet Irish gangland head on.

At 10.43 am on 6 December 2005, Moran, along with Noel Slattery and Tony Rothwell, flew out of Belfast City airport direct to Milan's Malpensa Airport arriving into terminal two after a two-hour flight. The three men hailed a taxi as they started towards the city centre located twenty-nine miles from the airport. The men checked into the Hotel Da Vinci in the heart of Milan's Navigli area or "the Venice of Lombardy", which is part of the ancient canal system that served Milan.

Seamus Delaney had arrived a day earlier along with Timmy Kelly, Micky Donnelly and Tony Dunne and had booked into the Capitol Hotel close to Milan's Duomo, the world's largest collection of marble statues along with the famous golden Little Madonna statue. Of course, not one of the men registered under their real names.

That same day, 6 December, Moran sent word to Delaney through one of the Milan-based Camorra crew, one Giuseppe Montello. Montello was a close acquaintance of Philippe Garrone and was a very senior figure of the organisation that ran all operations in Milan so when he got the call to help his friend, he agreed to contact Delaney without any questions as to why they were in Milan. It was 11.55 am on a bright but chilly Milanese morning when Montello arrived at the Capitol Hotel; he headed straight into the bar area where he found Delaney with Kelly, Donnelly and Dunne sitting in the exact spot Montello had asked to be met.

'Buon giorno Mr Delaney and friends, it's good to see you.' Montello shook hands with all four men and as he started to sit down, Delaney looked the exceptionally well-dressed man from head to toe.

'And buon giorno to you too, bud,' Delaney replied in a poor Hollywood-style Italian accent. 'So who the fuck are you then?'

'I am the man to arrange this meeting between you and Mr Moran, are we okay with this?'

'Yes, yes, we are good. So when and where?'

'A tempo debito, Mr Delaney, all in good time, relax, gentlemen, enjoy Milano. Come have some wine with me, *Capocameriere bottiglia di vino!*' (Waiter, a bottle of wine.)

Montello was talking about the weather, football and just about any random issue for an hour and a half and two bottles of wine later, Delaney ran out of patience with Montello and asked him, 'So this meeting, Mr Montello, where and when?'

'Okay, okay. Tomorrow at 8 pm and you will have to take a cab to get to the meeting place. You will be meeting in Vineyard restaurant in the Navigli area of the city so remember the name, Mr Delaney.'

'The Navigli, I will remember.'

'So shall I tell my man that you will be there?

'Yeah, yeah, tell that cunt I'll be there.'

'*È cattiva educazione tirarsi indietro all'ultimo momento*, Mr Delaney.' (It is bad form to back out at the last minute, Mr Delaney.)

'Speak fuckin English, will ye, for Jaysus sake.'

Montello changed his tone and looked into Delaney's eyes and told him, 'Just make sure you're there, Mr Delaney.'

'Look, just fuckin let Moran know I'll be there.'

'Okay, at the Vineyard restaurant, 8 pm. Do not forget, the Navigli area.'

'Yes, the Navigli, Vineyard restaurant, don't you worry. I will be there.'

'*Arrivederci*, Mr Delaney.' Montello stood up and left the bar, never to be seen again.

It was 6.45 pm on a freezing cold Milan night as the time was rapidly approaching for the arranged meeting when Thomas Moran, Noel Slattery and Tony Rothwell all departed their hotel and met up with Philippe Garrone, Frankie McCann and Dennis Scully. All three men had arrived in Milan on separate flights via Amsterdam, Dublin and London earlier that day.

As pre-arranged, Philippe Garrone had already collected a parcel from Giuseppe Montello at Milan's Central train station, or Milano Centrale. The parcel consisted of four Glock-17 19mm model handguns for the unsuspecting Delaney who was about to walk into an ambush that he had never expected in his wildest dreams; thinking that there was no way in hell Moran would ever try anything in Milan.

Moran and his gang arrived at the Navigli but did not go inside the Vineyard restaurant as arranged; instead, they took positions in wait for Delaney while hidden within the shadows of Milan. At the end of the street, Rothwell and Slattery waited in the getaway cars, keeping the engines running as Moran, Garrone, Scully and McCann lay in wait for their foes to arrive. At 8.07 pm, Moran's heart skipped a beat when he spotted Seamus Delaney approaching with Timmy Kelly, Micky Donnelly and Tony Dunne.

When all four men were walking through the narrow street only one hundred yards from the Vineyard restaurant, Moran stepped out from the shadows and pointed his gun at Delaney, who froze with fright,

'Goodnight, Seamus, you cunt,' whispered Moran and within a second, Seamus Delaney was shot by a single bullet to the head and he died instantly in the narrow Milanese street. McCann opened his chamber on Tony Dunne who died suffering from gunshots to the neck, torso and the fatal bullet that went straight through his skull, killing him instantly while Dennis Scully's gun jammed as he was about to pull the trigger on Micky Donnelly. Kelly was hit by Garonne's gunshot in the shoulder and chest and hit the ground as the bullets passed through his body but he would recover from his wounds. Donnelly, knowing he got lucky, ran and dived into the nearby canal taking cover away from the attack.

'Fuck that, let him off, we've gotta get the fuck outta here now so come on boys, move!' ordered Moran.

Donnelly, not taking any more chances, made his way to his hotel and quickly changed his clothes and headed straight back to Dublin by road, travelling through France to catch the Eurotunnel Shuttle via the Channel Tunnel and on to Britain away from the watchful eyes of the Italian authorities. On his return, he quickly alerted the rest of the gang. Moran's plan had worked out well as he had now taken out his greatest rival and his right-hand man but there was still work to be done to completely rid Dublin of all his rivals and that was just what he was planning to do.

Within hours of the assassinations, Moran fled to meet up with his wife Jean who was still residing in Spain while his men were all back home in Dublin the next morning as Irish TV and radio aired the news of the attack in Milan reporting:

'According to the Milanese police, masked men walked into the street in the Navigli area of Milan last night at around 7 pm Irish time and fired a number of shots, killing two men instantly while another man is in a critical condition. Both of the men are well-known Irish criminal figures from Dublin and the assassins are thought to be professional hitmen who escaped the scene before the alarm could be raised.

'Italian Police say they are studying more CCTV footage from the street and general area but so far, they have failed to identify any of the killers. Senior Gardaí in Dublin fear that this could be a revenge killing for the murder of gangland figure Brian 'Pudner' Smyth only a few weeks earlier.'

After Delaney's death, his gang fragmented for a time until ex-IRPP man Kelly and other dissident Republicans joined forces with the remaining members of Delaney's crew and swore revenge on Moran. Stewie Carroll, Terry O'Keeffe, Derek O'Neill, William 'Willow' Ryan, Tony Fox, Mickey Naughton and Ian 'Bouncer' Howe all signed up to support their new boss as did Micky Donnelly, his brother Gary Donnelly, Paddy Gallagher, John McDaid and Billy Masterson who all agreed to stay on board and bring down the Moran gang.

Once again, Moran and his gang gave a two-fingered salute to the system but this time there was going to be payback, D'Arcy had his trump card ready to play and he hoped Moran was about to lose this all-important hand.

Chapter 27
In the Dock

It was in the small hours of 1 January 2006 on the biggest party night of the year as the Garda Special Unit were making a move on Noel Slattery's brothel on Benburb Street. It was at 3 am when members of Operation Downfall led by Inspector D'Arcy raided the building, finding what D'Arcy called 'a den of debauchery and filth' that was filled with sex, drugs, underage prostitutes and drug addicts working to feed their habits. To D'Arcy's delight, the operation was a success as 22 people were arrested in the raid along with the seizure of four kilos of cocaine but to D'Arcy, it was somewhat frustrating as there was no Slattery present that night.

What was to frustrate and humour D'Arcy even more was when the Investigation Unit tried to pin the brothel ownership on Slattery, they discovered that the building was cheekily registered under the name of the Minister for Justice, John O'Connor TD. On receiving that information, D'Arcy nodded and gave a wry grin at the brazen act the gang showed but he was not finished, not by a long shot; if Moran thought 2005 was bad, 2006 was about to put it firmly into second place.

On 10 January 2006, two days after Moran returned home from Spain, D'Arcy arrested him in his Crumlin home on drug smuggling offences. Also arrested were Noel Slattery and Frankie McCann but both men were soon released from Garda custody without charge when evidence against them failed to materialise. For D'Arcy and Minister O'Connor, they were happy enough to try and get the one conviction they wanted—Thomas 'Little Don' Moran.

D'Arcy knew that the Dean Coyle court case was finally approaching and he also knew that Moran had heard nothing true in relation to circumstances that surrounded the aftermath of the Coleman and Coyle arrest. The State was ready to go after its biggest gangland figure and they wanted a conviction, no matter what, with Dean Coyle the jewel in the State's crown.

D'Arcy was well aware that Moran did not know about the incorrect information funnelled down to Tony Rothwell that Coyle had been put under the Witness Protection Programme. All that Moran was aware of was that Coyle had turned state witness against him but the actual fact was, as stated before, Coyle had never spoken to the Gardaí and he had never gotten the word that he was to meet up in Limerick for a clear-the-air meeting with Thomas Moran.

Instead, he went to Galway on a holiday with his girlfriend to get away from the troubles he had in Dublin. Moran was also unaware that D'Arcy, learning of the mix-up in information, had sent word to Dean Coyle telling him that he now had a one-million-euro price on his head because Moran thought he had ratted him out.

The information D'Arcy gave to Coyle about the hit was in part true because the order to take him out by Moran came long after his meeting with D'Arcy. Again, Coyle did not know the order was given under the ill-informed knowledge that he had turned on Moran, thus sending Coyle into the open arms of D'Arcy. Under the threat of assassination, he went into hiding and there was no way D'Arcy was going to tell Coyle about the mix-up in communication as the possible downfall of Moran was too close on the horizon to mess anything up. All D'Arcy could do was hope Coyle would never find out how sloppy the Moran operation was as crossed wires and people not carrying out their duties put him on the stand to take down Moran, and D'Arcy was happy to keep it that way.

D'Arcy, not wanting anything to go wrong, frantically worked around the clock to make sure all the paperwork was in order and that his men knew their jobs off by heart, knowing all too well that this was his big chance to finally get his man. Everything had to be one hundred percent accurate including times, dates, surveillance documents and much more.

To D'Arcy's delight, the justice Minister went one step more by adding another string in the bow of 'Operation Downfall' when the Department of Justice was to oversee the introduction of the assets-seizure legislation that could seize goods and property gained by illegal means. Along with this was the use of new legislation that was established a few years previous, called the Criminal Assets Bureau, otherwise known as CAB. This all was to be another giant step for D'Arcy's taking down of Moran as the Criminal Assets Bureau was to be the major armour in the government's and Gardaí's overall plans as they were now legally permitted to gain access into their financial networks in Ireland but also, thanks to European law, they could access accounts abroad.

CAB was established in August of 1996 but was given full statutory powers on 15 October that same year under the Criminal Assets Bureau Act 1996. In addition to CAB, there is the European Bureau know as Europol, Europe's criminal intelligence agency, that became fully operational on 1 July 1999. The agency started limited operations on 3 January 1994, as the Europol Drugs Unit or the EDU but was now a major international crime unit fighting serious gangland figures from across Europe and it was from here that D'Arcy could obtain the information on Moran's European operations.

Meanwhile in London Magistrate Court, George Mayweather was given a seven-year sentence for the importation of illegal drugs, thanks to Charlie Butterfield when he was arrested in London while trying to board a flight to Amsterdam with a briefcase full of money totalling £330,000 and two kilos of pure Columbian cocaine that he carried by hand. As Mayweather faced a seven-year stretch in Wormwood Scrubs prison, back in Ireland, Slattery and some of Moran's men listened as the early morning news led with the story in relation to Thomas Little Don Moran. 'Right lads, shut the fuck up,' screeched Slattery.

'Good morning, it is 8.00 am on Wednesday, 4 February. This morning's headlines are:

'The trial of a Dublin man known as Thomas 'Little Don' Moran will open today in the Four Courts and it will be surrounded by massive security due to the recent spate of murders across the city.

'Mr Moran is on trial for drug trafficking offences including importation with intent to sell, multiple murder charges and being the leading member of one of Ireland's leading gangland outfits.'

The newsreader continued:

'Today will see the start of the trial in Dublin's Four Courts involving Thomas Moran, who is believed to be the leading figure in one of Ireland's criminal underworld gangs. Mr Moran from Crumlin in Dublin is accused of running a massive drug dealing operation in Ireland over the last number of years and is also being questioned in relation to his involvement in more than ten murders in an ongoing vicious Dublin feud. Additional charges including his alleged involvement in money laundering, prostitution and fraud are to be put to the judge.

'State witness Dean Coyle who is an ex-member of the alleged Moran gang had been put under the Witness Protection Programme after his arrest in a sting operation by members of the Specialist Unit known as Operation Downfall. 36-year-old Thomas Moran has pleaded not guilty to all charges. The trial is expected to last at least a month and Thomas Moran is due in court at 11 am today.'

'Coyle, you're a dead man, you fuckin rat cunt! Fucking cunts, the lot of them,' roared Slattery as he sat and watched the news unfold on the TV.

Later that day, Moran's uncle Seamy Conroy sat with Moran's mother Marie and his wife Jean in the court awaiting his arrival into the courthouse having spent the night on remand in Mountjoy Prison.

'Court is now in session,' called out the bailiff.

In charge of the trial was 63-year-old Justice Dermot Conlon and as he took his seat, he began to speak directly to the jury:

'The State is relying on hard evidence, not circumstantial or hearsay. So that means we cannot be influenced by the media carnival that surrounds this trial so no adverse interferences should be drawn against Thomas Moran, nor could we speculate on what answers the prosecution might have anticipated from such witnesses.'

Moran just sat and listened with care as the judge continued:

'The issue on all matters for the State is to be one hundred percent clear that you are under no doubt in your mind that this man who has is accused of running a massive drug dealing operation in Ireland over the last number of years and also his accused involvement in more than ten murders, money laundering, prostitution and fraud is indeed fact. So be clear, be very clear that you are in no uncertain terms that the man standing in front of you, Thomas Moran, is either guilty or not guilty by only listening to the evidence given in this court and only from this court.'

So it was made very clear to the jurors that a jury's role is not to make the law but to uphold the laws that have already been made. The judge told them that while making decisions about a case, a jury must follow the precedent set by the law society with respect to the situation and conditions of the case presented in front of them to stand by and include the common law in statutory law but still relating to the original principles created. The same rules were also put to both the prosecution and defence due to the interest in the case before them.

Firstly, fighting the case for the State was the State Prosecutor Damien McIntyre while Moran had Diarmuid Corrigan to fight his corner. Moran knew that the Garda Síochána Special Unit had only the word of Dean Coyle against him and that they had to sell this to the jury. On the other side of this judicial coin, D'Arcy knew that Coyle was not the best witness due to his involvement in the gang and knowing all too well that Corrigan would go right after him when in the witness box, citing him as a liar who was only trying to help his own case.

Justice Dermot Conlon called for the opening statements from both parties and first up was State Prosecutor McIntyre: 'The accused Thomas Moran is part of an investigation led by a special Garda unit in conjunction with the Criminal Assets Bureau into drug trafficking by major drug gangs across Ireland. Yes indeed, Mr Thomas Moran, also known as 'Little Don', was arrested under these charges and taken to Crumlin Garda station, where he was held under the Criminal Justice Drug Trafficking Act of 1996.'

The Criminal Assets Bureau believes that Mr Moran has spearheaded the importation of tonnes of illegal drugs and laundered millions of euros of drug money in Ireland and across Europe and beyond over the last decade. Now Mr Moran pleaded not guilty to a total of 23 charges, which included twelve charges of drug smuggling and six charges for firearms smuggling dated from October 1998 to September 2005. Another key figure in this gang who continues the money laundering and drug smuggling side of Mr Moran's operations is a known Dutch contact (Dirk Van Der Beek) who we cannot name for legal reasons but make no mistake, this contact has kept up Thomas Moran's method of drug importation and other dealings such as betting on horse races and other sporting events, placing huge amounts of monies on these. This Dutch contact since the arrest of Mr Moran has disappeared off the radar and we believe he is in hiding somewhere in Europe. Mr Moran's gang is international and this is why I'm highlighting his European contact—'

'Objection, Your Honour, this man is unknown and has no actual link to my client. The right honourable gentleman cannot even name him; is he real?'

'Sustained; stick to Mr Moran and not any phantom associates you may want to bring up.'

'Indeed, Your Honour. You will also hear during this trial that Thomas Moran has pleaded not guilty to the murder of one Mr Andrew Russell on 20 September 1998. He also denied receiving shipments from a shipping trawler named *The Spirit of St Christopher* on dates in March 2005, July 2004, January

2002, February 2000 and April of 2000; all information has been presented from the man who moved the drugs for Mr Moran, a Mr Dean Coyle. We will present evidence to you over the coming days and weeks to prove that Thomas Moran is the leading figure in Ireland's underworld and Thomas Moran is a man who cares for nobody and nothing and he must be brought to justice. Thank you.'

Diarmuid Corrigan then opened by saying, 'The investigation unit has now turned gang members and associates into government witnesses just before they were about to be indicted for serious crimes that would see them put away for a very long time; interesting, wouldn't you think? My client Thomas Moran was an easy target for Mr Coyle to get time off under the Witness Protection Programme. Of course, it is so because Mr Dean Coyle, right after his arrest for drug smuggling offences on 3 June 2004, became a Garda informer. Mr Dean Coyle is all too aware of the art of informing on others to save his own neck because he saw a way out of having been caught with a huge amount of drugs and that way out was my client, Mr Thomas Moran.'

'Careful where you are going with this, Mr Corrigan, let us remember that Mr Coyle is not on trial here,' warned a stern but cautious Justice Conlon while giving Corrigan a wry look over his spectacles.

'I was just making a point, Your Honour, and as my illustrious colleague also stated, there is a ghost ship named *The Spirit of St Christopher*! Now the funny thing is, in his statement Mr Coyle clearly on a number of occasions told the Gardaí that he did not know any of the crew nor did he know any of their names. Odd, do you not think?' Corrigan played the jury and the room, waving his arms in the air in a way to say, *really*.

'Now in addition, what my colleague also failed to inform you, the jury, about is that this boat is not registered in any European port, so am I wrong in saying that the defence is actually rendering Coyle's statement as fictitious and only trying to blacken Mr Moran?' Again, Corrigan, arms out wide, looked across the room.

'Right okay, you may ask, am I making this up? Well, ladies and gentlemen of the jury, let me tell you this; right here on my desk I even have a report from Interpol about this phantom drugs ship. Yes, Interpol, the International Police Force, stating that they have no records of any such ship, boat, whatever you want to call it because it is not real. I leave that thought with you, the jurors. Thank you for your time.'

Corrigan completely dismissed the State's argument about the ship as the report from Interpol buried that. As the trial wore on, Damien McIntyre continued to stack the evidence against Moran and all Moran could do was sit and listen as McIntyre called his first witness. With his face covered so to hide his identity, Mr Jack Collins from the Financial Regulators Office in conjunction with the Criminal Assets Bureau took the stand.

'Mr Collins, can you please explain the reason why you are an expert witness here today to the court, please?'

'Yes sir, I can, I am a financial expert and a member of the CAB team.'

'So a financial expert in illegal moving of funds in Ireland and can you explain why you are here?'

'Yes, I am and the reasoning for my evidence is that in May of 1995, a piece of legislation was produced where under the law, all financial institutions including banks and building societies were obliged to report anything they considered to be suspicious activity in a bank account to the Gardaí. But the bank officials did not have to inform the customer that they had reported the activity to Gardaí. They were, however, legally obliged to make a suspicious transaction report if anything unusual was happening in an account.'

McIntyre continued to question the witness, 'But what has this got to do with Thomas Moran, Mr Collins?'

Collins explained, 'A bank official noticed at the Lucan branch of the AIB that the account of one Mrs Jean Moran had an enormous amount of money put through it over a short period of time and took it on to investigate it. The level of activity in the account of the woman puzzled the bank official because her only source of income had been disability benefit arising out of an insurance claim following an accident in 1995. Yet, up to one million euros in cash lodgements had moved through the account over the previous year.'

McIntyre cut in, 'One million euros on a disability benefit! That is an awful lot of money, don't you think, Mr Collins?'

'Yes, yes, it is and we agreed that a suspicious transaction report on Mrs Jean Moran's bank account would be forwarded to the Garda Bureau of Fraud Investigation after it was flagged by the bank.'

'And what came from this investigation?'

'Gardaí ascertained that Jean Moran was married to Thomas Moran, the man whom they expected to be Ireland's number one drug trafficker.'

'Objection, Your Honour, he is not an expert on the case and is being led by the prosecution.'

'Sustained, keep to your witness's level of expertise please, Mr Collins. The jury will disregard Mr Collins' last statement. Please continue but only about the bank account.'

'Yes, Your Honour.'

'Please continue.'

'By September 2005, members of the Garda fraud squad had held a meeting with the Garda National Drugs Unit as they came to the conclusion there could be few sources for such a large amount of cash.'

'So what you are saying, Mr Collins, is that you can see no other reason for this large amount of cash going into the account other than illegalities of which Thomas Moran was involved?'

'Mr McIntyre, I'm warning you; stop leading the witness and the jury.'

'Apologies, Your Honour, and thank you, Mr Collins, I am finished with my witness.'

'Mr Corrigan, have you got any questions for the witness?'

'Yes, yes, I do, Your Honour, yes I…do,' replied Corrigan.

'Mr Collins, may I take this opportunity to thank you for taking the time to come here today. I have just two quick questions for you.'

'That is fine by me, Mr Corrigan.'

'Thank you. Now this money you speak of, was it under the name of Jean or Thomas Moran?'

Collins paused. 'Well, it was not—'

Corrigan cut across and again asked the question, 'I will ask you again, Mr Collins. This money you speak of, was it under the name of Jean or Thomas Moran?'

'Jean Moran, it was under the name of Jean Moran,' answered a clearly disheartened Collins.

Corrigan now with a more stern tone to his voice, 'So what you found in this bank account was nothing to do with Thomas Moran, Mr Collins?'

'No, it was not proven that the money was directly linked to Thomas Moran but only to his wife Jean.'

'Thank you, Mr Collins. The defence will rest, Your Honour.'

The testimony of Collins and the lack of evidence of *The Spirit of St Christopher* had backfired on the State and round one went to Thomas Moran but round two was going to be a lot tougher. Even though he was held on remand, he was not going to take things on the chin while sitting in a cell.

Chapter 28
A Woman Scorned

It was now March 2006 and the trial continued, to Moran's annoyance, at a very slow pace as he listened to pretty much the same evidence being presented day by day. For him, the one tiny bit of comfort he took from all this was that the media focus had simmered down somewhat for now and he had a small bit of freedom on entering and exiting the courts, but this solitude would soon come to an end. On 5 March, during the case, Moran found out that he was soon to face down another media onslaught as the State prosecution was getting ready to call to the stand their number one witness—Dean Coyle.

Coyle had been hidden away in protective custody and had not been in court for the hearing at all thus far but this was all about to change as he would soon come face to face with his old gang boss. Over the next few days for the first time since his arrest for possession of drugs, Coyle would be in the public eye, and for once, the State had Moran rattled but for a man like Thomas Moran, he was not going down without an almighty fight.

A couple of weeks previous to the news of Coyle's imminent appearance, while inside the courthouse and away from the media, Diarmuid Corrigan pulled Moran aside. 'If, now I'm saying if, this boat, *The Spirit of St Christopher* was real, I would get rid of it. And I mean yesterday, understand, Thomas?'

'Understood, but look, while I have you here, Diarmuid, I need you to do me a favour.'

'A favour?'

'Yes, I need you to get in contact with Tony Rothwell—'

'What! Tony Rothwell? Are you out of your bloody mind, Thomas, I'm a man of the law. I can't be contacting one of the biggest drug smugglers in Europe—'

'Shut the fuck up and listen to me, you took our money without question, you know who we fucking are so stop with this holier than fuckin thou bollox. Now this is Tony's number, call him and arrange to meet up.'

'And tell him what?'

'To sort out this fuckin problem we have with Coyle and soon. Money is not an object so tell him to do what it takes.'

'Thomas, I can't be part—'

'Fuckin do it and also tell him to sink the lady. Clear.'

'Thomas, for heavens sake, I can't—'

'You can and you fuckin well will.'

Corrigan, beginning to sweat and trying to catch his breath, agreed, 'Okay, okay, shit!'

'Good man, it's not that I do not trust you not to get me off but ye know, no loose ends. You understand?'

'Oh yes, I understand. I understand all too well, that's the bloody problem.'

Three days later, after a brief call from a disposable phone, a nervous and reluctant Corrigan met up with Tony Rothwell in the Welsh capital city of Cardiff and passed on all the information he had received from Moran. Unknown to the authorities, Rothwell had swiftly sent word to Ibiza to have *The Spirit of St Christopher* disposed of.

On 21 February 2006, Danny Moore received a call from Tony Rothwell.

'Sink the old lady now, it's too hot.'

Within hours of the phone call, the crew of *The Spirit of St Christopher*, Captain Mark Lowe, Edmund 'Eddie' Baxter, Casper Von Bommell, Terry McLaughlin and Danny Higgins, sailed two boats—*The Spirit of St Christopher* and *San Michelle*—out to the middle of the Mediterranean Sea miles away from watching eyes, set *The Spirit of St Christopher* alight at sea and watched as it burned.

It was in the early hours of 25 February 2006 that *The Spirit of St Christopher* sank into the sea, never to be seen again. Not one piece of evidence was left to chance, with everything from the trawler including all paperwork along with shipping logs going down with her. As the court case continued, Tony Rothwell purchased a similar trawler, naming it the Saint Marie after Moran's mother and in a matter of time, the new boat was being readied, new plans were being put in place to ship in more drugs to Ireland's shores.

With so much going on in the background away from the court case, Moran could do nothing but hope everything was going to plan on the outside. Information could not be passed on to him as it was far too difficult with the State monitoring his every move and contact while he was inside. He need not have worried because not long after the sinking of the trawler following on from the Cardiff meeting, Rothwell promptly contacted Sam the Turk, explaining all about Thomas Moran's woes in Ireland. Sam told Rothwell that he knew a person who could help Moran out with his little problem and a meeting was arranged where Tony Rothwell was to travel to the Czech Republic on 4 March to meet a man called Alexei Ivanov in the city of Prague.

Originally from St Petersburg, Russia, Ivanov had previously trained as a sniper in the Russian Special Forces and after leaving the military, he became one of Prague's many expert guns for hire. Tony Rothwell was in Prague to hire Ivanov for that very reason.

At 7.45 pm on a drizzly March evening in Prague, Rothwell arrived at the meeting point, the Grand Hotel situated next to the Art-Nouveau Municipal House in the heart of the city. The deadly assassin made his way to the hotel walking up through the Na Prikope shopping street as tourists milled about; oblivious to this man among them.

It was at 8 pm when both men first sat down together and it would also be the last, but on first impressions, Ivanov was not the type of man Rothwell was expecting; he was a quiet man, only speaking when spoken to; he stood about five feet five inches tall and dressed very conservatively, donning a dull grey pinstriped suit; also on his person, which Rothwell thought odd for a sniper, Ivanov was wearing prescription spectacles.

Rothwell thought to himself, *This man looked more like a schoolteacher than an assassin* but that was all irrelevant when Ivanov sat down as he took a handkerchief from his breast pocket and began to wipe the rain speckles from his glasses and looked up at Rothwell, making eye contact for the first time and asked, 'You look a bit uncertain, Mr Rothwell, is there a problem or a worry you need fixing by me?'

'No, not at all, I just—'

Ivanov, without lifting his head as he continued to dry his glasses, replied, 'You were expecting a fucking movie star, was it, Mr Rothwell? This is not a Hollywood movie we are acting out, you know.'

'I'm well aware of that.' Rothwell slid an envelope across the table and spoke, 'Here are all your details of where and when the job should take place, the money has been transferred to your account and this is our last meeting, good day, sir.'

And that was it, Dean Coyle's destiny was written in the beautiful city of Prague by a drug smuggler and an assassin.

Ivanov arrived in Dublin on 10 March on a direct flight from St Petersburg, Russia, travelling under a false passport in the name, Petri Smolarek. When Ivanov met Rothwell in Prague, he received a city blueprint of the buildings and underground sewerage system of the general area because he wanted to memorise the complete area surrounding the court.

During the afternoon of 11 March 2006, Ivanov walked every inch of the streets that surrounded the court to do a reconnaissance on the locality. For a professional like Ivanov, it was not long until he found a perfect position to take down Coyle. Ivanov entered the main door of the Motor Tax Offices on Blackhall Walk, Queen St and it was there he spotted Maureen Gallagher.

Gallagher, a plain looking 33-year-old single woman, who lived alone worked at the Customer Information counter and he decided to approach her while inquiring about his fictitious car tax. Using all his charms, Ivanov had the gullible Gallagher eating out of the palm of his hands. Later that day, the unsuspecting young woman was followed by Gallagher on leaving work from a corner where he had discreetly lain in wait. The young woman was heading off on a night out on the town with friends and work colleagues. In one of Dublin city's many clubs, Ivanov pretended to bump into Gallagher and proceeded to charm her into his bed that night; As she slept, he stole her swipe card that gave him access to every door in the Motor Tax building. The next morning, Gallagher woke alone and Ivanov would never return to that room.

On 13 March 2006, Dean Coyle was to make his court appearance to testify against his former boss, Thomas 'Little Don' Moran, in Dublin's historical Four Courts. At 12.30 pm that afternoon, Coyle was taken from his hideaway in a small cottage in Avoca, County Wicklow, from where under an armed escort, Coyle made the journey to Dublin city for the trial. Coyle was physically sick with fear and nerves as the armed escort made its way along the M11 onto the M50 coming off at Exit 9 Palmerstown and then heading towards the Quays and into the courthouse.

As Dean Coyle made his way to testify against Moran, Ivanov got into position in a storage room he found on the southwest corner of the building directly facing the back entrance of the court where, according to the information gathered by Rothwell, Coyle would enter. Ivanov set up a CZ-700-M1 sniper rifle holding ten round detachable box magazines that could hit a man from over a mile away; this was, of course, not your everyday run of the mill gun you buy in a local store but one only such a professional would use.

Ivanov, now in place, heard the echo of the sirens approach the courthouse and he got into position to take his shot. Under the media circus once again surrounding the trial, the van carrying Coyle quickly entered through the back entrance to the court, concreting the information Ivanov had been given.

Just before 1:40 pm as Coyle exited the Garda van under a massive security entourage, he was quickly ushered across the yard and as he approached the backdoor to the courthouse, Ivanov fired two shots in quick succession. The sound of the gunshot was drowned out by the noise of the everyday comings and goings of Dublin city as a bullet entered the left side of Dean Coyle's head while the other hit the wall as Coyle fell; on impact, he fell backwards into the arms of Special Investigation Unit Officer John McDonald, covering him in blood and brain scraps.

Screams and shouts rang out as it was apparent Coyle had been shot dead by a sniper hidden away under the cover of Dublin city. Armed Gardaí ran around like headless chickens trying to find the assassin but to no avail. Ivanov had already made his getaway on an Irish rail train heading in the direction of Belfast Airport and back to Prague, away from the fallout in Dublin. A serious blow had been struck against the Irish judicial system and the State as Moran once again gave them a two-fingered salute.

D'Arcy felt the most helpless after the main witness in his case to bring down Ireland's most notorious criminal came to a violent and dramatic end. On hearing the news, Justice Minister John O'Connor TD once again lost his smile and the Garda Commissioner Gerry Daly was taking it in the neck from Parliament Buildings.

From his prison cell, Moran had Slattery arrange another hit on the night of 19 March 2006 only days after Coyle's assassination, thanks to a local St Christopher's man, Martin Fay, who was released only days after the assassination and upon orders from Moran got word to Slattery. Gerrard Coleman, the man arrested with Dean Coyle, was out on bail and was making his way home from a friend's 40th birthday party when he was ambushed by Dennis Scully who executed him in cold blood when he ran up behind him and fired a single bullet to the back of his head and then sped off on a waiting motorcycle.

Moran was ruthless and left no links behind but D'Arcy knew with Coyle and Coleman dead, the State had no case against Moran and his fears became a reality when Moran walked free on 1 April after the State's case fell apart.

The whole of Ireland was in a state of utter shock and disbelief that anyone would have the audacity to carry out such a public assassination at the Four Courts. Not only were the Four Courts the home of the Irish judicial system but it also stood as a cornerstone of historical significance in Dublin's long and bloody fight for freedom and independence. To a city that could always bounce back against anything life could throw at it, standing tall against every foe and circumstance that had ever tried to break her spirit over centuries gone by could not hide its shame, this one hurt, this time it was different as the Irish underworld had struck a deadly blow to a city's heart as once again, Moran told the residents that the city was his.

The good citizens of Dublin were now feeling extremely vulnerable with the blatant disrespect for anything or anyone as the barbarous acts of murder by these gangs seemed to have no boundaries. The result of years of neglect and disregard by the powers that be on its most vulnerable citizens meant it was now time for a city to turn on one of her own children, Dublin had had enough and something was going to give.

As the old proverb goes, 'hell hath no fury as a woman scorned', and this woman was the city of Dublin and Dublin was getting ready to fight back.

Chapter 29

Ice

Sitting alone in his Crumlin home one evening not long after the trial, Moran decided he needed to get out of Dublin as he was being constantly interrupted by the press either calling at his house or tracking his every move; for him, this was more intense than the Garda operations against him and they were even more persistent than any State operation put in place against him.

For Moran, another problem had come to the fore for his gang as they found many people who they had gained trust with in the past had now turned their backs on them, Coyle's murder was the last straw for many who would have shown nothing but support in the past. So, tired of all the unwanted attention, Moran decided to find solitude away from Dublin where he could get both rest and room to work without the authorities and media snooping around his every move.

In September of 2006, Moran flew out to his private villa on Spain's Costa del Sol where his wife Jean and mother Marie were now officially full-time residents as they basked in the sun-soaked Spanish Riviera.

On 15 September 2006, Thomas Moran left Ireland and arrived at his visually spectacular villa in Malaga known locally as 'Corazón Del Mediterráneo', or 'The Heart of the Mediterranean'. Only hours after touching down in Spain, Moran was contacted by Tony Rothwell informing him that a property on a Spanish website had caught his eye and not a man to let an opportunity pass, saw this as a perfect way to add to Moran's property portfolio plus an additional way to launder money for the gang.

The property was a prominent nightclub on the island of Ibiza named 'Ice' and as soon as Rothwell told Moran about Ice, he jumped on the opportunity, he still had a love affair with the island of Ibiza. Only a week later on 25 September 2006, Moran, Slattery and Rothwell entered the offices of 'Spanish Home and

Properties' in Ibiza to inquire about one of the island's famous, or to some infamous, dance clubs.

Moran knew well that the island of Ibiza was a haven for music lovers, clubbers and partygoers for many years; sure, he had played his part in it during the 90s and understood its place in club culture across the globe. Ice was not just going to be an investment but a trip down memory lane for him as he was to hopefully soon become the owner of one of the first Super-Clubs on the island of Ibiza. The club had first opened when a young 23-year-old Frenchman purchased the premises in 1988 and pumped a million pounds of his wealthy father's money into the site. It was an instant success.

Knowing the men had arrived on the island, Danny Moore was not going to let the opportunity to see his old friends go and he quickly organised a massive party at his villa. The following night, Ibiza's resident expats and people of importance drank and danced away to the sounds of the island's most famous dance tracks.

However, with the celebrations in full flight, not everyone was participating and having a good time. Unknown to the majority of the guests, a private gathering was taking place in a room to the rear of the house; now, if Inspector D'Arcy ever wanted to raid a room it was this one but unfortunately for him, he was 3,000 miles away in Dublin.

Present at this meeting along with Moran, Slattery, McCann and Rothwell were the leading operators of the most sophisticated drug smuggling operation across Europe. The men were Philippe Garrone, Dirk Van Der Beek, Marcel Kromkampp and Danny Moore along with crew members from the new trawler Saint Marie, Captain Mark Lowe and Casper Von Bommell.

'Okay, listen up, lads,' was the order from Tony Rothwell.

Moran and Rothwell explained that a huge shipment of drugs, Glocks and AK-47s were to be imported into Ireland from Ibiza via Turkey through Dirk Van Der Beek within the next few months. Moran gave the floor to Van Der Beek who continued to explain about the shipment and when and where they wanted it to go. When Van Der Beek finished, Moran again took over.

'What is spoken about in here is to be kept in here so that means everyone is to keep his fuckin mouth shut about this, got it? This is way too fuckin important to get fucked up because as you all know back in Dublin, some silly cunt decided to open their fuckin hole and caused way too much fuckin trouble, so everyone keep it fuckin shut!

270

'I am still fuckin fuming about this little cunt Dean poxy Coyle and I tell you all this so listen and listen very fuckin carefully and that includes every cunt in this room. If any of ye open your fuckin mouths to the Garda or any other fuckin law agency, I will have your fuckin families slaughtered. Got it! I'm not goin through all that court stuff again. I'm up to me bollix with all that shite, I'm fuckin sick of it. I've had nothing but fuckin coppers and fuckin slimy fuckin newspaper cunts all over me, so take what I fuckin say seriously!'

The men had never seen Moran so animated before as he spelled it out clear that he had had enough of the ongoing problems within his gang. Silence in the room was met by nodding heads and groans of 'hear you, Tommy, agree boss.' Everyone knew he was pissed off.

'Okay, we will be in touch when you're needed for this operation. This conversation, lads, ends here, okay? Now get the fuck out and enjoy; after all, it is a party.' The gang members left the room and two days later, Moran, Rothwell and Slattery had a pre-arranged appointment at 1 pm at Ice with a local estate agent, Mr Alfonso Gomez. When they arrived, they found the club in pristine condition and Gomez began his sales pitch:

'This nightclub is exceptionally well presented and furnished with a main bar area, cocktail bar and VIP lounge with a capacity for 950 guests. It also boasts sound and light system costing in excess of twenty thousand euro, a DJ booth, monster size dance floor, twelve TVs and a massive projector screen. It was totally reformed not so long ago and decorated in a warm and colourful Mediterranean style and is totally soundproof. The new furniture is trendy, modern and of a high quality consisting of stylish barstools as well as cosy sofas. During the high season, the takings are an average of eighty thousand euro a night or two million euro a year!'

Moran interrupted Gomez, 'I want it.'

'Excuse me, Señor Moran?' asked a bemused Gomez.

'Are ye deaf? I said I fuckin want it.'

'Señor Moran, you see, this luxury club is an exceptional—' continued Gomez.

'Yeah, I know that and I want to buy the fuckin thing so can you shut the fuck up and sort it now? I'm a very busy man.'

'Sí, Señor Moran, and the nine million euro asking price, is that okay?' asked a stunned Alfonso Gomez.

'Yeah, sound, cash okay for ye?'

'Sí, yes, cash is very good, Señor Moran.' Gomez replied, stunned.

'Tony, sort that, will ye? I'm meetin Jean in town; she arrived this morning from Malaga. Nice doing business with ye, Mr Gomez, right, I'm off. Oh, here look, Tony, come here for a sec, will ye? I need you to find me a pair of stupid cunts we can use, okay?'

'Gotcha, for?'

'A maritime diversion, Tony.'

'Ha-ha, yes, no bother, so we need a couple of wannabe gangster gobshites who will cover up a certain load heading for a certain destination?'

Laughing Moran answered, 'Exactly, my friend, exactly. You are a clever little steamer, ain't ye.'

'That's why you hired me, Thomas. Anyway, I got you.'

After his conversation with Moran, Tony Rothwell visited Danny Moore inquiring if he knew any sailors or if he knew where he could find interested parties to take a cargo to Ireland, no questions asked, of course.

'By people to take a cargo, Tony, do you mean people who we can trust?'

'Well, yes, kind of, Danny, we need a diversion to keep the coast guard away from our main shipment.'

Thinking aloud, Moore spoke, 'Right, right, I see, Tony. Right, leave that with me.'

'They will not know who it's for, by the way, Danny.'

'Oh, you made that clear, Tony.'

Not long after Rothwell was given the name of two young Irishmen who were moored in Ibiza Harbour, students Donnacha Feely and Fergal Byrne. Both came from middle-class families in the Ballyboden area of Dublin and were sailing around Europe while on a sabbatical from their studies in Trinity College.

When Feely and Byrne met up with one of Danny's men, Pedro Gonzalez, in a harbour-side bar, it became clear the two were struggling for cash having been heard asking other sailors for any spare fuel they may have had. Pedro Gonzalez had previously met with Moore before heading to the bar when Moore told him of Rothwell's offer and he was offering the students fifty thousand euro each in cash to sail to Ireland with a cargo of five kilos of cocaine. At first, Byrne was totally against the idea but Feely and Gonzalez soon talked him around.

'Okay, look we'll do it but what if we get caught?'

'Senor, you will not, we have a detailed run for you, fuel for your boat and a two-way radio to keep you in contact with our man in Ireland.'

'Come on, Fergal, fifty grand apiece for Christ sakes, simple stuff.'

'Okay, okay, we will do it.'

'Yes!' Feely punched the air in delight.

'Who are we running it for?'

'You do not need to know, we clear?'

'Yes clear, come on, Fergal, we do not need to know.'

'Okay, gentlemen, we are good to go.'

'Yes, yes, let's do this!'

'Great, take this mobile and await my call.'

On 2 October, Feely and Byrne received a call from Gonzalez explaining to them that the shipment was ready to go and the package would be ready to collect at 11 pm. Gonzalez met the students at the harbour and began to explain, 'When you get within thirty miles of the Irish coast, you will turn on this radio so you can make contact with our man who will be waiting to offload the cargo.'

'Sounds good and when we arrive, will he explain to us what to do?' Feely questioned.

'When you make contact, set anchor and he will come to you, then you disappear into the night with your money. Now take this, it's your coordinates to Ireland and the drop-off point where you set anchor. Take care, gentlemen, won't you and remember, you have fifty thousand euro each in this bag so enjoy it.'

'Yes, yes, yes. My friend, your package will be in Ireland in no time. Goodbye.'

It was in the early hours of 3 October 2006 that the Irish coast guard began to monitor a radio signal coming from a small boat heading for the County Dublin coast. Feely and Byrne began to try to make contact with the fictitious man on the Irish coastline, the line was an open line and it was heard by every enforcement agency from Dublin to the moon. At 5.13 am, the boat holding the two men was boarded by the Irish coast guard aided by the Irish naval frigate *Lara*, stunning the two amateur drug smugglers who were arrested on site.

Students Donnacha Feely and Fergal Byrne both were sentenced to three years in prison even though they had never been involved in drug smuggling before while Moran had an overwhelming success as he once again flooded the streets of Ireland with drugs and guns; at 3 am on the morning of 3 October, a fishing trawler named Saint Marie was unloading a massive cargo of guns and drugs off the coast of County Wexford. Unlike the students, Moran's cargo was clear from sight of the Irish navy and coast guard, all thanks to two foolish students—Moran was back in business.

The flow of drugs into Ireland is a never-ending one with its constant stream of coke, marijuana, heroin and prescription drugs that the government does their very best to limit, seize and destroy but they can't catch everything. So D'Arcy once again had failed to stop Moran's importation of drugs, and on top of that, every time they caught a drug smuggler using some new, previously unknown method for stashing and shifting drugs, a new method was born. Like any smuggler, Moran adapted and changed his methods; in this instance, he changed the boat when it was pinpointed by the authorities and business continued.

As Moran told his men, 'It's adaptation, lads, the survival of the fittest where only the strongest survive.' Inspector D'Arcy was about to get a reality check and if he or the Minister for Justice thought that they had Dublin's gangs on the back foot they were quite wrong. Moran was not finished, not by a long shot when during the same night of the meeting in Danny Moore's home on 25 September 2006, Moran called his closest men aside.

'Right, all this shite back in Dublin, I've a pain in me bollix with it, a massive pain in me bollix. So Frankie, I want you to send word back to Dublin that I want that cunt Kelly to know I've not forgotten about him. And I mean send a very fuckin strong message. Find those still loyal to us, let them know I've a pain in me bollox and get them sorted, the rest of them if they are not onside, well, fuck em. I'm really tired of all this fuckin shite; it's doing my head in and it's stopping me from fuckin sleepin, fuckin sort it.'

'I hear you, boss, I fuckin hear ye loud and clear.'

'Good man. Tony, whatever he needs, yeah?'

'Say no more, Thomas.'

Chapter 30
Loose Lips

In early December 2006, Moran returned home to Dublin from his self-imposed Spanish exile to find that the media circus from his court case had cooled down somewhat and the investigation involving the assassinations of Gerard Coleman and State witness Dean Coyle went unsolved. But only days before his homecoming, the order he had previously given to Frankie McCann in Ibiza was followed through when on 30 November, a motorbike was speeding towards Swords in North County, Dublin.

It was a damp and cold night when Noel Brady pulled his motorbike up outside number three, St Brendan's Park in Swords as the gunman Dennis Scully dismounted from the bike and walked towards the front door of the house. This was the home of Gary Donnelly, the brother of one of Moran's main gangland rivals—Micky Donnelly. On this night, if anyone had thought that Moran had gone away or become weak, he was about to send the word out loud and clear that he was still number one and nobody was going to take that away.

At 8.15 pm, Scully rang the doorbell, pulled up his visor from his helmet, took two steps backwards and waited for Donnelly to answer the door. Seconds later Gary Donnelly opened the door, to see a high-powered handgun pointed at his face. Donnelly froze with fright and in the blink of an eye, Scully fired two shots into the head of his target. Scully quickly turned and ran to the bike and in no time, both men were speeding up the motorway towards Balbriggan and out of the eye of the Gardaí. The following day, the bike was found burnt out on the beach close to Balbriggan train station.

The 30-year-old father of two lay dead in a pool of his own blood as the screams of his wife and children rang out across the cold winter night on the Northside of Dublin city. Within minutes of the hit, Micky Donnelly heard that his brother had been murdered and of course, he was furious and wanted nothing more than to see Thomas Moran and all his men dead in revenge for his brother's assassination. Once again Dublin had seen a major killing and Moran had struck right at the heart of the newly formed Timmy Kelly gang.

With the Special Unit on high alert, it was to be some months later on the day after St Patrick's Day, 18 March 2007, in one of the Dublin clubs owned by Tony Rothwell, the circumstances surrounding a conversation would change the whole landscape in the fight against the Dublin underworld.

It was at Rothwell's nightclub where undercover officer Shaun Ryan aka Stephen Trimble was out socialising with Dennis Scully and Noel Brady who, to his amazement, both began to speak freely about the killing of Gary Donnelly even telling him about the motorbike driven by Brady to the murder.

'Hey Stevie boy, you're alright, kid. Did ye like that bit of work over in Swords a while ago, buddy?'

'What was that, Dennis?'

'The Donnelly cunt, bang, bang in the fuckin head and let me tell you, that cunt got what he deserved.'

'You did Gary Donnelly, Dennis?'

'Did ye not know, Stevie? Ah, here you're not in the know at all, for fuck sakes.' Scully and Brady broke out into laughter and continued to openly tell an undercover Garda that not only were they the main suspects in a gangland killing but boasted to him about the shooting in complete detail.

On top of this, they told him all about a massive haul that was soon to be hitting Ireland's coast but they did not have the final details on it.

'Here, I'll tell ye what we have a fuckin massive haul comin in soon, massive.'

'Really, when?'

'Jaysus, Stevie, you get told fuck all, don't ye.'

'Sure lads, I'm just the new kid on the block; what would I know?'

'Very true but look, this haul is fuckin big, we ain't 100% sure; Tommy is staying tight-lipped on this one but word is that it's going to be fuckin huge.'

'Happy days, boys, god bless Tommy fuckin Moran.' Trimble raised his glass to his new-found information.

Two days later, Trimble was sitting in a coffee shop on Pearse Street in Nenagh, County Tipperary, with Inspector Niall D'Arcy as he explained in detail the whole conversation he had with Scully and Brady in the nightclub. D'Arcy could not believe his ears as the detail of the killing was completely in line with the investigation carried out by the Garda forensic team.

'Inspector, I have to say that I have a bad, bad feeling that all hell is about to break loose out on the streets, I mean, absolute mayhem. Donnelly is not going to let things go after the murder of his brother Gary, by all accounts, Donnelly's going mental and Kelly has lost control over him.'

'Did Brady and Scully say this to you too?'

'Yes, pretty much, they were saying that a few incidents did occur but nothing bad enough that made the news or our attention.'

'Okay, fine, fuck, this is going to be a mess.'

'To add, Sir, there are now real fears—from talking to gang members, especially after the Coyle murder—that both sides are reaching out to European criminal contacts for assistance in carrying out high-impact attacks aimed at reaching the senior figures in the groups.'

Ryan also explained to D'Arcy that he was told by the two men of a major haul that was close but the details he had gathered so far were very patchy at best.

'Okay, okay, Shaun. Look, stay on it and keep your head down and your eyes and ears open. Anything you hear on this shipment, let me know straight away. I'll be in touch.'

'Will do, Sir.'

'Okay, get back to Dublin.'

With the information gathered by his man, D'Arcy was able to secure a warrant for the search of the homes of both Scully and Brady but not wanting to compromise Trimble, the warrants were issued for a house search for arms and hoped he could find something during the searches that would allow him hold one or both of them.

He hoped that if he got either man into custody, he could try getting a testimony secured in relation to the Donnelly murder but D'Arcy understood all too well that it would be difficult, plus he had to play it clever, not letting them know how he had heard about their part in the above murder.

After a short surveillance operation, the intelligence unit reported back that both men were at home and in the early hours of 25 April 2007, under the watchful eye of Inspector D'Arcy, members of the Emergency Response Unit backed up by local Gardaí raided the homes of both men. Caught by surprise, both Scully and Brady were quickly taken away to separate Garda stations under heavy security. During the raids, D'Arcy got a lucky break when his men discovered €10,000 in cash at Brady's home and Scully was caught with a sizeable amount of cannabis valuing €2,000 in his bedside locker; it was enough to arrest and charge both men on drug-related charges.

In the early morning news bulletins, the press was all over the story and reporting:

'In Dublin, two pre-planned early morning raids by the Emergency Response Unit have seen two men arrested and brought to separate Garda stations across the city. Sources say that both men are well known to Gardaí.

'Both men are suspected of being involved in an organised crime gang. In a statement from the Garda Press Office, it has been reported that both men are helping Gardaí with inquiries. We will bring you more news in later bulletins as details arise.'

In fact, neither man knew anything of how the inner workings of the smuggling operations were actually run. To D'Arcy's absolute frustration, neither man broke under fierce interrogation.

Even though the interrogations were going badly, D'Arcy still thought he had enough evidence to have the men remanded in custody for a longer period so he could put them in front of the courts. In the court hearing, to D'Arcy's utter dismay, the court case backfired when Justice Fintan O'Keeffe granted bail as the prosecution had nothing bar a few thousand euro they could not prove was from illegal gains and a bag of cannabis with, as the judge put it, a modest value of 2,000 euro.

'Due to the lack of any evidence on behalf of the State, I see no reason but to grant bail for both men at 5,000 euro each. Court is adjourned.'

'Are you fucking on the take, Judge?' barked a clearly angry Inspector D'Arcy.

'I'll pretend I never heard that, Inspector.'

Justice O'Keeffe, understanding the anguish of the inspector, let his outburst slide but called him aside, 'Inspector D'Arcy, a moment of your time please.'

'Sorry about the remark, Your Honour, I did not—'

'Stop a moment, nothing to do with that remark but my advice is to be careful in front of judges in the future.'

'Yes Sir.'

'Now what I do want you to clearly understand is that within these walls, we take the justice system very, very seriously, Inspector, so what I am simply saying to you is that when you get something concrete on these people, we will hit them with everything we have, and I mean everything, got that?'

'Yes, Your Honour! We will get them.'

'Good, good, you do that, now have a good day, Inspector.'

Not far from the courthouse, shortly after the court hearing had finished, Noel Slattery spoke to Scully and Brady who explained about what D'Arcy wanted to know and his line of questioning about Donnelly worried both men who feared they might have a mole in the gang or close to it. On receiving the information, Slattery went to see Moran and he explained to his boss that the two men could not understand why D'Arcy questioned them albeit just a couple of questions about the shooting of Gary Donnelly.

'The lads said he asked questions about the hit and got a vibe that D'Arcy knew it was them who done it.'

'Yeah, that's odd; it is very odd that they picked up those two out of everyone and mentioned Donnelly.'

'It's not a fucking coincidence, Tommy.'

'It certainly is not, Noel, it certainly is not.'

With this information in hand, Moran sent orders to Scully and Brady that they were to go into hiding to avoid being arrested again because if D'Arcy did know about the Donnelly murder, it worried him exactly how much more he might know. 24 hours after the court appearance, both men were hidden away on the West coast of Ireland and out of touch of D'Arcy and hidden away from the Garda Special Unit. Little did Moran know that it was they who had unintentionally told the mole on that night in Rothwell's nightclub.

Moran was content for now as he headed back to Spain for the summer but deep down, he knew that more problems would be certainly brewing and yet again, he was correct.

Chapter 31
Turning Point

Unperceived by both Thomas Moran and Timmy Kelly, a coming together of a different kind would once again see them cross paths. In Dublin, working from behind closed doors, a certain young gangster was planning a double-cross of both the Dublin gangs as he began to organise his ragtag band of thugs and wannabe gangsters. Stewie Carroll had been gathering a gang of carefree and violent young men who were a mix of streetwise thugs, thieves, murderers and drug addicts, all of whom had an unhealthy passion for violence and mayhem. Once again, Dublin city was about to become a threatening and deadly place because a young gangster had his eyes firmly set on the ultimate prize—Dublin.

What made Carroll and his gang even more intimidating was that they had nothing to lose as many of them came from broken homes with a history of violence and neglect, just like the Moran gang in their early days. This group was fearless with an unstable hostility that was increased due to the level of cocaine and anabolic-steroid concoctions they were using, a lethal mixture that produced greater levels of aggression and extreme levels of paranoia. Not a good mix for young gun-yielding gangsters with a youthful cocky bravado and itchy trigger fingers.

Carroll's main gang members included Pat Stacy, a 22-year-old cocaine addict from Killarney Street in Dublin's North Inner City. Stacy, a colossal-sized young man, had trained as an amateur bodybuilder while using anabolic steroids to increase his performances. The cocaine and steroid mix made him very aggressive and it was widely known that he beat his girlfriend Carla Quinn quite regularly. Stacy had served time in St Patrick's for aggravated assault and robbery and was known for his exceptionally short but extremely fierce temper.

The next gang member was a Scotsman named Maxi Rodgers, a 23-year-old native of Glasgow who moved to Dublin after meeting his Dubliner girlfriend,

Lisa Keane, on holiday on the Greek Island of Crete in the summer of 2006. Rodgers was working as a security guard in Dublin City Centre and befriended Stewie Carroll when they met through Carroll's sister Brittney who was close friends with Keane. Rodgers had no previous convictions in Scotland and he joined the gang to make extra cash.

Along with Stacy and Rodgers were Jeff Turner and his best friend, 20-year-old Gavin Noone. Noone hailed from the Oliver Bond flat complex that sat on the banks of the river Liffey on the Southside of the City while 21-year-old Turner came from the School Street flats, a mere ten-minute walk from Oliver Bond. Both young men were recruited by Carroll as they were well known to the Gardaí and both had notorious reputations for violence. Already on the radar of Dublin's Gardaí since they were 12 and 14 years old respectively, the two youngsters were chronic cocaine abusers and had a file that even made the hardest of criminals look like a boy scout.

Next gang members were 20-year-old Keith Murphy and 19-year-old Freddie Hayes, both of whom grew up with Carroll and were two of his closest friends so they automatically followed him. Both were extremely violent and had served time for assault and battery along with small drug possession charges.

A close associate to Carroll was 43-year-old Pavel Predovnik, a Serbian national who was living in a rented apartment in Dublin's highly sought after IFSC area located in the heart of Dublin city. Predovnik had met Carroll through Rodgers as they both worked the same shifts in the security company they were employed by, having moved to Ireland in early 2001.

Predovnik, much older than the rest of the gang, had gone on the run after the Serbian authorities put out a warrant for his arrest when it became clear he was a member of the notorious Arkan's Tigers, a ruthless paramilitary unit that fought in the Eastern European wars in Croatia, Bosnia and Herzegovina in the 1990s.

Last but not least was 29-year-old cocaine dealer Gary 'Gaz' McCarty or as people who knew him, 'The Modfather', due to his absolute love for the 1960s music and fashion genre known as the Mods. McCarty dressed like a Mod, wore his hair like a Mod and spoke with an odd put-on London accent; he had two Vespas and one Lambretta and was an expert in replica guns.

Carroll, through McCarty, quickly began to organise the importation of replica guns to Ireland via Odessa in the Ukraine. On arrival, McCarty was then able to turn these guns into live weapons with ease and they were a lot cheaper plus, as Carroll saw things, it was less risk compared to importing actual firearms into the country. McCarty also explained to Carroll that convertible replicas were widely available across many European countries that did not require identity checks like genuine guns did. The added bonus for Carroll was that these replicas did not carry a jail term if found in the possession of such guns and this suited him.

He was now ready to get to work after he approached Kelly about the gang.

It was Saturday, 18 August 2007 and Slane Castle was hosting legendary rock band *The Rolling Stones* for the second time but behind the rock spectacular, 20-one year-old Stewie Carroll had organised a pre-arranged meeting with Timmy Kelly about, as he put it, 'The direction the gang was going'.

At 8.30 pm, Kelly arrived at the cooling off area in Slane with Ian Bouncer Howe, Micky Donnelly and Billy Masterson to see exactly what was so urgent.

'So what is this all about, Stewie?'

'I am not happy with the way the gang is going and I want to play a more senior role, simple.'

'What! Go and fuck off, ye little cunt. You came all the way down here to fuckin tell me this, fuck off, ye prick!' raged Kelly.

'No, listen to me for a sec, Timmy, we have got to be taking over the city and it's plain to see that you're letting that dirty fuckin scumbag Moran walk all over ye.'

'Will you ever go and fuck off, ye little cunt. You're the fuckin big man, Stewie, a fucking big man. You actually want us to go right at Moran? Are ye fuckin kidding me, you would not last two fuckin minutes out on the streets with that attitude, you stupid little cunt. Moran is no fool and he has a strong gang around him, we got to bide our time, Stewie, that's how it fuckin works.'

'Ah here, Timmy, ye right? The Stones are comin on, this is bollix here.'

'Yeah, you're right, Bouncer, let's go. Stewie, we're here to see the gig, not listen to your shite, now fuck off.' Kelly laughed in Carroll's face as he walked off with Howe, Donnelly and Masterson. Outside in the main concert area, Kelly shouted into the ear of Howe, 'Keep an eye on that little bastard.'

Carroll was furious at Kelly's flippancy and utter disrespect when he tried to discuss the future plans of the gang and he went directly from Slane to the flat of friend and fellow gang member, Gavin Noone,

'I want something done and soon. We'll show that wanker who would not last on the streets,' fumed Carroll with a look of murder in his eye and murder was exactly what he had in mind.

For Carroll, it was now clear to him that, Kelly was never going to take him seriously and he was never going to harness the respect within the gang he so dearly craved. A self-serving megalomaniac, Carroll wanted it all, he wanted nothing more than to take over Dublin city and her ill-gotten gains and be the man everyone spoke about and feared.

So if Kelly was never going to give Carroll the time or respect, it was now time for him to earn his stripes and gain the respect from his peers by taking out his nearest rivals. Not long after the meeting at Slane Castle, Carroll organised the members of his gang to put some plans in place that would send out a clear statement plus it would put both Kelly and Moran on the back foot.

The young gangster's plan was simple; he wanted to develop a catalogue of events that would see both the Moran and Kelly gangs once again go at each other. Carroll's plans began to fall into place when things came to a head within a three-day period, starting on 24 November 2007.

It was late evening when Jeff Turner collected two handguns from Pavel Predovnik in Dublin's city centre and it was from here that he headed off to meet up with Carroll and Maxi Rodgers at a warehouse they were renting on the Ballymount Road, Walkinstown, on the southwest side of Dublin just off the M50 motorway. On arrival, Turner handed the guns over to Carroll who then told both his men about information he had gathered about one Ken Fox. Carroll explained to his men that Fox lived in Artane and he was one of the Moran gang.

Carroll continued to explain that they were to, 'take out Fox and make it look like it was a planned gangland hit, and for fuck sake, boys, don't be recognised at any time by anyone, now if it happens that you're spotted, pop the cunt too, yeah.'

At 8 pm, Carroll's men made their way across Dublin city in a stolen BMW car towards Ken Fox's home and at approximately 8.43 pm, pulled up outside his house. Pulling on balaclavas, Turner and Rodgers got out of the passenger and back seat of the car respectively and as both men entered the garden, Turner spotted Fox in the downstairs front room and pointed it out to Rodgers. Turner and Rodgers turned their guns towards the house and opened fire indiscriminately, discharging a hail of bullets that smashed through the window; as the bullets flew, Ken Fox was shot five times in the neck and upper body.

Another of the Moran gang had just fallen and questions would have to be answered but it was only Stewie Carroll who had the answers.

Later that night, Carroll anonymously sent out word to Moran that the hit on Fox was ordered by Kelly, and word spread across Dublin via social media, texting and good old-fashioned gossip that it was the Kelly gang that had carried out the attack. Carroll's crazy plan was working. A few days later Carroll, Maxi Rodgers and Pavel Predovnik were out on the town with Kelly gang member, Mickey Naughton.

On 27 November 2007, after a hard night's intake of drugs and alcohol to continue their partying, all four men headed to a flat in which Maxi Rodgers frequently used to bring women back, away from his girlfriend. Things took a turn when a heavily intoxicated Rodgers full of alcohol and cocaine let it slip to Naughton that it was they who had murdered Fox and that they were going to be blaming it all on Kelly.

'So come on, join with us and help the lads in taking out Kelly.'

'Shut your fuckin mouth, Maxi, ye stupid cunt!' Carroll screamed at the loose-lipped Rodgers as Naughton began to get very edgy. Now full of cocaine and alcohol, he was becoming extremely paranoid and refused to collaborate with the men.

'You're all fuckin dead, you hear me, when Timmy finds out, he will fuckin kill the lot of yis.'

Carroll jumped up and pushed Naughton to the ground, warning him not to open his mouth but as he was struggling to gain his feet, Predovnik having heard the ruckus from the bathroom, leapt on Naughton from behind, repeatedly stabbing him with a meat carving knife he had grabbed from the kitchen. Naughton was dead and the three men stood over his body as it lay in a pool of blood on the floor. Carroll, in panic, began shouting at Maxi, 'Fuckin hell, Maxi, ye silly cunt; we said that we would say fuck all, didn't we, ye silly, silly cunt!'

'Sorry, fuck, fuck, fuck!'

'Okay, right boys, look, torch this fucking place and then get home and burn those fuckin clothes yis have on, in the mornin, go and have a sauna and sweat everything out of yis, right, let's do this.

'And keep your fuckin mouths shut, for fuck sake!'

The next day, the news reports were only snippets in the evening newspaper that read 'Drunk dies in house fire' as it was then unknown what was actually the cause of the fire. Like the Fox murder, Carroll again sent out word onto the streets but this time to catch the attention of Kelly that this was no accident but a hit ordered on Naughton by Moran in revenge for Ken Fox. Just like before when Moran had heard the news of the Fox murder, Kelly was also not very happy and swore revenge for his friend's untimely murder. Over the coming days, Dublin city was put on lockdown by both gang bosses in fear of reprisal but unaware to both men, Carroll ran free to do as he pleased.

A couple of weeks later, Carroll was to strike again on 20 December 2007, in the middle of the Christmas rush, Noel Slattery accompanied by Nailor O'Neill had just finished off some shopping. It was 2.15 pm when both men had returned to the car in Blanchardstown shopping centre; Slattery was now a good hour into a bad mood as he was supposed to meet up with Moran in Crumlin at 2 pm.

'Fuckin hell, Nailor, get the fuck in, he is going to be fuckin fuming, look, I've a ton of missed calls on me phone.' Slattery showed O'Neill the phone; putting the phone down, he turned the key in the ignition, but it failed twice.

'Ahh, me bollix, Nailor, not fuckin now, seriously, Tommy is going to go fuckin ape-shit I'm so fuckin late and now the fuckin car won't start.'

Slattery would not make the meeting on that very cold December afternoon. The Modfather, Gaz McCarty, armed with a controlled electric pipe bomb targeted Slattery by placing said bomb underneath Slattery's BMW on the driver's side for maximum effect. The bomb was formed in a tightly sealed section of pipe filled with gunpowder for a simple but deadly result but it was designed to produce a relatively large explosion, and the additional internal fragmentation of the pipe itself was created with potentially lethal shrapnel that included deadly ball bearings.

The bomb was a short section of steel pipe containing the explosive mixture and closed at both ends with steel caps and the fuse was electric with wires leading to a timer and battery of which McCarty processed the detonator. As Slattery eventually got the motor running, McCarty sitting a few cars away from his targets pressed a remote-controlled button and the bomb went off, injuring four passers-by and of course, Slattery and O'Neill. To Carroll's frustration, the bomb did not blow to its full effect and Slattery survived the blast but a number of the internal ball bearings lodged in his left leg would leave him with a permanent limp. O'Neill was only grazed from the blast.

While this passage of events was taking place, it was still unknown to Moran and Kelly that these were moves from Carroll's newly formed gang of reckless youngsters. However, not everything goes unnoticed forever and what Carroll forgot to realise was that he was up against seasoned professional gangsters and he and his gang were about to become stuck in a quicksand that was going to see his gang sink quicker than he could ever imagine, his plans were about to be seriously derailed.

Carroll's luck eventually ran out when only weeks after the two attempted murders of Slattery and O'Neill, Gavin Noone, stricken with fear that Kelly would find out what Carroll was up to, visited Kelly in fear for his life. Noone told Timmy Kelly exactly what had happened but to his amazement, Kelly was not too shocked to hear the news but was obviously furious at the audacity of him to tackle the two biggest gangs in the Ireland.

'Gavin, I'm tellin you here and now that you do not open your fuckin mouth to Carroll or you will join him and his little friends on a one-way trip to fuckin hell. Now I want you to stay in touch with me and tell me everything he does, no matter how small it may be, you even inform me when the little cunt has a shite, do you fuckin hear me, son?'

'I do, Timmy, I do loud and clear,' answered a visibly shaken Noone.

As Noone left the room, Kelly looked up and said to himself, *That cheeky little cunt.*

Carroll was now a marked man and his time was running out fast. The next step in this event was something that not one person in Dublin could have dreamt when Gavin Noone received a call from Kelly telling him he needed him to deliver a message.

It was Sunday afternoon on 25 January 2008 when Timmy Kelly sent Gavin Noone to see Thomas Moran with a proposition he hoped he might be interested in hearing. At 3.12 pm, Noone entered the Black Horse Bar only to be met by Nailor O'Neill.

'What the fuck do you want around here, ye little cunt?'

'Look Nailor, relax, I've got a message. I've been sent to see Tommy by Timmy Kelly.'

'A message for Tommy from that scumbag, is that right now? Okay, wait here,' ordered O'Neill. 'Lads, watch this little cunt very closely.'

O'Neill disappeared into a back room as Noone impatiently waited. When O'Neill returned, it was not Moran who accompanied him but Noel Slattery who approached Noone, visibly limping from the botched assassination attempt.

'Nailor tells me you have a message from Kelly?'

'Yeah, he wants to talk to Tommy about a situation—'

'A situation, what fuckin situation?'

'You'll have to ask Timmy about that now, won't you? I'm just his messenger, that's all, Noel, ye know?'

'Okay, then tell him to be here tomorrow night at eight, now fuck off.'

'Okay, I will let him know, Noel.'

The following night, as planned, Timmy Kelly and Paddy Gallagher called at the Black Horse to a meeting that saw Dublin's two main gangsters in the same room for the first time ever. With both men in the same room, it sent shivers down the spine of the patrons who sat in the bar in fear of what may come of this.

'So Timmy, what can I do for you?' questioned a cautious Moran accompanied by Slattery and McCann.

'A short-term truce.'

'Come again?' answered Slattery with a complete puzzled look on his face.

'You heard me.'

Moran leaned back in his chair and rubbing his nose calmly responded, 'Okay, go on.' Moran raised his right hand in the air as if to say, okay, I'm listening.

'Right then, here it goes, Tommy, it was Stewie Carroll who caused all this recent shit.'

'What?'

'Yes, you see, he wants to be a boss and he is a right little cunt who will do anything to get it.'

Again, Moran paused and answered after a short breath, 'Well, that is interesting, very, very interesting indeed.'

'I found out that it was Stewie Carroll and his men who murdered Naughton and Ken Fox.'

'Reallllly.' A sarcastic tone from Moran but Kelly was not impressed as his volume increased.

'For fuck sakes, Tommy, look, the little bastard put the word out that we had done it making it look as if it was just another hit by us. This little cunt actually wants to take over Dublin.'

'You will have to take more control of your men in the future, Timmy, it looks very bad on your behalf.'

'Yeah funny, Tommy.'

'Okay, leave it with me for a bit. Sit easy and have a gargle on me. I won't be long.'

'Oh, by the way Noel, he did the pipe bomb attack on you too.'

Moran, Slattery and McCann disappeared into the back office of the bar.

'Tell him to go and fuck himself, Tommy,' fumed McCann. 'Let him sort out his own shite. I have a good mind to slit his fuckin throat, the cheeky cunt!'

Moran was in deep thought and nothing was getting through to him as McCann again aired his voice of caution, 'Fuckin hell, Tommy, tell us you're not gonna help these cunts?'

'Yes, I think I am. Once we sort this problem, and let's be honest here now, lads, a little cunt with pipe bombs trying to kill us is a fuckin problem in my books.'

'I don't know, Tommy, can we trust this fucker?'

'I guess we will have to for now, Noel.'

And it was from that moment that Moran who—without thinking unlike he normally did on such issues—agreed to help Kelly sort Carroll and his men. As he saw it, it all made sense, including a short-term truce.

If Slattery and McCann were cautious, it was nothing near the feelings of Micky Donnelly who was not happy about the arrangement. After all, it was Moran's men who had murdered his brother but following a brief discussion with Kelly, Micky agreed to go along with the operation in the end but refused to work alongside any of the Moran crew.

Moran understood all too well that Carroll and his gang were causing far too many problems for him and right now, he needed these problems like he needed a hole in the head. The meeting of two gang bosses would now see the most notorious gangs in the history of Ireland's gangland ready to work side by side if only for a short spell to take down a common enemy; the days of Stewie Carroll and his gang of young thugs were now officially numbered.

Chapter 32
An Unholy Alliance

Within days of the meeting with Kelly, Thomas Moran decided to contact Tony Rothwell, informing him to put all shipments from Europe on hold until further notice. He explained further by telling Rothwell that there was far too much information openly floating around the city and he was not one hundred per cent certain of what information the Gardaí actually knew.

'Tony, this place is ready to go off big-time and to be honest, I am worried because we could be on the verge of a fuckin bloodbath here and the heat from the pigs will be far too fuckin risky to jeopardise any of our shipments.'

'I hear you, I'll hold everything until I hear back from you.'

As Moran was contacting Rothwell, they were unaware that over in Leinster House, Inspector D'Arcy was reporting to the justice Minister that they had received intelligence reports from their inside man informing that serious trouble lay ahead.

'Minister, I have recently met with my inside man and he told me that something big was about to go down in the city, now the thing is, Minister, he has not found out the exact details. But one thing he told me was that from listening to loose talk around the gang, it is certain that more blood is about to spill on the streets of Dublin, now this he could guarantee for me.'

'Okay, Inspector, keep at it and keep me informed. Any detail let me know. More blood would spill, he said that?'

'Yes Minister, those are the words he used.'

'Fuck me, okay, thank you, Inspector.'

It was only days after Moran cancelled his latest drug shipments from fear of being intercepted by customs that his paranoia would be strengthened after he got news from Tony Rothwell. On 17 February 2008, Rothwell rang Moran informing him that one of his main traffickers working through Britain and on the Continent, Englishman Tommy Sprake, was arrested by Interpol agents at a lock-up in Düsseldorf, Germany, carrying a passport under the name of Matthew Kirby.

Identified by Interpol, Sprake was charged with being a member of a major drug trafficking organisation when he was caught in a sting operation, which led agents to a lock-up in the Derendorf borough of Düsseldorf. They found 35 kilos of cannabis, 22 kilos of cocaine and 14 kilos of heroin along with numerous false passports, small quantities of cash and firearms.

'Thomas, I have no idea how they found our man but I am beginning to believe you about this leak.'

'I fuckin knew it, Tony; right, fuck this, hold everything and I mean everything until I sort this Dublin thing out.'

It was not a leak as Moran thought, nothing more than Interpol doing a good job on tracking a major player involved in international drug trafficking; Sprake was sentenced in a German court and would serve eight years in prison but for now, Moran had other problems that needed taken care of. Another incident would completely change Moran's mind about Carroll when on the morning of 20 April, he all but sealed his death warrant.

It was a typical sunny afternoon as Moran's wife Jean and his mother Marie left their Malaga home by foot to make a routine trip to the local store. On the short walk, they were stopped at a junction by a man holding a clipboard and dressed in holiday rep clothing. As the women stood at a traffic light, the man stepped up in front of the unsuspecting women.

'Ahh no, you're grand, mate, we are not tourists, we live here,' explained Jean, thinking he was a rep for a local bar or one of the many restaurants located in the area. However, the man holding the clipboard raised a handgun from behind it and pointed it towards her head and pulled once on the trigger. At that moment, time froze still for both women but for some reason, the gun jammed and the gunman panicked, dropping the gun and running off into the busy morning crowd.

Within seconds of the incident, the two women dropped to the ground in shock, holding onto one another as passers-by ran to their help and soon after, they were taken away to a local Spanish police station. It only took a couple of hours for news to reach Dublin when two uniformed members of An Garda Síochána greeted Moran as he answered his door.

'What the fuck do you scumbags want now?'

'Mr Moran, we are here to inform you that today, an attempted assassination was made on your mother Marie and wife Jean in Malaga.'

The blood ran from Moran's face as he replied, 'What the fuck did you just say?'

The second Garda continued, 'It's true, Mr Moran, someone tried to shoot them in a shopping area in Malaga but they are fine, if not shaken, and by all accounts, the gun jammed...'

Moran angrily told the Gardaí to get out of his garden and minutes later after a brief phone call, Slattery was on his way to collect Moran and both men had only one destination in mind—Malaga.

After a couple of days in Malaga, Moran spoke to Timmy Kelly asking if he knew anything about the attempt on his wife and mother.

'Not fuckin us, Tommy, not by a fuckin long shot, we have our differences but not that, no. I fucking swear on my kids' lives, never ever would I go after your family, never.'

After that conversation and a few days, one name came back to Kelly and that name was once again Stewie Carroll. Kelly had uncovered a plot by Carroll when Pat Stacy's girlfriend overheard him talking to two of his associates, fretting over the botched assassination in Malaga. Sick of Stacy and his ill treatment, she asked to see Kelly so she could once and for all get Stacy out of her life.

'Come on in, Carla, what's up, you good?'

'Yeah, I'm grand, thanks Timmy.'

'That big cunt give you that shiner, love?' asked Kelly as he brushed her long hair from her face, she was clearly trying to hide a black eye handed out by Stacy.

'It's okay, like it's grand.'

'It's fucking not, Carla. So tell me what did he say?'

'He'll fuckin kill me, Timmy,' fretted Carla, clearly terrified of Stacy.

'No, he fucking won't, you're under my protection now, love. So go on tell me what was said.'

'That one of Carroll's fellas went to Malaga to kill Tommy Moran's missus but he fucked up and that Stewie was goin fuckin mad over it.'

'That's what he said, yeah?'

'Pretty much yeah and Stewie told him not to miss but he did. I'm not in trouble now, am I, cause I'm not like them?'

'No, not at all, for fuck sake, ye done good. Okay, grand, Carla, head off and say fuck all to anyone. Look, before you go, ye got somewhere to crash?'

'Just the apartment with him.'

'Well, ye can't stay there, look, go get some clothes sorted. I'll get you a place away from him for now.'

'Sound Timmy, thanks. If ye ever want me or anything, just giz a shout, ye know.'

'Yeah, no bother, now go on.'

Donnelly came into the room and asked, 'What you up to sortin her out or are ye lookin to sort her out, ye dirty bastard?' Both men looked at each other and broke into laughter.

'Well, she is a fine little thing in fairness, Micky, and she did say if I need anything, so fuckin sure I will.' Winked Kelly. 'Right, I have a call I need to make.'

Minutes later, Moran received a call from Kelly about the information that was passed on.

'I'll be quick, it's that problem we spoke of. Our friend was that problem you had recently in Spain, I got told by a very close source who heard it said.'

'Sound, look, let's fuckin sort this out and soon, let me know what's needed.' And that was that.

It was 9.25 am on 20 July 2008 that Stewie Carroll received a call from Micky Donnelly telling him to meet with Timmy Kelly. Donnelly told him, 'Stewie, meet Timmy at the Cup & Saucer Café on the North Circular Road for 2 pm, it's a two-minute walk from The Joy near Mater Hospital on the corner, don't be fuckin late. He'll explain everything to you when he talks to ye later. Bye.'

As per the phone call, Stewie Carroll, with fellow gang members Freddie Hayes and Gaz McCarty, arrived at the Café bang on 2 pm where on arrival they found the solitary figure of Timmy Kelly sitting in wait. When the three men entered the Café, McCarty pointed Kelly out to Carroll as he sat at a table in the dull corner of the room under a television that looked as if it had not been used for many a year gone by. Without batting an eyelid, the ice-cold gangster waved to Carroll and his men and calmly called out and invited them to be seated.

'Alright lads, take a seat here, I've got some great news.

'Lovely Timmy, I love good news so what is it then?'

'Well, Stewie, I have a nice little number for you and your lads.'

As the meeting progressed, Kelly explained that a sizeable heroin consignment was expected into the country from the Netherlands within the next couple of weeks and he wanted Carroll and his men to move the shipment. Kelly clearly explained to the youngsters that whoever moved the gear for him would become pretty flush with cash overnight. Carroll and his men became very giddy and Kelly had to tell them to, 'Keep the fuckin tone down, ye silly cunts, do yis want the whole fuckin world to know what we're doing?'

'Sorry Timmy, just this is fuckin deadly news, bud.'

'Still shut the fuck up and listen, ye dozy cunt.'

After they calmed down, Kelly continued to explain, 'Now listen, for fuck sake, on arrival in Dublin, the drugs are going to be delivered to an as of now unknown destination, it's best that way. Stewie, your job will be the supply of a van to move a consignment that will contain 27 kilos of heroin valued at three million euros, street sales.'

'Holy fuck, three million!'

'Will you shut the fuck up? Now you lot get twenty grand each for the job.'

'Yess! Timmy, I know exactly where I can get my hands on a van for the night.'

'It cannot be traced back to you, can it?'

'Fuck no, Timmy, no.'

'I'll take your word on that. But I'm tellin ye it fuckin better not be.'

'Honest Timmy, it won't be.'

'Okay, Stewie, you fuckin sort the van. I'll be in touch, goodbye.' And with that, Kelly got up and left the Café. Part one of this outrageous and murderous joint operation was now in place.

Only days after the meeting in the North Circular Road Café, Terry O'Keeffe called on Kelly and reported to him that he had been out with friends in one of Dublin's popular nightclubs where he had met Pavel Predovnik. O'Keeffe explained that Predovnik told him that Pat Stacy and Maxi Rodgers were going to be waiting for Carroll the night of the drop off in The Horse & Carriage Bar in the North Strand on Dublin's Northside. He further explained that they were going to help Carroll move the gear to an unknown location that Kelly was yet to give them but the date was also unknown. When they got the date and address, Carroll would contact them after the pickup and they would make their way to the delivery destination.

Kelly was furious that Carroll's men were already mouthing off about the operation so soon after they were told about it. Wasting no more time, he swiftly got word to Moran about the possible whereabouts of two of Carroll's top men on the night of the operation. Moran, keeping to his word, organised to take down both men. With the Carroll men mouthing off, Kelly and Moran decided that the weekend of 3 August 2008 was the date that Carroll and his gang were to be taken down. They could not take any more chances with the Carroll gang so the quicker they were gone, the better.

As all the pieces of the puzzle had begun to fall into place, Carroll was unknowingly going to his death and Moran and Kelly had formed an unholy alliance to carry out the deed. Dublin was once again sitting on the dawn of a gangland bloodbath and nothing was going to stop it, not even an insider undercover Garda. The word inside the main members of both gangs was nobody was to speak a word of what was going down or they would join Carroll and his men; as only a handful knew about the operation, mouths were sealed as tight as a door on a submarine.

The morning of 3 August finally arrived and Thomas Moran left his Crumlin home to meet up with Noel Slattery, Frankie McCann and Nailor O'Neill for a pre-arranged meeting at the builder's yard at 9.30 am while across the city, Timmy Kelly was organising his men.

At 10 am, Stewie Carroll received a text message from an anonymous number telling him to meet at the Hellfire Club at 11 that night with the van and to let the number on the phone know all his gang's details. Following on from the text message, Carroll then got his men together and arranged all the collection and meeting points of which he then forwarded to Micky Donnelly (the person who sent the original text message), who then forwarded all the details to Tony Rothwell.

Donnelly laughed to himself when he received the message. *Those stupid cunts.*

Both Moran and Kelly now knew all of the Carroll gang's movements and whereabouts for the whole day and night; it was so easily laid out for them. Carroll and his men were about to meet their maker at a place of legend, which in folklore is known to house the devil himself.

The meeting point was the notorious Hellfire Club, an old abandoned building located in a forest on the Dublin Mountains overlooking Dublin city; the club is more famous for its urban myths than its scenery. The site was commonly used for the practice of 'Satanism' and other occult activities, and legend boasts that the devil himself had made a brief appearance there at some unspecified time in the past.

Unknown to Dubliners, evil was about to make its second coming to the Dublin mountains in the form of gangland killers. Devious as Kelly was, he picked the Hellfire Club for this meeting for a reason because he wanted Carroll to look at the view as it would be the last thing he would ever see—the city he could never have.

The day before the meeting, Kelly's man Ian Howe had already visited the Hellfire Club on a reconnaissance trip so that he could identify entry and exit points for his men. While at the Hellfire Club, Howe strategically placed weapons in and around the building and woodland area; if stopped by the Special Investigation Unit, better to not have any weapons on their person.

At midday on 3 August, Stewie Carroll headed straight to his brother-in-law Barry Keys, who was the owner of an old junkyard on the N7 Dublin to Galway Road to collect the van Timmy Kelly had previously requested. The van had been off the road for a while now and on request had been fitted with false plates along with fake tax and insurance discs.

After Carroll collected the van, he parked it up and with nothing but time to kill decided that both he and Predovnik would go over to the flat of fellow gang member, Keith Murphy. On arrival, both men were met by Murphy and Freddie Hayes and that afternoon; all four men relaxed and watched movies while occasionally playing computer games. Their fine happy mood could not be broken as the notion of a large quantity of money coming their way brightened up an already beautiful long weekend.

'What yis gonna buy, lads?' enquired a chirpy Carroll as he sat back with feet up on the coffee table while never moving his head, staring directly at the TV screen as he played a video game.

'Your ma,' joked Murphy as the three men burst into uncontrollable laughter.

'Cheeky cunt, yeah Keith, well, ye couldn't afford her,' replied Carroll. For the next hour, jokes were flying about the room and games were played but all that was to come to an end. As night began to fall on that warm summer's weekend, Dublin city was coming to life as revellers began to descend on their favourite bars and clubs across the city. Unknown to all, Dublin's underworld was planning murder and the city was about to see a mass bloodbath within the next few hours.

Timmy Kelly gathered his men for the last time to make sure everyone knew their jobs and also to put the final plans in place. When his men had gathered, he began explaining that all the hits were to be carried out at 11 pm so nobody in Carroll's gang could be tipped off in the process. While Kelly was putting his final preparations together, across the city, Moran was at home likewise getting ready to go as all his men knew their jobs and were already in place.

As agreed, Donnelly was not working with any of the Moran gang so the coastal town of Balbriggan on the far Northside of Dublin city was his port of call. Under orders from Kelly, he was to meet up with two of Carroll's men, Jeff Turner and Dickie Walsh, and it was also organised that he was to meet up with fellow gang members, Paddy Gallagher, John McDaid and Billy Masterson. The arranged time for this meeting was 10 pm at Balbriggan train station, where they would then head to a lockup at a small industrial estate on the Drogheda side of the town.

Carroll received a call from a Kelly gang member with the details of the lockup and he then relayed the information to Jeff Turner and Dickie Walsh. Carroll also told the two men to expect a call from Pat Stacy about the shipment being delivered to the lockup and he would let them know when he was on his way, to Carroll and his crew all was going well in their minds.

Carroll, along with Predovnik, 20-year-old Keith Murphy and 19-year-old Freddie Hayes set off at 9.15 pm from the Oliver Bond flats complex towards the Hellfire Club. A giddy journey was had as a fire was burning in their stomachs with the absolute excitement of the welcome but all too unexpected windfall. When Carroll and his men arrived, they parked the van and then proceeded to make the short trek up the steep mountainside to the Hellfire Club. When they reached the top of the climb, a light breeze caught their faces while the moonlight shone through the pine trees as they seemed to glide and dip on a breeze and the rustle of branches softly broke the silence of the mountain air. As the Hellfire came into sight, the calm silence was broken when Timmy Kelly called out.

'Welcome to the Hellfire, gentlemen.'

'A pleasure, Timmy, a fuckin pleasure' was the reply from a very upbeat Carroll, still full of excitement.

'Okay, let's go straight into the business at hand, shall we?' questioned Kelly.

'Let's,' again answered Carroll.

'Its five to eleven, Timmy,' was the comment from Howe as he appeared from a brush behind the gable end of the building.

'What the fuck, Ian fuckin hell, buddy, ye frightened the shite outta me.'

'Are you afraid of the dark, Stewie?' Howe was enjoying his haranguing of the youngster.

'Okay, enough play. Ian, go and give all the lads a bell and tell them we're on.' And with the order from Kelly, Howe once again disappeared into the dark of night to make that call to Thomas Moran and Micky Donnelly in Balbriggan.

'So Stewie, you think we are a bunch of silly cunts, do ye?'

'What? What d'ye mean, Timmy?' The colour started to run from Carroll's face as Terry O'Keeffe, Derek O'Neill, Tony Fox and Ian Bouncer Howe all appeared from the forest and behind the club building.

'We know it was you and these silly little bastards you call a gang that done Naughton and Daly. By the way, Tommy Moran is fucking fuming about the attempt on his wife and ma.'

'No Timmy, no, for fuck sake, you have it all wrong.'

'No, no, not at all, Stewie, I don't fuckin think so.'

In a blind panic, Keith Murphy tried to make a run for it when Howe pointed his gun at him, fired three times and killed him as he ran. In the next second, Kelly gave an order, 'Okay, have fun, boys.'

'No, no!' The terrified screams of the remaining three men rang out as the bullets began to fly when all of the well-armed gangsters opened fire, killing Carroll, Predovnik and Freddie Hayes where they stood instantly. Not happy they were dead; Kelly stood over the body of Stewie Carroll and emptied his gun into his head as he lay dead on the ground.

'Okay boys, let's get the fuck out of here,' ordered Kelly.

Away from the mountains, The Horse & Carriage Bar was full of red-skinned people and some even had their white bits showing, an Irish suntan as it's more widely known. Pat Stacy, Maxi Rodgers and his fiancée Debbie Keane sat waiting for Carroll to call but the call never came and what did come, they never expected in their wildest dreams. Moran had organised his men to play their part but told them to be under extreme caution as Kelly was not to be trusted.

'Do this fuckin job, boys, and get the fuck offside,' were Moran's only words to his men.

Frankie McCann, Gerry Dunne, Ken Fox and Dermot Behan all met up in the Phoenix Park where they had previously parked up two high-powered

297

motorbikes to use in the bank holiday operation. At 10.30 pm, they drove out of the Park towards the North Strand for the 11 o'clock deadline. As Pat Stacy and Maxi Rodgers sat in an alcove just close to the bar enjoying the sounds bursting out from the DJ's box, they were oblivious to what was happening outside as two motorbikes pulled up to be met by Nailor O'Neill who had previously entered the bar, pinpointing the whereabouts of their targets.

Without breaking his stride walking past McCann, Nailor told him, 'In the left corner of the bar in an alcove close to the DJ.'

With the bike engines still running, McCann and Fox dismounted their bikes and walked through the pub doors directly to the area where both Stacy and Rodgers were seated. Without blinking an eye, McCann shot Stacy twice in the head while Fox missed Rodgers with his first shot, hitting his fiancée Debbie Keane in the shoulder. The second bullet made contact with him in the chest, McCann quickly noticed the problem and opened two rounds into Rodgers' head and within seconds of entering the bar, the two assailants darted for the door as panicking customers screamed and ran for cover.

Within the hour, Frankie McCann, Gerry Dunne, Ken Fox and Dermot Behan were miles away from the scene, drinking pints in a bar in Dundalk, at the 21st birthday party of a close associate in County Louth. Three men met the bikes as they arrived at the outskirts of Dundalk and two of the men quickly disposed of the bikes while the other drove the four men to the party; as they entered the bar, McCann gave Moran a nod and he knew all was well. Their alibis were sorted and solidified as Garda Shaun Ryan or, as the gang knew him, Stephen Trimble was to arrive with Paddy Bird and Philippe Garrone not even ten minutes after them. Inspector D'Arcy had actually given the Moran gang it's alibi.

Back in Balbriggan, Micky Donnelly received a call from the Hellfire Club from Ian Howe and five minutes later, two young men lay dead from a single gunshot to each of their heads; Jeff Turner and Dickie Walsh were slain as they stood waiting at the lockup. The bodies were removed and dumped on top of each other on a narrow but frequently used Country Road near Balbriggan town centre.

The following morning, as drops of moisture were glistening in the early sunlight, a morning hike by John Garland and Anna Hopkins was abruptly interrupted when they came across the bodies of Stewie Carroll, Pavel Predovnik, Keith Murphy and Freddie Hayes.

Not long after this discovery, a Garda patrol came across the bodies of Jeff Turner and Dickie Walsh. Within hours of the news reaching the streets, Gavin Noone, fearing for his life or a lifetime in prison, went on the run to his uncle in New Zealand, never to return to Ireland's shores again.

The media frenzy around the murders of eight gangland figures in one night over a peaceful long weekend saw Inspector D'Arcy come under fierce pressure once again and the Minister for Justice wanted answers.

'Well, Inspector?'

'Intelligence has nothing concrete but I can bet Moran or Kelly is involved.'

'You are joking, Inspector? I mean in all seriousness you're saying nothing concrete, fucking hell.'

'No Sir, sadly I'm not, we have no solid leads.'

'You fucking knew something was coming; how did you miss it? And what about your inside man, has he added anything to this?'

'You see, how can I put this. He is actually Moran and his men's alibi; they were at the same party that night.'

'Oh, for fuck sake. Pull them all off the streets, Inspector, I want answers. And for fuck sake, try not to fuck this up.'

The arrests came and went as a silence once again came across Dublin, not one person was charged and the public again slated the authorities for failing to combat gangland crime.

Adding to the mayhem, Gaz 'The Modfather' McCarty was found dead at his home but Garda put it down to a robbery that went wrong as no evidence was to be found to say any different, but McCarty was number nine in the long weekend murder case involving members of the Carroll gang after Frankie McCann had paid him a visit.

Chapter 33
The Persian Gulf and Expensive Cars

Months had passed as a very sombre Dublin ruefully stumbled back to some sense of normality after witnessing the mass murders of the now notorious 'Bank Holiday Massacre' in August of 2008. Inspector D'Arcy was relentless in trying to bring the killers to justice but all he could really do was hand out orders to the Emergency Unit to constantly raid homes and premises known to the gangsters and arrest members on sight in hope that somebody would crack. The ongoing interviews, harassment, interrogations and raids failed time and again as he never gained any information to his increasing frustration.

To make things even more annoying for D'Arcy, not long after the murders, Moran decided that it was best to get out of Ireland and away from the hotbed of Garda activity that did not look like coming to a halt anytime soon. Under orders in Dublin, a crew would still run business as usual but they had to contend with Kelly and his gang but mostly the threat came from D'Arcy. Those orders from Moran were clear to all of his gang members:

'Keep heads down and operate in the shadows but take no unnecessary or stupid risks.'

Those gang members knew and clearly understood that in Moran's absence, operations would continue but what was also clear was that the gang would only move small to medium loads of drugs due to the severe pressure from the Garda drug squad and the Garda Emergency Units. Moran deep down was worried because he could not risk his business being compromised if one of his men got arrested; Dean Coyle had proved that to him. The one positive thing in his mind was that not everyone knew of the plot to take out the Carroll gang and this gave him some comfort as it was only his senior men who knew.

Moran had Rothwell contact the mainland European smugglers who were informed, 'Shipments on a large scale are suspended as the lady will be tied up in Ibiza for the foreseeable future.' In addition, they were told to be careful while making sure operations ran smoothly across Europe with an added warning of threat from Interpol and Europol.

This information was cemented when Dirk van der Beek contacted Captain of the *Saint Marie*, Mark Lowe, and gave him one message, 'Mother cannot make it home today.' And from that moment, Lowe knew that the possibility of sailing the *Saint Marie* was too dangerous, informing him of when authorities were too close to the gang.

Now that everyone knew what was happening and what was to happen, it was in September of 2008 that Moran headed to Spain to his wife and mother while many of his senior men soon followed his temporary exile as they all went their separate ways during the winter and spring of 2008 and 2009 to different locations across the globe and clear of D'Arcy. One of those men was senior figure, Tony Rothwell; it was in April of 2009 when he travelled to meet a friend in the United Arab Emirates capital city, Dubai, that something got his mind racing.

Located in the eastern part of the Arabian Peninsula on the coast of the Persian Gulf, Dubai was fast becoming a major city in the world of business and tourism. This all was part thanks to UAE's huge oil revenue that helped accelerate the development of the city; in time, its massive revenues would come from trade, tourism, aviation, real estate and financial services.

What caught Rothwell's attention was that the Dubai government's decision to grow the city by way of service and tourism made real estate and additional developments become even more valuable resulting in the property boom that presided in 2004-2006 when construction on a large scale turned Dubai into one of the fastest-growing cities in the world.

For Rothwell, he once again got lucky because in 2009, many construction real estate projects were suspended or abandoned, due to the worsening financial crisis. This, to Rothwell's delight, caused property prices to fall considerably throughout the United Arab Emirates, but most notably in Dubai; after a couple of weeks in Dubai and some homework, Rothwell made a call.

It was on 26 April 2009 when Thomas Moran spoke to Rothwell.

'Get a flight to fuckin where?'

'Dubai, Thomas, the United Arab Emirates.'

'Why and were the fuck is that, Tony?'

'It's in the Middle East on the Persian Gulf, get here as soon as you can. I got a business opportunity for us, gift horse this one.'

'Yeah okay, can I fly there?'

'Fucking hell, Thomas, I'll sort your flights, where are you?'

On 3 May 2009, Thomas Moran flew out of Malaga airport on a Turkish airlines flight direct on a ten-and-a-half-hour flight to Dubai International Airport. Now, the thing was that Dubai in May, the start of the summer, temperatures are at a sizzling 37°C, and occasionally exceeding 42°C.

'Holy bollix, Tony, its fuckin roastin here, what the fuck!'

'It is hot, it is certainly hot.'

'Fuckin hot!'

'Okay, let's get your pasty Irish arse out of the sun, Thomas.'

It was not long after Rothwell got Moran back to his luxury apartment in Dubai he began to explain, 'Okay, this place is a goldmine with property prices dropping all over the place, it is soon to be one of the most sought-after real estate locations on the planet as soon as this global economic crisis is sorted.'

'Oh?'

'Interested, are we, Thomas?'

'Yeah, what's the story here then?'

'You hired me to do deals to better our situation but to also invest in ways we can hide our cash, yes?'

'Of course, now get to the fuckin point.'

'So I have been in contact with the developer of a couple of prime locations here in Dubai, one is named the 'Palm Resort' and the other the 'Dubai Coral Apartments', both close to where we are. In fact, you're standing in one of the apartments from the Dubai Coral right now.'

'Fuck me,' was the reaction to Rothwell's news as Moran looked around at his surroundings in awe because this was an extremely high-end property.

'Work started in 2006 and the first residents were to arrive in November of last year. But the developer went tits up so I contacted them in New York and made an offer for both apartment blocks. Thomas, these are the most sought-after properties in this part of Dubai with big trading companies and bankers and oil kids wanting to live here.'

'Fuck me, how many are there?'

'The Palm Resort has seventeen apartments; this one has nine. So a total of 26 apartments located on Oceanside Dubai.'

'What's the fuckin price for this lot then, Tony?'

'Well, we have two, three and four bed apartments here, we rent them out for a few years and then sell when the prices come back up, and they will.'

'For fuck sake, Tony, how fuckin much!'

'All for the 26 apartments, €65 million.'

'How fuckin much!'

'Look, we can get an average of €120 grand a year each for them so that's a total of €3.1 million per annum. So in five years, you have fifteen and a half back, when the prices go back to their actual value, they cost on average €110 million if sold. So in all you can make a clean fifty million in five to ten years.'

'You sure?'

'Of course, I'm fucking sure, Thomas.'

Taking a moment in thought, Moran turned to Rothwell and told him, 'Okay, fuck it, do it.'

'Perfect. I'll get the paperwork sorted and set us up as a property management company in the morning.'

'Cool. I'll leave you to it so.'

What Tony Rothwell was doing was going to be nothing odd in Dubai as the city was to become the new destination of choice for gangsters to clean up millions of their ill-gotten gains because the lack of regulation in Dubai meant it was to become a money laundering centre for global gangs. And property was king and Rothwell took a moment to take the piss out of his boss.

'Look at you, a little shit from the Inner City flats in Dublin becoming a property owner in Dubai. Another thing, Thomas, cars.'

'How much will this cost me?' Laughed Moran.

Another of Rothwell's business ideas was to purchase high-end cars from Dubai due to the momentary crash in the financial institutions because he wanted Moran to set up a network of garages across Ireland and Britain to sell cars to launder their drug cash.

After a few days of deals and viewing vast numbers of cars, Moran was onside; over the next year, high-end garages were opened up in Dubai, plus Paris, Rome, Milan, Dublin, Munich, Edinburgh, London, Liverpool, Manchester and Madrid. All in all, this venture cost a staggering €75 million to get up and running but Rothwell, knowing his market, opened showrooms in some of the more important retail areas across Europe's main cities.

Professional staff was hired and two well-known motor experts ran the business but, of course, not knowing who the owner was. The clients too did not know nor did they care who the owners were because the cars were sold to business people, famous sports stars, bankers and rich kids all looking to spend, spend, spend.

The cars included Bugatti Veyron 16.4 Grand Sport, Koenigsegg Trevita, Ferrari 458, Lamborghini Gallardo, BMW M5, Mercedes-Benz SL63 AMG and top-end Range Rovers. This venture and the Dubai property were to be extremely lucrative for Moran and Rothwell, business was looking up but problems in Ireland still needed sorting.

Chapter 34
The Beginning of the End

It was now March 2011 and having spent eighteen months building his Dubai property portfolio and his European car business, Moran knew well that he needed to get back to Dublin as he had been absent for a time. It was on the afternoon of 25 March 2011 when Noel Slattery and Tony Rothwell got the word from Moran that they were once again to get ready to start importing drugs and he wanted both men to bring all the main Irish gang members together to organise their next shipment.

Moran, wasting no time, two days previous to speaking to Slattery and Rothwell, contact had already been made with the crew of the Saint Marie, Sam the Turk, Dirk Van Der Beek and Marcel Kromkampp about the organisation of a shipment coming in from Ibiza via Morocco in the winter of 2011 so he needed his Irish crew ready. Hours after the initial contact from Moran, Noel Slattery got word out to the rest of Moran's crew that a meeting was organised for a date in April and it would be at the end of the west pier in Dun Laoghaire, South County Dublin.

It was on a cool crisp clear night as the moon shone down on the harbour when at 10.15 pm on 10 April 2011; Noel Slattery arrived in Dun Laoghaire and made his way towards 'The National Maritime Museum of Ireland'. This had been planned the day before with Rothwell to discuss the final details of the agenda before meeting the other gang members. As Slattery arrived at the entrance of the Museum, he found that Rothwell had already arrived.

'Evening Noel, it is freezing here, why on earth did Thomas not get a nice warm room for us?'

'Stop your fuckin moaning, for fuck sake, and let's get down to business.'

'Okay, Noel, was only asking, my friend, so have you got all the details to hand of who is taking on the tasks and with whom they are to work with?'

'Yep, all here, Tony, but we'll leave that for a later date just in case anyone fucks up. Plus this rat thing, Tommy still isn't so sure if we have one or not.'

'Okay, let's walk.' both men started off towards the pier discussing the details of the meeting before they met up with the gang members. Slattery explained to Rothwell that when the original contact was made to all, 'The one thing that Tommy was clearly ball bustin about was that if anyone suspected they had a Garda tail, they were not to come anywhere near the meeting. They better have fuckin listened.'

'Yeah, he told me that too, Noel, so hopefully that should be clear as hell but yes, you're spot on.' But nothing is as ever clean cut with the line of work these men were in because the one thing that Slattery had not worried about was that the Special Garda Unit were ordered to stand down because Garda Shaun Ryan or as he was known to the Moran gang Stephen Trimble was also invited to the gang's meeting. When he got word of the meet, Ryan contacted Inspector D'Arcy about the gathering and D'Arcy wanted all the information Ryan was about to receive so taking no chances, pulled all units off the gang for that night.

The only people who knew of the meeting outside of the gang, Ryan and D'Arcy were the Minister for Justice who without hesitation gave the all clear for the blanket silence across the board. Not even the Chief Superintendent knew of this operation and that was how D'Arcy wanted it played out, the less who knew the better.

Earlier that day, Ryan met with D'Arcy to lay out their final plans for the night ahead and with a pat on the back and best wishes; away he went to collect Paddy Bird. It was now 10.23 pm when Garda Ryan parked up close to the pier; and as he and Bird arrived at the meeting point, he could not believe his eyes when he saw the entire Dublin crew of the Moran gang. At long last he also met the infamous Tony Rothwell when Slattery introduced him, no member of the Gardaí to his knowledge knew his face until now, but to his frustration, there was no Thomas Moran.

Also present were Frankie McCann, Gerry Dunne, Ken Fox, Dermot Behan, Philippe Garrone, Seamy Conroy, Paddy Bird, Dennis Scully, Nailor O Neill, Paddy Agnew, Jimmy Greg and Noel Brady. Once the men all settled down after greetings and handshakes, Rothwell explained, 'Okay lads, I will be quick, I do not want this group hanging around here too long and it is fucking freezing so listen up. Now, the drugs will arrive later this year all going well aboard the Saint Marie so we have not got much time to get things sorted from this end. She will anchor two miles off the coast of Cork sailing from Ibiza and we must move its cargo of cocaine, heroin, marijuana and guns as quickly and as efficiently as possible. Noel wants a quick word.'

'Okay, whats gonna happen is that a few days before she sets anchor, you will all be contacted but for now, keep low and stay out of bother. We will sort out jobs closer to the arrival date so I'll be in touch. Nobody make any fuckin arrangements for November, December or January; plus not a fuckin word of this to anyone outside this group and I fuckin mean not one solitary fuckin word, if I hear of a leak, you're all fuckin dead, yeah. Okay, now get the fuck outta here.'

As the details were discussed, Ryan knew his only problem now was that the main instigator Moran was nowhere to be seen and he needed to link it all to him. Even though he had the proof for his superiors of a major drugs and arms shipment coming in after Rothwell basically gave to it to him, he still could not get near Moran. After the meeting when Ryan dropped Bird home, he contacted D'Arcy who on hearing the news saw the opportunity to finally get his man. It was now just after two in the morning when Ryan met up with D'Arcy in Trim County Meath.

'The boat is a fishing trawler named Saint Marie, Inspector, but I have no dates as of now. What I do know is that it will be setting sail out of Ibiza between November and January, anchoring off the Cork coastline.'

'Fucking hell, Stephen, oh sorry son, Shaun,' joked D'Arcy with a new-found vigour on hearing this news.

'This is fantastic work. Ibiza! I should have known, Moran has history with that place. Okay, we have a chance to fucking get him, the smug murdering little bastard, we can fucking have him this time and along with all his scumbag gang.'

'But he was not at the meeting, Inspector.'

'I know that. Now we must connect him to the shipment, that is vital, okay, okay, look, get back to it.'

'Will do, Inspector.' Even though this was a major break in the case against Moran and his gang, D'Arcy knew the courts would demand hard evidence that Moran was behind the importation. The fact was, and D'Arcy was all too aware, that the gang boss had not been present at the pier arranging his men to import the drugs and this news was tearing him up inside. But the chance that D'Arcy and Ryan were looking for was about to come sooner than they had ever hoped when a major breakthrough came their way.

It was only a few months after the meeting in Dun Laoghaire when Tony Rothwell contacted Stephen Trimble a.k.a. Garda Shaun Ryan to go on a business trip with him because, as Rothwell believed, Trimble was an expert in weapons. Rothwell explained that they would be travelling to Edinburgh to meet up with none other than Moran's top smuggler, Dirk Van Der Beek. Ryan nearly fell down on hearing this news and without delay contacted D'Arcy.

'Inspector, you are not going to fucking believe this but I'm meeting Dirk Van Der Beek in Edinburgh with Tony Rothwell.'

D'Arcy's heart was thumping out of his chest as he just could not believe his ears when Ryan explained the news and his reaction showed it.

'What! Rothwell and Van Der Beek, holy fucking shit! Okay, okay, fucking hell, okay, do it and meet me after, I'll be in touch and for Christ sake, be careful!'

'Yes sir.'

Sitting in his office, D'Arcy put his hands on the table in front of him flat down, took a deep breath, staring into the abyss, and spoke to himself, *Holy fuck*.

D'Arcy without delay visited the Minister for Justice alongside the chief superintendent and highlighted to both the men the information at hand.

'Minister, our man is meeting up with two of Europe's most wanted, Tony Rothwell and Dirk Van Der Beek, in Edinburgh soon.'

'Holy shit, Inspector, this is huge. Can we get Scottish police to observe or even Europol offices in case he is compromised?'

'I am not sure, Minister, but we can inquire; personally, I would rather Europol due to security reasons, you understand, Sir?'

'Of course, of course, Inspector D'Arcy.'

On the afternoon of 12 October 2011, Rothwell and Trimble met up with Van Der Beek in a fashionable café bar in one of Edinburgh's most vibrant areas, Murrayfield. Sitting under the shadows of the famous Scottish rugby ground, Rothwell and Van Der Beek quizzed Trimble on what weapons were the best to smuggle in for a possible street war at home in Dublin.

Rothwell was aware that the gang had imported guns in the past but also knew that the market changes and 'guns were not cheap'.

Ryan found this quite amusing coming from a man who was making in excess of one million euro a month. Lucky enough, he had a fair grasp on modern weaponry so Trimble came across as knowledgeable and professional. After a brief encounter with two of Europe's most wanted men, Ryan departed Scotland

and back to Dublin with Rothwell heading off to Istanbul for a meet up with the notorious Sam the Turk. Two days after the meeting in Edinburgh, Ryan met with D'Arcy in London's Piccadilly Circus, away from prying eyes in Dublin. He explained what had gone down at the meeting with Rothwell and Van Der Beek in Scotland and told D'Arcy, 'During the meeting, Sir, they would mention a "third party" go-between on the transaction and I believe without doubt this was definitely Moran. Now again the thing is, Rothwell never mentioned his name and only referred to him as the boss.'

All D'Arcy could do was listen and nod.

'I know Moran was involved in the purchase of the weapons but I can only prove Rothwell was the money man, as you know, Inspector, I helped him organise to get them into Ireland so I am more to blame than Moran at present with the information we have at hand.'

Again D'Arcy just sat and listened to his man's detailed account of the meeting as he was told that Moran's name was kept clearly out of any conversations involving the guns and the drugs.

'Adding to this, Sir, I'm certain that it was Moran who called as we sat in the Café and thanked Rothwell for helping him get the deal done but I just cannot prove it.'

Ryan continued to explain, 'As you know, Sir, I was present at a meeting in Dun Laoghaire where Rothwell briefed the gang about a huge drugs and arms shipment he and the boss are in the process of sending to Dublin. This is possibly our best ever chance to get him.'

'Indeed, we know that, son, indeed we fucking do.'

Not to let things turn cold, D'Arcy organised to meet up once again with Ryan but this time, it was a more high-profile meeting than the London outing, he was meeting directly with the Minister for Justice, John O'Connor.

Garda Shaun Ryan explained the whole story word for word to the Minister as he had previously done with D'Arcy. He told him that he had also found out that the gang through Rothwell organised to have a huge shipment of drugs along with the weapons imported into Ireland through their European contact Dirk Van Der Beek. Minister O'Connor though ecstatic with the news and the massive progress made by the young Garda, like D'Arcy was not completely happy as Moran once again kept his fingerprints away from the shipment.

'My word Inspector this is unbelievable news. Moran is staying well under the radar but I think we can get him this time. Okay, we need to make this information work to our benefit?'

The Minister for Justice on hearing this ground breaking news backed Garda Ryan without question and gave the go ahead for additional Garda and coastguard personnel and overtime to assist D'Arcy in his operations. O'Connor in a private undocumented meeting went to cabinet with the information and unanimously got its support. Another bonus came from Cabinet for O'Connor when he got clearance and received the backing from the Minister for Defence, Enda Cooney giving clearance to the Irish Armed Forces to support the Special Unit to take down Moran's gang if and when needed.

Now all D'Arcy could do was just sit and wait for Garda Ryan to contact him and this time he knew he had to bring down Moran.

Chapter 35
Operation Godfather

Paris in the winter is one of the most delightful places on earth as locals and tourists alike bask in the glory of this beautiful city while visiting her many famous landmarks located across this vast Metropolitan. On 19 January 2012, one such tourist was sitting in a Parisian bar located just off the Champs-Élysées when his mobile phone rang. 'Hello,' said the man.

It was 3.30 on a beautiful winter's afternoon when the voice on the other end of the phone spoke, 'Mother wants you home.'

'Okay, see you soon.'

That short phone call was a call to the Captain of the Saint Marie, Mark Lowe, and the voice on the phone was none other than Moran's Mr Fix-It, Tony Rothwell. Lowe had just been given the code that would see the Saint Marie set sail for Ireland with a cargo of illegal drugs and weapons for sale and distribution for Thomas Moran and gang. Within 20 hours of that phone call, Lowe and his crew were boarding the Saint Marie, which was then moored in Malaga awaiting further instructions from Rothwell; they did not have long to wait for more instructions.

On 21 February, as the crew were getting the Saint Marie ready for her maiden voyage, Rothwell once again contacted Lowe telling him that the sailing and pickup instructions were in a mailbox located at Malaga post depot.

'Go to the depot and collect the key for deposit box A-327, it is under the name of Carlos Alonso.'

'No problem.'

'Now, what you will also find there is the coordinates and pick-up location, destroy all that when you know where you are off to.'

'Will do, bye.'

'Good luck.'

That was to be the last contact between Rothwell and Lowe and on that same night in Dublin; Noel Slattery sent word to the men that a meeting was to be held in the backroom of the Black Horse pub. Slattery told the gang, which included Stephen Trimble, that 'the lady was about to sail' and would be heading out of Ibiza very soon. After Ryan left the meeting, Inspector D'Arcy received a single-word text from Ryan—the one word he had patiently waited for—'Corleone'—and D'Arcy knew that was the code word that signalled the Saint Marie was about to set sail.

Without delay, D'Arcy contacted all the concerned parties to let them know what was going on as the Gardaí, the coast guard, Irish Customs, Irish Navy and Europol were all put on red alert but Inspector D'Arcy had one more trick up his sleeve.

One of the main organisations in tracking down European drug traffickers is the Maritime Analysis and Operations Centre on Narcotics based in Lisbon, Portugal. The MAOC is an international agency set up to coordinate anti-drug trafficking action by several European Union states with financial support from the European Commission and works closely with Europol and Interpol. Ireland's representation is a combined one from the Irish Drugs Joint Taskforce of An Garda Síochána, the Irish Customs Service and the Irish Naval Service, but it was from Lisbon—thanks to a call from D'Arcy—that a coordinated operation with Dublin had begun to take down the Saint Marie and her crew. But as ever with Moran, nothing ever went according to plan for D'Arcy as he was soon to find out.

The thing was that what Garda Ryan had told D'Arcy was only part correct as the Saint Marie had already sailed but what he did not know was, the Saint Marie was not yet in Ibiza as it was currently headed for Malaga to collect the details of her operation from the deposit box as per the phone call to Lowe, which both Ryan or D'Arcy knew nothing about.

Secondly, after leaving Malaga, it was not sailing directly to Ibiza where they thought it would be found because Ibiza was only going to be a stop off for fuel and supplies during its journey to Cork. The information was part correct but the Saint Marie was going to go missing.

The crew arrived in Malaga on 25 February and Mark Lowe went to the deposit box where he did indeed find the information needed for the sail and once again like with *The Spirit of St Christopher* many years previous, the crew on-board the Saint Marie's first port of call was to the port of Al Hoceima in

Morocco, a six-day journey, before it hit Ibiza and a window in which the MAOC, Europol and the Irish authorities would have lost complete contact with the boat for a number of days. The crew set sail from Malaga on 26 February 2012 on a three-day sail to Morocco.

Panic set in when word came to Dublin via a French Europol agent named Pierre Lecarde who was stationed in Ibiza to solely track the Saint Marie. Lecarde explained that the boat was not in Ibiza as originally thought and this had D'Arcy in a complete and utter rage because this was his time to take down the operation once and for all. What D'Arcy also did not know was that Lecarde was the Europol officer who was part of the European operation to take down Moran's gang on the mainland plus he was the agent in Edinburgh on request from the Garda Commissioner to keep tabs on the meeting with Garda Ryan, Tony Rothwell and Dirk van der Beek.

D'Arcy felt that the information he had received was all wrong and the operation was in jeopardy and to top things off, he had organised a mass operation across many European agencies.

'What the fuck, it's not in Ibiza? Then where the fuck is it?'

'We have no idea, Inspector. It's vanished,' explained Lecarde.

'Vanished, you have got to be fuckin kidding me, Agent.'

'It's not in Ibiza like we thought; it's gone somewhere but where, that we do not know.'

'Christ! Okay, keep in touch, Agent Lecarde.'

D'Arcy, hanging up the phone, could not hide his frustration. 'Fuck! Fucking Moran, ye fucking prick!'

But his frustrations were about to turn into joy when on 4 March 2012, an amazed Interpol agent Pierre Lecarde could not believe his eyes when the boat that near enough every Interpol and Europol agent was looking for sailed right into Ibiza harbour and moored with one of the most infamous drug crews in Europe aboard. Without delay, Lecarde issued a bulletin that the boat had arrived in Ibiza albeit days later than expected but now nobody cared as Lecarde contacted D'Arcy personally and told him, 'Inspector your boat has arrived in Ibiza in the last few minutes. It's here right now; I am looking at it!'

'What! You're fucking kidding me, okay, stay with it and for fuck sake, do not let it out of your sight. If it sails, you swim after the fucking thing if you have to. I'll send one of my men over to Ibiza today.'

'Okay, Inspec… Oh, you are gone.' D'Arcy hung up before the agent could finish his sentence.

D'Arcy looked across his office and called out, 'Okay Devlin, get your passport; you're off to Ibiza. Pronto.'

'What! I'm going where?'

'The Saint Marie has fucking arrived in Ibiza so off you get to the airport now. I'll sort your flight.'

'Yes Inspector. And how long will I be gone?' asked the confused and surprised Garda member.

'As long as it fucking takes, now go.'

D'Arcy contacted Lecarde in Ibiza and told him that Garda Devlin was on his way and eleven hours later, Devlin arrived in Ibiza where he met Lecarde in a café that was overlooking Ibiza's San Antonio harbour, directly looking at the Saint Marie.

'That's your phantom ship, Monsieur Devlin, see the green and blue trawler moored in the harbour? That is the Saint Marie. Shall we get a closer look?'

'Let's do so, Agent Lecarde.'

'Okay, look, Garda Devlin, we must not speak to or interact with them at all. Your accent may worry them, you know, so best just to look and not speak.'

'Understood.'

As both lawmen walked the pier, they noticed a hive of activity on the boat as boxes were loaded and supplies were put on board. Under the cover of a couple holding hands and frolicking on the pier, the men even took photos of the boat as passers-by were asked to take their pictures, which also handily had photos of the Saint Marie and her crew clearly in the background. Later that day, Lecarde forwarded the pictures to Europol headquarters so that it would also help the Maritime Analysis and Operations Centre track her voyage.

Back in Dublin, Stephen Trimble was given instructions from Slattery that he was to go to Wexford with Jimmy Greg and Gerry Dunne to help offload and load the drugs into awaiting vans. The collection point was at Saltmills, a small village located in the southwest corner of County Wexford that had a landing area neatly sitting at the head of a small inlet that entered Bannow Bay, out of sight of residents in the tiny village. The small beach was a perfect place to offload the drugs away from prying and unwanted eyes.

After receiving his instructions from Noel Slattery, Garda Ryan was stunned to find out he was to be part of the landing crew and moving quickly, he sent a registered letter by courier marked 'Urgent' to the office of Inspector D'Arcy. When D'Arcy opened the envelope, he found the exact details of the landing crew's destination, arrival time and position that the Saint Marie would set anchor off the Irish coast from Ibiza. Without hesitating, D'Arcy got onto Justice Minister O'Connor to sort out what plan of action was best to intercept the cargo with the hope of finally taking down Thomas 'Little Don' Moran.

It was 11 pm on 6 March 2012, days later than scheduled and nearly one year after the original meeting in Danny Moore's Ibiza home that Captain Mark Lowe and his crew of Edmund 'Eddie' Baxter, Casper Von Bommell, Terry McLaughlin and Danny Higgins sailed a trawler called the Saint Marie on her maiden voyage towards Ireland with a cargo of illegal drugs for the Irish and British market. At the same time, Agent Lecarde and Garda Devlin contacted Dublin and Europol, informing them that the Saint Marie had finally set sail to Ireland.

Agent Lecarde contacted Lieutenant Michelle Baptiste of Europol who informed the Maritime Analysis and Operations Centre, who then alerted the French, Portuguese and British Navy and coast guards to monitor every movement of the trawler. In a joint operation working from the MAOC headquarters, Europol the Portuguese, French, British and Irish coastal authorities all put a full surveillance on the Saint Marie and from the moment the trawler hit Portuguese waters, the unsuspecting crew was now doomed to fail.

As the crew set course for Ireland, the Garda and European police agencies were all over the voyage as all of the European agencies kept in contact with each other via the private military international airwaves. There was no chance the Saint Marie was going to win this game of cat and mouse, no matter how good this crew was and it was very, very good.

In Dublin with Inspector D'Arcy leading the entire operation, a Garda briefing on Operation Godfather was taking place with members of the Garda Emergency Unit, Customs, Coast Guard and Irish Navy; D'Arcy was ready.

Everything fell into place when following a late-night emergency meeting of cabinet, the Irish Minister for Defence Enda Cooney gave the go-ahead for the deployment of the Irish Navy and it was at 1.45 am on 7 March that Commander Finbarr Mullen of the Irish Army Frigate *Róisín* deployed his ship to the Irish south coast to aid and support the Irish coast guard. It was at 3.44 am when word came through to Commander Mullen that the Saint Marie was now entering Irish waters and would arrive at the expected time, 5 am. Commander Finbarr Mullen told his crew, 'Set course as planned, gentlemen!'

Mullen was now given sole charge of the operation and keeping a safe distance, the *Róisín* approached the Saint Marie in attack mode, ready to pounce. In relatively calm seas just sitting off the Irish south coast, the Saint Marie anchored and the coast guard were given the go-ahead to intercept by Commander Mullen as the Navy backed them up.

'Okay, full ahead, Mr Keogh. We are to assist the coast guard unless we are told otherwise. This is not a drill, gentlemen, this is full on interception of an enemy boat,' was the order from Mullen.

As the Saint Marie had anchored at its point of destination, Captain Mark Lowe as vigilant as ever had his binoculars in hand and spotted the coast guard in the distance to the stern of the trawler while the Irish Army Frigate *Róisín* was lurking just a mile off the portside and both ships were approaching the Saint Marie at high speed.

'Oh, you have got to be fucking joking me.'

Lowe called his men together and explained. Pointing out to sea, he began telling the crew, 'Okay gents, listen up; it looks as if we are done for.'

'What you on about, skipper?'

'Fucking Navy and coast guard, they have us. Look out to sea; they are all over us and both ships are coming in hard from all sides. We ain't going anywhere so no heroes, just take what comes. It's been an absolute pleasure sailing with you all but now it ends. Fuck!'

Lowe, a vastly experienced sailor, knew all too well that there was no way on earth they could outrun the much faster boats nor could they unload their cargo in time. It was apparent to him from that moment that they were done for and he openly surrendered his boat and crew to the Irish coast guard and *Róisín*.

At 5.22 am on 7 March 2012 the coast guard personnel on board the *Eleanor* supported by the Irish Army frigate *Róisín* stormed the Saint Marie, finding its all but beaten crew sitting on a cargo of cocaine, heroin, marijuana and guns destined for the Irish and British market.

Moments before the Saint Marie was boarded, Lowe in a last-ditch effort had tried to warn off the crew on the beach but it was to no avail as right before the boat was boarded, Irish Army personnel, aiding members of Operation Godfather, swarmed the stunned and unsuspecting Paddy D'Arcy, Noel Brady, Jimmy Greg and Gerry Dunne.

The thing that was unknown to the men, a certain Garda Shaun Ryan had an extra surprise when it was him who made the four arrests.

'You're fuckin dead, ye cunt Trimble, fuckin dead!' screamed Gerry Dunne.

'Take them away, lads.'

During a long summer's night, the Saint Marie bobbed around on calm seas off the Wexford coast as she was found carrying the biggest haul of drugs ever seized in Ireland in excess of €100,000,000. At 6.12 am, the crew of the Saint Marie, now on board the *Róisín*, were escorted into port where on arrival at the pier, they were arrested and driven away at speed to Dublin to face questioning from the Garda Emergency Unit. As the men were whisked away, Gardaí carrying Uzi sub-machine guns along with Irish Army personnel patrolled the pier inside a sealed-off area where the Saint Marie was finally moored alongside the naval vessel.

As the boat moored, a few hardy locals woken by the noise coming from the coastline looked on as the Saint Marie was then handed over to the members of the Gardaí forensics unit to examine and photograph the haul. Not long after the Saint Marie was brought into the harbour, officers from the various agencies formed a line handing the tightly-packed bales to each other until a stack of drugs stood at well over a metre high on the pier.

A Naval PR spokesperson gave a brief interview to the waiting media, who had gathered on the pier after an anonymous tip went to certain newsrooms,

'More than fifty Garda, Navy, Army and Europol officers were involved in the joint operation, which led to the biggest seizure of drugs in the history of the state. At this time, we do not know the exact value of the haul but the sheer volume tells us it's huge. The navy's intelligence operation was led by Commander Finbarr Mullen, who, with around a dozen land-based staff, coordinated the seizure of the Saint Marie fishing trawler twenty kilometres off the Wexford coast.'

As the interview was ongoing, heavily-armed Gardaí and Army personnel accompanied the drugs as they were transported to Garda headquarters in Dublin but D'Arcy was furious that the Navy did an interview as they had not yet arrested Moran and his senior men and he was right to be annoyed when at 7.37 am, Moran got a call from Rothwell explaining what had happened.

'Thomas, it's all gone tits up; get the fuck out of Ireland.'

'What the fuck are you talkin about, Tony?'

'The *Saint* was boarded and the lads were all arrested, Garda, Navy and coast guard arrested the lot of them. We were fucking grassed up; they got the lot.'

'Fuck! Fuck, fuck, fuck!'

'Right Thomas, I'm off; best of luck, it's everyone for themselves now.'

On hearing the news, Moran immediately gathered some possessions as he quickly got offside before the Gardaí arrived at his Crumlin home and while in transit, he contacted Slattery and McCann and explained to both men what had happened.

'The ship has been taken, the Gards know fuckin everything so get on your toes, Noel!'

'Ohhh bollox, Tommy, bollox. Right, I'm off, see ye again someday, buddy.'

It was pretty much the same call to Frankie McCann as they all went on the run but as of then, unknown to all three, this would be the final time the friends would ever speak to one another again. In the rush, Moran even left his Crumlin home front door wide open and after a few hours, he found himself on a private boat heading to Liverpool having paid a local fisherman ten thousand euros to sail to England. Before D'Arcy caught breath, Moran was in the Channel tunnel heading towards the European mainland to Spain's Costa del Sol while Noel Slattery and Frankie McCann both went on the run, using the many contacts they had encountered over the years as they found themselves leaving Ireland behind forever to start new lives abroad.

Hours after the seizure of the Saint Marie, Minister for Justice John O'Connor called the Dáil to sit on the morning of 7 March 2009 to pass emergency legislation that would give the courts the authority to finally take down Moran and his men after he felt that they had now enough evidence to bring the gang boss and his men into custody on drug trafficking charges.

Later that day in a hail of media coverage, Inspector D'Arcy and the Garda Commissioner stood alongside the Minister for Justice John O'Connor TD as he announced the breaking news:

'Not long after 5.00 am this morning, members of the Irish coast guard aided by the Irish Navy captured the boat known as the Saint Marie. In a combined operation, a total of nine arrests were made including members of the crew and additional land crew members of this organised crime gang. A cargo of illicit drugs was found on board the boat that was in excess of €100,000,000 along with a cache of guns and ammunition.'

He continued:

'Myself and the Garda Commissioner on behalf of the Special Investigative Unit that was led by Inspector Niall D'Arcy here to my left have issued warrants for the arrests of senior gang members including Thomas Moran, Tony Rothwell, Noel Slattery and Francis 'Frankie' McCann. Additional warrants were issued for other gang members we would like to interview in relation to drug trafficking. All four men are known to the Gardaí and in addition to the Irish warrants, we are now seeking European arrest warrants for these men through Europol.'

The Moran gang were today's news as every detail of the fugitives appeared all over the screens and in all the newspapers in Ireland and additional European media. The Irish State had struck a massive blow against international drug trafficking after the biggest and most ruthless gang Ireland had ever seen were now for the first time firmly put on the back foot.

Inspector D'Arcy's operation was not an absolute success because he did not get the main players—Moran, Slattery, Rothwell and McCann—which still got to him.

Chapter 36
My Brother's Keeper

Within 24 hours of the news hitting the streets, Moran and Slattery had arrived in different parts of Spain, Moran in Malaga and Slattery in Seville who was organising to make his way to Asia. In Malaga, Moran was trying to get to Ibiza to meet up with his wife and mother who had moved there not long after the news was released but to top this all, he was furious when it became clear to him that Stephen Trimble was actually Garda Shaun Ryan. In a fury, he put a reward of €1,500,000 on his head but the order would never be carried through as the gang was in complete disarray.

It was not long after the arrest warrants were issued that Dennis Scully was found hiding out in Amsterdam and within days of his arrest, he was immediately deported back to Ireland to stand trial thanks to the information gathered by Garda Ryan. D'Arcy knew that Scully was done for and the new legislation passed in parliament on the importation of drugs and weapons was more than enough to put Scully and any other members of the gang away for many, many years to come. In conjunction with the Irish and European warrants out on the Moran gang, Europol put out additional European arrest warrants on the heads of Dirk Van Der Beek and Marcel Kromkampp, thanks to intelligence gathered over the years, pinpointing them as two of Europe's main drug traffickers who worked alongside Thomas Moran.

After the collapse of the gang, Moran and his wife Jean eventually settled down together, moved to the island of Ibiza and took residence in a plush villa given to them by Danny Moore. Moran was now running his club, Ice, on a full-time basis while realising he could never return home to Ireland again and how true this was to be.

During the early hours of 18 June 2014 as the fresh Mediterranean air gently blew a soft breeze across the island, the last of the party-goers made their way back to their apartment blocks situated around the San Antonio resort. That night as per usual, Thomas Moran was closing up his club when he did not see a man come from behind him; startled by the man in the shadows, Moran called out, 'Fuck off, we're closed.'

'Is that right, Tommy?' answered a man standing in the shadows with a distinctive Northern Irish accent.

A curious Moran called out, thinking it was one of the staff or possibly one of his boys paying a surprise visit. 'Who the fuck is that then?'

As the man stepped out of the shadow and into the gleam of moonlight reflected from the windows of the club, Moran instantly recognised the man who stood before him—none other than rival Dublin gangster, Micky Donnelly. Donnelly was tipped off about Moran's whereabouts back in Dublin and he had boarded the first available flight to the island to confront his foe.

'Well, well, look who it is, I never thought I'd be seeing you again, Micky.'

'Then you guessed wrong, Tommy, didn't you?'

'Sure looks that way, it sure does look that way, Micky.'

Moran momentarily turned away from Donnelly, knowing exactly why his foe was in Ibiza; as he placed his tablecloth on the bar, he took a deep breath, turned around, looked Donnelly in the eyes and asked, 'So what now, Micky, I guess you're not here to fuckin reminisce about the past now, are ye?'

'Correct, Thomas.'

'So are we going to get this over with quickly, Micky?'

'Oh yes, Tommy, oh fuck yes, it won't take long.'

'Ahh well, I never guessed it would end this way but fuck it, I had a good run.'

Moran was standing in front of the man who had escaped him and his gunmen in Milan and it had now come back to haunt him after the one thing Thomas Moran had never done before—let a witness go. As Moran picked up his glass, he took a sip from his final drink and said, 'Well, come on then, ye cunt, let's have ye and I hope ye die screamin like your cunt brother as you burn in fuckin hell.'

It was at that moment that Donnelly pulled out a Glock already with silencer attached and shot Thomas 'Little Don' Moran point-blank with a single shot to the head. Moran fell to the floor dead as Micky Donnelly stood over his victim and said, 'Thats for my brother, you cunt!'

Donnelly then turned and walked out of the club back to the airport where he boarded a plane three hours later to Dublin.

It was on a beautiful Mediterranean night that Thomas Moran lay dead and alone in a pool of his own blood on the floor of his nightclub and it was here where he lay until the next morning when one of the staff members discovered his body. The news about the demise of the infamous Thomas 'Little Don' Moran spread like wildfire across Europe but to Inspector D'Arcy, this was not a victory as he had wanted to bring Moran to justice and it was not the outcome he wanted. For a man like Niall D'Arcy, who was an exceptional Garda member, he put the death of Moran behind him knowing his work was not yet finished due to the fact members of the Moran gang were still at large and he was not going to rest until they were either dead or imprisoned.

In government buildings, Minister O'Connor spoke to D'Arcy the day after the death of Moran, 'Well, Inspector, a job well done, this is a great victory for the Garda Special Unit and now that Moran is dead and his gang on the run, we must stay on top of things and control all gangland activity in Ireland.'

'A victory, Minister, this is no victory. Moran and his men have left many a family with drug addicts or the loss of a loved one. I say there is no winner here.'

A very solemn and heavy-hearted D'Arcy continued, 'But yes, I completely agree that our job is to bring all his men to justice and maybe, just maybe, at least for the families who suffered under these scumbags, they can have some sort of closure.'

'Yes Inspector, you're correct. Everything you need to bring them to justice I will help you with.'

D'Arcy nodded and gently spoke, 'Thank you, Minister. But remember, we are far from done here.'

D'Arcy knew well that Thomas 'Little Don' Moran's life on earth had ended on 18 June 2014 but his life would never be forgotten by many, many people who mourned and cried, thanks to his gang and its drugs and D'Arcy hated him for that. He would never shed a tear for him, nor would he for anyone involved with him.

On the island of Ibiza, Moran was buried a week later on 24 June, many miles from Dublin city, the city he had terrorised and far from the streets he had controlled with fear. Two people turned up to the funeral and they were his wife Jean and his mother Marie. Even Danny Moore distanced himself from the

Moran family after his death, leaving Jean and Marie Moran for the first time in many years on their own.

In Dublin, many of her residents happily raised a glass to his death; for many families, his legacy would never leave them, especially for those who had crossed him or his products over his years of savage rule. Moran's mark on the city was much more than he could have ever imagined as many dead and living drug addicts and broken families that he had left behind would never forget him.

Moran tasted the world he envisaged with Noel Slattery when they met for the first time on that Halloween night many years ago or when he stood on top of the flats in St Christopher's with Jean looking down on his boys rioting in the streets as he promised the world to her. He certainly gave it a right shot but like many young gangsters, the rule of the street always catches up with them and someone else will without doubt be waiting in the wings to take over. Moran was gone but the prize of Dublin was still to be won.

Chapter 37
On the Run

With the demise of Thomas 'Little Don' Moran, the Irish authorities turned their focus towards bringing his gang to justice. With many of the major players still at large, the Irish and various European police forces worked hand in hand with Interpol to bring them to justice but it was not going to be easy as the gang were now scattered across the globe. D'Arcy knew he had to go hard after those who had gone on the run but first of all, he wanted to tie up the cases he had against the crew of the Saint Marie and the men arrested on the beach in Saltmills, County Wexford, on the night of 7 March 2012. The justice Minister also wanted to get the cases to court as soon as possible and with backing from cabinet moved the case times ahead.

It was on 12 February 2015 in Dublin's Special Criminal Court that D'Arcy watched on as Captain Mark Lowe and his crew of Edmund 'Eddie' Baxter, Danny Higgins, Casper Von Bommell and Terry McLaughlin were all sentenced on multiple drug smuggling charges with intent to import, sell and supply in the Irish market. Additional charges of importing weapons were added to the case by the State prosecution as the chief justice handed out the sentencing.

Mark Lowe was given a 15-year sentence while the rest of the crew all got 12 years apiece. Those gang members who were arrested on the beach in Wexford while waiting for the drugs to arrive were sentenced three days later on exactly the same charges as the crew of the Saint Marie. On 15 February, Inspector D'Arcy again watched in court as Paddy D'Arcy, Noel Brady and Jimmy Greg were all sentenced to eight years each while Gerry Dunne got an additional two years for threatening to murder Garda Ryan on the beach when he was arrested. All nine men were sent to Ireland's maximum-security prison at Portlaoise prison.

Other members of Moran's gang had encountered very different lives after his death. Dubliners Ken Fox and Dermot Behan continued working on small-time drug deals across Dublin city but they never got to the levels they had while working under Thomas Moran. Corkman John Joe Daly was stabbed to death in an argument over football in a pub brawl by an 18-year-old man in September 2016 while Tinker McFadden continued to run Limerick with an iron fist as he tried to calm the gang war that plagued the city.

After the news of the Saint Marie being boarded found its way to Jan Kromkampp, he quickly fled Holland. Kromkampp in fear of arrest found a perfect hideaway in southwestern Montenegro at the Bay of Kotor, which is situated on the banks of the Adriatic Sea. Following his retreat, Kromkampp did not quit his drug dealing lifestyle as he continued to work with known smugglers across Europe from his Montenegro base. Over the coming years, Kromkampp would make huge amounts of cash and he would also find himself become one of Interpol's most wanted men; the brilliantly elusive Jan Kromkampp would never serve a day in prison.

Another of Moran's major European operators, Dirk Van Der Beek, found his way to Bloemfontein in the free state province of South Africa. Van Der Beek found safe cover in his native South Africa as he had gathered a number of contacts who he had become close with through his dealings in the Northern and Eastern parts of Europe. Away from Interpol's reach, Van Der Beek became a successful businessman, opening up a chain of very successful coffee shops across the planet as he retired quietly from the world of drug and gun smuggling. In April of 2015, he was officially announced as a legitimate millionaire by the South African banking industry.

Italian Philippe Garrone returned home to Italy under the cover of the Alps and back to the Camorra in Naples. On his return to Italy, he remained in Naples moving from safe house to safe house while working alongside the Camorra. In October of 2018, he was shot dead in a shootout with Italian police after a botched armed robbery.

Brian 'Nailor' O'Neill and Seamus Conroy turned the builder's yard into a legitimate business following the death of Moran with both men making a very good living out of the yard. It was in November 2014 that the surveillance on the yard was halted by the Garda's Special Unit after D'Arcy gave up, realising that O'Neill and Conroy had actually gone legitimate. Neither man would ever serve a day in prison.

Leading underworld figure Timmy Kelly was charged with being a major figure in Irish drug smuggling but he was also charged with the murders of Stewie Carroll and Pavel Predovnik. It was on 1 December 2017 when he was sentenced to 20 years in Portlaoise prison but Kelly would later die of a heart attack in prison, only serving a sentence of 23 months.

Another of Kelly's gang, Ian 'Bouncer' Howe, returned to Belfast where he ran a major security firm that controlled many of the Loyalist affiliated bars in the city. Howe never returned south again as the British government ignored D'Arcy's call to have him taken to Dublin for questioning in the murders of four men at the Hellfire Club. The PSNI let him do his everyday business while ignoring his involvement with the Kelly gang.

Terry O'Keeffe worked with Tony Fox, pulling off small robberies after the arrest and imprisonment of Kelly but they were back in business when Micky Donnelly had all his charges eventually dropped by the Director of Public Prosecutions in June of 2013. The case collapsed due to a lack of evidence as charges that included conspiracy to sell and supply drugs failed to materialise, all to D'Arcy's annoyance. None of the men would ever serve a day in prison.

Other members of the Kelly gang had not so much luck. Paddy Gallagher was shot in a gangland hit in October 2014 after he grassed on a major player in Ireland's illegal diesel trade. John McDaid and Billy Masterson continued doing small jobs but both men just disappeared off the radar as work ran out. In August of 2014 after months away from gangland activity, in a bizarre twist, Billy Masterson was gunned down in a random Dublin shooting in a murder case that would never be solved.

In December of 2015, Derek O'Neill was found dead in his apartment in Dublin city centre after he had overindulged in the festive activities. Doctors found massive amounts of cocaine and alcohol in his system courtesy of his heavy partying during the Christmas period; it was put down to excess and the case was closed.

D'Arcy wanted the mass murderer, Frankie McCann, but this was never to be as he disappeared off the face of the earth. Frankie McCann was to become Ireland's most wanted man who, over a 25-year period, took the lives of what the Gardaí calculated as at least sixteen people. Unknown to all, McCann travelled to Copenhagen, Denmark, via Scotland and booked a flight on a false passport to South America. He eventually set up home on the peaceful island of Aruba, a paradise in the Caribbean Sea off the coast of Venezuela.

It was a world away from Dublin's Inner City where he settled in Aruba's capital city Oranjestad. The multiple murderer McCann completely changed his lifestyle, living as a recluse, never to be seen out in public, bar the odd excursion to the local market and then home. Inspector D'Arcy searched long and far but the psychopathic killer McCann had disappeared, never to be found.

As gang members were on the run, going legitimate, getting acquitted or being killed off, D'Arcy was feeling frustrated about the lack of convictions. He felt that nothing was going to plan since the first major trial involving the nine members of the Moran gang and the trial of Timmy Kelly but in April 2015, Inspector D'Arcy was about to get a welcome surprise.

At 9.45 on the night of 29 April, D'Arcy was contacted by Interpol with news he thought he would never hear—Tony 'The Fairy' Rothwell had been arrested as he sat drinking a cappuccino in an Athens café.

Interpol were contacted after a report from an Athens airport security check flagged a man carrying the passport of a dead man. Interpol told the airport to let the man through as they did not at the time know who the man was and where he may lead them. When images were closely scrutinised by members of Interpol's identity fraud unit, one man's name kept appearing and that was the name of international drug smuggling's Mr Fix-It, Tony Rothwell. Inspector Claude Bentsen was given the order to approach with caution and make the arrest.

On 28 April 2015 at 13.45 pm, a unit from Interpol assisted by members of the Greek police force moved in and surrounded Rothwell.

'Tony Rothwell. My name is Inspector Claude Bentsen of Interpol. I believe you to be the man we have been searching for on drug smuggling charges after you fled the Republic of Ireland.'

At the time of his arrest, Rothwell had significantly changed his appearance so the Interpol officers were informed by the identity fraud unit that they were not one hundred per cent sure if this actually was him. Wearing a brown wig and having grown a goatee beard, Rothwell had flown under the radar until now. When arrested, he was also carrying a fake Canadian passport plus a driver's licence in the name of Terence Harper.

Rothwell, knowing that he was done for, looked Bentsen in the eye and arrogantly stated, 'Well done, Officer, you just got a promotion.'

On 12 May 2015, Tony Rothwell was extradited back to Ireland via Athens under a heavily guarded private charter plane. Upon his arrival he was handed over to Irish authorities by Interpol agents and was again arrested in Dublin airport by Inspector D'Arcy and charged with drug smuggling, money laundering and the importation of weapons. A month later on 29 June in Dublin's Special Criminal Court, Tony Rothwell was sentenced to 25 years in Portlaoise prison, he would never see the outside of the prison walls again.

The last member of the original Moran gang was his right-hand man and best friend, Noel Slattery, a man D'Arcy really, really wanted and he was about to get his man. On 11 March 2016, Noel Slattery was living in Sydney, Australia, and while out shopping, he was spotted by an ex-Garda from Dublin who was now working for the Sydney police department. As he sat in wait for his partner, the officer recognised a familiar-looking man with a slight limp making his way to his car, and curiosity got the better of him.

'Control, this is car 091, can you give me a reg check please.' and he proceeded to read out the car's registration plate.

'Control to 091, that car is registered to a Miss Anna Canning. No previous on that plate, guys.'

'Cheers, control.'

As his partner returned to the car, O'Rourke explained, 'See the red Ford across the way? I got a feeling about the driver, I know him and it's really running wild in my head.'

'Right, so mate, let's go have a chat then. Let him pull out then turn on the lamps and siren.'

As Slattery pulled away, Officer John O'Rourke followed him and within yards of driving, he pulled the car over.

'Step out of the car please, sir.'

When Slattery got out of the car and stood in front of O'Rourke, he realised it was in fact notorious Irish drug smuggler Noel Slattery. In a panic, O'Rourke stood back and pulled his gun, pointing it at Slattery. His partner in a spin had no idea what was going on and also drew his weapon and assisted his partner.

'Noel fuckin Slattery, it's fuckin you, ye bastard, isn't it?'

'Go fuck yourself, ye silly little cunt,' was Slattery's beaten reply.

Slattery was arrested at gunpoint as O'Rourke explained to his partner that they had just made a massive collar. After two weeks of legal wrangling, Slattery was on a flight back to Dublin to face trial just like Rothwell for drug smuggling plus conspiracy to murder charges. On 17 April 2016, in a holding cell at Dublin's Mountjoy prison, Noel Slattery committed suicide before his trial had begun. Another of the notorious Moran gang had gone and once again, Dublin did not mourn this loss.

In Ibiza, Jean Moran and Marie Moran ran 'Ice' as it remained one of the most popular clubs on the island with both women becoming quite wealthy from the takings.

Last but not least, the so-called fool of the gang became a wealthy and successful businessman as Danny Moore ignored his past and got on with his busy life on the island as he closed his book on gangland activity.

Dublin city had a void and voids need to be filled and with Moran and Kelly gone, a massive drug operation in Dublin was left and somebody had to fill it. In May of 2015, Sam the Turk was meeting up with an Irishman on a boat on Lake Geneva, Switzerland, organising the importation of guns and drugs to Ireland.

That man was Micky Donnelly.